CALIFIA—THE WEALTH OF THE LAND, THE POWER TO BE GAINED IN FREEDOM—IT DREW THEM LIKE A MAGNET . . .

SAM BRANNAN—The visionary who led his outcast flock to the new Zion. He dreamed of freedom, yet risked it all for the only love that could enslave him.

SUSANNAH MORRISON—A fiery beauty torn between two proud men. Her own passionate heart would force her to challenge the stern commandments that bound—and betrayed—her.

CAMERON GENTRY—A California aristocrat, he would have both the land and the woman on his own uncompromising terms: total surrender.

SEAN McKAY—Misplaced trust had cost him his farm. Had he erred again, placing his family's lives in the hands of the Donners, following their strange route westward?

EZRA MORRISON—He did his duty to God by casting out his children and marrying his son's wife, only to find eternal damnation in the guise of love.

TOLERANCE MORRISON—She was the model of rectitude until she cut all ties with the past and unleashed an ambition and sensuality that threatened them all.

THEIRS WAS A DAZZLING VISION OF THE FUTURE . . .

THE MAGNIFICENT DREAM

Books by Day Taylor

**THE BLACK SWAN
MOSSROSE**

THE MAGNIFICENT DREAM

Day Taylor

A DELL BOOK

Published by
Dell Publishing Co., Inc.
1 Dag Hammarskjold Plaza
New York, New York 10017

Dell ® TM 681510, Dell Publishing Co., Inc.

ISBN: 0-440-15424-3

Printed in the United States of America

First printing—September 1984

Part I

Chapter One

The Mutual Improvement Association meeting had just ended. The usual atmosphere of camaraderie was heightened by news which, until this evening, had been mere rumor. Laughter and excited chatter broke out all over the room as the young people gathered in little circles.

Susannah Morrison was the focus of one such group. At seventeen Susannah was gay as a cricket and as pretty as a spring morning. Her black hair shone with good health, and dancing in her blue eyes was a sparkle and zest for life that attracted the attention and friendship of both men and women.

Bertha Brown, not endowed with beauty, found herself standing next to Susannah. She smiled up at her, a peasant gazing in worship at the stars. "Oh, Susannah," she said, "isn't it just *immense* about the new settlement in California! I suppose your family will be one of those chosen to start it."

Susannah barely hesitated before she smiled confidently, showing even white teeth. "I suppose we will," she agreed happily.

A slender red-haired girl spoke. "The Goodwins are going. How blessed they are! Can you imagine how wonderful it would be to be among those chosen?"

"Your family isn't going?" Susannah asked.

"No, Papa would have told us by now, I'm sure. We'll probably just stay here in New York City."

"Thomasine, I would miss you so!" Susannah declared. "But perhaps you'll come with the next group."

7

"Oh, I hope so. I would like so much to take part in it."

"Not everybody is going to get to go, Susannah," Bertha said, a bit nettled. "After all, there will be only one ship, and we cannot get all the Saints on it. Some of us must stay behind to do our work here."

"Well, it won't be me!" Susannah said, laughing.

"When did your father tell you your family would be among those to go?" Bertha asked suspiciously. "I didn't hear the Morrison name mentioned this evening."

"They named only a few," Thomasine put in quickly.

"Papa hasn't spoken of it yet," Susannah admitted, then added quickly and brightly, "but he will."

Bertha snorted. "You aren't going at all! You're just talking. You're no different from the rest of us ordinary folk."

"Look!" someone called from over near the row of windows. "That's Elder Brannan!"

All the young men and women in the room moved toward the windows, with Susannah crushed among them. Pushing a bit, she managed to get to the window just as the man who would lead the Saints to California had passed. But even the sight of that tall dark-haired figure moving purposefully down the snow-covered street was enough to make her heart pump faster.

She went back to the clothes rack and found her cloak and bonnet. As she tied the ribbons fetchingly under her chin, she looked at Bertha, a devilish sparkle lighting her eye. With a self-assured little smile, she whispered, "The Morrisons *are* going to California, Bertha. You'll see!"

Susannah stepped outside the meeting hall into the snowy New York street, tossing her head back to let the thick, moist snowflakes drop upon her face, cooling her flushed cheeks. Going to California! The whole Morrison family! Even though Papa had not yet announced it, she was sure they were going. God would not deny her!

To a chorus of modest and amused giggles of her friends, Susannah twirled about in the snow, making little circles on the sidewalk where her boots dug into the soft newly fallen flakes. She laughed aloud, enjoying being the center of attention. Since she had seen Elder Brannan pass by the building, she had become a new girl. Her clear blue eyes sparkled as she remembered. She had seen him! The Lord had let her see him, and in a way He had let her see herself. She would be one of those chosen to go to

8

California with Elder Brannan. She was sure of it! She could not—would not—be left behind! She skipped around in the snow, scooping up handfuls of it and tossing it at anyone nearby, unable to quiet the elation she felt within her.

She didn't even mind when her intense, overweight, overeager stepbrother, Asa Radburn, came from the meeting hall and tried to match her exuberance with a pretense of his own. He came bounding up to her, his hungry dark eyes glowing. "Hey!" he cried, announcing to all on the street that he was entitled to the company of this desirable girl whenever he chose. "Isn't this great?" He made an awkward running skid in the snow, his arms waving frantically as he flew past her, then managed to catch his balance. "Come on, Susannah, let's race! We can pretend we're skating! Come on, everyone!"

Susannah laughed. Asa took it as a rare cheerful response to his presence. Susannah whirled around again, then ran a few paces, and Asa came to her, caught her and lifted her into the air. For a moment, a brief moment, Susannah Morrison imagined she was being lifted by a tall man who had been touched by the voice of God. But, clumsy in everything he did, Asa stumbled, and the two of them crashed to the snowy ground. Even that, and the shattering of her momentary illusion, did not dampen Susannah's spirits. Covered with snow, she rolled over and got to her feet, called to Asa, and ran down the street on her way home. She was eager to talk with her father, for she was certain he would reveal that the Morrisons were among the elect families, and she didn't want to miss that. It wasn't every day that one was chosen to make a journey for God to found a new nation for the Church of Jesus Christ of Latter-Day Saints.

Susannah's father, Ezra, was grappling with the same thoughts, and more, but from a radically different viewpoint. He was not quite so sure of his position in God's plan as was his daughter. He had lived too long, and had been too often scarred by fear and experience, to share her exuberance.

Ward Bishop Lorenzo Waterman, who had just departed, had left Ezra much to think on. Before he spoke of these momentous things to his wife, Prudence, and to Susannah and Asa, Ezra wanted to get straight in his own mind just how he felt about the double honors that had been bestowed upon him and his family. At the moment he was so awed that he seemed unable to think at

9

all. How did one simply give up a living it had taken a lifetime to build and go to an unknown land called California to begin over again? He could not envision it. He was numb.

Some voice in his mind kept saying that this was an honor. The distinction called forth in him the earnest desire to perform, but at the same time it reminded him of the worst times in his life. The Saints had tried other times, other places to find their niche. Ezra had lived through the horror of such an attempt in Missouri. He had come out of that experience with no more than life and limb, and had been thankful God had granted him so much. Even thirteen years later he wasn't certain he should tempt the fates again. He had never doubted the Prophet, or his community of Saints, but the tests of strength and courage they had to endure tried Ezra's soul. His great weakness, which he fought day and night, was fear. He dreaded living through a nightmare of persecution again. But his great strength was the knowledge that he was one of God's chosen, and he would always serve his God.

He sighed, reminding himself of the joy of service, and began another circuit of the room. Ezra had been pacing slowly, but now he was moving with great speed. His mind was beginning to make lists of work to be done before sailing. He was no longer thinking of the move as a possibility, but as something to be planned for. The date was three months away, in February, but to Ezra it was already looming up as soon as next week. Feeling rushed, he started for the door to tell Prudence.

Then he thought of the other honor, and stopped dead, his heart beating in a rapid, excited way quite at variance with the solemnity of the duty that the Church of Jesus Christ of Latter-Day Saints expected of their capable people.

He—Ezra Morrison, forty-two years old in this year of 1845, married and father of two adults—was to marry again, not merely one woman, but more than one if he could find them unmarried and suitable. And, more important, he was to father as many children as the Lord saw fit to send.

The thought made him weak; his forehead and hands were clammy. He had always accepted the tenets of his faith. He had always known all the men of the Church were priests, but for Ezra that duty had been a minor one, a daily task composed of ordinary kindnesses. Now he had truly been called to be a priest. He tried to think of the souls of future Saints waiting for their

10

turn to enter *Time* on this plane. He thought of his duty and privilege to give them their chance. He was truly blessed, but the idea of his place was awesome.

He began pacing again, breathing shallowly, his faraway gaze touching the objects in the room without seeing them. Nervously he rubbed his hands together. It was a frightening honor. Siring children was one thing, but fathering them was quite another, and dealing with several wives at once was perhaps the most frightening thought of all. He and Prudence were comfortable enough together despite their having no mutual children. He had not terribly minded the absence of wet diapers and little feet and little screamings. Surely the Lord knew what he was about.

His face grew grave. He knew himself to be attractive—tall, straight and slender, self-confident—and wealthy. He had been a faithful husband. Nonetheless, he had observed the gleams in women's eyes when they spoke with him, and had answered smiles of invitation with smiles of regretful refusal. Now—if he obeyed the Church's orders—all that would change. In his middle age he would be once more a hunter, competing with young, less-encumbered men for the favors of maids scarcely older than his own daughter.

Ezra stood in front of the fire, flexing his hands in its warmth. Without his willing it, his mind roved dreamily over the unmarried women he knew. Bertha Brown, plump and giggly. Merit Winestaff, cool and slender, with those luminous gray eyes that ate into a man. Ezra shivered with excitement and dismay. Lust had no business entering into something essentially holy—but confound it, if a man couldn't feel *something*, how could he perform the necessary actions? He thought of Susannah's friend Thomasine Barnes, a girl just waiting for her man. He could feel his face growing warmer as his thoughts of Thomasine developed, and he felt compelled to move.

He paced more rapidly. A nervous sweat had broken out on him, making his skin clammy even under his long woolen underwear. Soon he had to break the news to Prudence, and he was no more ready than he had been an hour before.

Prudence was in the small sitting room. Ever thrifty, even when her husband's considerable wealth made it unnecessary, she had cut worn-out clothing into strips and was hooking a rug for her son's bedroom.

He was chilled again. With a muttered exclamation about the

weather, Ezra went to the fireplace, the tail of his frock coat lifted to the heat. He looked at Prudence in the lamplight. Her hair was blond, a little faded now that she was forty, parted down the middle, and drawn into an uncompromising coronet around her skull. Her eyes squinted a little when she looked closely at things, but they were still the same merry blue they had been when he married her. Her small nose and her small mouth ill became her breadth of shiny forehead, and her chin was a little too large and firm. Nevertheless, Ezra found the familiarity of her homeliness vastly reassuring on this miraculous night.

He wanted to tell her so, but what came out was, "You've kept your figger very well, Prudence my dear."

She glanced up at him, amused but flushing. "Whatever made you think of that?"

He winked and shrugged, and tried to smile. Prudence returned to her work, and left him to deal with a silence that grew large and heavy. He cleared his throat. "I have—Brother Waterman brought me—some news, Prudence. Exciting news."

"I *thought* he stayed rather long," she said comfortably. As was her habit when Ezra needed her attention, she put her work aside and folded her hands to sit quietly.

He took a breath. "It is—a great honor. We've—our family has been chosen. We are to—to carry on the work of the Lord."

She smiled faintly. "That can hardly be news, as we already do that." She had learned long ago to remain undemonstrative, but inside herself Prudence was anxious. Her eyes were fast on Ezra.

"I—I know it will be hard for you, leaving your friends and doing without comforts, but I will be at your side." Thinking of how these honors would affect her, Ezra swallowed hard, and hastened on. "I promise you, it will be exciting. And I *will* be at your side—always."

What Prudence was beginning to feel was more than anxiety, it was fear. Why wasn't Ezra saying straight out what Ward Bishop Waterman had told him? She found it difficult to control her voice as she said, "Could you tell me just a little bit more?"

Ezra was little more comfortable than she, but he was supposed to be strong. "I'm trying," he said. The fire, which had been so cozy, suddenly seemed too much, and he began to pace back and forth in front of her. "This comes straight from President Brigham Young," he assured her. "He and Brother Waterman conferred only a few weeks ago. You know that Elder Samuel Brannan is fitting out a ship to take emigrants to California? Naturally they are choosing a few, um, well-placed Saints—men of good judgment, substance, and influence. These are Brother Waterman's words now, not mine. And when my name came up, President Young immediately got a revelation. The Lord has told us, dear Prudence, to sell everything and go to California to settle new territory for the Church!'' Ezra's eyes lit up.

For a moment Prudence thought her heart had stopped for good. She struggled for breath, and to regain control over herself. She forced a smile to her lips, and tried to make her voice sound hearty, but it came out weak and frightened. ''Isn't that splendid? Tell me about California, Ezra. Are there other Saints there? Or is it a well-established Gentile community like—'' She couldn't bring herself to say Independence. For a moment she thought she'd faint. Hideous flashes of the terrible night Heber had been killed, and she and Asa had fled in terror, flitted before her eyes. Had she been able to speak she would have told Ezra right then that not even for the Lord could she again face the horrors she had lived through in Jackson County, Missouri.

It was true that the Lord had seen fit to give her Ezra in her time of direst need. She shuddered as she thought of what would have become of her and Asa had Ezra not seen them as he fled by carriage with his children from the blazing Mormon community at Independence. As long as she lived she would never be able to muffle the sounds of pain, death, and fright she had heard that night. She'd never be able to forget the sight of a man racing wildly, insanely, down the street, his body blackened with hot tar and covered with feathers. She had seen her neighbor's daughter crushed beneath the hooves of one of the nightriders' horses.

Ezra watched the unusual play of emotions on Prudence's face. He wished there were something he could say that would make her feel better, but he knew from his own thoughts and night-mares that there was nothing that could erase that last night in Jackson County. He sat on the arm of her chair, and took her hand in his. They sat together that way for several minutes, neither saying anything. ''My faith should be stronger,'' she said finally.

Ezra sighed. ''I have thought the same thing. I wonder how much the children recall of that night?''

Prudence looked into the fire, then away. It reminded her too much of her own flaming house that night. "Asa will remember. The Devil touched him that night and taught him to hate. Do you realize how adamant he is in his hatred of Gentiles?"

Ezra shook his head. There was a great deal he didn't know about Asa, and he preferred to keep Prudence ignorant of the fact that there was a great deal he did not care to know about Asa.

"Susannah was quite young, only four," he said. "Perhaps she has been spared the scars of that night. I'm less certain about Landry. He was nine years old. I think he remembers, for he refuses to hear mention of Independence."

"Then we can be sure he remembers. For those who were not there it is a curiosity, and for those who were, it is something to be buried deep in forgetfulness. Are we likely to encounter something like that in California, Ezra?" Prudence's hand clutched his a little tighter.

He patted her hand and moved to the sofa, the arm of her chair having become uncomfortable. "Well, I don't know a great deal yet. The little I do know indicates otherwise. From what I've heard, the weather is satisfactory. There are no Saints there yet. In fact, I believe it is hardly inhabited at all by civilized folk. It sounds as though we'll truly be starting all over again, Prudence. We will have the immediate advantage. There will be much land, which we can claim for ourselves, and there will be timber to build our houses. The land is said to be fertile, so we can grow crops, and have cattle and sheep—"

Prudence burst out giggling. "You, Ezra? A New Yorker born and bred, you'll grow wheat and corn? And milk cows?"

Nettled, he replied evasively, "I'll start up my bakery there. I'll be the only baker, so it is a fine business opportunity. The more we discuss this, Prudence my dear, the more I feel that this journey will bear no resemblance to our time in Jackson County. Oh, and I had nearly forgotten the greatest news of all. California is not a state. Do you realize what that means? It means we people of Mormon can live there and no longer be persecuted for our faith—not murdered, like the Prophet Joseph Smith, nor driven out of the town, as we were in Missouri and as were the people in Nauvoo. We have been frightening ourselves with our memories, and the fear of losing the small security we have in New York. God, indeed, is directing us. I can see that now. I must confess I feel the fool for having doubted. We'll be

14

free-at last to worship our God in our way, the way that was revealed to the Prophet Joseph.''

"The Lord be praised," said Prudence, tears standing on the rims of her eyes. They sat silent for a moment, then she asked, "But why is it that President Young will not lead us? If it was revealed to him—"

"In a sense he will, my dear. He'll be leading a party overland and will meet us in California. There is some urgency to our getting there as quickly as possible to claim the land. Elder Brannan has boasted that with a hundred armed men we can take the whole of the territory!"

"Mercy! Is this to be a military settlement? If there is no danger of attack from Gentiles, why must we be armed? I can't say I like the idea, Ezra.''

He smiled patronizingly at her. "Don't alarm yourself. We must be armed and trained, of course. But it is not for the reasons you fear. The inhabitants are Mexicans and native Indians, who are not expected to put up resistance.''

"But—but—at Relief Society there was talk about war coming with Mexico.'' Prudence, confused and uncertain, now wrung her hands. "Were we given no alternative? Could not some younger family go in our place? Is the bishop dissatisfied with our work here?''

"On the contrary, he praised our efforts—yours as well as mine—and he said he looks forward to a like performance in the new land. But as for an alternative, no. It was a *revelation*. The Lord revealed our names to President Young, and we are among the chosen. I need not remind you of our position in the Church, dear wife. We have been recognized as pathfinders to this miracle of Zion. We'll follow the word of the Lord as it was given to us. And we'll do it with pride, and strength, and faith.''

"Of course," Prudence said automatically. She sat looking unhappy for a few moments, then brightened and said, "It is just that the Lord's mind runs so much faster than mine. I'm sure I shall adjust to things.''

Ezra filled his lungs with air. There would never be a more propitious opening. Prudence had managed with the first revelation better than he had expected. Perhaps it would be the same with the second. He began, "And there is yet another revelation. I—I must admit that I don't quite know how to cope with this

15

myself." He hurried on. "I—we—have been chosen to enter into celestial marriage."

"Oh, my dear!" Prudence jumped up and started to give him a hug, but was so embarrassed by her own forwardness that she settled for just squeezing his arm. "I've always wanted that—to be sealed to you for eternity, to continue our marriage in heaven—to bear your children in eternity as I have not been able to on this time plane."

Ezra stared at her. Her blue eyes shone with tears, happiness, and a deep, deep love. He had some idea of what it had cost her to agree to go to California, and not to try to dissuade him. He knew the dread she felt, and now he had an idea of the depth of her need for him. Perhaps it would be better to tell her of the other honor at some later time. He needn't cause her any more consternation at this moment. Tomorrow or the next day would be soon enough.

"Well!" he said heartily. "This has been quite an evening. I might even break the Word of Wisdom and drink a cup of coffee. How about you?"

Prudence smiled up into his face. The Prophet had stated that true Saints would not drink liquors, coffee, tea, or hot drinks, but on a cold winter's night many a Saint warmed his innards with a forbidden beverage. "To celebrate?" she asked, her eyes twinkling.

He chuckled, and hugged her before letting her go.

Prudence wheeled the tea cart in near the fire. She had brought delectable slices of hickory nut cake to enjoy with their coffee. On an elegant silver tray were the silver cream pitcher and sugar bowl. The fine Bavarian china with its hand-painted border of shamrocks was so thin that the firelight made shadows through it. Handling her beautiful things with prideful care, she remarked, "I suppose I'll have to pack these very carefully if they're to survive an ocean voyage."

"I'll order some barrels," Ezra replied absently, not yet feeling at ease with his thoughts.

The front door was opened and closed noisily, and Susannah's bubbling laughter rang out, joined by the braying of Asa. Ezra frowned slightly. His daughter and her stepbrother usually did not get along well, and that was all to the good. Asa was so openly infatuated with Susannah that it repulsed Ezra nearly as much as it did his daughter. He could obey nearly all the demands the Lord made of him, but he doubted he could bear the

16

burden of Asa as his daughter's husband, should that come to pass. It was unthinkable.

Still laughing, covered with snow, they entered the sitting room.

"Coffee!" Susannah laughed. "I smell coffee!"

Ezra looked at his daughter appreciatively as she undid the wide ties of her bonnet and shook snowflakes off its elaborate feathers. Quick as a sparrow, she took a piece of hickory nut cake and popped it into her mouth. Ezra should have disapproved, but he smiled instead. He could seldom resist her, and rarely denied her anything. Her wine-colored velvet bonnet and merino cloak especially became her, setting off the perfect cream and peach of her complexion and enhancing the pure blue of her eyes. Her hair, now freed from the bonnet, sprang to life, refusing to lie fashionably smooth but instead curling into fine black tendrils that framed her lovely oval face.

Asa seized the opportunity to reach out his clumsy hands to brush the snow from Susannah's cloak. He did not trouble to hide the hunger in his eyes.

Light as down she spun away from him. "You'll mark my cloak, Asa," she said, removing it and shaking it lightly. Unaffected by her rebuke, he took the cloak from her to place it on a hanger in the hall armoire. Around the corner from the sitting room, he pressed his face into the silken lining, breathing in her scent, mentally possessing her and all that was hers.

He returned in time to hear Susannah's voice. "Yum! That hickory nut cake is delicious, Mama." She nibbled at another piece. Her eyes, however, were on Ezra. He smiled benevolently at her, but said nothing. Finally she could stand it no longer. "Is there something you are going to tell us? A surprise?"

"What surprise?" Asa asked as he sat down and looked over the serving tray. He said maliciously, "Coffee, Brother Ezra? Tut, tut."

"If you disapprove, Asa, I suggest you report our indulgence, and refrain from joining us." Ezra stared at his stepson, daring him to live up to his implied principles. He watched in fascination as Asa took a large chunk of cake in his fingers and made three large bites of it.

Noisily, Asa licked his fingers. "Any more, Mama?"

"Asa!" Susannah cried in disgust. "You are annoying everyone, and I want to hear what Papa is going to tell us!"

Asa accepted coffee from Prudence, stirred in ample cream and sugar with many clickings of his spoon against the cup, and drank it all without stopping. Heaving a satisfied sigh, he clanked the cup into its saucer. A glint of hostile enjoyment flashed in his eyes as he saw Susannah struggling with her disgust.

Susannah turned to her father. "You do have something to tell us, don't you?" she asked, hope naked in her eyes.

Ezra's eyes crinkled at the edges as he looked at Susannah. Of all those blessings God had granted him, Susannah and his son, Landry, were the most treasured.

He broached the subject of California. However, with Asa present, he showed none of his pleasure at what he had earlier called an honor. No one noticed Ezra's curbing his enthusiasm, for Susannah more than made up for it. She jumped up from her seat and threw her arms around her father's neck, kissing him quickly on both cheeks, his forehead and eyes, until he had to beg for mercy. "I knew it!" she cried, subsiding only slightly. "I've had a feeling all evening long that we'd be going." She turned suddenly, her mouth open in thoughtful surprise. "Landry! We must write to Landry right away, Papa. Will his mission be completed?" Without waiting for Ezra's answer she went on, clasping her hands in pleasure. "We'll be a family again! Oh, what fun it will be with Landry along!"

Ezra smiled, pleased that memories of Independence did not immediately flash into Susannah's mind as they had for him and Prudence. Perhaps God was merciful, and she had been too young to recall. He watched the smiles and dimples come and go on his daughter's face as she spoke of the fun she and her brother would have in California.

But before she built up her expectations only to be disappointed, he interrupted her. "I have reserved space for Landry, Susannah. However, the ship will not wait for him. If he tarries in Canada once his mission is completed, we shall have to sail without him. I don't want you to place your hopes too high. Landry is a grown man now, and may have plans that will not be in accord with the family."

Susannah gave him a mischievous look. "Oh, Papa, you know Landry wouldn't miss an adventure like this for the world! And anyway, he'd never make plans that did not include me—us. But I'll write him tonight, just to be sure."

Asa had been sitting back in his chair, boldly watching Susannah. With mention of Landry, his least favorite person in all the world, save Ezra, Susannah had shattered his dreamy reverie. He had been immersed in fantasies of the two of them, inseparable for the long months of the voyage . . . Susannah falling in love with him. With Landry along, she would not even look at him. He sneered. "Adventure, bah. Though certainly Landry would find that far more attractive than honest labor."

"Don't be uncharitable, Asa," Prudence reproved him, but her eyes met his with understanding.

Susannah swung around to glare at them both. "Honest labor!? You should talk, Asa. Just because my brother is too clever to work with his hands, and you can do nothing else—"

"Children, children," said Ezra.

Asa went on as though Ezra had not spoken. "Sweet Susannah, has it never entered your head that your dear brother is lazy? Have you never questioned that he seems clever at nothing, either with his hands or his head? This so-called mission of his is no more than—"

"Asa! Enough!" said Ezra. "We are not all called to the same purpose in life, and it is not your duty to judge others. Although—"

"You were not called to anything," Susannah hissed.

"Susannah! I will not be interrupted," Ezra said angrily. "Asa, you seem to have taken God's right of judgment on yourself. As your stepfather, and your guide as an elder, I suggest you get your excess in this matter in hand."

Asa's shrewd brown eyes slid from Ezra to Susannah and back. In Asa's view, Ezra already monopolized too much of Susannah's affection. Nothing was to be served in uniting them further. "My apologies," he murmured. "Possibly I have mistaken Landry's finer motives for mere lack of application. I certainly did not mean to overstep my bounds."

"Oh, Asa, you do this all the time! You're always petty and peevish," said Susannah in exasperation. "We were having such a fine time—and now you've spoiled it!"

"The truth is so often unsettling to hopeless romantics," Asa said, reaching for a third piece of cake.

"I knew you didn't mean that apology!" Susannah said triumphantly. Then as he lifted a large bite to his mouth, she added, "But go ahead and make a hog of yourself, and see if

19

anyone cares. At least we hopeless romantics care about each other. We do have friends."

Asa glared at her, his round face reddening. Then with great care he laid the loaded fork back on the plate and placed the plate on the tea cart. He folded his hands across his fat belly. "You have friends? Or is it that you only think you have?"

Susannah left the room in a huff, and Asa picked up the plate again.

Chapter Two

Landry Morrison awakened, stretched, and then immediately regretted putting his arms outside the comforting warmth of the blankets. He retreated into the depths of the bed. He reached for his wife, running his hand along her hip. He did not want to get up. He did not want to face the eager dedication of his mission partner, Phineas Wade. He was tired to death of being made to go out into the cold, day after day, to convert the rugged, ill-educated men of these faraway parts to a religion they laughed at more often than not. He found it depressing.

He lay in bed, putting off minute by minute the inevitable point when he'd have to get up, dress, and go out to preach. His thoughts offered no comfort. There was little in his life these days that he didn't find confusing or tedious or mechanical, except for his new wife, Tolerance. Phineas Wade was tedious—treading only the straight and narrow Mormon way. Phineas was Landry's age, twenty-two, but so much more in earnest that Landry often envisioned him as a goose trussed for roasting.

Pushing that thought aside, Landry gave more serious consideration to his predicament. He had some weighty problems, and not the slightest idea of the way to solve them to his own satisfaction. Though he had a certain pride and a need to be independent of Ezra, there were times, like this morning, when he wished desperately that he was at home under his father's roof, with Ezra to see to the sticky, prickly thorns of responsibility.

With a deep sigh, unable to bear one more serious thought,

21

Landry rolled over and nuzzled his face into the warm soft skin of Tollie's back. His fingers played along her ribs until he had her fully awake and giggling. Squirming and laughing, she managed to roll over just in time to receive a face full of kisses. "I don't want to go out in the cold to talk with Brother Dillon, Tollie," Landry complained. "Brother Dillon doesn't like me. He hates Phineas. He doesn't like Saints. I don't even think he likes God a whole lot. Save me, Tollie. Love me and tell me I may stay in your arms all day long."

Tollie tried to frown, but she couldn't stop giggling. "You're going to be late, Landry. You already are! Get up!"

He kissed her, then looked deeply into her eyes. "Do you want me to leave you?"

She made a face at him, then smiled. "You are being unfair again. I dare not answer that, and you know it. Sometimes I think you would truly lead me astray if I'd allow it."

"I would," he said cheerfully. "I'd allow you to lead me astray right now. I'm sure Phineas will get along much better without me."

Tolerance didn't have the ability to play on the wrong side of responsibility as Landry did. As Bishop Weber's daughter, she had been reared to be elite, and try as she might, her sense of obligation to that higher order always won. She pushed back the covers and placed her feet squarely upon the cold floor, leading her husband by example to righteousness.

By the time Landry had managed to dress, eat a hearty breakfast, and walk the four miles to Dillon's cabin, Phineas, who had preceded him there by half an hour, had managed to irritate both Dillon and himself.

Cephas Dillon liked young Morrison, liked arguing religion with him. At least there was a trace of humor in him, unlike Phineas. He spat luxuriously into the fire at the thought, then shifted in his rump-sprung rocker closer to the fireplace so he could better see young Morrison. "Bet you been doin' somethin' more interestin' than Phineas an' me."

Landry arranged his face into serious lines as he dared a glance at Phineas. He was very cautious these days about what he allowed Phineas to know or even to surmise about him. He already regretted the error of confiding his fears and doubts about some of the Prophet's visions, and of miracles. Phineas had taken it upon himself to be Landry's mentor, and his rigid and diligent savior. That had been the most depressing of many depressing happenings since he had come on his mission to Canada. Assured that Phineas was not paying much attention to him, Landry turned bright mischievous eyes to Cephas Dillon and nodded.

Landry let his mind wander as Phineas droned on about religion. The man irritated him, and though Phineas admitted to only the highest motives, Landry occasionally had his doubts. He felt used by Phineas. Landry, with his handsome face, his wavy brown hair, and his utterly captivating smile, was the advance man, the bait to capture the interest of householders long enough to get them talking about the Church. Phineas called that the work of God, but Landry had come to think of it as whoring for Mormonism. Of late everything about his mission had taken on a sordid cast. He had lost sight of the bright promise of Joseph Smith's visions, and the miracles that were a part of daily life.

When he had been within the security of his family, with the constant support of his father and the warm companionship of his fun-loving sister, everything had been clear to him. Now he knew only indecision and dismay. Doubts sprang from every nook of his mind to haunt him, and to tempt him into saying and doing rash things. Landry sighed, and tried to pay attention to Phineas's new line of attack.

"Tell me, Brother Dillon, have you given any thought to your salvation?" Phineas asked in his mechanical way.

Landry winced.

Dillon gave a wry smile. "Reckon I have off and on, 'specially when I happen to get caught in the woods benighted, or in a blizzard. Troubles like that make a man think a lot about God an' hisself. But I'll tell you, not once did God come an' get me outta trouble. It was always a man, sure enough."

"Has it not occurred to you that the man was sent by God to save you, Brother Dillon?" Phineas asked, leaning far forward in his seat.

Dillon scratched his head. "Mmmm . . . I 'spect that could be, but I can't say. None of 'em laid claim to it."

Landry grinned, but Phineas's face took on a look of severity, and he shifted direction earnestly. "We must not call upon the Maker only when we are in dire need. What we are talking about, Brother Dillon, is a closeness on a daily basis. Saying your prayers, tithing to your church, doing acts of charity, so that you may attain the divine state."

23

It did not occur to Dillon to associate his own openhanded neighborliness with an act of charity, so he said quickly, "Naw, I don't do any of that. You boys're wastin' your time tryin' to save an old codger like me. The only hope I got of gettin' into heaven is if the gatekeeper gets called out o' town."

"Now there you are wrong," Phineas said. "You have a wife, and you have a large family, both of which are required for exaltation."

Dillon slapped his knee and gave a short bark of laughter. "Well now, that's a good'n. Knock up the old woman every winter and I got me a claim on a throne. Sure sounds like a easy church t'me."

Landry moved uncomfortably in his straight, hard chair. Doubts and dark thoughts were assailing him again. What Phineas saw as a means of salvation, Dillon saw as a physical act, and Landry saw as a nonsensical turmoil. He felt like shouting, Who cares which is right? Nobody has an answer! No one cares if there is one!

Phineas's face had gone ashen white. His voice was deadly earnest as he said, "I'm afraid there is more to it than that, Brother. Orson Pratt, one of the Twelve, an Apostle and a Gauge of Philosophy, said, 'All who will not now repent, as the authority is once more restored to the earth, and come forth out of the corrupt apostate churches and be adopted into the Church of Christ and earnestly seek after the blessings and miraculous gifts of the gospel, shall be thrust down to hell, saith the Lord God of Hosts.' "

Dillon's eyes squinted, and his mouth was tight. "You don't say. That's kinder a mouthful, ain't it, Wade? What d'you think all that palaver means? Everybody's gonna be damned but you Mormons?" Dillon slapped his knee. "Think mighty fond of yourselves, don't you?"

Phineas's eyes were bright with the clarity of absolute faith. "We are God's chosen people," he declared. "There can be no salvation outside the Church of Jesus Christ of Latter-Day Saints."

"*Saints,* now!" Dillon howled derisively. "How far you gonna take this?"

Landry smiled and leaned forward in his chair, gaining Dillon's attention. "Let me tell you why we believe this." He looked directly at Dillon and waited until the man relaxed back into his rocker. "Joseph Smith," Landry began, "was an ordinary coun-

24

try boy, born to a big family. He worked as a well digger, and he used peepstones to locate treasure, and after his miracles happened, he was known as the Prophet, and he has guided us."

Dillon's eyebrows rose, but he remained calm. "Say on, Morrison. What did he prophesy? It must have been a doosey to get all of you out on the road insultin' other people's way of praisin' the Lord."

Landry kept his smile in place. "Well, sir, when the Prophet was fourteen, he wanted to join an existing church, but he saw they were all fighting amongst themselves, every church saying it was the only true church. He went to the woods and knelt down and began to pray to God. And here, Brother Dillon, his miracles began. Suddenly two Personages appeared. One of them pointed to the other and said to the Prophet, 'This is My Beloved Son. Hear Him!' Then the first Personage told the boy that he wasn't to join any sect, since they were all wrong, and all their creeds were an abomination in His sight. The Personage went on to say that all those professing their faith in the sects were corrupt and hypocritical."

Dillon sucked at his teeth. "Don't sound like much of a miracle to me. Seems like any man can ask God and get an answer to his likin', 'specially if he's the only one around to hear. S'posin' I was to tell you a *Personage* come to me an' said you an' Wade here was full of horse manure?"

Landry flashed an engaging grin and went on. "But that wasn't all. He was being prepared, but the next miracle didn't happen until September twenty-first, 1823. At Brother Joseph's bedside appeared a Personage who was glorious beyond description. He said he was the Angel Moroni. He told Joseph Smith that God had a work for him to do. The Angel Moroni said that a book had been written on golden plates, giving a history of early peoples on this continent, and detailing the Everlasting Gospel which had been delivered to these peoples by the Savior himself."

Dillon rubbed the stubble on his chin. He looked at Landry, a twinkle in his eyes. "Now, you're talkin' the first real miracle. I'da thought that boy'd sell them plates for the gold."

Phineas's nostrils pinched tighter, and a white line showed at the top of his upper lip. "Don't you think that if you had an angel by your bedside, you might be careful what you did?"

Dillon snorted. "Boy, if I had an angel by my bed, I'd start rememberin' everything I had to drink the night before."

Landry cleared his throat. This was the one part of Joseph Smith's story he could not be skeptical of. By its merits hung his faith. "Let's not get to arguing again," he said mildly, and smiled at Dillon. "With the golden plates, said the Angel Moroni, there was a pair of miraculous spectacles, *two stones set in silver bows*. Using these blessed spectacles, Joseph Smith would be able to translate the golden plates. That is very important, Brother Dillon, for without the Lord touching him, the Prophet could not have read them." Landry's eyes held fast to Dillon's. He waited, not breathing, hoping that Dillon could present no argument, no cynical remark to shake the wonder of the ignorant country boy being able to read with stone spectacles.

When Dillon remained silent, Landry spoke again with more enthusiasm, working out his own salvation more than Dillon's. "Next morning Joseph went outside the village to a hill called Cumorah, and found the golden plates and the spectacles in a stone box just as the angel had said. The Prophet was nearly twenty-two then, a grown man with a wife."

"I don't see how them stones could be spectacles," Dillon puzzled.

Landry said, "That was a miracle. *It had to be a miracle—* wouldn't you say?"

"If he truly saw through them, it surely was. Nearest I ever knew to somethin' like that was Old Woman Chenez, out in the country, used to read some mighty and awful things in water."

Landry moved to the edge of his seat. "But at least water is clear. The Prophet used stones. No ordinary man can see through a stone! He did use the spectacles to read the golden plates. Brother Dillon, think about it. This isn't an ordinary book. This is the Book of Mormon, the most important book in the whole world. It never had any errors in it. The Prophet said the Book of Mormon is the most correct book on earth, and that a man could get nearer to God by abiding by its precepts than by following those of any other book."

"Now ain't that funny, some preacher here a couple years ago was tellin' me the very same thing about the Bible."

Phineas sensed corruption around him. He leaned forward and spoke earnestly. "The Bible, Brother Dillon, is not the *authoritative* Word of God. Mind, I did not say it was not the Word of God, just that there are many errors of translation, and many important

26

facts left out. In fact, the authority was given to Joseph Smith to correct some of these mistakes of early translations.''

Dillon eyed him coldly. "He was a mighty important fella to God, this Smith. Wasn't he the one that got murdered in jail two summers back? Where was them angels then?''

Landry felt the customary sickness begin in the pit of his stomach. He believed in God, and wanted with all his heart to serve, and yet always there came the ridicule that made his chosen religion appear so shallow, almost laughable. He looked at Phineas, and could see that Phineas suffered none of his shame or doubt.

Dillon reached out and laid on another log. "Wade, you an' Morrison here got a imitation Bible and a imitation religion.''

Phineas was mortally offended. He was seeing the face of Evil, hearing the Voice of the Tempter. "Shall we take our leave, Brother Morrison? 'For behold, my beloved brethren, I say unto you that the Lord God worketh not in darkness.' Second Nephi, verse twenty-three.''

Dismissing Phineas, Dillon turned on Landry. "What about you, young fella? Don't quote me nothin' now, just give me a honest answer. Do you believe everything you been sayin'?''

Landry felt as though he were being torn in half. He wished with all his heart that he could deafen his ears and blind his eyes. He wanted to be a good Saint. He wanted the security of his own salvation.

"Can't you give me a honest answer?'' Dillon prodded, his eyes steady on Landry.

Phineas took Landry's arm. "We must be going, Brother Morrison. We have work to do, and it is not in this house.''

"You can't think much of this religion of yours if you're gonna turn tail an' run every time a man questions, or disagrees with you.''

"That's true, Brother Phineas,'' Landry said. "I think we should talk further with Brother Dillon.''

The white line of strain appeared across Phineas's upper lip again. "It is time we left.''

Dillon began to chuckle softly, mockingly.

"I want to stay a bit longer,'' Landry said. "You go ahead. I'll catch up with you.''

"Our mission is together, Brother Morrison. I must insist you come with me.''

"Let the boy be!" Dillon said gruffly. Taking Phineas by the arm, he ushered him to the door.

"Brother Morrison! You are committing a grave error! Come with me now, before it is too late!"

Dillon closed the door on Phineas and walked back into the room, smacking his hands together. "Well now, let's hear what you have t'say on your own."

"I can't stay long. I must catch up—"

"What's the matter, Landry?"

There was great pain in Landry's eyes as he looked at Dillon. "I don't know all the answers, Brother Dillon. I am weak in my faith. I beg you not to judge the Prophet's word, or the Lord's word as it was given to the Prophet, by me."

Dillon sat down comfortably in his rocker, the mischievous hostility gone from his expression. "That's the first sensible thing I heard come out o' either of your mouths today. I ain't gonna be one o' your Latter-Day Saints, but I can respect a man who's willin' to serve his God as best he knows and is willin' to say right out that he don't know all."

Landry smiled, but did not trust himself to answer. Finally he said, "How about a few words of prayer before I leave?"

"Thanks, but don't happen I b'lieve in it. Now you cut across Widder Myers's cow pasture, an' take the loggin' road from there to Buster Fodor's and turn left, an' you'll save two miles walkin'."

"Much obliged, Brother Dillon."

Landry pulled up his collar and wrapped his scarf around his ears. The sun had gone behind the clouds, and the barren landscape, hidden under four inches of snow, looked as cold and inhospitable as the moon.

By the time Landry reached the bishop's house it had become pitch dark. As he neared, he saw Tollie's anxious face at the window, her smooth dark hair haloed by the lamplight. Quickly she came to meet him at the back door.

"Hello, honey," he said, smiling, and pulled her into his arms to kiss her. She made the kiss brief, and whispered, "Father's very worried with you, Landry, and angry as well." Then, trying to keep her voice light, she said aloud, "We were wondering what happened to you. Brother Phineas just left."

So he had stopped. Landry said easily, "Brother Phineas

decided the Devil was at work, and ran off to nurse his cold. I expect I forgot the time.''

Sister Weber slammed the serving dishes on the table. The bishop came from his study and stood by his chair. His grace before dinner was even longer than usual, and rather pointed in the direction of apostate missionaries and the wiles of evil. During the meal the only voices were Landry's and Tollie's, and hers was muted. She did not look at either of her parents, and when she looked at Landry, fear and speculation were in her expression.

Landry tried to appear cheerful. His best defense, he decided, was an offense. He talked of Brother Dillon, God, and the Devil, not hesitating to say that temptation had been rampant, and emphasizing that Phineas had run from it, but he had not. ''I knew the Lord was with me!'' he said triumphantly. ''Dillon threw all the tricks of the heathen at us until I found the right time to tell him of the true faith and the true path to the Lord God.''

The bishop stood up. ''Brother Morrison, you will come to my library immediately.''

Landry crammed down a last bite of fowl and dressing, and scrambled to his feet. In the bishop's library the door behind them closed; he waited for his father-in-law to meet his eyes. Before he dared go further in his own defense, he had to know how seriously Bishop Weber had taken Phineas's complaints and worries.

Bishop Weber began abruptly. ''Of all the young men I have had to castigate, the one who grieves me the most is you.''

''Castigate? I don't really think you should take what Phineas says too seriously. He wasn't feeling well, and I really was working very hard with Brother Dillon. I believe I explained . . .''

Bishop Weber watched his agitated son-in-law. He didn't doubt Landry's sincerity. It was genuine—yet there was something that always rang false with Landry. Was it possible to be too sincere? He cleared his throat. ''I believe it would be wisest if I brought you and Brother Wade together.''

Landry looked alarmed. ''He's sick. He can't come out tonight. I don't think we should bother him.''

''I'll be the judge of that,'' Weber said. ''I have already sent the housekeeper around to inquire.'' He looked up at a knock on the door.

"I didn't bring him, Brother Weber," said the woman. "His landlady said he had taken a fever and 'twould be death to bring him out on a night like this."

Weber turned to Landry, and was dismayed to see the relief written in every line of his young and handsome face. "Our talk will have to be postponed. I think it would be prudent if you were to suspend your missionary activities until then."

"Why can't you just take my word?" Landry asked softly and pathetically. "I am not lying. I was trying my best to enlighten Brother Dillon."

Landry went to find Tollie. He needed someone to talk with, someone to whom he could tell his story as he wanted it to be. He trusted Tollie's faith. It was as pure and uncluttered as his was haunted and twisted with doubt. Perhaps if she saw him as God's man, so could he.

He found her in their bedroom. She was such a beautiful child, he thought, looking at her fondly. But he couldn't talk to her either. Though he was twenty-two to her sixteen, he sometimes felt ages older than she. To him she was so loving, so unworldly, so vulnerable. Her gleaming dark hair, sleek as a blackbird's wing, and her soft dark eyes, and her small chin that trembled whenever she was embarrassed or bewildered, all combined to lock her fast inside his heart.

Paradoxically, he needed Tollie so much more than she needed him. Love welled up in him, along with the dreaded malaise of fear that was always sitting in the pit of his stomach, waiting to spring forth. Whatever might happen to him, Landry knew he'd be a better man, a more whole man, if Tolerance were with him. He looked vacantly across the room, his hand still caressing Tollie's arm. He had always relied upon a woman to determine his worth for him. For so long it had been his sister, Susannah. He had always known he'd be all right, that he'd make it through the trials of life, because in Susannah's eyes there was a portrait of him that served as guide and goal. Now it was Tollie. He squeezed his eyes shut for a moment. Dear God, I need Tollie, he prayed silently.

He stood suddenly, and pulled her up from the side of their bed into his arms. "Oh, darling, wouldn't it be wonderful if we had these days alone together? Just the two of us? Just you and I—"

"And the baby?" she said, blushing radiantly. They had been married only a few months. Their child was due in April.

His smile answered hers, and tears of pleasure moistened his eyes. "Of course, the baby. Our little daughter."

"I thought men always wanted sons."

Sons. One son. One child who would be untarnished by doubt as his father had been tarnished. One son for the father's salvation. Landry suddenly felt the fear rise up. He felt trapped and hemmed in. He could imagine Phineas's voice condemning him, accusing him, misunderstanding him, in the meeting to come with Bishop Weber. He wanted to run. He couldn't allow Phineas or Bishop Weber or anyone else to pressure him right now. His thoughts and his feelings about God and himself were too fragile. An idea popped into his mind fully developed. "Won't your aunts be delighted to hear about the baby? I expect you can hardly wait to tell them."

"Well, I did write, but I only hinted. I wasn't sure then."

"And now we could tell them ourselves. That is—"

"Yes!" Tollie exclaimed, and laughed. "You won't be doing your mission work for a few days! We could, if Father—oh, I am going to ask him right now. Come with me!" Excited, she clasped his hand, and raced toward her father's library.

They left before daybreak the following morning. In the back of the wagon were Tolerance's trunk and Landry's bag, along with a ham, some apples, and other supplies the bishop wished to send to his sisters. Landry had stuffed into his one bag nearly everything he owned. He had not been able to do the same for Tollie, for he couldn't tell her his plan quite yet. He had talked her into packing as much as he could without making her ask questions he dared not answer.

It was a beautiful day after a light snow the night before. The sun lurked behind the trees, sending out fine reddish rays from its hiding place. Ahead of them a cardinal flew from branch to branch as though leading the way. The horse moved along at a good pace, its breath making little regular clouds in the frosty air. Landry took a deep breath of relief and satisfaction. Not a bad omen to see. If God guided by the signs of His own creatures, his decision had been good. He was doing what was right.

"Oh, Landry, I'm so happy!" Tollie declared. "I wish we could ride on forever, just us!"

31

He smiled into her lovely child's face, and basked in the reflection of himself he saw in her eyes. "So do I, sweetheart."

They snacked on cold pancakes and sausage, not wanting to be too full when they arrived at Aunt Lavinia's. But as time passed, Tolerance began to be fretful. "I don't think you're going the right way, Landry. Shouldn't we have turned off before now?"

The turnoff was several miles behind them. Landry let the horse keep up his pace as long as he could. He said finally, "Tollie, did you mean it when you said you wished you and I could go on forever and ever, just the two of us?"

"Of course I meant it," she said petulantly, "but I'm trying to tell you we've missed the turnoff."

He glanced at her face, her short nose and sensitive mouth, then away. If she failed him now . . . but she couldn't do that. They had to go on together. He needed her. He glanced again at the expectant look on her face. He didn't want to see that expression change. Now that the moment was here, he was finding it difficult. After a false start he asked, "How would you like to go visit my parents in New York?"

He shouldn't have been watching her face. He could barely stand the appalled shock he saw there. "Landry, we can't do that! We told Father we were going to see Aunt Lavinia and Aunt Eunice."

Landry kept the horse moving, though it showed signs of tiring and he would have to rest it soon. He hadn't known he was capable of hurting so much. Yet her reaction was normal—to be expected. He told himself to be patient, to talk with her, to tempt her with the adventure—but reason wouldn't take hold. Fear already had a grip on him. He *had* to get away before Phineas accused him, and Bishop Weber condemned him as an apostate. He had to escape, and he had to have Tollie with him. He felt too desperate and hemmed in to be nice.

He said, hating himself for every word, "I'm going to New York now. Do you want to go along, or shall I turn around and take you to your aunts'?" There, he had said it. If she refused him, he had no idea what he'd do.

Her eyes were awash with tears. "Why are you doing this? You told Father—"

"You told your father. I said nothing."

"Landry, I don't understand. How can you do this? You let

him believe that we—that you were planning to take me to my aunts' house. How can you be so deceptive?''

He looked at her and saw the hurt and uncertainty in her eyes. He said firmly, ''You once said you'd follow me to the ends of the earth. Did you mean that, Tollie?''

''Of course I did, but . . .'' Her chin was trembling too hard for her to go on.

''Tollie, I must leave Canada. Phineas plans to do me great harm. What he'll tell your father is a distortion of the truth. I don't know how to defend myself, Tollie.'' He turned to her and looked her fully in the face. ''I want you with me more than anything, but no matter what you decide, I am going home to New York.''

The tears were running down her cheeks now. ''We shouldn't run away, Landry. No matter what Phineas says about you, Father would help you. He knows you.''

''He doesn't know me!'' Landry nearly shouted. ''I can't go back! Give me an answer, Tollie! Are you going with me or not?''

''What if I don't?'' she asked, and nearly choked on the words.

''I don't know,'' he said in a near whisper. ''I won't desert you—I'd take you to your aunts' . . . and then I'd go on . . . and I don't know what would happen.''

She was quiet for a time, tears streaming from her eyes as she wrestled with her private thoughts. She finally took her hands from her muff and wiped away her tears. ''It isn't true, is it—what Phineas said? You didn't apostatize?''

He looked at her squarely, his heart beating hard against the walls of his chest. ''I'm still true to the Church. But you prove my point, don't you? If my own wife must ask me to swear my faithfulness to the Church, wouldn't others who love me less be more doubtful of me?''

Tollie's eyes continued to meet his. In them he saw a strength and rigidity he hadn't known was there. Her voice was steady and cool as she said, ''I am afraid of evil, Landry. If I thought you were not faithful to the Church, I couldn't—I wouldn't go to New York with you.''

''Does that mean that you are going?''

''Yes, it means I am going. If you say it is necessary for you to get away from Phineas, I'll believe you.'' She looked away, then stared down at the muff. ''Landry, please don't lie to me.''

33

Chapter Three

The avenues of New York were clogged with slush tinted hazy gold by the flaring gaslights. Shops lined the narrow streets. There was as much traffic now in the evening as most cities boasted at high noon. New York never slept. As one neighborhood sleepily turned down its lights, another flashed into life. Music could be heard seeping through windows closed against the cold. Carriages skidded and maneuvered around each other. Men in evening wear helped ladies in sumptuous gowns and furs to the curb.

Tolerance watched the bustling activity in awe. She would be terrified to walk along these congested streets. She watched until she could no longer stay awake. Her head drooped close to her husband's shoulder, touching him now and then, annoying him for some strange reason as he tried to keep the horse going. He leaned forward so that perhaps she would wake up, and quit nudging him. If he could stay awake, why couldn't she? He was just as tired—and he had done all the driving.

She sat up. "Landry, I'm so tired and hungry. Can't we stop somewhere? So many houses—surely someone could feed us and the horse."

"This is New York, Tollie, not the country. You don't stop at people's houses and ask them to feed you and your horse."

"But I'm tired and hungry, Landry!"

"We both are," he snapped. Then, relenting a bit, he said,

"But I recognize all the streets now. We'll be knocking on Papa's door in half an hour."

There were no lights on in his father's house as Landry pulled the wagon into the driveway and back toward the carriage house. It was close to midnight. Tollie, open-mouthed, stared up the three stories to the jutting tile roof. He helped her down, and took her hand as they mounted the steps. He turned the familiar figure-eight handle, and in the center of the house a bell pealed.

After some time the door opened and Ezra stood there in the light of a small lamp, blinking. As Landry stepped forward, his father took several steps back. "Landry? My God—Landry?" Ezra shook his head, trying to clear the cobwebs of sleep. He thought suddenly of the disturbing letter he had just received from Bishop Weber. He said querulously, "What are you doing here in the middle of the night?"

Landry laughed exultantly. "Now I know we're home! How I have longed to be chastised by you!" He put his arms around his father and hugged him mightily. Sheepishly Ezra returned his embrace.

"It's good to have you home and safe," Ezra muttered, for the warmth he felt at his son's exuberance touched him deeply. He showed them into the kitchen, lighting lamps as he went. "I expect you'll be hungry," he said, remembering his son's appetite.

Landry was still smiling. His eyes were bright with happiness. "Papa, I'm so glad to be home!" he declared. "I've missed you all terribly. Where's Susannah?"

"She's already retired—" Ezra began, but Landry, leaving Tollie in the kitchen with his father, bounded up the stairs.

"Susannah! Susannah!" Crying her name, he burst into her room.

Susannah was standing by her bed, trying hastily to find the sleeve of her bathrobe. As he opened the door she dropped the robe and ran to him. "I thought I heard your voice!" she cried.

Landry's arms went around her, pulling her tight to him. They kissed, drew apart, laughing with the joy of seeing each other again, embraced and kissed again.

Just as they had when they were young children, Susannah bounded away from him, jumped on her bed, and patted it for him to sit cross-legged beside her. How often they had sat thus, talking over all their secrets, their dreams and fears.

Susannah sat smiling at him, her eyes bright and sparkling.

35

"Oh, Landry! Landry, thank God you are safe! I've missed you so much! Come talk to me. Tell me the good things that have happened first, and then we'll talk about—the other. We'll find the answers together. It will be just like it used to be."

Landry, still standing, was suddenly uncomfortable. He drew his tongue across his lips, then took hold of Susannah's wrists and pulled her to her feet. "We can't lock ourselves away up here talking tonight! I've just arrived—Tol—Papa is downstairs waiting."

She let him pull her toward the door. "Oh, all right. I'll share you tonight—but tomorrow we talk!" She thought for a moment. "Wait, Landry. One thing I think you should know." She looked up at him, her eyes glowing, her black curls down around her shoulders. "Papa got a letter from Bishop Weber. He was very angry, and so is Papa, I'm afraid."

His eyes met hers sharply. "That old fox! He didn't trust me at all. I can imagine the picture he painted of me for Papa. But Papa didn't say anything just now—"

"Maybe he didn't want to spoil your first night. You know how considerate he is. Thank God Asa isn't here, or the whole thing would be out in the open tonight."

"Well, thanks for warning me." He tucked Susannah's hand under his arm. "Let's go down. I want you to meet Tollie."

"Is that all you're going to say? You are going to tell me everything that happened, aren't you?"

"Of course, but not now."

She hung back. "Landry, are you happy? Is she a good wife?" His smile was bright. "Very happy," he declared.

Susannah squinted her eyes. "I don't believe you. Something is wrong. Why did you run away?"

Landry squeezed her arm. "Not now!" he whispered hoarsely.

Prudence was coming out of her bedroom, a ruffled nightcap covering her hair, her heavy nightrobe half swallowing her little figure. Landry deserted Susannah and her questions to catch up his stepmother and swing her around him, while she protested indignantly.

Prudence, her feet safely on the floor again, straightened her clothing. "Watch your step, young man! You're not too big for me to box your ears. Ten minutes home and the house is in an uproar," she scolded, but her eyes were gleaming. She tried to keep it well hidden for Asa's sake, but she had a soft spot in her

36

heart for Landry. She knew well that Ezra was too lenient with both his children, and fostered irresponsibility in them, but she was not much help, for they were both likable. Prudence looked at Landry's shining, happy face. She thought about being a bit sterner, in view of the bishop's letter, but she didn't have it in her.

Downstairs Susannah and Tolerance took appraising looks at each other. Susannah was all Landry had told Tollie, and more. Susannah Morrison was beautiful, and she had an easy confidence and friendliness that comes only to those who are sure of their places in this world. After a moment both girls smiled and gave the impression of instant friendship. With measured gaiety, Susannah brought forth a stream of chatter and giggles as she helped Tollie off with her wraps. She said chidingly to her father and brother, "You men would have allowed her to sit here all night in her coat!" She looked at Prudence. "I imagine that is why God provided us with marriage—men could not get along without someone to look after them."

Ezra chuckled appreciatively. He looked at Tollie out of the corners of his eyes. "Will you listen to my daughter? Her modesty is true and deep."

Tollie smiled, but said nothing. She viewed Susannah with more than awe. She was unaccustomed to hearing a young woman speak so freely in the presence of her elders, and even more unaccustomed to hearing the adults accept such impertinent comments with good humor. It would take some doing for her to become used to this family.

She looked up a bit startled as she realized Susannah was offering to show her upstairs to her bedroom and a bath. She smiled again and got up to follow.

As Susannah took her to the bathroom, then showed her to the guestroom, she kept up a stream of questions about life in Canada and all that could be told about her brother. By the time Landry had returned from stabling the horse, Susannah had reached the conclusion that Tollie was a bit rustic, certainly not sophisticated, but nice. If Landry had to be married, Tollie seemed the sort she might like to have for a sister, the sort who would be companionable but never competition.

Ezra was strangely unsmiling after the girls left. He didn't know what to do, or think. His son was home at last, and before the Morrison family was laid the greatest adventure possible—the trip to California—but it might all be blighted by Landry's disgrace. Ezra wanted desperately to believe that Bishop Weber had overstated his case. He was even tempted to say plaintively, "You did not do or think what the bishop claims, did you, son?" But he said nothing. He would sound foolish, and he shrank from the answer.

As they heard sounds that told them Tollie and Susannah were returning, Prudence served the hot tea and sliced bread, cold beef, and cheese. The family sat down to eat. Two or three times Tollie glanced at her tea, but finally asked for water.

"Tollie's family follow the Word of Wisdom, Mama," Landry explained. "They are far stricter than we. Am I glad to be home! I'm so glad to see something hot, I could drink the potful!"

Ezra stared down at his hands. Was that the explanation? After all his care, and all his faith in his Church, did something so small as being lax on what he considered minor rules lead a child to apostasy? Was Landry's weakness, after all, Ezra's own? This wasn't the first time he had suspected it. And if it were so, who should take punishment—Landry, who at his age should be master of his own soul, or himself, who had not guided him properly to begin with?

"You haven't much to say, Papa." Landry's eyes showed puzzlement.

"We'll talk in the morning," Ezra said.

"Landry!" Susannah gasped. "Did you get my letter? About California?"

"California? No. What about it?"

Susannah's face glowed. "We're going there to found Zion. We will be the first Saints! You too, Tollie. It's very exciting, isn't it? Papa was chosen by the bishop—and President Brigham Young himself!"

Landry's eyes lighted with pride. "Papa, what an honor!" He put his hand over his father's. But his next thought was not so honorable. It would be perfect for him. If he went to California with his family, he, too, would be honored; and he would be well away from Bishop Weber and Phineas's accusations. Part of his thought he said aloud. "A brand-new start for all of us."

Ezra glanced at him, then away. "We'll talk that over in the morning too."

Landry's face grew red. "Papa, what's come over you? I don't understand you at all. Aren't you glad to see me? Aren't you glad

38

I brought Tollie into the family? You'll be a grandpa in a few months—don't you think that's wonderful? You're acting as though I were an outcast or something."

Ezra fought to keep his conflicting emotions under tight control, as he had been doing ever since he had received the bishop's letter. Now they threatened to burst forth in all directions. He could not look his son in the face. "You're home now, with a lovely wife, and I am grateful to the Lord for your safe return. Excuse me now. I haven't been sleeping well. I suggest we all go to bed—it's very late. Coming, Prudence?"

"Papa?" said Landry softly.

As Ezra walked from the room without answering or looking back, Tollie laid her buttered bread on the plate and burst into tears.

Susannah and Landry comforted her until her weeping subsided to an occasional sniffle and she sat wiping her eyes again and again. It was as though, without leaving the room, she had withdrawn from them both. Susannah exchanged a glance with her brother. "Maybe we ought to go to bed now."

Landry shook his head. He ran his hands through his hair. "I've never seen Papa this way. What did Father Weber tell him? He really must have made up some story."

Susannah shrugged. "I think Papa is most upset at your running away. Why did you? What happened in Canada?"

Landry laughed shortly, Tolerance all but forgotten. "Nothing to warrant all this breast beating and hair pulling, I can promise you."

"Then why did you run? Why didn't you face your accuser and straighten it out?"

Landry's eyes drank in her sureness, her beauty and innocence. He smiled and knew hers wasn't the innocence of purity, but that of a single-minded belief in self. Susannah was a survivor in every sense. He was beginning to see that he was not. "Perhaps I would have, if someone like you had been there to help me see what I should have done. But I didn't see it, Susannah. I never see things like that! I'm not even sure I did anything wrong— except run away. I felt alone. Everything was closing in on me. I can see why Phineas said the things he said about me, but he was mistaken. At least, I didn't mean what I said the way he took it."

"Whatever did you say?" She nearly laughed. She was beginning to understand how Landry had gotten into his predicament. He could always see both sides to a question, but rather than enlightening him, it only confused him. When Papa heard all of it, he'd understand too, and take care of it as he always did. Susannah felt much better now. It didn't seem nearly so serious as she had feared.

Landry marveled at her ability to find amusement in something others took so seriously. "Well, I didn't say anything so bad. It was more that I laughed, and didn't say things. We were at the house of a man named Dillon, and he said some disparaging things about the Prophet and some of his miracles. Phineas began preaching—my God, he was all but frothing at the mouth—but I didn't join him, and he thought I had been touched by the Devil." Landry sighed and looked heavenward. "Maybe I have been, because to tell the truth, Susannah, I think some of the Prophet's miracles are pretty laughable."

"You don't believe?" Susannah asked without shock or surprise.

"Of course I believe, but must we be so deadly earnest about it—all the time, with every word, every breath? Isn't there any time to just live and be normal?"

"Like the heathen are, you mean?" Susannah giggled.

Landry managed a genuine laugh too. "Yes, exactly like the heathen are." He paused. "And like you are. Why is it that no one ever questions your faith, little sister?"

Susannah raised her eyebrows. "Why should they? I never tell anyone what I believe."

They had forgotten Tollie, but now she turned on both of them, her hands over her ears. "Do you know what you're saying? I can't listen to this! I won't hear it!"

"Oops!" Susannah whispered to Landry. "I think we should have gone to our rooms. Goodnight, you two. I'll see you in the morning." At the door she looked back at Tollie. "I left one of my nightgowns on the bed for you, Tollie. Don't take too much to heart what Landry and I said. If you think about it, all we said was that we like to laugh a little—and that's not a sin, even for the strictest Saint."

Landry looked after Susannah with something akin to awe on his face. Why didn't he think of something like that to say? Even if it wasn't the exact truth, it wasn't exactly a lie either. She was so smooth.

Now he looked back at his wife, and saw the hurt and disappointment and suspicion in her expression. He helped her out of the chair without saying anything. He felt condemned by her eyes.

Landry Morrison, sinner and confused rebel against God, and his bride Tolerance, daughter of a Mormon bishop, walked in silence and loneliness up the stairs of Ezra's house to the neat room waiting for them.

Exhausted and miserable, Tolerance began to shiver violently. Landry jerked the blanket off the bed to wrap around her. Tollie resisted him for a moment, then moved closer to him. He was trembling too. They sat on the edge of the bed, holding each other and staring out the window at the snowy night.

Tolerance buried her face in the hollow of her young husband's shoulder. He wrapped the blanket around them and held her tight against him. He wished his love of his religion and his Maker were as simple as this. He loved Tollie with all his heart, and the child she carried was more his life and his salvation than anything he himself might become or do. He caressed her, aware of every pain he had ever caused her. He knew she was sad and homesick, still chilled from the journey, dismayed by his father's distantness. She was ashamed of having come to the Morrisons in a manner she thought dishonorable.

He could do nothing about any of these things, except to warm her, and later to make love to her. His Tollie was a tender blossom plucked perhaps too soon from her parents. But he had needed her, and so he had taken her.

Her fingers stroked his cheek. "I am going to write to my parents again tomorrow. I want to tell them everything that has happened."

Landry kissed her. "I think you should. I don't mind now. Papa will help me see what is right. Everything will be all right now, Tollie, you'll see. I just had to come home."

Tollie nodded and smiled, then bravely threw off the blanket and removed her dress and shoes. Landry had shed his trousers and shirt, and shivering, they scrambled into bed.

"Would you add to the letter I write Father? He will not worry quite so much once he knows you are working toward salvation."

Landry agreed, but it struck him as odd that never once had Tollie worried about what her mother might be thinking. His hand found its way through the layers of underclothing and caressed her full, warm breast. He began kissing her neck, moving down her throat, unbuttoning the heavy clothing until his lips found her erect nipples. He teased them with his tongue while his hand went to other places and began pulling down the layers.

Tollie turned toward him, her breath warm in his hair, her gentle hands fumbling at his buttons. They moved carefully, trying not to make revealing noises. "Landry?"

"Yes, darling?"

"Do you love me?"

"Silly goose," he said affectionately. "Don't you know?" Slowly, deliciously, he titillated the inside of her warm, round thighs. His mouth met hers. He ran the tip of his tongue over her lips.

"Tell me," she whispered.

"I love you," he said into her ear, and kissed her once more, lingeringly, exploring gently. "Love me?"

A bit breathless with what he was doing, she gasped, "Yes—yes! We'll be together always, won't we? You'll never leave me—ever?" He moved his mouth down to her nipple again, sucking hard, his caresses becoming regular, until he felt her small explosion of warmth and moisture on his fingers. He went on more slowly as her spasms diminished, but did not move away from her. His own arousal was still unsatisfied. He could feel the roughness of her underclothing against his hot nakedness.

He continued to caress her, to kiss her breasts and explore her mouth with his tongue. Then, when he sensed that she wanted him again, he joined their bodies, and together they moved effortlessly, finding realms of unparalleled delights. They went to sleep thus, slack in each other's arms, replete.

Landry woke up some time later and moved to a position beside Tollie. He adjusted the covers and prepared to drift off to sleep again. But sleep eluded him. He could distract himself with pleasures momentarily, but always the feeling of being hounded returned to him. All his life he had tried desperately to do what was right, but it never seemed to work. He didn't see or under-stand things as others did, and somehow his difference always made him wrong.

He squeezed his eyes shut. This time was the worst of all. This time he had not been entirely honorable. He had tricked Tollie into coming with him. And the charges Phineas was so eager to lay against him had some truth in them. He had denigrated the Church. He couldn't help it. There were some things he just couldn't accept. He didn't know how to, and remain an honest man.

More sins came to haunt him. He thought of the fifty dollars he had stolen from the bishop's desk. He thought of the horse and wagon that was outside now, and of Tollie herself, the bishop's only child. Hadn't he stolen her too?

He didn't know how everything had gone so wrong. He had meant well. He had never wanted to hurt Tollie—in fact, he had tried to spare her anguish. He thought of the talk he would have with his father tomorrow. Perhaps he and Papa could go together to the elders and arrange for some different means of fulfilling his promise of two years' missionary work. It wasn't that he was unwilling to serve the Lord; he simply wasn't cut out to convert the heathen.

As if reciting a litany, Landry, lying warm beside his young wife, told himself it shouldn't matter whether or not a Saint believed in every single one of Joseph Smith's visions and miracles, or the correctness of the Book of Mormon. Even President Brigham Young often took it on himself to explain what the Prophet had meant in a certain passage. Was there some reason why a serious young missionary couldn't do the same? According to Mormon Doctrine, he was a free agent, in charge of his own salvation. He could believe whatever he believed. And if he was wrong, may the Angel Moroni come right down out of heaven, and stand by his bedside, and tell him so.

"I have never felt so ashamed in my life," Ezra declared, angrily shaking Bishop Weber's letter in front of his son. "Ever since this—this report arrived, I have been asking myself where I went wrong, what awful sin I have committed, that I am cursed with such a son as you."

Stricken, Landry looked in silence at his father.

Ezra felt Landry's pain, and his own, but couldn't allow himself to give in to the love that welled up in him. "You have blasphemed! It says so in this letter! Is it true?"

"I don't *believe* it's true, Papa, but I don't know how to defend myself. That is why I left. I needed you—your guidance. I came home to you for help. I need help. You said my mission was the salvation of my brother's soul, even that of Phineas. If that is true, then my salvation is your mission as well."

Ezra stared at the wall, feeling out of hum. He wanted to

believe that there was still some hope of salvation for his son. If he never asked Landry exactly what he had said or done, perhaps he could forget Bishop Weber's accusations. Perhaps hope would remain. For the first time in his life Ezra Morrison dodged an issue.

He shifted his gaze to his son and kept it there so long that Landry lowered his eyes. Finally, with no softening in his face, Ezra said, "I will help you. Each evening for one hour, you and I will meet privately and read over the Book of Mormon and the Doctrine and Covenants. We will continue until all doubt has been banished from you, until all trace of the influence of evil on your thoughts and your soul has been crushed."

Landry fell to his knees and kissed his father's hand. "Thank you, Papa. I pray you can succeed. I never meant to do wrong. I—"

"Stand on your feet! We shall begin this evening at eight o'clock."

Ezra sat for some time, pondering the enormity of the task he had undertaken. He had to succeed for his son's sake, for his own sake. There *was* no salvation for those outside the Church. This was Landry's last chance. If he failed, Ezra had no choice but to turn his back on his son forever. It was Ezra's duty to take care of those who still believed in the Church, and let the Devil take his own.

Chapter Four

The meeting hall was crowded on a frigid night in mid-January, 1846. Nearly a hundred men and women were seated; about as many children roamed, squirmed in their seats, or engaged in minor personal confrontations around the periphery. In the warmth of the room people were holding their coats on their laps.

There was a crackling of tension and excitement in the air. Most of the people were anxious, but tried to hide it, which only added to the charged atmosphere. They chatted among themselves with a well-practiced sophistication, always trying to glean information or feelings from their conversation partners. Mothers kept wary, alert eyes on their offspring. Men, not so adept at cool sophistry, wished they had time to go outside and have a chew or a smoke. But no one moved from his place. They were waiting for eight o'clock, and the appearance of their leader, Elder Samuel Brannan.

Ezra's family had arrived early, as Ezra had agreed to help usher. Prudence and Susannah sat in the front row where Ezra had placed them, a position that befitted his wealth. Ezra's mood, glum of late, lightened immediately as many men reached out to shake his hand and talk with him. Susannah was immediately surrounded by other young women and men of her age, all talking excitedly about what they might find in California and what kind of clothing might be appropriate aboard ship. Asa tried to join in, but was commandeered to place additional chairs in the already crowded hall:

"I'm certainly not going to look like a drudge aboard ship," Susannah said pertly, with a condescending glance for one girl who had been preaching prudence in dress. "Just because we are en route someplace does not mean life stops. *I'm* going to enjoy myself!"

As the other girls began tittering and talking about clothing, Susannah looked anxiously around the hall. Landry and Tolerance were supposed to be here, but she hadn't seen them yet.

A sort of truce had been called within the family regarding Landry. Each member had his or her own opinion about the handling of the matter, and no one agreed on anything. To quell the squabbles and hard feelings that were developing, Ezra had called an end to discussion. They would give Landry a chance to redeem himself, and to prove he was not an apostate. In Ezra's mind, it was all up to Landry.

Ezra was still mightily upset by his son. His fears did not seem to lessen, only deepen. He had had several prayer meetings with Landry, and they seemed to go fairly well, but that was all that had gone well. Landry had insisted on establishing his own home, so he was not living under his father's roof, but in a small cold apartment of his own. He worked for Ezra in the bakery, and did his job well enough, but without any dedication or sense of belonging. It was in that Ezra saw the danger. He feared something had happened to his son that had permanently separated him from those who loved him. Ezra feared that Landry really did not belong—not in the bakery, not in the family, not in the Church.

Just as Ezra was about to sink into morbidity, there was a stir at the main door. The loud noise of the crowd abruptly quieted, and all that could be heard was the sound of rustling material as all turned to see the man entering. The children milling around stilled and drew back as a tall man strode past them to a small platform in front. Behind him scurried Bishop Waterman.

Susannah's eyes and mouth were open as she stared at the man she had seen one other time, from the back and in a snowstorm. She felt a warm, rosy blush of pleasure reach her cheeks. She couldn't take her eyes off him. Thick waves of rich brown hair curled around his head, framing his face. His sideburns and goatee were luxuriant. His pearl-gray frock coat and trousers were the latest in elegance, fitting the breadth of his shoulders and the slimness of his waist perfectly. Even the way he walked, mas-

46

sively yet gracefully, showed his complete awareness of himself as a man. Susannah's heart pounded.

He fairly crackled with vitality. Susannah had already begun falling in love with him. Then he turned to the audience, raising his hands in greeting and smiling, and her thralldom was complete. He was exceptionally handsome, with flashing brown eyes and an infectious smile that revealed even white teeth. She had never seen a man like Sam Brannan before.

Susannah was in such turmoil that she did not hear the prayer that opened the meeting, or Bishop Waterman's words of introduction. Her whole inner being was stopped, still and waiting for the words that would come from Elder Sam Brannan's mouth.

When at last he spoke, she thought she would faint. His voice was compelling, authoritative, full and deep. He said, still smiling in that joyous way, "Praise the Lord!" And every face in the hall smiled back, and every voice cried, "Praise the Lord!"

Not satisfied with mere joy, he called again, "Praise the Lord! You are His chosen ones! Give Him praise!"

Wildly exuberant calls of praise rose and echoed against the walls. The tensions and fears in the room were being shattered and tossed away by the powerful, charismatic man who commanded all attention and trust.

Quieting, Brannan went on in his melodious, carrying voice, "I am gratified to see so many of you here tonight, especially with the weather threatening. We are the vanguard! We, the strong, are here—to do God's work!"

"Amen!" the people shouted above the din of clapping hands.

"We came here as strangers." Brannan's voice was pitched low. "But we will not leave as strangers. We are brother Saints." He began to stalk the small stage, electrifying expectations. "Brothers! Sisters! Turn to your left and shake hands with your neighbor! Tell him your name. He is your best friend! Your success depends on his success! Now turn to your right, and meet your best friend on that side. Laugh, brothers! Bring joy and courage to one another." As he continued speaking, Sam leaped down from the platform and worked his way along the front row, shaking hands, exchanging a word with each person.

When he reached Susannah, she felt the pressure of his hand. She wondered if it were her imagination, and dared look into his eyes. He gazed into her face, and she knew he felt what she felt.

47

With a slow smile he said, "This is a great, great pleasure. You are my best friend. Our success depends on each other." He paused for a moment, then asked, "Sister—?"

She had to swallow first, but he waited until she said, "Susannah Morrison. I—I am so happy—" She had meant to say more, but he smiled and moved on before she could. She looked at her hand. It felt different now that his fierce grip was gone. Now he was holding Prudence's hand in both of his. Susannah thought she would burst with pleasure. The look from his eyes had been like a caress she could feel all over her body.

He moved back to the platform again. The showman was gone, and in his place there was a serious, down-to-business, practical Sam Brannan, a man prepared to explain details and answer all questions. "Brothers and sisters, we have a lot of ground to cover in this meeting. I know you are eager to hear about the ship. We sail on the *Brooklyn*, a cargo vessel of five hundred tons. The master is Captain Richardson. I am pleased to tell you the captain is a recent member of the Church. The ship is now nearly completely converted into a passenger ship to carry two hundred persons. Many of you have helped to sustain the cost of this conversion, but we're going to need further contributions for that work.

"Now, as to the cost of the voyage itself. We've been conferring with Brother Richardson, figuring the cost per person. Our original estimate of seventy-five dollars for each adult has proved correct. That's fifty dollars passenger fare, plus twenty-five dollars for food. You can bring all your children for half fare.

"We had to make a choice when it came to room," he went on. "We want to take as many Saints as possible, and when we get to California we're going to need supplies of all kinds—food, tools, armaments, personal furnishings, equipment for a settlement. So we've divided the cargo space and the passenger space in the way we thought best for the service of our mission. You're going to be a bit cramped in your cabins, and I don't want you to expect otherwise—"

"There goes your beautiful wardrobe, Susannah," one girl whispered.

Susannah grinned. "Uh-uh, I'm a wizard at packing."

"There are two very important pieces of machinery going with us. One is the Washington printing press that belongs to me," Sam said. "The very press on which we used to print *The*

Prophet, and on which, when we reach California, I intend to print the first newspaper in the West!'' Cheers greeted the statement.

''The other important machinery belongs to Brother Ezra Morrison. It is a large flouring mill, bought especially for this emigration, which will be put to use for the benefit of us all as soon as we get it erected.''

Susannah found herself blushing again. Sam Brannan looked right at her. She was in love. Surely this was love. It had to be. Anything more exciting would cause her heart to stop. With a rush of vanity, she was glad she had worn her rose-colored silk blouse and the wine-red skirt that went so well with it. The outfit was very becoming to her complexion and her hair. It was almost as if this night, this meeting Samuel Brannan, had been foreordained. She wondered if it was. Was it a revelation? How did one ever know the truth of these things?

An old woman had asked, ''How come Brigham ain't going with us?''

Prudence leaned over and said, ''I've wondered that too.''

Brannan said, ''President Young is leading another party overland, out of Nauvoo, Illinois. He especially asked us to take this party around Cape Horn and meet him in California, right on the Pacific Ocean at San Francisco Bay.''

''Thought I heard you didn't get on with Brother Brigham,'' said a man.

Sam Brannan did not look disconcerted. ''I'm sorry you heard that, brother. Rumor is a nasty weapon. It's a hard thing for a man to fight. What you heard wasn't true. We are all good Saints together. Brother Brigham and I will work together for God. And it is a fact that I was good friends with that respected patriarch, William Smith, the Prophet's brother, and with the Prophet himself.''

Asa Radburn didn't care who got along with whom. He leaned back in his chair near the rear of the hall. His mind was full of visions of a slimmed-downed version of himself as a Danite, wearing a black cloak, a red scarf, a ferocious look in his eyes, and power in his very being. Someday . . . someday people would look at him, and know he could call down fear—of God, of course.

''How long will the voyage take?'' a woman asked.

''About five or six months. It is going to be a long, arduous journey, but take heart. It's not like going to the Dark Continent. You needn't do without forever. You may make arrangements for all your household items to be shipped on other vessels. We'll have many, many businesses and dwellings there, and you'll be glad of your grandma's old rocker.''

Elder Sam Brannan's eyes skimmed the room, his gaze lingering briefly on Susannah. "No more questions? Very well. I want to see the brothers who have cattle and livestock. When you are ready to leave, Brother Asa and Brother Ezra will be at the door to take your free-will offering to complete the renovation of the ship. Remember, 'He doubles his gift who gives in time.' I'll be here for a good while after our prayer, so come right up and take my hand.''

Susannah arrived at Landry's apartment at lunchtime. She found Tollie sitting dejectedly at the kitchen table, her eyes puffy, her soft pink mouth ravaged with crying. Recovering from her surprise, Susannah began taking off her gloves and hat, and laid her coat on the unmade bed. She said, "I don't suppose you've eaten.''

Tollie's gaze met hers and skidded away. "I'm not hungry.''

"Well, I am. And even if you're not hungry, you should eat. How'll you have a proper baby if you don't take care?" Finding nothing in the empty cupboards, Susannah broke bread into two bowls and poured milk on it. "Sugar? Or molasses?''

Tollie stared at her blankly, not answering.

Cheerfully Susannah spooned up her bread, talking with her mouth full. "I'm sorry you didn't come to the meeting last night. It was important to you and Landry. That couldn't be what is troubling you today, could it?''

Tollie looked at her through puffy, reddened eyes. "That's part of it . . ." For a moment a bright gleam of hope lit her face, then died away.

Susannah said quietly, "You can confide in me, Tollie. I know we don't know each other very well yet, but we are sisters-in-law. In a way, whatever worries you affects me. We are all one family.''

Tollie bit her lips as tears began to leak from her eyes again. "Susannah, I just don't know what to do! I love Landry very much, he is everything to me—but maybe I did marry too soon. I don't seem to understand what he needs, or thinks. I . . . nothing is right. But I don't know why, or what to do about it." Again hope came to her face. "Would you think me awful if I told you there are times when all I wish is that I were back under the protection of my father?"

Susannah shook her head. "I wouldn't think you awful—but neither do I think you really mean it. I wish you'd be a little more specific about the trouble you and Landry are having. I'd like to help if I can. I know Landry pretty well."

"He's told me how close you and he were when you were young."

"It's true. So tell me—what is my brother doing to make you unhappy?"

Tollie's sweeping gesture included all of the poor abode. "You can see how we live, and we can't even afford this! Landry goes on as if nothing is wrong, as if nothing bad can happen to us. He seems to think your fath—" She looked down self-consciously, not yet accustomed to calling Ezra "Papa." "He thinks Papa will take care of everything once he is over his anger at Landry."

Susannah blinked, not seeing the problem. "But Papa is helping out, isn't he? He'd never allow Landry to want!"

Tollie hesitated. "Well, yes, he did pay the rent, and he gave Landry his old job back—but when Landry got his first week's pay, he spent most of it on a gift for me!"

Susannah's face was completely blank. She gave a small smile. "But why does that make you unhappy? It seems to me that means he loves you."

"Oh, he does! He does. But he promised to pay for it in four payments, so we are living on bread and potatoes and corn meal mush! We are both always hungry, and cross with each other—and all because of a silver teapot! Look at this place! What use do we have of a silver teapot? Shall I serve high tea with my milk and mush? I simply cannot live this way! Something is wrong with a man who thinks like that."

"Nonsense!" Susannah said brightly. "The only thing wrong is that Landry is trying so hard to prove to Papa he can handle everything on his own that Papa isn't aware of how you are living. The minute he realizes what a burden it is, Papa will take care of it."

Tollie put her head in her hands. "You don't understand! It isn't Papa's help we need! It's Landry who is wrong. He values

51

the wrong things. He seems to get everything backward. I'm so afraid that Phineas's accusations are true. What will happen to us if they are, Susannah? I'm so frightened. If Landry really loved me, he'd be thinking of me and the baby. He wouldn't allow us to go hungry, and he wouldn't let a breath of doubt touch us with the Church members. He just wouldn't!''

Susannah patted her hand sympathetically. "You are making too much of it, Tollie. Landry is a good man, and he has always desired to serve the Lord. Whatever has gone wrong, he and Papa will fix it. As to the other, I can help a bit." She got up and found her reticule, then poured out the contents, about three dollars in coin. "Take this and buy some food. Buy some cheese and a little meat. Be sure to ask for bones, to make soup. And liver is free, and makes a fine meal. Don't start crying again, you goose!''

"But I shouldn't be taking from you. This is Landry's duty."

"Nonsense! Men never know what is needed for a household. That is a woman's task. Not only must we see to the running of the house, but we must also instruct the man in his part in it. A woman must do whatever is necessary! From now on, you tell Landry to give you what you need for some frivolity. That will make him feel manly for giving, and then spend it as you like—or need. With the extra I shall get from Papa, and what you get from Landry, we'll have your house in order in no time."

"But that is dishonest!"

"I wouldn't know," Susannah said indifferently. "I do know crying at breakfast and being hungry every day is wrong. Isn't it just as dishonest to have the means to correct such a situation, and not use those means?"

Tollie's earnest eyes remained steady on Susannah. "You and Landry have such a way of turning everything to suit yourselves."

"And you have such a way of bemoaning your fate, and doing nothing constructive about it, Tollie. I don't think you're in a good position to judge my actions. I am at least trying to keep you and Landry healthy. What are you doing?"

"I am trying to preserve my soul—my salvation! Everything Landry says goes against all that I have been taught from birth! And you are the same way!" Tolerance wrung her hands; her lips worked in emotion. "I don't want to make you angry, Susannah, but I don't understand—and I'm too frightened to think straight. I love Landry so very much, and I cannot understand how I can.

He may well be an apostate—no, he *is* an apostate. I know he is. He—he doesn't mean to be, but he can't help it. I—I must talk to someone in authority. Perhaps the bishop here—''

"For heaven's sake, don't go talking like that outside the family! Landry is in enough trouble as it is! You're his wife, you're supposed to help him, not condemn him!''

"But I am first a Saint!''

Susannah looked at her in angry amazement. Tollie was a trifle too holy, and it all sounded far more like betrayal of her brother. "Don't take this to the bishop, Tolerance. If you must talk to someone, why not my father? Or have you decided he's an apostate too?''

Tollie began to cry again. "I've made you angry.''

"Yes, you have. Landry is no agent of the Devil, and neither am I. You've gotten yourself so overwrought that you see evil everywhere. You are about to cause a great deal more trouble for our family.''

"I don't want to cause trouble.''

"Then don't betray your husband and call it salvation! I'll ask Papa to come here this very afternoon. You can talk to him.'' She donned her coat and bonnet. "If you start now, you'll have enough time to make yourself presentable for Papa.''

Susannah ran into the bakery. She brushed Asa aside and went to find Landry.

"Susannah! What brings you here?'' Landry, getting a good look at her, hurried her to the privacy of a storeroom. "What is wrong?''

"Your wife!'' Susannah cried without preamble. "How stupid can you be, Landry? One would think you are trying to bring trouble down on yourself. Tollie thinks she is going to lose her immortal soul to damnation because she loves you, and you are an apostate.''

"But I'm not!''

"She believes you are! And she can cause chaos—more than Papa can smooth over for you. Until you're free of suspicion, you must do and say whatever is necessary to quiet all this furor! I am going to ask Papa to go to your apartment at two o'clock to talk with her.''

"Oh, God, no, don't do that!''

"If not Papa, she intends to go to Bishop Waterman. Would you like that better?''

"What should I do, Susannah?" It was like the old days, when he had relied on Susannah to save him.

"Tonight, when you go home, make up to Tollie. Take her a present—from the butcher shop, not the silversmith's. Then talk to Papa. Convince him that the angels, the Prophet, and anybody else you can think of healed you of evil, and you are the most saintly Saint that ever lived."

"But that would be untrue—"

"Then lie!" she hissed. "Now, I've got to see Papa."

Ezra arrived at Landry's apartment promptly at two. Tollie invited him to sit on one of the kitchen chairs.

"Well, Sister Tolerance, you are an excellent housekeeper. I am pleased to see you so capable."

Tollie's cheeks grew pink. "Thank you, Brother Morrison."

"Now, now, don't be so formal! You may call me Papa, or Ezra, or Brother Ezra if that suits you better."

"Brother—Ezra." He noticed she gave the final *a* of his name a long sound, making it come out Ezray. He found Tollie's way of saying it most delightful.

"It was good of you to come. I know you must be busy, getting ready to sell your property and move to California."

"My property is sold now. Brother Denton and I signed the papers this morning. You are the first to know. Now there is only time between the Morrisons and the voyage to California."

Tollie looked down at her hands. "Landry refused to attend the meeting last night."

Ezra gave her a reassuring smile. "Is that your trouble—that you were unable to get your husband out into the cold last night?"

She glanced at him. She hardly knew where to begin. She murmured a fervent prayer for guidance, then said, "That's only a part of it, Brother Ezra. Landry is truly in turmoil. He even hints of leaving the Church."

Ezra sat straighter in his chair. "Do you think he means it?"

"I think that for now he is trying it out to see if it will shock me." She raised her grief-stricken eyes to him. "It does. Even if he doesn't mean it, it still shocks me that he would say it. I am frightened that he may already be beyond salvation."

Ezra nodded, unable to voice his sorrow. He wouldn't have believed this if anyone else had said it, but he had to believe his son's wife. Who would know better than she?

Tollie stumbled on her words, but went on. "And I'm frightened also because we are sealed for eternity. My fate is his fate. There is no salvation outside the Church, and if I am sealed for eternity to an apostate, I am damned as he is damned." Tears came to her eyes. "Landry says I am foolish, but, Brother Ezra, I am terrified. God is good, but He *knows* what is happening. He knows I am living with a man who—" She burst into racking sobs.

Ezra sat quietly, holding himself in, trying not to cry right along with his daughter-in-law for the lost soul of his only son. Finally, with a breaking voice, Ezra said, "My dear, this has gone so far that it is out of your hands and mine. We must choose Landry or our Church." He sighed. "I am helpless. This must be presented to higher authority for judgment."

Tollie suddenly remembered Susannah's angry words. "Ezra, please! Talk with Landry first."

"Of course we shall give him a chance to speak. His sins against the Church are many, but the Lord knows what is in his heart. If Landry is pure in God's eyes, he shall be guided. If it is His will, we shall all work together to save one we love."

"But if His will is otherwise—"

"Then it will be revealed to us, and we shall act accordingly."

In the following week, Ezra's time was greatly occupied with the pressing matter of his son's salvation. Landry tried to take Susannah's advice. He said whatever was necessary to answer Ezra's questions accurately according to doctrine. At the end of the week he was frustrated, and disgusted with himself.

Ezra said, "I do not know what to do, Landry. You seem able to spout doctrine until daybreak, but from your lips it does not ring true. You tamper with mysteries! And you do not repent. By that you are overthrown!"

Landry looked at him with strangely innocent eyes. "Is that the answer, Papa? Is it that I have tampered with the mysteries?"

"The Devil has your mind!" said Ezra savagely. "We do not need such as you in the Church!"

Landry said pleadingly, "But I need the Church."

"I have no choice. I must take this to Bishop Waterman. I have already risked my own standing in the Church by supporting you. I can no longer justly delay."

"Papa, please! If we have the answer, if it is that I have tampered with mysteries and overthrown my own faith, then I can restore myself—I'll never think of another mystery as long as I live! I promise!''

"For God's sake, Landry! This is no game! This is no small matter of a father chastising a son, and a promise, and all is put right. This is your soul, and mine—and Sister Tolerance's!''

"Then let me go with you. Let me speak on my own behalf. Papa, I don't want to be put out of the Church! Please.''

Ezra, still righteously angry, glared at him. Then he said, "Very well. Perhaps you're entitled to that consideration. Perhaps God will touch you and heal you. I pray it will be so.''

When Ezra left Bishop Waterman's office with Landry, he had a sick feeling deep in his stomach. Only Susannah had argued that Landry's problems should be solved within the family. Only she had said that Landry was being betrayed by those who loved him, and that there was no danger of discovery from outside. Now Ezra was bitterly regretful and sad.

Bishop Waterman, it turned out, had never received any communication from Bishop Weber. He was totally unaware of any improprieties while Landry was in Canada. Weber, Ezra saw, had chosen to protect his daughter and his son-in-law rather than reveal Landry's weakness publicly. But it was too late now. Ezra, Landry's father, had been too righteous and too frightened of the threat to his own reputation. He had betrayed his own son.

Waterman had assured Landry and Ezra that had he known one of his elders on mission was sowing seeds of doubts among the Gentiles, he certainly would have settled the matter promptly. Landry had done his best to present his own point of view, but even Ezra could see things had gone too far for anyone to listen to Landry now. Bishop Waterman had become a man with a cause—the scourge of the infidel—asking question after question of the most direct kind, never being satisfied with the answer, or with the sincerity with which it was given.

At length Bishop Waterman had said ponderously, "I have formed an opinion. But let me first submit it to the Lord, seeking His will. I shall see you both, and Sister Tolerance as well, on Thursday.''

Ezra prayed as he had never prayed before. For the first time in his life, he felt a sinner, and his sin had been committed against his own son. He had set in motion a force that he could no longer stop.

On Thursday the Morrisons were back in the bishop's study. Landry and a very pale Tolerance sat close side by side on the sofa. Ezra sat by himself, nearest his son. He glanced at Tollie and Landry, and all he could see was two frightened children.

Landry Morrison could feel his heart thudding inside his chest. He knew the power the bishop wielded, and now it was going to be brought to bear down on him. Perhaps this was where his fear and doubt had always been, and never with God, or God's laws. Somehow Landry had always known that this benevolent power would be turned to crush him. Now the time had come.

Bishop Waterman began abruptly. "Whenever it is necessary to dismiss a member, it is not only that member who loses—it is the Church as well." As Tollie drew in a sharp breath, he held up his hand for silence. "Landry Morrison, in front of these witnesses, it is my duty to inform you that you have been cut off from membership of this Church. You are stripped of your position as an elder. You will no longer be permitted to enter our houses of worship, nor to participate in the sacraments. You will not be admitted into God's grace, though we pray that God will have mercy on your soul."

Tollie, wailing, clung to Landry, crying, "No! No! Please, God, I never meant for this to happen!"

Landry, white-faced, a beading of sweat across his nose and forehead, held his arm firm around his hysterical wife. "Bishop, you are wrong! I don't want to leave the Church, I—"

"You forget yourself, boy! You are in my private home! If you do not get yourself and your wife under control, I must ask my manservant to usher you both out."

"You mean your Danite bodyguard!" Landry shouted. "Why is it, Bishop, that all you holy men need bodyguards to protect you from your people? Why?"

Ezra had been sitting as one struck dead, his eyes staring blindly, his mouth sagging open. But suddenly he turned his head, and in a voice of thunder he cried, "Hush! May God Almighty forgive you!"

Still ashen, Landry glared at his father. Their eyes locked. Ezra's began to water as for the first time he saw hatred in his son's eyes. What had he done? Could this be God's work?

Waterman stepped forward. "You have confirmed our opinion of you, Morrison. Now I should like to conclude this unpleasant task and have you leave my home." He turned to Ezra. "Brother

Ezra Morrison, you are reprimanded for failing to report to me immediately the conduct of your son.''

"Your fellow bishop didn't report me,'' Landry interrupted, no longer caring what he said. "Are you going to reprimand Bishop Weber too?''

Waterman closed his eyes, a long-suffering look on his face. "I have taken into account your valiant efforts, Brother Ezra, to return him to the fold. Therefore, no reparation will be required. Your good standing in the Church will not be impaired as soon as you have completely disassociated yourself from this man. He shall be as though he had never been.'' Waterman turned momentarily to Landry, a look of triumph in his eye.

Ezra nodded, but kept his eyes down, to hide his tears of shame.

"Sister Tolerance, now we must come to you.'' The bishop sat back in his chair and looked at Ezra, Landry, and Tollie. "Landry Morrison, you may leave my house.''

"I'll escort my wife home.''

The bishop said easily, "Brother Ezra will see her safely home.'' Waterman stood up. "You must leave now.''

"Tollie?'' Landry asked, pleading with his eyes. "Together?'' His voice was desperate, and he reached for her.

Waterman coolly placed his hand on Tolerance's arm, pressing it to her side, away from her husband. He rang a small bell on his desk. Instantly two menservants appeared at the door to his office, and moments later Landry Morrison was standing alone on the street outside the bishop's home.

Waterman got right to the point with Tolerance. He was tired of this and wanted his lunch. "Sister Tolerance, you are sealed for eternity to a man who has apostatized. Yet you love your own salvation, you love the Church and its teachings. You will have to make a choice—a choice between this marriage and the salvation of your eternal soul. You cannot have both.''

Tollie, hunched miserably in her chair, swallowed against the knot in her throat. "But if he repents—if he rejoins the Church—''

Waterman waved his hand. "You have heard him. He did not even trouble to prevaricate about his apostasy. He has truly left the Church of his own free will.''

There was a long silence while Tollie sat with her eyes downcast, her lips and chin trembling, and tears running down her face.

Ezra, feeling his own anguish as well as hers, swallowed hard several times, and dabbed at his face with his handkerchief.

At length she cleared her throat and wiped at her tears. "I am ready to give you my answer. I—I—" She could not bring herself to say the words, and the tears returned, with an odd mewing sound that she couldn't stifle. "I—will remain with the Church."

The bishop nodded. "And how have you arrived at this decision?"

"I prayed for enlightenment. I prayed that Landry would heed God's will and serve Him. I prayed that God's will would be made known to me. I prayed for guidance from those members of the Church who are close to God. God's answer came clearly to me."

"You will not regret it," the bishop assured her. "I will attend to the details in connection with your divorce from Landry Morrison."

Solemnly, Ezra took Tollie home to Prudence. He hadn't known what else to do with her. He could not return her to Landry. Landry . . . My God, what a day! He no longer had a son. Tollie no longer had a husband. And their child no longer had a father.

Seated in his comfortable carriage, Ezra felt deathly ill.

Bishop Waterman praised the Lord, and thanked him for having imparted to him the wisdom to deal with the apostate in so satisfactory a manner. Then he went to join his wife and family for his midday meal.

Chapter Five

Prudence came to the front hall when she heard Ezra enter the house. Busy with all the preparations necessary to moving a household across the country, she was less than pleased to have a wan, bewildered houseguest thrust upon her. She wasn't fond of Tollie to begin with—too much of a whiner, in Prudence's opinion. She opened her mouth to question Ezra, then instantly shut it as she looked at her husband's strained and drawn face. Except for the nightmarish flight from Missouri, Prudence had never seen Ezra like this.

Tersely, Ezra explained that the bishop had divorced Tollie and Landry, and that the girl needed time to recover from the severance before she could go on with her life. Prudence recognized that this was only a small portion of the truth, but wisely she did not press for more information right then.

Ezra brooded over the bishop's decision and its consequences for three days. It was not until Monday of the following week that he decided what he would do, and he allowed Prudence access to his thoughts.

Prudence had already known of Ezra's attempts to guide Landry back into grace. But she had not known they had gone to see Bishop Waterman. "I never dreamed this was going on," she breathed, scandalized at the enormity of it, and shaken to her marrow at the thought of an apostate within the family. "And so the bishop has dismissed Landry. May the Lord have mercy on his soul. What will come of him, Ezra? Where will he go? What will he do?"

Ezra wouldn't allow her to see his eyes. "I don't know, Prudence. Landry—I don't know where he is. He didn't come in to work on Friday. I have heard nothing. I don't suppose I ever will. He hates me for what I have done."

"But you did right! Ezra, you had no choice. We must choose God above all. We must be faithful to the Church."

Ezra laughed tensely. "Landry doesn't see it that way."

Prudence bowed her head. Ezra had been right in what he did. She knew that without doubt, but if it had been Asa, she, too, would have had difficulty accepting her duty. Ezra was a strong man, a man of great will and character. Her eyes teared with love and admiration. She gained control of herself. "And so now Tolerance is divorced, and the baby is on the way . . . and fatherless." Suddenly the full possibilities struck her, and she stared at Ezra with wide eyes and mouth slightly agape. "You brought her here," she said, her voice failing.

Ezra had once worried that Prudence would not be able to withstand the shock and the burden of the honor of his taking additional wives, so he had put off telling her. He hadn't been sure he could take it either. He still wasn't.

He cleared his throat; his eyes did not meet hers. "You perhaps recall the evening when Bishop Waterman came to call on me? When we learned we are among the chosen to settle California?" Prudence did not answer, merely went on looking at him, so he hurried on. "At that time he told me—it was a revelation given to him and President Young—that I was—I have been chosen to—save maidens from the loneliness of the hereafter. And, uh, to father as many children as the Lord sees fit." He sighed heavily, and looked upward. "It is a great and blessed work to bring Saints into the world."

Prudence swallowed painfully. "You are speaking of plural wives. Why didn't you tell me before?"

"I didn't—I mean, it didn't seem necessary. Bishop Waterman said that it would happen when and if suitable young women were found. I didn't think—I wasn't certain it would ever come to pass." He looked at his hands. "But it seems the Lord has seen fit—"

"—to take your son from you, and in his place leave you the wife and unborn child," Prudence finished for him, her voice a strangled sob. "Why did you have to get involved, Ezra? Why bring her here?"

Ezra took Prudence's hand. "My dearest wife, where else would I have taken her? Am I not now responsible for her? My son married her. It is my grandchild she carries within her. Because of a Morrison man, she is now friendless and alone in a land she knows nothing about, far from her own family, bereft of the protection she had a right to trust. Can the Lord be any plainer in stating His will?"

Prudence would not face the inevitable. She said, "How long will she stay here, Ezra?" Her voice was small and high-pitched.

Ezra said nothing. Prudence gathered her courage, and a shred of hope. "Will you send her back to her family in Canada? She *is* little more than a child." She knew what he was going to say; her mobile face revealed the dismay she felt.

"Prudence, I must fulfill my obligation to the bishop's request, and above all I must uphold the honor of the Morrison name. I am asking your permission to"—he almost could not get the words out—"to marry Sister Tolerance. I ask you to join with me in saving this young woman and—my grandchild. That child is a Morrison. He should be raised one. Humbly I ask this of you. Will you give her to me?"

Prudence dissolved in tears. Her small mouth stretched in an ugly way; her cheeks and throat grew red. She withdrew her hand from her husband's and turned away so as not to display her grief to him. There were no ways to guarantee that the pretty new wife would not supplant the homely old one in the affections of the husband they would share.

In her mind Prudence turned the entire problem over to the Lord, to take care of as He saw best. And just as quickly, it was no longer a problem for human contemplation.

She wiped her eyes with the backs of her hands and tried to smile at Ezra. She said shakily, "If it is the Lord's will, Ezra."

He put his arms around her and pressed her face down against his shoulder. "I'm doing a duty, Prudence, you must know that. She is a lonely, frightened, bereaved girl, but in time to come she will be a credit to both of us. We must remember that."

"Yes. All the same, I shall miss you."

They stood in an embrace for a long time. "Have you told Sister Tolerance of your plans yet?"

"No, I haven't. Perhaps all our worrying has been for naught. She may want to return to her parents."

"No, I'm sure she will agree to your proposal."

Ezra, relieved that the thing was settled, gave her a hearty kiss. "I shall talk to her in the morning. For now, I suggest you and I make our way to our own bed, snuggle close together, and talk of things more agreeable to our age." He held her close against his side as he turned out the lights.

The following morning he rapped gently on the door to Tolerance's bedroom. He was most uncomfortable, and with cowardly thought hoped she was still asleep and would not hear his knock. Just as he was about to go away, she opened the door. Her robe was clasped securely about her waist and wrapped at her neck so high it touched her chin. Ezra faltered. She looked more like a child he should dandle on his knee than a woman to whom he was going to propose marriage. "I can see you are not yet ready for the day, Sister Tolerance, but I would like to talk with you about matters of some importance. Will you please come to my study in fifteen minutes?"

As he waited in his study, Ezra tried to think how he could best approach this matter with her. Should he be authoritarian? The patriarch? He couldn't be romantic! Perhaps just being straightforward and factual was best. It was a rather cold approach to matrimony, but then these were not the best of circumstances.

He was still brooding over the problem when Tollie came in. She skittered over to a chair and sat stiff-backed, her hands folded in her lap.

"My dear Tolerance, I wish to speak with you concerning your situation. There is little I can say to ease your grief, so I shall come directly to the solution I believe will serve all of us best. I am—comfortably well off, and in a position to support a large family. The Lord never gives a gift unless he intends its use in His service. Since we find ourselves—our family—in such strange difficulties, we should look upon my wealth and position as the work of God. I realize that you have not as yet even considered remarriage, but there is the child to consider, and your own protection. I am asking you to be my wife."

Tollie sat silent for a moment, until she saw Ezra become uncomfortable, and saw hurt register in his eyes. She found her voice. "A sealing for time only?" A woman could enter heaven only when married to a man endowed with the priesthood; a man

63

became perfect in the next world only if he had several wives. Though Tollie could see that marriage would benefit both herself and Ezra, she wanted to be very careful how this was arranged.

"You would choose marriage for time only?" Ezra asked, somewhat puzzled, accustomed as he was to Prudence's delight in celestial marriage.

"Yes, I would," Tollie said shyly. "But I am already sealed for eternity to Landry."

Ezra could not look at her. His voice sounded gruff when he said, "You have been unsealed. Bishop Wa—"

Tollie began to cry.

Ezra fidgeted. He didn't know what to do. Had she been someone else, he would have held her, comforted her, but he could not stop thinking of her first as a child and second as his son's wife. This was going to take some prayer and meditation! His eyes lit as he stumbled across that thought. "Tollie, my dear, I have rushed you too fast. It is all this hurrying about over the California venture—it interferes with a man's good sense. You must rest, and pray, and seek God's guidance. Within a short time I am certain you shall have your answer. Perhaps a time marriage is just what is needed. For now we have answered the most pertinent question, and your child shall have a name." He suddenly smiled. "And I shall have fulfilled the bishop's request before I leave."

Tollie looked at him with new gratitude. "Thank you, Brother Ezra. I am so glad you understand that I am unable to give up hope for Landry. I have prayed so hard. I cannot give up now."

"I, too, pray that he finds his way, Sister Tolerance, but I must warn you, as I must frequently remind myself, false hope is the Devil's tool, and it is difficult to tell the difference between the real and the false sometimes."

In the kitchen Prudence moved quickly, cutting ham and putting it in the skillet to brown, cutting up cold boiled potatoes to put in with the ham. "Sister Tolerance must be hungry by now," she said to Ezra, as he stood by, watching her and enjoying the bustle. "I sent a tray up to her about noon, but she hardly ate a bite, and I haven't heard a word out of her. What did you say to her this morning?"

Ezra chuckled, and snitched a piece of ham from the skillet. "I think she took me quite literally, and has been praying for guidance. I shall have to learn to be careful with what I say to her.''

Prudence smiled weakly, then grew serious. "You must also talk—and carefully so—with Susannah. Surely you are aware that she has not spoken a word to any member of this family since she heard about Landry. Part of it is theatrics, of course, but she is truly enraged, Ezra.''

Ezra said nothing. Where Landry and his interests were concerned, Susannah's loyalties were always predictable. In her eyes Landry could do no wrong—at least, no inexcusable wrong. "Where is she now?"

"Taking supper with the young women of her sewing circle. One of the elders will escort her home about nine.''

Ezra tried to snitch another piece of ham, and received a smack on his hand. He sighed. He wished Susannah were not so adamant, or so bold, in allowing her feelings to be known. Perhaps he should have been trying to save Susannah all along, instead of Landry. One thing was certain: he could not make the same errors of leniency with her that he had with Landry.

The back door was jerked open and slammed shut. Landry, his cheeks red with cold, hat and scarf awry, his eyes hollow and wildly stricken, burst into the kitchen. He glared at Ezra, then at Prudence, then at Ezra again. "Papa!" he sneered. "She's here, isn't she? You took her! You wouldn't even let her come to say goodbye to me! My own father!''

Ezra moved quickly to block his son from going through the kitchen door into the hall. "You can't go up, Landry. Please! You'll only make things worse.''

"Damn you, old man! Get out of my way!''

"Lower your voice! You are in my house, and you will respect it as such. Those who live here are under my protection!''

Landry's voice was low and desperate. "I want Tollie, and I am going to find her.''

"Not in my house!" Ezra shouted. .

"You'd better move out of my way, because I'm going upstairs.''

Ezra stood his ground, righteous anger blazing in his eyes. Landry came straight at him, shoving him aside and making him lose his balance. Ezra stumbled into the kitchen table. He sprawled awkwardly and heavily.

A pain shot through Ezra's hip, but he got to his feet and ran after his son. The two men reached the door of Tolerance's room at nearly the same time. Landry grabbed the knob and tried to turn it, then tried to bash the door open. It was locked. He beat on it with his fists. "Tollie! Tollie, answer me! Are you all right? Tollie, talk to me! Tollie! Please!"

Ezra grabbed his son from behind and for a long time pinned his arms. Landry sobbed Tollie's name, then wrenched free of his father's hold. He began battering at the door with his shoulder. "Tollie! Speak to me!"

"Stop this disgraceful exhibition!"

"I know she's in there!" said Landry frantically. "Why won't you let me see her? Please! Did God tell you I couldn't see her, Papa? Papa! Father of mine! Can I have nothing of value? Tollie! Tollie!" Again he beat at the door with his body.

There was a cry from inside, and Landry stopped suddenly, his whole being listening. "Tollie—is it you?"

"I am here, Landry. I am safe . . . but I cannot see you . . . not now."

"But I've got to see you! Tollie, don't fail me now! I need you!"

Ezra backed up several paces, barely able to stand watching his son. Landry pressed his head against the door, listening intently, despair etched on his handsome young face. His voice broke. "Please, Tollie—"

Her voice sounded hollow and uncertain. "I cannot see you! You must go away, Landry, I cannot see you."

Ezra tried to pray, but his mouth was dry, and the words turned rancid and ugly in his mind.

"Tollie, I love you! I can't go away! I can't!"

"You must leave. Do you hear me, Landry? I will not come out. I will not see you."

"For the love of God—" he pleaded.

"It *is* for the love of God!" Tollie wailed through the door. "Let me be, Landry! I am trying to do what is right!"

"At least let me see that you are all right. Tell me what has happened—"

"Ask your father."

Landry whirled and faced Ezra. His eyes were bloodshot from crying and lack of sleep. "I have no father! I thought I had a wife—but I have no one!"

"Come downstairs with me, Landry," Ezra said more kindly. "This will do no good. Her mind is set."

Reluctantly, casting backward looks at the door, Landry, defeated, went with his father. In as few words as possible Ezra explained that they had been unsealed, and that very soon Tollie would be marrying a man in the Church.

Landry tried to stifle a sob, but couldn't. "She didn't wait long, did she? Three days ago she was my wife—for eternity—and now she is going to marry another man. And my child—what becomes of my child? I brought that child here to earth time. I am the father! Papa, what happens to my child? To me?"

Ezra was finding it difficult to speak. "You must try to find your way back to grace, Landry. Alone. It will be difficult, and—"

"You don't believe I can."

"You are very much like your mother. She laughed at the Church—and I cast her out! Long before the Lord took her from the earth plane *I cast her out!*"

"Just as you have cast me out." Landry laughed suddenly, hysterically. "Will you have any of us left, Papa? Of your own, you have only Susannah. Will you cast her out too, if she laughs or makes a mistake?"

Ezra's eyes met Landry's. "Yes, if she follows in your footsteps, I shall cast her out too."

Landry's face crumpled. Pale, his mouth set, he stared back at his father. "It's a good thing you have the bishop and his little god, Papa, because you have nothing else. It was my sin because it couldn't have been yours, or the bishop's, or the Church's. You've always had to have someone to blame, or nothing holds together for you, does it, Papa? I pity you, for you will never see anything for yourself as long as you wear the blinders of the Church. And I pity Susannah for the pain you'll cause her when she runs against your armor of false righteousness."

Landry had cut too deeply into Ezra's own fears for him not to strike back. "While you are pitying everyone, you might reflect on the losses you have sustained by your own clear sight, and ask yourself which is best. We are done, Landry. I have no more to say to you."

"What have I lost, Papa? A father who betrayed me? A wife who could not wait three days to find a new husband? Is that so much to lose?" Landry turned from his father, picked up his hat where it had fallen on the floor, and let himself out of Ezra's house.

Ezra stood staring after him, his face a stony white mask. Landry had the power of the Devil. Ezra could feel it. He could feel the temptation to doubt, to think as his son urged, but he would not. He would hold fast to the Church.

The following morning Ezra visited his attorney. He changed his will so that upon his death Prudence would receive half of all his real and personal property, Susannah one fourth, and any wives he might marry in the future would divide one fourth equally. Such was his wealth that even if he took five more wives, each would receive enough to live on in relative comfort for ten years or more. He disinherited his son. It was painful, but also rewarding, for as he disinherited Landry, Ezra felt sure he had cast out the Devil as well.

When he reached home that evening, Tolerance was in the sewing room helping Prudence lay out a quilt. There was little sign of tension between them, although Tollie's eyes were deeply shadowed and Prudence's eyes were bleak. Prudence greeted Ezra first, as was her right, and he patted first Prudence, then Tolerance, on the shoulder. Prudence seemed strained and self-conscious. Ezra tried to act natural, but he didn't know what that was: He had a quick vision of a corridor of years stretching out forever, down which he walked, always needing to be mindful of which woman he was to soothe, and who was to come first. He sighed and asked, "Are you improved, Sister Tolerance?"

"I am better, Brother Ezra, thank you," she said with a smile, and glanced at Prudence.

It was Prudence's turn to attempt to be natural. In a stilted voice she said, "Sister Tolerance and I have been discussing her future, Ezra." She waited, but Tolerance said nothing. "She has asked my permission to—" Her brave effort came to a sudden halt.

Tollie said, "Sister Prudence has given her permission for me to marry you, Brother Ezra." She kept her gaze down. Ezra could only guess at her turmoil, gauging it by his own.

He said, "Thank you, Prudence. Thank you, Sister Tolerance. God's will be done." He was glad it was settled. But he felt unfathomably depressed. He sat with his newspaper in a comfortable chair near to his wife. After a few minutes he looked up and asked, "Where's Susannah? I haven't seen her for four days now. She has had enough time to pout. It is time she joined the rest of us."

Prudence and Tollie exchanged quick glances. Tollie looked away first, leaving the telling to Prudence. Prudence took her time, then said, "She has gone to find her brother and talk with him."

Ezra sat straight in his chair and flung his newspaper to the floor. "By damn! That is a bold girl! She knows my wishes on this matter, and she dares defy me! Who has accompanied her?"

Tollie again glanced at Prudence, but this time the older woman appeared to be concentrating very hard on threading a needle. Ezra repeated his question, and finally Tollie admitted that Susannah had run out of the house alone.

"And you let her go?!" Ezra said in a near shout. "Where was Asa? Surely he could have—"

"Asa and Susannah argued. You know how Asa feels about apostates," Prudence said. "Susannah wouldn't have allowed him to come anyway. She has vowed to have nothing to do with any member of this family as long as Landry is ostracized."

Ezra rubbed his forehead. What was he to do with Susannah? His headstrong daughter was capable of any independent action she chose. There wasn't much he could do. He resolved to watch her closely until they were ready to sail for California, and hope that her natural zest for life would eventually overcome her outrage at what had been done to her brother. He might also pray that somehow her eyes would be opened to Landry's mistakes. Landry was wrong, Ezra repeated to himself. He had to be. Ezra's own integrity depended upon it.

Ezra married Tolerance in early January 1846. In attendance were Asa and numerous long-time Church friends of the Morrisons. Ezra, Prudence, and Tolerance were dressed in white wedding robes with a dark sash that crossed from the right shoulder under the left arm. On Ezra's head was a white flat-topped cap. The three of them knelt at the altar, Ezra facing the two women across from him. Around them were seated the wedding guests.

Bishop Waterman sat in a straight chair at the end of the altar. He said, "Prudence Morrison, are you willing to give this woman to your husband, to be his lawful wife for all earthly time?"

"I am willing," Prudence replied.

"Then you will manifest it by placing her right hand within the right hand of your husband."

Prudence took Tolerance's cool hand and placed it in Ezra's. Then she took Ezra by the left arm, completing the linking of the three of them. Ezra and Tolerance exchanged vows. Tolerance submitted her cheek to Ezra's kiss, and the new couple left the altar together, followed by Prudence on Asa's arm.

For Susannah the entire idea of the marriage was shattering, and she could not bear to be present at the ceremony, preferring the seclusion of her room. Her loyalties were in such a welter of confusion, she would not trust herself to watch as her father took her brother's wife as his bride. Not that she couldn't see the sense or the kindness in his action. She could. It was just that none of it mattered. Her father should never have been in the position of marrying Tolerance in the first place. She could not understand or accept any of the events that had taken place.

Poor Landry. Susannah's eyes gushed tears at the thought of the way these occurrences must be tearing him apart. Tolerance represented the first real and independent commitment he had made in his life, and even that had been seized from him—all because nobody would listen to him. If only his own father had given him time, allowed him to redeem himself! But everybody was so busy being right that no one could hear Landry. And now he had been left penniless, without wife or child, or family or community—and without her.

She searched her mind for something she could do for Landry. Not necessarily a sacrifice—though she would gladly sacrifice for his sake if it came to that—but something to show that she, at least, cared what happened to him. Just as she was sure Ezra was wrong in what he had done to his son in the name of righteousness, she was equally certain that she would find a way, some way, to help her beloved brother.

Part II

Chapter Six

Mary McKay had been standing at her front window for a long time before she saw her husband coming up the path from the barn. The sight of him still gave her a deep feeling of downy warmth, but this noon no smile came to her face. He was walking slowly, his shoulders slumped, his head down. These last few months had been difficult for him, and for her as well, for Sean had tried to keep their troubles from her. She had been waiting patiently for the day he would tell her, and she'd be free to talk with him—perhaps help him.

She took a heart-sore look at her husband. She hated seeing him as he looked now. For her he was a man of great inner strength, straight of back and mind, healthy in his spirit. But Sean didn't always see himself through her eyes, and now, not realizing he was being watched, he looked sad and defeated. As he came nearer the house, he lifted his head. She watched his smile come into place, and could even see the sparkle come to life in his gray-blue eyes. She quickly left the window and ran to the door, opening it before he had time to regain his composure, her arms out to him. When he didn't rush to her, she ran to him and wrapped her arms around his neck.

"Mary, Mary," he said, baffled, not knowing what had caused this. "Is—has something happened? Did you burn yourself cooking?"

Mary McKay shook her head and laughed. "No, I did not! I

wanted the comfort of your arms about me, and I thought perhaps you'd want the same of me.''

Sean removed her arms from around his neck, turned her, and began walking the last few steps to the house.

As soon as he had removed his coat and sat down at the kitchen table, she placed before him a steaming cup of hot chocolate and a bowl of soup, then sat down opposite him. ''Sean, I have done all in my power to remain quiet and patient, but I am no good at it. What is it that's been on your mind for so long?''

For the last two months every time Mary had brought the subject up, he had smiled and waved her concern away, but he couldn't any longer. He had seen the bankers in Springfield this morning, and Mr. Donaldson had told him he could have no more time. The bank was taking his farm. He put his soup spoon down, and looked at his wife. He couldn't think of a thing to say. He didn't know where to begin. For her, he had always wanted to be the man who strode the mountaintops, and here he was a failure, about to tell her he had lost their home right out from under them. He tried several times to formulate the sentence that would say it, and get it over with, but he couldn't speak.

''Whatever it is, Sean, we will see it through. We have before, and we can do it this time.''

Sean looked away, cleared his throat, and said gruffly, ''I've decided we could do better elsewhere. We're—we're going west.''

Mary sat stunned, her mouth open. Then she stood up, hands on hips, about to speak. She walked hastily around the room, and sat down again. ''I know you, husband, and you're not telling me the whole truth.''

''Need a man tell his woman all his business? Am I not still the head of this house, and is not my law the rule?''

Straight-backed, stiff-lipped, Mary said, ''It has never been necessary before, Sean. Why should such a rule be necessary now?''

''Because I have made a big decision—to move us west. I knew a houseful of three women would not want to move—it's a woman's way to want to nest, stay in one place.''

Mary's creamy white Irish skin was showing dangerous tinges of pink, and her green eyes flashed sparks. ''Sean McKay, it is bad enough you deceive me, but a worse matter yet that you should say such untruths about me and your daughters!''

Sean looked up in alarm, "Now, now, there's no need to get fussed—"

"You have not told me the truth!"

"The bank is going to take the farm from us," he said in a flat, resigned voice.

"The bank? What has the bank to do with us? Sean, *what has the bank to do with us?*" She felt a tremor of fear, and suddenly remembered a letter from his cousin, nearly two years ago. Why had she just now thought of that? A nervous laugh bubbled from her mouth. She had thought about it because even then she had known it boded no good for the McKays. "Is it your cousin Jack? You sent him the money?"

Sean looked at her for a moment. She never failed to surprise him. "You remember that?"

"I remember it," Mary said. "Is that our trouble now? You mortgaged the farm and sent him the money to come to this country to get started?"

Sean took her small, soft hand in his large, work-toughened one. "Mary, if you remember the letter, you also remember what it was like in Ireland before we left. We were lucky—we had our own means of leaving. The Lord blessed us when he led us to our first little plot, and then to this farm. Not once since we've left Ireland have we gone to bed hungry, or feared that the girls would be cold in their sleep."

His hair was gray now. Every so often, like now, she would look at him and see him as he had been, his hair a deep rich brown, curling about his head, always going its own way no matter how much he tried to tame it with comb and brush. It was still curly and unruly, and its pale color served to heighten the blueness of his eyes, and the weather-tanned bronze of his face. But what had attracted her to him had always been the inner light that shone through his features. Sean McKay was a good man. He always understood and cried for the sorrows of others, and because he was good he always tried to help, never understanding that those others only too often suffered their plight because they made no effort to help themselves. "Tell me what you did, Sean."

He looked down at their two hands joined on the tabletop. "I didn't have enough to bring him and his family here, so I mortgaged the farm. He promised I'd have the money to make the payments."

"He didn't keep his word?" Mary asked, a bit surprised. That didn't sound like Jack. A lazy ne'er-do-well, perhaps, but not a dishonest man—not a liar who would see his cousin lose his farm.

"He's sent me every penny he could scrape together, but he bought his land sight unseen from a man who had returned to Ireland after a spell in this country. It's a rock patch. He's lost his miserable plot, and mine as well." Sean sighed and leaned back in his chair, releasing her hand. "Now you know all. I have done bad by you, Mary."

"We just got the air cleared of untruth, Sean, don't start anew by cluttering it up again," she said tartly.

"I've told you all there is to tell! The truth—all of it. There's not a disgraceful scrap left to tell. I've failed you."

"You've done it again!" she said, her cheeks pink. "I'll not have it, Sean! You have not failed me, and I won't hear it said by anyone, not even you. How much time do we have?"

"We must be gone by the end of April," he said. "Even now the bank is dealing with another buyer."

It was already February—not much time to pack up the family and make arrangements to find a new home. "You said you had told me everything, Sean, but you haven't told me where we'll be going."

He gave a vague wave of his hand. "West. I was told of some men who are planning to take their families west too, so I went to see them last week. George and Jake Donner are brothers—each has a large family."

"But where are they going?" Mary insisted. "West" meant nothing to her. The next farm over was west.

"The Donners are headed for California, a Mexican land where a man can purchase huge tracts for nearly nothing. It is a good place for us to begin again. Another man and his family will be going, and perhaps they'll join others on the road. The Donners are nice enough folk. They've welcomed us, if we care to travel with them."

"What is wrong, Sean? You don't sound very enthusiastic. Don't you like the Donners?"

Sean shrugged. "I liked them well enough. But I can't say I thought much of James Frazier Reed, the other fellow. He's an uppity man, him and his three names and his high-nosed

76

wife. But the Donners are pleasant, and we'll need to travel in company."

"What is it that bothers you?"

He scratched at his chin. "I don't know, Mary. I guess it's that I can't figure out why they are leaving prosperous farms behind to make such a journey. The Donner brothers are not young men—Jake is an old grandfather—and they've got no need to go, as we have." He shook his head. "If I had their prosperity, I wouldn't be leaving."

Mary smiled. "You're a good man, Sean."

He smiled back at her. "A failure, Mary. And I'm dragging the girls and you with me."

"All right. You've said it. Let that be the end of it. We cannot begin life anew with you complaining to God that you want the old back. We've been blessed. Now let us begin to live the new blessing."

"This is no blessing, Mary!" Sean said with a little heat. "We have lost everything, and it wasn't God who lost it for us. I did it! Me and my cousin Jack. We are not blessed, my girl—we are near penniless, and without a place to live."

Mary crossed herself, her way of telling him she was deaf to what he said.

When Sean had finally given up trying to make her see the darker side of their situation, the view he considered the realistic one, Mary said, "I will talk to the girls after a while. You let me talk to them first, then I am sure they will want to ask you many questions about their new home. You should be better prepared to answer them than you have been to answer me. We McKays are not going to set our foot on the road to a new home with long faces! Do you hear me, Sean?"

"I hear you, Mary." He grinned and leaned back in his chair, his eyes twinkling. He loved her very much, and once more seeing himself as she saw him, it did seem that perhaps his feet might touch only the mountaintops. He spread his arms to her, and Mary fitted warmly into his embrace. She was still sitting on his lap when Fiona and Coleen came in from the garden.

The two girls exchanged glances and began to giggle. Coleen was a pert eighteen-year-old with her father's dark brown hair and blue eyes. She had a wide, full mouth ready to smile, and a look in her eye that said she was looking for the man who would be for her what Sean was for her mother. "Working hard, Mama?" she asked saucily, putting her basket of turnips on the table. "Any hot chocolate left?"

Mary started to get up from Sean's lap, but he tightened his arms around her and held her in place. "See for yourself. Your mother and I are having an important talk."

Fiona laughed. "I'll make the chocolate. You sit there and stare at them, Coleen."

"Fresh, fresh girl!" Sean growled, but his eyes were warm. He loved both his daughters, but Fiona was his favorite. He made no effort to keep it hidden. At fifteen she reminded him of Mary. She was petite and well-formed. Her deep auburn hair shone in the sunlight as she moved gracefully from table to counter. Her eyes were merry, a bit greener than her mother's, but with the same ever-present wellspring of warmth and optimism showing through them. In eyes such as those a man would see paradise, for it existed within Fiona just as it did within her mother. Sean's only problem with Fiona was that he could not bear to think of her with a man unworthy of her, and so far he had never met a man or a boy who came close, or even showed promise.

Fiona brought two cups and sat down, both elbows on the table, her chin propped in her hands, her head tilted prettily to the side. "What is happening? Are we going to a social?"

"What would make you think that?" Mary asked with a laugh.

"Well, you and Papa are planning something, and it must be a good thing, so I thought it might be a social. And of course Coleen and I would need new dresses."

"Oh, you would, would you?" Sean exclaimed. "And what for? You're too young to be bringing the eyes of men to yourself."

Fiona's eyes grew wide. "Papa! I wouldn't!"

Coleen made a face but, at a warning frown from her mother, said nothing.

"Well, Fiona, you are right. Something good has happened, but it is not a social." Mary got up from Sean's lap. "If your father would be so good as to return to the land and do a good day's work, we women will have a talk about the new fortunes of the McKay family." She pecked a kiss on his cheek. "Supper will be ready at sundown."

78

Sean stood up, looked at each of his women, then shrugged. "I've been dismissed."

Mary and the girls set to fixing the supper. As they prepared meat and pared potatoes and vegetables, Mary told her daughters what their father had said earlier. At the stricken look on Coleen's face, Mary spun round, her paring knife still in hand. "Before either of you make comment, you will listen to your mama. There is no tragedy in this family! Not now, not ever. We have our health, we have each other, and most important of all, we have our faith. I'll hear nothing else."

"When will we leave?" Fiona asked.

"Mama! Why must we go west?" Coleen cried. "Why can't we stay here? If Papa can get land out west, why can't he do the same here? I don't want to leave!"

"You don't want to leave Billy Beemis," said Fiona.

"What do you know!" Coleen yelled. "You're nothing but a baby. It doesn't make any difference to her, Mama. But what about me?"

Mary's eyes grew hard. "What about you?"

"Don't I have a say in this? I want to live here."

"Whatever the cost to your father's pride, to your family's well-being?" Mary asked coldly. "Get on your knees, Coleen, and ask forgiveness before you say another word. Your words must burn your tongue as they pass through your mouth. God forgive you!"

Tears stood in Coleen's eyes. With all her might she wanted to argue with her mother, but she couldn't say what she was feeling without sounding worse and seeming a more wretched, selfish sinner than she already did. "I'm sorry, Mama."

Mary nodded, then spoke in a softer voice, but still a voice of iron. Coleen listened, for though her mother's words crushed and frustrated her young and very potent desires and dreams of a future, Mary never spoke from cruelty, and more often than not she was right. Coleen forced back her tears as Mary said, "We will work together as a family, each of us bound to and responsible for the well-being and happiness of the others. In that we will find strength, and in that we will find this new fate of ours to be a good one. When we are gathered together, Jesus is among us, Coleen, not when we are all split apart trying to think only of our own satisfactions."

Mary walked over to her daughter, and took her chin in her

79

hand. "Alone we are so weak and powerless, Collie, that all manner of ills befall us. Surely you've lived long enough to have learned that. You might please yourself for today, but never can you find peace and love."

"But I don't want to be alone, Mama—I mean, I—"

Fiona giggled. "It's Billy."

Coleen flared at her. "What if it is? He's handsome, and—"

"Do you think you can find love with one by turning your back on others you love, Coleen?" Mary asked.

"But Billy won't be going west!"

"Your family will be," Mary said. "Will you leave all of us to have your own way?" She thought for a moment. "Or do you love him so much you'd give everything to be with him?"

Coleen glanced away, then down at her hands. Hesitantly she said, "He is handsome—and I like to be with him—and . . ." She thought about the sweet, tender kisses that came so readily in the pale light of the moon, and the warm, electric touch of his hand as it slipped around her waist when they walked home along the garden path. She could feel her cheeks getting red, and could say no more.

Mary smiled, her eyes warm on her daughter. "Keep Billy in your memory, Coleen. There will come a day and a man who will mean much more to you. Perhaps he will be a man of the West."

Coleen nodded, and now the tears fell in earnest. Mary hugged her. "When your papa comes in tonight, you may ask him whatever you wish about our search for our new home, but remember, he sees two sides to this. One is as it should be—we are about to seek the life God has given us. The other view, however, is fraught with dangers and sadness, for he also looks upon this not as a blessing, but as a failure of all he has tried to do with his life. It is our task to be certain no such evils blight our thoughts—or his."

After supper the McKays' parlor rang with laughter, and hundreds of questions about when they would leave, where they would go, and the people they would travel with. Mary was for the most part silent. She had accomplished her most difficult task of bringing her family together in harmony and optimism, and now it was time to think of the more tedious tasks of preparing for the trip.

Near eleven o'clock she looked up from her knitting and said,

"Sean, get your fiddle out, will you? I'd like for us to have a sing before we go to sleep tonight."

Obliging as always, and still pleased she liked to hear him play and sing, Sean tuned up his fiddle, and the McKays sang songs of Ireland, another home they had been forced to leave.

Chapter Seven

Mary wasted no time. She knew they hadn't much to waste, and she didn't want anyone dwelling on what would be left behind, or fearing what lay ahead. The very next morning she was up before sunrise and had breakfast on the table nearly half an hour before the others usually awakened. She called them all out of their sleep.

Sean was still rubbing sleep from his eyes when he came to the table. "What is it that's got us up before the roosters?"

"Oh, I thought you'd heard! Sean McKay is taking his family to a new home in the West. Foolish man that he is, though, he gave them only two scanty months to get ready!"

Sean shook his head. There were days he wondered how he could be so stupid. How many times did he have to experience Mary's whirlwinds of activity until he realized she would drive them all to exhaustion before she was satisfied they were ready to leave. He ate a hearty breakfast. He was going to need it.

Sean went out the door with orders to cut firewood for her cookstove. "We'll need to put everything up, or it will spoil on the journey," Mary said, all business. Turning to the girls, she told them to dig up every winter turnip and parsnip to be found.

Both girls looked out the window at the snow coming down. "Mama! It's too cold today," Fiona complained for both of them.

"And soon it will be raining," Mary said. "Would you rather

82

be a bit cold, or soaked to the skin and digging about in the mud?''

The girls donned their outdoor clothing and went without another word. Mary rooted all her large kettles out of the cupboards and hung each of them on a hook in the fireplace. Another she placed on the raised oven Sean had built in the middle of the huge fireplace, which she called her cookstove.

That first February morning was to set the pattern for all the other mornings that followed. Sean cut wood and hauled it to the house twice a day. Mary kept her kettles boiling. Fiona's and Coleen's fingers ached at the knuckles and were sore at the fingertips, for every evening they were given old clothing to mend and new to make. Coverlets were sewn with money in the lining. Others were made with special linings to keep them warm on nights they would have to camp out in the open.

Mary had her family go through every trunk, every drawer, every cupboard, setting aside those things no longer wanted or needed, or judged impractical to take with them. ''We will have an auction before we leave,'' she said to Sean, who was trying to sit quietly in hopes he would not be noticed and given another task.

''An auction? Now see here, Mary, we haven't got time—''

''We will need the cash! I want you to go through all the outbuildings and add to my household things any item we will not take with us. The sale will bring us plenty of added money. We'll have a fine place west.''

''I wish someone would tell me where west is!'' Fiona said. ''All you ever say is west, Mama! West, west, west! What is west?''

''The Donners are going to a place called California,'' Sean said.

''Are we?'' Fiona asked.

Sean shrugged. ''I have heard the Oregon territory is full of fine land, and it is a part of the United States.''

''Isn't California?'' Coleen asked.

''No, but there is talk of a war with Mexico to make it so.''

Fiona kept staring at her father. ''When will we make up our minds? Are we just going to—to go west and—''

''Would that be so bad?'' Mary asked quickly.

Fiona looked concerned for a moment, then her eyes lit up, and she broke into a broad smile. ''It might be nice.'' She stood up, and put on a quick little dialogue, playing both parts. " 'Why, Miss McKay, I heard you are going to a new home. Where will you live?' " She hopped to the other side of the fireplace. " 'I have no idea, dear sir, and won't until I have seen it.' 'But, Miss McKay, one must always know where one is going!' " Fiona scowled. " 'Must one? Why, dear sir, that is the most awful news, for in all my life I have never met anyone who truly knew where he was going. We must all be doomed to going no place . . . or someplace. Yes, that's it, dear sir. I am going to live someplace.' "

Coleen laughed. "Oh, do sit down, Fiona. You look like a grasshopper, and all you're trying to do is get out of mending."

Fiona glared at Coleen, and Mary smiled, handing back to her the bag of socks and underclothing to be mended. Under her breath Fiona muttered to Coleen, "You'll be sorry!"

Coleen gave her a superior look. "I'm not a shirker like some I know."

Fiona wrinkled her nose. "Maybe not, but I know other things you like to do instead of work! You just better watch out, Coleen!"

"Mary, your daughters are out of hand," Sean said.

Near the end of February Mary and Sean sat late at the kitchen table going over accounts together. Wearily, Sean looked up from the long column of figures. "Let's call it enough for tonight, Mary love. I am beginning to see figures where there are none to see."

Without a word she closed the book, but continued staring thoughtfully at the yellow flame of the lamp. "You have decided we will travel with the Donners?"

"Yes. I know of no other group going when we must, and the Donners have offered a welcome to us."

"Then I'd be glad if you would take us to meet them. I would like to talk with the other women, and see what provisions they'll be taking, and I'd like to know them. We'll be neighbors of a very close sort for a long time, Sean. It would be best if we could begin the journey in the company of friends rather than strangers. Are these people Catholic?"

Sean shook his head. "They're pious enough—I've seen evidence of it—but not Catholic. I doubt they'd mind that we are."

"We'll have to see Father Rooney before we leave, Sean."

"Aww, Mary, you've given us so much to do now, we'll never leave on time! Must we drag the priest into it as well?"

"Heathen! I'll not set foot in the wagon until it is blest—and not a scrap of our household goods go into the supply wagon until they are blest."

"I'll see to bringing Father Rooney out here for supper one evening. I'm sure he'd do a second-rate blessing if he were not properly fed, and given a little libation in his coffee first."

"I surely hope it's to purgatory you go, and not to hell for all your blasphemous words, Sean. I'd miss you if I could not see you again, or have hope of saving your wretched soul."

"I thank you for your kind thoughts, and all the prayers you'll no doubt be saying for me on your knees, Mary." He made a face at her. He began to get up, making a great show of stretching and yawning.

Mary got up too, blowing out the lamp and taking a candle with her to light their way up the stairs. "Don't you forget, you have given your word—we'll meet the Donners and the Reeds, Sean."

"I gave no word," he said, laughing.

"You did indeed, and I'll have you make it good!"

Still chuckling, he slipped his arm around her as they walked the upper hall to their room. Mary gave up the pretense of squabbling with him, and leaned against the comfortingly muscular man she had married and loved.

Whether Sean had given his word or not, he kept it. Three days later, after the noon meal, Sean brought the family wagon around, and the McKays, dressed in their second-best clothes, settled into their seats for the ride to the Donner house. All of them except Sean, who had already met the Donner brothers and their families, were a little nervous. The McKay women sat straight-backed and quiet, each of them trying to imagine what was to come.

As soon as they pulled up in the Donner yard, their fears were allayed. An assortment of dogs and children announced their arrival with barks and shouts of welcome. The front door to the Donner house was flung open, and a pleasant-looking woman stood smiling at them; an older man stood behind her. Though George Donner's expression was not so outgoing, he was a friendly man. Even before she had officially met him, Mary thought kindly of him. She thought perhaps she could feel comfortable honoring Sean's request to call the Donner brothers "uncle," the title of respect they favored.

Mary smiled as Sean helped her down from the wagon and then turned to do the same for his daughters. Alone, Mary approached Mrs. Donner. The two women introduced themselves and greeted each other warmly. George Donner's wife, Tamsen, was one to inspire confidence. She was a small, energetic woman of mid-years, with a ready smile at all times and open arms to all who came to her. At the moment she turned that smile and embrace on Sean's daughters. Coleen laughed a bit nervously, unaccustomed to such easy displays of affection from strangers, but to Fiona, Tamsen Donner was just another motherly woman, and she hugged her back.

Tamsen was favorably impressed with the McKays. Her first impression was of a family who was united, friendly to others, yet maintaining a bit of reserve, and that Tamsen liked—it was one of many signs of intelligence. Tamsen Donner had never lost the quick, curious eye of a schoolmarm, and most likely never would. It had always served her well, and informed her of the subtle language of unspoken messages that showed through the ordinary things that people did as they moved and thought themselves safely private in their thoughts.

Her other great quality was a talent for order, which was apparent as soon as one was in her house or around her family. Without the fussiness of a nervous housewife, she was able to keep her home clean, comfortable, and ready to be used for whatever activity the family might engage in, even moving across the country to an unknown territory like California. She made others feel confident and capable of sorting through the myriad necessities that would ensure success in this new place, because she was doing so in what seemed an effortless manner.

Mary was entranced as soon as she walked into the front room. She stared in awe at the wide variety and large quantity of calicoes and bolt linen and other yardgoods spread out across Tamsen's table and sofa. She gave a quick glance at Sean. Imperceptible to all but her, Sean shook his head. They did not have enough extra cash to purchase yardgoods. With a quick nod and smile, Mary picked up the calico, and looked at its weave more closely. She said to Tamsen, "I can see I still have a good deal of work to do before the McKays are fully prepared for this venture."

Tamsen kept her eyes on the fabric in Mary's arms. "I am sure we could spare some if you'd like to purchase it from us."

"Why, thank you, Tamsen, but I don't believe I am ready to make my choices yet. It is so difficult, with an entire lifetime of furnishings and favorite things, to decide how one can best use the wagon space. I am just not—" Mary looked up as there was a quick knock on the door. Another family entered.

Tamsen smiled. "My husband's brother and his family. Come, I want you to meet them."

Mary and her family were introduced to Jake Donner, a man older still than his brother, his wife, Elizabeth, and his children. The room was very crowded now, and no one could move without someone bumping another person or one of the piles of household necessities Tamsen had set out for packing.

Laughing, George Donner clapped his hands above the hum of talk. "Children! Children! All of you outside!"

A piping voice cried, "It's cold outside!"

"Run! Have a race, and perhaps we can persuade Mama to give the winner a prize hot from her oven!"

Tamsen smiled, shaking her head. "He is always doing this to me, always expecting that I shall be prepared no matter what or when."

Mary laughed. "It looks as though you usually are."

"With the Donner family it is best to be. Sometimes I think we live a bit too casually, but I wouldn't have it any other way."

The two women moved along the tables of goods, Mary's eyes sharp and intent on remembering anything she saw here that she had not already prepared for her family at home. Involuntarily she stopped, her attention caught by a large parcel almost hidden behind some cooking utensils. Books. Chalk. Slates. All the things a woman would need to teach her children.

"There will most likely be no schools when we first arrive, and the trip is a long one," Tamsen said. "I have been told it is a foolish waste of space to carry such things with us, but I don't agree. I will have these things for my children, and I believe the other families will be glad I brought them once we have arrived."

Mary couldn't resist squeezing Tamsen's arm. She liked this woman. "My own are grown and beyond the chalkboard, but we would all love being able to read books as we travel. It would make some long tedious evenings quite pleasant."

"Perhaps we could trade along the way. Between us we will probably have a supply that will last us all the way to California."

"Yes," Mary agreed readily. Then, biting her lower lip, she asked, "Are you pleased to be going?"

Tamsen Donner's smiling facade slipped for a moment. Her eyes searched for her husband. "I don't know. I have misgivings— not about California itself, or even of leaving Springfield. It is just a feeling too vague to tell exactly." She laughed nervously. "It is most likely maternal nerves. I worry about the young ones. It is such a long journey."

Mary's gray-green eyes bored into Tamsen's. For a time she said nothing; then she forced a smile. "Yes, that's likely all it is."

During the following two weeks Mary and Coleen and Fiona emptied their root cellar and preserved everything they could to take with them on the journey. Sean butchered and smoked all the meat they could manage to spare, making careful selection of the livestock he thought young enough, strong enough, and of good enough stock to take with them. The girls rooted in the cold, hard soil of the garden, taking from it the last of the winter crop. All the family were tired. For the first time, misgivings were creeping into the optimistic front Mary had maintained for so long. The time to leave was nearing, and she was too tired to be able to fend off her sorrow over losing their home.

Most of the time Sean McKay considered himself a strong and forceful man, something of a tyrant after his own fashion. That image slipped only on those rare occasions when circumstance butted him up against the mirror of man's ultimate helplessness, and he glimpsed the possibility of defeat. In those terrible times he counted on his Mary to give him a different view of himself and to set him upright again—but now it was she who had seen that awful mirror, and he wasn't sure what to do. When Sean entered the front door of his two-story clapboard farmhouse, he was aware, as he always was of late, that it was one of the last times he'd do so. He found his wife staring wistfully out the window at her flower bed. He could not see her face, but he knew her great gray-green eyes were misty, and that her mouth was turned down at the corners to hold back tears.

Her garden was barren. The little that had been left there to remind them of greener days through the winter had been taken to make food for the trip. Now there was nothing except the still cold and hard earth of winter.

Sean started to speak and raised his hand to her back, but then let it drop. He felt so helpless. It was difficult to be forceful with a woman like Mary. It was like doing battle with freshly whipped honey butter. A man got lost in the softness and the sweetness before he knew he had lost. This time he couldn't lose. He couldn't let her soothe him, because this time she needed him. He had to restore to her the bright outlook for the future that was normally so much a part of her makeup.

She sensed his presence behind her, and turned to him, tears spilling off her long dark eyelashes. "April hasn't softened the earth, Sean—it's still cold." She pressed her face against his shirt. "Will it be like they say in California? Will I have a garden with flowers blooming all year round? No cold soil from the winter?"

Sean blushed as he put his hands on his wife's back and held her gently against him. Fiona and Coleen watched from the front room, their eyes dancing. His voice came out gruff, a contrast to the gentleness of his touch. "For the love of God, Mary, you're blubberin' all over my clean shirt. No one's said we're going to California. We'll decide when we get there. It may be Oregon."

Mary took a deep breath and cried harder. "Why can't we know where we're going?"

Sean patted at her. He hated for her to cry. He didn't know what to do. "Would it make you happy to know our destination?"

Mary sniffed and looked up into Sean's face. He was forty-two years old now. The wind and the sun, the long hours of hard work and worry, had taken their toll on the outward man. His thick wavy hair was more gray than brown, and around his eyes were the lines of years of smiles, and around his mouth was a deep line of laughter. Only in his eyes, his brilliant blue eyes, could she still see him as he had been when they first met and fell in love. All of her Sean lived in his eyes, the past, the present, the future. Now his eyes were telling her desperately that he needed her to be happy about their move west, because he couldn't do it without her.

Her gaze on him was warm with love and a deep trust. "Just tell me I won't miss my garden, Sean—tell me we are going to a better place, and then I'll know everything is all right."

As Sean held his wife so warm and close, his heart had begun to pound. He tried to muster up some anger or humor that would distract him. She had no shame looking at him like that when he could do nothing, and talking to him in her low, husky voice while his daughters were right there to see and hear. He glared ferociously at Coleen and Fiona with no result, so he tried glaring at Mary, willing her to release him, but she smiled. Then, understanding his plight, she began to laugh. It was a tiny sound at first, then, with merry teasing eyes, she was laughing hard.

He began to laugh too. He couldn't help it. But when his daughters joined in as though they understood all that had taken place, it was too much for him. "Coleen! Fiona! You're a lazy bunch at best! Not a room in this house is packed for leaving!" He stomped dramatically into the front room, pointing out stacks of household goods, opening drawers still filled with linens and supplies. "If I'd been blessed by the good Lord in His wisdom with sons, every wagon would be ready to roll!"

"But you weren't blessed with strong-backed sons, Father dear—you must have been a sinner!" Fiona said, laughing. "Better see Father Rooney and confess!"

"Mary, do something with your daughters! Will you stand by and allow them to show such disrespect to their father?"

He had been teased enough. Mary, knowing his limitations, shooed her daughters away. "Back to work, girls. Pack the kitchenware we'll need on the road, and keep them separate from the rest." As soon as the girls were out of sight, and presumably out of earshot, she turned to Sean. He was still nursing wounded pride. "There is no man alive, Sean McKay, who has greater love or respect from his family than you."

"Hrummmphh," he growled deep in his throat, and cast her a doubtful glance.

She kissed him on the cheek. "You're fishing, Sean," she said gently.

He grinned. "And what is wrong with that? If a man doesn't cast his line every now and then, how will he ever get anything?" Happy again, he went briskly toward the door, then remembered his original purpose for coming in. He rushed back to Mary, and placing his hands on either side of her head, looked searchingly into her eyes. "Are you happy now, my Mary?"

On tiptoe, she kissed him lightly. "Very happy, Sean."

He left the house with the air of a very busy man.

Mary went into the dining room, where Fiona and Coleen were

working. She looked at the linens, some of which had been made by her grandmother's own hand by candlelight in a peat-smoked cottage in County Cork. The linens were the treasure of the household, and the girls handled them gently, carefully folding and wrapping the precious cloths in paper before placing them in cases that would protect them from rain and dust on the trip.

Soon Mary stepped back and looked at her daughters. She felt an overwhelming pride in them. Coleen, in her eighteenth year, was broad of face, taking after Sean. Her eyes were vivid blue, the blue of a tropical ocean, and wide-spaced. Her long wavy auburn hair had a mind of its own, always slipping from the neat braid she labored over each morning. Mary's eyes misted again as she saw a soft reddish curl near Coleen's temple. It made her think of her daughter as an infant. That was a part of Coleen that would remain Mary's own special possession as long as she lived.

Fiona began to giggle. Her large green eyes caught her sister's. "Mama is mooning again. It's not the garden still, is it, Mama?"

Mary sniffed and laughed with them. "No, it is not the garden. I was remembering you girls as infants—when I'd hold you in my arms, and you'd reach up with tiny hands and your wee fingers would wrap around mine, and . . ." She sniffed again and dabbed at her eyes. "I have no more to say."

Fiona put the linen case on the floor and came to her mother. "Are you really so wary of our move, Mama? Do you want so much to stay here?"

Mary shook her head. "No, I don't want to stay here, Fiona. I'm just feeling it for the last time." She took a deep breath and looked around her, her eyes still misting, an occasional tear spilling. "Whenever something new comes into our lives, something old must go from it. But every now and then, the Lord sees fit to allow us to see our past, and what will be lost before it is actually gone. I'm looking at my past while still living in the present. I can't help being a bit sad." She laughed self-consciously. "I sound touched, don't I?"

Fiona said nothing. Solemnly her eyes locked with her mother's. Slowly she shook her head.

Mary hugged her youngest daughter. She had no babies left. Fiona was near womanhood. She was but fifteen, but the promise of a womanly body was already in evidence, and the girl had a depth and an aura about her that was wholly, provocatively

91

female. She worried for Fiona, seeing in her what Fiona could not see in herself. Fiona was the universal mother, with her quick sympathy and warmth, but she was also the temptress, and thinking herself above all dangers, she was a tease of the worst kind, unaware of her own power.

Fiona was still young enough that she wore her hair down, and it curled riotously about her face as though a halo of flame always engulfed her. Her skin was the pure milk and roses that only the Irish could produce, and her eyes sparkled after the gem for which the isle was named.

Mary held her tighter. For the moment Fiona was still her child and could be tucked under her nurturing wing, but soon, too soon, Fiona would enter the world of the woman, and that journey, too, might be a difficult one.

Chapter Eight

Mary McKay and her daughters were so busy during the last days before the journey was to begin that they had no more time for misgivings or moments of nostalgia. Packing the entire household into two drays and the family wagon was no mean task, and the work wasn't aided by the uncooperative weather. Spring was late; the ice of winter seemed not to want to let go of the Illinois countryside. Small pools of water stood in the yard, morning ice forming on them in defiance of the increasing power of the sun. The McKays could not pile their goods and stores in the yard, but had to take everything directly from the house and barn to load in the wagon. Everyone was edgy from overwork.

"Mary, we cannot take all this heavy furniture," Sean growled, kicking at the front of a large chest filled to bursting with winter clothing. "They don't even have winter in California, and I've heard it's mild in Oregon as well."

"Sean! Some respect for my mother's furniture, if you please! And where did you learn so much of the West? And what of the journey out?"

"For the love of the saints, Mary, most of the journey will be made in the heat of summer!"

"Is that a fact! Then why are you standing out here shivering?"

"Because you're a stubborn woman who won't see reason, and insists on standing outside to argue the point! The farm implements go in this wagon, not this blamed chest. That's my final word on the matter, woman!"

Mary went back into the house. She never doubted he'd find space for her chest, but this was no time to press him about it.

All of them knew the impending departure had drawn their nerves taut. They were wise enough to realize that the sound of Sean yelling at the oxen to start the trip would cure them, but for the time being each day was a trial filled with decisions and tasks that seemed to multiply as the final hours came near. In only one respect did Mary have misgivings that she could not explain away with good common sense. Sean's instant and strong dislike for James Frazier Reed could bode poorly for a journey during which they would all be in constant contact. From the little she knew, the members of the wagon train resembled a large, sometimes unwieldy family. To begin with animosity toward one of the main members of the train was not to her liking. Yet Mr. Reed could not be all bad, for he was taking his ailing mother-in-law with them without complaint.

Mary handed Sean the small boxes of family treasures—her few pieces of good jewelry, a small tapestry Sean's mother had sewn, some Irish lace doilies she planned to put on her divan in her new home.

"He's a damned arrogant son of a bitch! Who does he think he is, lording it over the McKays? Dear God in heaven, Mary, the man's all but named himself captain of the train, and we've not even set out yet! I won't stand for it! We'll do it the democratic way—by vote. I won't be a part of the Reed train, by God!"

"Calm down, Sean, nothing's been decided yet. The Donners don't seem the sort to be pushed around by the likes of Mr. Reed. Most likely he'll settle in too. He's probably just eager to be going. He'll be more tolerable once the journey has begun."

"Have you set eyes on the palace on wheels he thinks he's going to drive to California?" Sean fumed. "I'll wager he'll be wanting every man-jack of us to be pulling it up over the hills before we're ten miles out. The man should be ashamed to put it to the road, and instead he struts around so stiff you'd think he'd break his back. I do believe the fool's proud of it. Have you seen it?"

"Yes, yes, Sean, I've seen it." She handed him a nearly square package. "Wrap these carefully in the quilt I gave you before you put them in the trunk. They're our paintings; I don't want the glass broken." She sorted through some other breakables as Sean followed her instructions. "You know, Sean, he's a wealthy man, and his family is used to extravagance. Perhaps he doesn't see his excesses, for he's never known anything but.''

"And what am I? A pauper? No, by God! Sean McKay can stand proudly by the side of any man!''

"You're not in question,'' Mary said quietly. "You are a good man, and true. It is plain for all to see. No one snickers behind your back as they do Mr. Reed's, nor do they slyly curry your favor, as they do his. He's an ignorant man, Sean, and not worth all your fretting.''

Sean was pleased by what she had said and had to admit he agreed with her. Sean was a fair man, and all who knew him knew that. He was also a sensible man—at least most of the time. But he frowned at her, his blue eyes looking dark and serious. "He'll cause trouble. You mark my words, wife, before the end of the journey we'll have heard more than we wish of Mr. James Frazier Reed.''

On the appointed day the McKays piled into the family wagon with the carriage hitched behind. Sean stood looking over the land he had farmed for the past fifteen years. Rapidly he tried to think over every square inch, every cupboard, every storage place, to be certain he had taken with him all that he would need to begin again. Taking a deep breath, he cracked his bull whip in the air over the backs of his lead oxen.

The household wagon lurched. Fiona clutched her stomach. They were on their way. A wave of sadness-gladness swept over her, and she clutched her sister's arm. In Coleen's eyes she saw the same tentative excitement she felt in herself.

Sean walked at the side of the animals for the better part of a mile, until he was certain all was as he wished it. He waved the butt of the whip at his drivers, then hopped aboard the family wagon. As the McKay wagons rolled across the familiar countryside, neighbors came to the road to wave goodbye and to wish them well.

Fiona's eyes grew wide as she saw a tall square-shouldered youth standing at the gate to his father's farm. She blushed, and waved at him. For a moment she tried to stare straight ahead as they moved past, but she couldn't. She climbed into the back of the wagon to look out and wave goodbye once more to Toby Walker. How could she have forgotten that she'd be leaving him behind? She hadn't thought of never seeing these Illinois people ever again. So often she and Toby had talked of the wonderful land in California, and the great adventures before them, that she had automatically included him in all her thoughts. It was only today that she realized that all of it was just talk, and he'd be left behind. She was a little downcast when she resumed her seat beside Coleen.

Coleen smiled and hugged her close. "Don't pull such a face, it might get stuck, and then I'd have an ugly sister. You'll meet other boys better than Toby. I had to leave Billy, and you showed no sympathy for me."

"But I'll miss him," Fiona said sadly.

"No more than I'll miss Billy, and you have more years to find the right man than I have. I'm already at marrying age, and haven't a beau in sight. How would you like to be in my shoes?"

"You, you just talk!" Fiona said, sniffling and then giggling. "Boys always fall in love with you!"

Coleen made a face. "When there are any boys. Did you see the men Papa hired to drive for us? I think he picked them to be sure we'd not look twice at them. Not a one is under sixty, I'm sure."

Fiona, still giggling, had to think hard to regenerate her sorrow over the loss of Toby Walker. Her eyes kept scanning the horizon. She had never been far from home, and had often wondered what the rest of the world might look like. So far, all she saw was more of the midwestern countryside, greening in spring, lavishly lush with its rich dark-brown earth glistening moistly in the spring sun.

By midafternoon they had caught up with the nine wagons of the Donner party. Each of the Donner men had one family wagon and two supply wagons, as did the Reeds and McKays. Reed's enormous house wagon lumbered along, towering over the others, its canvas cover flapping against the ribbed top as the wind hit it.

"Can you imagine what it's like riding in that?" Fiona breathed. "Virginia showed me the seats. They're on springs and it doesn't even feel like you're in a wagon. You can bounce up and down on them."

"You were inside that wagon!?" Coleen asked, with ill-disguised jealousy.

Fiona gave her a smug smile. "Virginia Reed took me all through it when I went with Mama to the last meeting. Too bad you didn't want to come."

"Why didn't you tell me? What's it like?"

"Like a house. There's a sitting room right in the middle, with a cooking stove, and chairs to sit on and lounges to lie upon. There is an upstairs where the Reeds sleep, and Mr. Reed has an office right in the wagon. Virginia has a sister, Patty, and two little brothers, Thomas and Jimmy. And they have a dog too, named Cash. You can't imagine all the things they have in there. Mrs. Reed is a fusspot, though. She came in while Virginia was showing me around, and first off she asked me my name, and how many servants we were bringing with us. You would have thought I'd turned into a cockroach before her eyes when I told her we'd have only the men to drive the other wagons, and no one to wait on Mama and us."

"Papa can't stand the sight of Mr. Reed. Have you met him?" Coleen asked, her voice pitched low so that Sean wouldn't hear. "Mama said that just laying eyes on Mr. Reed at a distance gets Papa's Irish up."

"I didn't get to meet him. He dresses like he just came out of the tailor's shop, though. I saw him the day I went through the wagon. He looks very important, and the other men are always running around saying, 'Yes, Mr. Reed, no, Mr. Reed, whatever you say, Mr. Reed.' He likes it, you can tell."

The first night in camp was a pleasant, lighthearted one with the four families getting to know one another. Mary dug out the china from one of the trunks when she saw that the Donners and Reeds were going to eat on the trail more or less the way they did at home. The crockery dishes that Mary had expected to use were put away for another time. "Don't you breathe a word that I even thought of the crockery," she whispered to the girls. "We'll not have anyone thinking that the McKays are less than anyone else in this train."

"Yes, Mama," the girls chorused, knowing when not to argue with Mary. They helped unpack the china, and over the stove that they unloaded from the wagon, the three women cooked the first McKay dinner on the trail.

Many people from the neighboring area came to bid the travelers farewell. That night they camped on a hillside; a lush spring breeze carried with it the first scents of budding trees and spring flowers, and the music of fiddles and harmonicas blended with the voices of the travelers and friends.

Coleen, fourteen-year-old Virginia Reed, Fiona, and Leanna

and Elitha Donner sat together a little away from the main campfire watching the adults socialize. Jacob and George Donner were obviously brothers. What they lacked in similarity of appearance, they made up for in the sameness of character. Jacob was the elder brother, sixty-five years old, father of five, and had in his company two stepsons of fourteen and twelve. His wife, Elizabeth, was a large woman, in all ways the wife of a well-to-do farmer. All who knew Jacob Donner called him Uncle Jake, and quickly all on the wagon train knew him by that name. He elicited confidence, as well as a kind of protective liking, for his health was frail, but his spirit was enduring and bright. Fiona had decided long before they had actually begun the trip that she liked Uncle Jake Donner. He reminded her of the grandfather she had never met, but of whom her mother had endless stories.

Fiona looked among the people for her mother. She heard Mary's laughter before she saw her. She was standing with Tamsen and George Donner and two other couples Fiona didn't know. It was nice to see her mother smiling again. During the last few days a smile in the McKay household had been hard to come by. Now even Papa was regaining his usual ebullient spirit, and maintaining it as long as he wasn't confronted with Mr. Reed.

"How long will it be before other wagons join us?" Fiona asked the girls.

"Papa said we'd be having people join us all along the way," Virginia Reed said, then giggled. "Just imagine how many old 'uncles' we'll have by the time we reach California."

Fiona's face looked closed, her eyes filled with ponderings. She was wondering if she should take the word of Mr. Reed via Virginia. She was sure Sean would not.

Elitha Donner smiled and said, "My father said we wouldn't have many until we reach St. Louis."

Fiona smiled. Coleen said, "I hope some young men are in the new groups. All we have are little boys and old men."

Virginia looked up at the starry sky, a wistful smile on her full young lips. "I wonder what it is like to be in love. Have you ever loved someone, Coleen?"

"Almost."

"Mama said that love is a very good thing," Virginia said, "provided the man also has the means to keep you in the proper

98

style. She says that when you have to choose between a kiss and a hungry stomach, almost every time the kiss will lose out.''

"Ugh!" Fiona groaned. "That's not romantic! Why can't you have both?"

The girls giggled. Leanna, usually shy and retiring, blushed and said, "Well, tonight we can all wish on a star, and the five of us will find our true loves and they will all be wealthy."

"And handsome!" Fiona added.

"And madly in love with us," Virginia said.

"I want to marry a pirate," Elitha said, and burst out laughing.

As if the girls' laughter was a signal, the heads of several mothers turned, and the younger children were called back to their wagons to retire. Coleen and Fiona walked slowly down the hill and climbed into the family wagon. It had been a good night, and the feeling of closeness with the others lingered. "How many more days do you think it will be before we leave United States territory, Coleen?"

Coleen shrugged. "I have the strangest feeling. I know all of this is happening, but it doesn't seem real. I keep thinking I'll wake up one morning, and the rooster will be crowing, and Papa will be singing as he goes out to the barn, and everything will be like always. But . . . for a long time each day is going to be different, and we'll always be in a new place, one we've never seen before and perhaps will never see again. Don't you think that's an odd thing to think about, Fiona?"

"I never thought it," Fiona said, and screwed up her nose in an effort to follow Coleen's mental processes. She hated being left behind or being left out of anything. She yawned and gave it up.

Fiona snuggled down into the warm quilts her mother had provided her and closed her eyes, anticipating dreams of tomorrow's adventures. The McKays were heading west! With their old home out of sight behind them, all Fiona could think of was the great expanse of road and trail that would lead them to a new home. She was smiling as she drifted off to sleep. This was a wonderful time . . . a happy time . . .

Part III

Part III

Chapter Nine

The wharf where the *Brooklyn* lay was thronged in the days before the Morrisons sailed on February 4, 1846. There were big drays bearing goods to be unloaded and hustling men shouting "Make way! Make way!" as they carried their burdens onto the gangplank. Seamen completed last-minute chores. Trunks, boxes, and hampers lined the narrow walkway. There were families: mothers with babies in arms and two or three little ones clinging wild-eyed to their skirts while the older children dodged among the luggage in eternal games of me first; harried fathers overburdened with bundles to carry and things to remember yet to do; young couples beaming with delight at the adventure ahead of them, and knowing that were they older, they would do far better than those they saw on the pier struggling to get their unruly families aboard; maiden aunts and wrinkled grandparents who could not be left behind in New York City and therefore were emigrating with their children.

En masse, and *en famille,* the Saints were voyaging westward. This was not merely a migration of the fit and the Church-obedient. It included everyone: the leaders, the followers, the truly pious, the skeptics, the teetotalers and the hard drinkers, the optimistic, the cantankerous, the richly dressed, the raggedly dressed, and the scrimped-up dandies. Poor as some undoubtedly were, all had somehow raised the passage money to the promising new land where their beleaguered religion could have breathing space.

Susannah Morrison felt neither religious fervor nor relief as her family waited their turn to be checked onto the *Brooklyn*. In the first place, she could not think of this group of people with whom she was standing as a family. There was no Morrison family. She could not imagine that there ever would be a Morrison family again. All that was left was betrayal and anger . . . and disappointment and more anger. She was angry with both her father and Tolerance: Angry that Tolerance had married her father, angry that her father would see to Tollie's needs, but not to those of his own son, angry that Ezra had allowed Asa to take the position of eldest son of the family, the position that should be Landry's and no one else's.

Whenever Susannah was forced to be with her family, as she was now, standing in line with them for all to see, her view of the trip was bleak. Fortunately there was another aspect of the trip that aided her in throwing off the grief and turmoil every now and then. In one small, precious corner of her heart there was an excitement that kept stirring within her, protecting her, soothing her. That excitement was over Elder Samuel Brannan. For months she would be aboard the same ship with Sam. She would see him, get to know him, become part of a great adventure with him, and perhaps . . . She couldn't go on with the thought. She lost herself in a blur of emotion and visions of Sam so near to her that her mind couldn't comprehend the feelings.

Susannah had never been in love before, had never before spent hours lying awake dreaming of a man and hungering for embraces she had never experienced, thinking of the hard muscles hidden under his elegant garments and fantasizing the moving silkiness of them under her hands. She was ready for love and loving now, and she knew it. Elder Samuel Brannan was the man who would explore with her this new world of delight she so wanted. She knew that too. There was a part of her that had already entered into a communion of love with Sam Brannan.

Thinking of this, she felt her cheeks flame, and she turned away from the others and looked at the ship. To her unpracticed eye it looked small and ugly compared to the other ships in port, and its masts seemed inadequate to hold sails bellied out with the great winds of the Atlantic. But it was clean, and freshly painted.

After a long spell the line moved on. Elder Drake, whom Susannah knew, was marking down names, sending families with a guide to their cabins, and issuing the first of many warnings.

"There'll be no cooking in the cabins, Sister Morrison," he said, looking at Prudence. "Elder Brannan has hired a cook and a steward. He's paying them sixteen dollars a month." His eyes showed what he thought of this unexpected extravagance.

Prudence said, "Thank you, brother."

"Brother Radburn, you are assigned to sanitation duty. You will perform and supervise regular morning cleaning of the entire ship. You report to Brother Preserved Hart, who will explain the extent of your duties. We do not want any illness aboard where cleanliness would prevent it."

"I assume that inexperience in this type of employ will prove no hindrance?" asked Asa. His tone was respectful, but Susannah noted that his face was sullen.

"Not at all," replied Elder Drake cheerfully. "Brother Morrison, you are needed to organize a study class of men aged thirty to forty-five. Sister Prudence, we are asking you and Sister Tolerance to make up and teach a sewing class for girls up to age twelve. Sister Susannah, I have no activity scheduled for you. However, you'll soon be assigned." He looked up from his schedules and gave them a tight smile. "There'll be no idle hands aboard the *Brooklyn*."

Their guide stood waiting to conduct them below, so they picked up their bundles and followed him down narrow companionways and through narrow corridors frequently interrupted by the transverse bulkheads. These were heavy partitions that stretched the width of the ship, subdividing the hull into compartments, and always awaiting the unwary head. Cut through the bulkheads were doorways. Single file, and scrunched down to make themselves smaller, the Morrisons stepped high over each threshold. Ezra had the worst of it, for even in the most spacious areas belowdeck he could not stand or walk upright. "I shall have a permanently rounded spine by the end of this voyage," he grumbled as he rubbed his forehead—penalty for having forgotten to duck. Asa growled an agreement. Though he was of average height, he too was walking hump-shouldered, and had taken several knocks on the head. Their tempers were already being tested, and they hadn't even left port.

At a particularly low door their guard said, "Watch your head," but it was too late, and yet another *knock* and muttered exclamation came from Ezra.

Prudence turned to offer him sympathy, lost her balance, and fell against the bulkhead. Aside from tipping her hat askew, she suffered no damage. "My gracious! There certainly isn't much room in these halls. Thank goodness the bedrooms will be larger."

"Not much, sister," said their guide. "Here is yours." He indicated a cabin and stood to one side as they all tried to crowd toward the opening to peer in.

"Where is our other cabin?" asked Ezra, the last trace of good humor vanishing as he looked about the cubicle. "We were to have two. I hope the other is larger."

"You have only one cabin. As you see, there is accommodation for all."

"But this is impossible!" Ezra exclaimed. "Five people—why, our pantry was larger!"

"So was mine," said the guide ruefully. "But we will have two hundred and forty passengers, so doubling up had to be done. Be grateful you are all one family. Quite a number are sharing with strangers."

"Do you mean a stranger might be crammed in here with us?" Prudence asked.

"Well, you did originally reserve space for six, and you have only five—"

"No!" Ezra roared. "We shall have no one else brought in here!"

"We shall manage, if you just leave us as we are," said Tolerance, surprising everyone, especially Prudence, whose mouth was open to say the same.

All of them moved at once, bumping into each other with their bundles, cracking their heads in the darkness on the various projections designed to hold their possessions. After a few false starts they all crowded into the abysmally tiny cabin.

Susannah's eyes teared, partly from the bump on her forehead, and partly because she missed her spacious bedroom at home, with the elegant four-poster bed, the heavy linen draperies, and the fine ruffled curtains, and her own large closet. Here she would be stuffed into a nook hardly fit for a cat, and sharing it with four other people, all of whom she hated. Unintentionally, her swimming eyes met Tollie's. Quickly she looked away, wanting no contact with her sister-in-law-stepmother-traitor.

She turned her attention to the cabin. There were three narrow bunks, one attached to each wall. Their trunks had already been brought down, and occupied the greater portion of the floor

106

space. There was no porthole, no aperture of any kind to let in light or to look out of. The darkness was relieved but little by the light filtering in from the corridor. There was no place to put things, no way to stand up straight and comfortably, no chairs, and, as they would soon discover, there was no end to the motion of the ship in the water.

Ezra struck a match, found the covered light mounted on the bulkhead, and lit it. "Ah, that's better!" he said heartily, and nearly laughed at how quickly he was learning to appreciate small comforts.

"Yes, well, we must put our things away," said Prudence dubiously.

"Where are we going to sleep, Mama?" asked Asa.

Prudence's eyes flicked to the bunks. "Papa and I will sleep there. Asa, you may have the bed in the center. Susannah and Tolerance, the one there." She was very pleased that she had arranged it so tidily, without once considering the marital state of Ezra and Tollie. She hurried on, before she began to think too much. "Asa, you and Papa can find a place to put the trunks. We won't be needing anything in them for a while. Susannah, you and Tolerance make up the beds. I will devise a way to create some privacy for us."

For some minutes they attempted to do their work all at once, but after several collisions, which had everyone laughing but Susannah, Prudence asked the men to be seated on a bunk while the women finished the immediately necessary chores.

"Did anyone say where the water closet is?" Tollie murmured.

Susannah had already noticed a door tucked into a corner, but she said nothing. Let Tollie figure it out for herself. Served her right for being so—so sanctimonious. Susannah couldn't change things for Landry right now, but she needn't be helpful to any of these treacherous people. No one, not even her father or Tollie, had so much as mentioned Landry's name. Susannah resented it deeply.

She glanced at the members of her family, her mouth set. They had gotten their way, and they thought they were free and clear of Landry and all responsibility for what had happened to him, but they were wrong. She hadn't forgotten, and she never would. Landry would get his share of the family bounty somehow—she would see to it. Sullenly she completed her chores, keeping her eyes lowered, and avoiding all contact with the others.

Tollie emerged from the water closet, and stood near Susannah. Susannah coldly turned her attention to Prudence, who had strung bedding up in front of each bunk, providing the occupants with minimal privacy. As the others admired Prudence's handiwork, Susannah stepped unnoticed into the corridor. She moved quickly through the low doorways and mounted the steps of the companionway. Somewhere on this ship was Sam Brannan, and she meant to find him. He alone might make this trip bearable.

As it turned out, she could hardly avoid him. He was highly visible, standing on deck, looking grim as a severe-faced young woman complained, "It's not enough that you force me on board this mean little boat—oh, no! I want you to come down with me right now and look at our room! Why, you can't curse a dog in there without getting a mouthful of fur! And there are no cooking facilities! What are you going to do about it? And don't dare say you expect me to eat the common food!"

She broke off as Susannah stood at a tentative distance, hoping Sam would see her and indicate that he would like to talk with her next.

"What does *she* want?" demanded the irate woman, glancing suspiciously from Sam to Susannah.

Sam brightened as he glanced at Susannah. He said, "Excuse me, my dear, I'll just find out. I am responsible for these people, after all. She has a right to my attention."

"That's right, put everybody's and anybody's convenience before mine!"

Sam moved easily toward Susannah. "Sister Morrison, what a pleasure to see you!" He smiled at her, carefully keeping his distance, but his eyes danced with a light that gave Susannah considerable hope. "How may I serve you?"

Aware that the woman was listening, and a little taken aback that Sam did not introduce them, Susannah felt unsure of herself. The woman's attention was so keen as to border on nosiness. "I didn't mean to interrupt—in fact, I just happened on you by accident—but what I mean is—when we boarded, everyone was given a job—but me. I thought there might be some mistake . . ."

Sam studiously ignored the young woman; he had almost entirely turned his back on her. His slow smile was devastating to Susannah. "It's simply that your task is—different from the usual. Someone will talk with you about it this evening."

An exciting chill ran through Susannah. She'd had no experience in intrigue, but she felt certain that Sam himself would be the one to talk with her this evening—and perhaps what else? She tried to behave normally. "I'll—my family—will be in our room— our cabin after dinner." It was terribly difficult trying to act normal when she couldn't breathe, and her head was swimming with the possibilities of what might happen later tonight. She tried to smile and took an awkward step back.

Sam inclined his head slightly, his thick vital brown hair moving as he did so. "Then good day, my dear."

It hardly bothered her that she had heard him use the same term to the other woman, for that tenderness was in his eyes. She said, "Th-thank you," and moved off down the crowded deck as one in a sweet dream.

She heard the woman's voice, soft, mocking, dominating. "Well, well, Sam, what have we here? Another of those helpless sheep you've got to feed?" And then shriller, "This one is a bit obvious, isn't she?"

And Sam's clear reply: "Has it never occurred to you, Ann Eliza, that your temper and jealousy reflect only on your own character?"

Susannah felt a pang of fear. The woman was someone he knew well enough to use her Christian name. His wife! Susannah whipped around to stare behind her, but they had gone.

She stood by the rail, shivering with excited tension and cold, for she had forgotten her cloak in her eagerness to leave the crowded cabin. The sickly February sun had slid down behind the buildings on shore and taken with it the minor warmth of the day. But she didn't want to go back yet. She wanted a few more minutes to savor her memories of the handsome lines of Sam's face, the meaning in his glances.

A lean and unkempt man was standing near her, looking with empty eyes at the flurry of activity on shore. There was a strange smell about him, a strong smell like that of fermented fruit. He said, "You ought to see the guns and ammunition they took on board."

Startled, she said, "On this ship, you mean?"

He gave a dry chuckle. "They got enough to mount a war if they'd a mind to. Reckon Elder Sam'l could take that Californy by might after all. He's not a man to fool with. He's got power and ain't afraid to use it."

Susannah did not know what to make of the man's statement. She began shivering again. "I must go in, if you'll excuse me."

As she went swiftly down the companionway, she had in her mind not a picture of Sam as she wished, but instead that of a lonely, neglected-looking man standing all by himself at the rail in cold dusk. She shivered again, wishing she had a spot all her own to which she could go.

As she expected, Prudence and Ezra both scolded her for slipping out, and Asa, not to be forgotten, added chidingly, "Why, Susannah, you had only to ask, and I would have accompanied you."

"I didn't want company," she said rudely. It was her first response to anyone.

Ezra spoke harshly. "Susannah, I will not have this. You have always been a loving, dutiful daughter. Now suddenly you are changed. Are you trying to make life miserable for those around you?"

Her eyes sparkled with angry hurt. "Well, you've certainly made it miserable enough for me! Disinheriting my brother! Marrying his wife! Just because he questions! Why—"

Ezra no longer met her gaze. "It is not your place to judge." Uncomfortably, he moved in the small cabin space, then said, "It will soon be time for the evening meal. As Sister Tolerance is looking quite peaked, she will rest until it is ready." Ignoring Prudence's look of exasperation, he took Tollie by the arm and led her over to the bunk.

Prudence said acidly, "I'm going upstairs, where the air is fresher."

"Susannah and I will accompany you," said Asa. He took Susannah's arm, though she protested and tried to jerk away. "Brother Ezra and his new bride have hardly had a moment together." With a smile he darted a sly glance at Ezra.

Susannah felt ill. She allowed Asa to lead her outside.

After they had gone, Tollie smiled and said, "Ezra, come over here with me."

Ezra was so astonished he hardly knew what to do. Though it was true that she was his wife, she had remained in his mind his daughter-in-law. After a moment he went to stand outside the makeshift curtain beside Tollie's bunk. "Yes, Sister Tolerance?"

"Pull the curtain aside, and sit by me. I am your wife, even though we have not yet shared a bed."

110

Ezra blushed deeply at her outspokenness, but gingerly ducked under the sheet and found the two of them enclosed in a cozy bower. He could not meet her gaze. In all his experience he had never been in a situation that felt so intimate—or so unnatural. He couldn't help thinking of Landry, nor could he bring himself to think of Tollie as his wife—not in the full sense. He had intended only to protect her, and now with her lying beside him, flat except for the mound of her belly, he realized that he could not just protect her. She was his wife, and somehow he was going to have to learn to think of her that way.

Tollie's clear blue eyes with their fringe of dark lashes were fixed on him. "I have several things to speak of, husband, and until now I have never had the chance." She paused, her pink tongue running across her lips. "First of all, I must try to express my gratitude to you for—for pulling me out of the jaws of Hell—"

Ezra suppressed a smile at the extremity of her language. "Sister Tolerance, I—"

"Please call me Tolerance, or Tollie. When you call me Sister I feel as though you are holding me at a distance from you. Now that I am your wife, I—when the time comes—I want to share with you all the warmth that a man and wife should share."

Ezra took her hand in his. Her fingers were cold, and he put them to his lips for a moment in reassurance. With a pang he again thought of Landry. Tollie could be very endearing. He murmured, "I look forward to it—Tollie. But do not feel you must sacrifice yourself to me."

Her eyes met his. "I want to be your wife, Ezra," she whispered. "I want to turn my back on evil completely and begin anew. That is the only way."

Ezra felt a peculiar chill come over him. She was putting him at war with himself. As he gazed at her now, he saw his son's wife. He saw the mother of his first grandchild. And he saw a seductive woman whose youth, beauty, and nearness tempted him.

Her arms came up around his neck as he bent to take her sweet lips. Then his hand went under her head and neck to support her, to pull her body against his as their kiss set off long-dormant passions in him. He pulled away for a moment, to take in a gust of air, and felt her breasts against him as he kissed her again. It was like forbidden fire, this kiss with Tollie.

At last he held her away from him. In the half-dark her eyes were languorous, her lips parted. He said harshly, "They will be back soon. Tomorrow, Tolerançe. I'll arrange for us to be alone, and I will come to you." Her mouth still tempted, and he met it with his again. This time his tongue found its way in, to touch and slide smoothly against hers. When he let her go he was quaking, his face hot. "Tomorrow, Tollie—"

"Yes, Ezra. Oh, yes." She held on to his hand.

Ezra gazed at her. He had thought this sort of passion was dead in him. He thought he had become for all time the middle-aged man who was so peacefully settled with Prudence. Now his eyes fixed on Tollie's belly. He felt a sense of possession for both her and the child she was carrying. It might have been his child under other circumstances, and in a way the child *was* his. God had given this unborn to his care. He suddenly smiled and squeezed her hand. "What a surprise you are, my lovely Tolerance." He kissed her once more, but drew away when he felt his passion rise again. He whispered, "Tomorrow, my little darling. Tomorrow we will be man and wife."

She smiled at him. "Yes, Ezra." She trailed her fingers down his coat sleeve, smiling dreamily.

Ezra felt the pressure as though she were caressing his very flesh. With an uncontrollable shudder, he stood up, ducking out from behind the curtain. As he was adjusting certain body parts and smoothing his clothing, he became aware that Asa was lying on his bunk, one arm flung over his head. Asa's eyes missed nothing of Ezra's motions, and a little smirk etched the corner of his mouth.

Ezra's anger was so instantaneous, it was all he could do to control it. His face was red with the effort, and with the fury at being invaded. He had never felt this way before, but he had a sudden possessiveness of Tollie he hadn't suspected, and he did not know how to deal with it. He managed to control his voice. "You should have made your presence known, Asa."

With greater confidence than he normally had, and less deference than he usually showed to Ezra, Asa said lazily, "It was so quiet I thought you had gone out, Brother Ezra." His smirk deepened.

Ezra had the wild desire to double up his fists and to pound on Asa. He jerkily turned away and said gruffly, "Next time, knock!'' He stalked out of the cabin and walked as swiftly as possible to the deck. His sudden irritation at the close quarters, and his equally sudden craving for privacy, caused him to miss dinner. He knew this would cause a great deal of questioning by Prudence later, but at the moment he didn't care. He was a man with a new obsession, and he wanted to plan how he could be alone with her tomorrow.

Sam Brannan came to the Morrison cabin about eight that evening, bringing with him a tough, tired-looking woman past the bloom of life. He introduced her as Sister Flora Humphrey. With a casual grace, as if he were accustomed to the odd situation of having to sit on the beds, Sam seated himself and the others followed suit. Sister Flora sat like a grand Turk on the floor. Susannah, seated beside Tollie on their bunk, avidly watched the changing expressions on Sam's face.

At last he looked directly at Susannah. Her heart surged with pleasure. His eyes were merry as he said casually, ''Sister Susannah, I expect you've been wondering what your tasks will be.''

''Yes, I have, Elder Brannan.''

His look of amusement deepened, as though he knew that she had a dearer name for him. ''I'm told you are a capable seamstress. Is that so?''

Susannah was aware of Prudence's eye on her from across the narrow room. She said, ''I am competent, yes.'' She had a sinking feeling, hoping that he was not going to stick her for the entire voyage with Prudence and Tollie and their young girls' sewing class. He couldn't do that to her! She'd never get the chance to see him, and she was so sure he was going to do something special for her.

His eyes twinkled again, and she caught the look. ''With good eyes? And strong hands?''

Her mood swung again. It was uncomfortable to be so out of control, with her moods swinging from wild happiness to deep despair, depending on the tone of his voice and the look in his eyes. Now she wanted to smile. He was praising her beauty, not her accomplishments. The corners of her mouth curved slightly, deepening the dimple at one side. She said boldly, ''Yes. And I have perseverance too.''

''Excellent. Now the reason I brought Sister Flora is that she has, until this week, earned her family's living as a sailmaker and tentmaker. We will have to have tents available for all the families to move into as soon as we reach California. So Sister Flora agreed to sail with us, as she knows how to make patterns and assemble the pieces. She will be in charge of the work. You, Sister Susannah, will be her first assistant.''

Susannah was torn with feelings of pride and inadequacy and a halting feeling that perhaps Sam didn't care, for no matter how important the tents were, it was not a glamorous task. She had not expected this from him. She said diffidently, "I-I'll have so much to learn.''

Sam smiled, his dark brown eyes sparkling. ''You can do that much for the Lord, can't you, sister?'' He stood up suddenly, missing the shelf just over his head. ''Keep your seat, Brother Ezra, I'll see my way out. I've asked Sister Flora to talk with you, Susannah—Sister Susannah,'' he amended easily. "She'll tell you everything you want to know. And I will stop by from time to time and check on your progress. The tents are vital to our success. Goodbye for now, and may the good Lord be with us.'' Then swiftly, before Ezra could get to his feet to shake his hand, he was gone. Susannah heard his quick, sharp footfalls going down the passageway.

There was a moment of silence, almost of bereftness, after he had taken away the tremendous vitality of his presence. Susannah was so restless she couldn't sit still, and as soon as she could get away without appearing to follow Sam, she wished aloud to take a last look at New York City. ''After tomorrow we may never see it again,'' she said.

Flora got up off the floor and moved near to her. ''We'll talk in the morning—plenty of time then. You go say your goodbyes. I was young once; I remember what it was.''

Susannah threw her a grateful smile and hurried up to the deck. She stood by the rail for some time before she realized someone was standing a little down from her.

Tollie's voice sounded light and childish on the night air. ''I didn't think I could bear looking at the city. It is like saying goodbye to Landry all over again. I'm glad you came. I couldn't have done this by myself.''

Susannah pulled her heavy cloak tight about her. ''I'm not here to help you! If you'd stayed with him—''

114

Tollie jumped back quickly from the rail, her eyes flashing. "Let me tell you something, Susannah Morrison! I have a respect for God's will, even if you don't! It isn't my fault Landry couldn't do what he was supposed to do!" With that, *gentle* Tollie ran for the companionway, awkwardly making her way through a large group of people coming up to view the city.

Susannah stared after her, then ran to catch up with her stepmother-sister-in-law. "Liar!" she said softly so others wouldn't hear, but loud enough that Tollie would.

Tollie looked at her, hurt and angry, tears shining on her cheeks. "You don't understand, do you? You'd tie me to him forever! You truly don't understand!"

"No." Susannah turned and walked back to the rail, alone.

With a pang she thought of Landry, living alone in a rented room, searching in Gentile stores and factories for work because the Saints did not want his taint of apostasy rubbed off on them. As she fought back easy tears, her anger at Tolerance and Ezra refreshed itself. No matter what they said about Satan or temptation or God's will, it was their fault that Landry had been thrown out of the Church. No matter what, she'd never forgive that.

In bed that night with Tolerance, Susannah could not sleep. Tollie was large enough now with Landry's child that she was very restless, besides having to use the water closet two or three times. After the third time Susannah, exasperated and sandy-eyed beyond measure, took one of the comforters and wrapped herself in it to sleep on the floor.

She awakened early in the morning, aching in every joint and bone, and feeling strange in the stomach. She unwound her covering and looked out the door to the passageway to see if it was light yet. It was gray, the color that in varying shades would filter down from the deck throughout the voyage. She poured cold water from the pitcher into the basin and, shivering and goosepimply, washed in it. Using her nightgown as a tent and herself within it, she struggled into her clothing.

Soon the others were awake. "I don't want any breakfast, Sister Prudence," said Tollie weakly.

"Nor do I," said Ezra. "Something has upset my digestion."

Susannah, relieved that the others did not feel well, realized that it was mild seasickness, and that they were under way.

Those passengers who were not too ill to leave their bunks attended worship services on deck that morning. After that they went to their assigned tasks.

Sister Flora's cabin, no larger than any other, had been designated as the tent factory. Flora's children, ages nine through fourteen, were absent that first morning, though they seemed to be constantly underfoot as the voyage continued. There was room enough for Flora, Susannah, a winsome girl named Mary Addison, and a quiet young wife named Alma Davis. All were experienced seamstresses.

Each was seated on the floor cross-legged, their knees ballooning out the sides of their skirts, as Flora taught them. There was much laughter and squealing as the young women tried to adjust to the new seating. As the morning progressed, it became necessary more and more often for the girls to rise for a few moments and regain the circulation in their legs and bottoms. Flora teased them good-naturedly, and sat in the position as though glued. In and out through the stiff canvas flashed her needle, pulling the strong thread. No one else accomplished much, however. They had to overcome the awkward new motion of pushing the needle with the sailmaker's palm, a device one slipped over the thumb and fingers. It was a reinforced leather hand protector, with a socket against which the eye end of the needle was pressed with each stitch.

True to his word, Sam looked in on them briefly. Susannah observed that Mary was nearly as smitten by him as she was herself. For a moment her misgivings flared up, then died down. There was no particular warmth in his eyes for Mary as there was for Susannah. She smiled up at him, all her own feelings plain for him to see.

Soon after he left, she realized the time. "Excuse me, Sister Flora, I must go to our cabin."

Sam had not been the only person to read the message of her smile. Mary Addison's smile was warm and teasing. "Elder Brannan is a comely man, isn't he?"

Susannah flashed her a startled glance, then recovered nicely, she thought, to say, "Oh, do you think so? I must take a close look sometime."

"Is that why you're leaving now, to see if I'm right?"

Susannah felt exposed and vulnerable, but there was little she could say in retaliation without antagonizing Mary, and she didn't want to do that. She said quietly, "Some of my family are seasick, and I must relieve my stepmother of their care for a while. I'll come back after our meal, Flora, if I can."

Chapter Ten

It had been many days since Susannah had taken her final look at the city of New York. She had no idea how far away the city actually was, but the distance was so great that New York seemed a part of her past. Now the ship and the sea and her duties were her life. She was leaning over the rail, just enjoying the feel of being on the sea. Over her head loomed the tall, sturdy masts, today laden from top to yards with canvas swelled fat by the fine wind that whistled in the rigging. Below her the prow of the ship cleft the gray seas, halving the waves and sending froth back along the hull to join the white boil of foam trailing at the stern. All week the skies had been blue and enormous; today they were small and low, the clouds clumped together in heavy gray layers as depressing as dirty flannel. But with every hour that passed, the ship leaped forward under the full press of sail, her constant, gentle side-to-side rocking so much a part of daily life that only a few still noticed it.

During the first two weeks of the voyage Susannah had quickly grown accustomed to the cloistered routine of shipboard. She still grated occasionally at the lack of privacy and freedom, however, and was still speaking to her family only when spoken to. To her dismay, they all seemed to accept such treatment as perfectly natural. It gave her apprehensions and doubts. Landry had been done away with so thoroughly, and seemingly without regret, that she sometimes wondered just how secure she herself was within her own family. What would happen if she made a mistake, or

118

did something of which Ezra or Prudence, or even Tollie, disapproved? She wanted and needed to talk with someone about her worries, and the one person above all she wanted to be near was Sam. Though it was difficult for her to see Sam romantically, she, like all the other Saints, had access to him as a leader and guide. She knocked tentatively on the door of his small office. Almost before he had completed his welcome, she poured out her worries about her family.

With bemusement and sympathy, he said, "Susannah, there has never been a sect that so dearly loves a scolding as the Saints. It makes them feel beloved of God."

She looked at him curiously, her attention momentarily distracted by the nearness of Sam himself. "What do you mean by that?"

He got a faraway look in his eyes, the look of a man who has heard almost everything, seen too much, and has been disillusioned by others too often. "It's the Old Testament pattern— doom and destruction if you disobey the Lord, constant testing of one's fitness to enter the kingdom. You are continually testing your family by your attitude, and they are continually proving themselves more worthy than you."

"But they don't even know my reasons! Not really. How can they—"

"In this, my dear, you are wrong. Unlike them, you have not yet formed any soul-deep philosophy. You have no consistent code of ethics."

Her eyes flashed at him. "How charmingly shallow you make me sound! And unjustly so! I am loyal to those I love, and I cannot imagine how it could be pleasing to the Lord for Landry to be abandoned and deserted and rejected and—and—left to the powers of evil just so Papa could marry his wife."

Sam put his hands on her shoulders. "Calm down, my dear, you are saying things that don't make very good sense."

Even the touch of Sam did not still the angry hurt inside her. She wanted to shout, and accuse every member of her family— except Landry—of terrible, hateful behavior. But Sam was smiling at her, and his voice was low and soothing. "You have many worthwhile attributes, my little Susannah Morrison. Your sweetness, your loyalty, your courage in pursuit of right as you see it, your unquenchable optimism that life goes on and you will go on with it. So many of the things you represent are the things

I feel in my own heart, and for that reason there is this—closeness between us.''

Susannah's heart leaped with gladness. Regardless of how Sam saw her attributes, she had not been feeling so courageous, or certain of what was right, and certainly not optimistic of late. She needed reassurance, no matter how slight. She needed to know that someone could love and appreciate her as she really was. She smiled at him, but something else came to mind. "Sam, is it true that you were once expelled from the Church?"

He glanced at her, then again there came into his eyes a faraway look, the look of a man who had been deeply wounded. "Yes, it's true. Some things were said about me . . .'' His voice trailed off for a moment. "I suppose there was a trace of truth, but wildly exaggerated, and I suddenly found out I had been ousted.''

"But here you are, leading the Saints in good standing.''

He smiled the charming smile that quite melted her heart. "Isn't it obvious, Susannah? I was accepted back into the Church.''

The first real ray of hope for Landry grew strong in Susannah. "You make it sound so easy. It couldn't be so simple, could it?''

There was an ironic twist to his smile. "All I did was ride horseback from New York City to Nauvoo, Illinois, and appear before the Council of Twelve. I begged most desperately for a return of my rights and standing as a Saint. Thanks to President Brigham Young, I was reinstated and sent back to New York. Quite soon after that, I was put in charge of the exodus of Saints from the East Coast to the West.''

"You must have been very persuasive before the Twelve.''

"Susannah dear, I was. I felt very strongly about the Church at that time, and my emotions lent eloquence to my pleas. My reinstatement meant going on with my life as I envisioned it.''

"How—how do you feel about the Church now?''

"About the same,'' he replied lightly.

"About the same,'' she mused. "I wonder what that means?''

He didn't answer her question, but said, as much to himself as to her, "You love Landry very much?''

She nodded. "He—what happened to him is part of the reason I both fear and love the Church, but I have never felt that I could count on it. It seems that all the Morrison luck with the Church is bad. Wherever we have settled, there has been bloodshed and brutality and mob actions. I don't understand—and I'm afraid of

120

it. If that is what it means to be a Saint, I—I haven't the heart for it."

"Yet your family are all Saints, so you are looked upon as one of the faith. I am surprised, Susannah, that you have confided in me to this extent. You could be expelled for what you have told me."

The corners of her mouth lifted briefly. "I know. But I am placing myself in your hands, Sam. I trust you not to betray me—in any way. I believe that you of all people should understand my feelings and doubts. And if you do not, then there is little hope anyway."

The pupils of his eyes grew dark, and she knew that while the Church was included, neither of them was referring only to that. Wanting to protect her, wanting to lend his strength to hers, he said huskily, "You may depend on me, my dear. Susannah, my Susannah, I shall—" Sam's mobile face became serious as there was a rap on the door. A quick look of regret as he bowed to her, and he opened the office door.

Afterwards Susannah recalled every word, every sound, every nuance in her voice and Sam's, but most of all she recalled the look in Sam's eyes. That look meant love to her, safety, a promise there was hope that the bright future she so often dreamed about could come to pass.

From that day on Susannah allowed herself to dream on a bit. She warmed herself again with the look in Sam's eyes. He was in love with her, as she was with him. And loving led to marriage. She squeezed her eyes shut and took a deep breath. She thought of herself in Sam's arms, her lips against his, his hands touching her naked flesh as they gave themselves up to an all-powerful passion.

Susannah's lips parted, her eyes sparkled, and her cheeks suffused with pink bloom. She looked up at the sky and knew that the gray and gloomy day was brighter. It was always brighter when she thought of the man she loved.

Behind her she heard men's voices and their footsteps moving in cadence, then the thump of rifles. It was difficult now to remember only the beautiful parts of that day with the military reminder at her back. Standing in little clusters, tough looks on their faces, were young boys getting ready to imitate the older men as they all went through morning military drill.

Sam had put two men, Samuel Ladd (whispered to be an Army

121

deserter) and Robert Smith in charge of military training. The rumor she had heard was right. There were indeed guns and ammunition aboard the *Brooklyn*, and the men were learning how to handle the rifles and how to maneuver their feet and bodies in the seemingly easy routine of marching under arms.

Susannah turned to watch them. There was a certain beauty to the regimentation and rhythm the men achieved, but there was something else—something she did not like so well. She sought and found Asa in the ranks. She stared at him, watching the intensity with which he took his directions from the erect, straight-backed Ladd. Asa had changed a great deal since the beginning of this voyage, and Susannah was not comfortable with his transformation. The man she had always thought of as puling, begging, and hopeless, had become harder, more secretive than ever, and was gaining a bearing that was tough, sometimes to the point of callousness. It was almost as if Asa had awakened one day and decided he would take whatever he wanted from the world. He was no longer begging.

She looked away and thought of the number of times he had practiced his maneuvers in the tiny cabin, placing the rifle on the proper shoulder, standing erect. How often had he stood holding his breath, eyes growing wild and distressed with the effort, his gut sucked in until Susannah knew it had to hurt.

Even now as she watched, Ladd went straight to him. "You!" he said. "Ain't got no more idea how to stand than a cow. Now remember what I been sayin'. Shoulders back, chest out, belly tucked in, butt tucked in, feet like this. *Balance* your stance. Do it right, and right becomes easy." His attention was diverted. "Brother Hascall, put your weight evenly on both feet and straighten up them shoulders. Brother Pell, keep your eyes on me. Brother Nichols, I know you got to blow your nose, but it don't have to be now. You're at attention, hands at your sides."

The two sergeants—Ladd at one end of the ranks and Smith at the other—began to walk up and down, adjusting the way the men stood. Once more Ladd came back to Asa. Ladd's voice was very quiet as he looked Asa up and down. "Brother Radburn, your stomach is bigger than your chest." Suddenly he moved his head forward, like a snake's, until he was nose to nose with Asa. Ladd screamed, *"Pull it in!"*

Hastily Asa attempted to obey, while the men around him tried not to snicker. Ladd looked around with a quelling glance that stopped mirth in its tracks. Even the women and girls standing on the sidelines felt the tension mount in the air. But Susannah saw something she was sure the others had not. Asa's face was cold and hard. Not long ago, Asa would have been humiliated and embarrassed, but he was not so today. He struggled, not very successfully, with the bulk of his belly, but inside him, the part of Asa that showed only through his eyes was becoming a hard man, a man with a lean heart and soul, a man whose feelings for others were being pared down.

Susannah started to walk away from the rail, but Ladd spoke and she stopped again to watch. Ladd's voice was pitched conversationally low. "All right, you men can relax now. But stand where you are. We've only got a few months to get you toughened up. Today we're gonna start exercises. A few weeks from now, when I tell you to suck in that belly, you'll know how to suck it in and keep it in. It's all a part of your discipline in military preparedness. First—five laps around the deck! Everybody ready? Follow me."

Susannah's eyes were on Asa. His face turned scarlet after the first half lap, and by the second it was beginning to blotch a pasty white, but he kept up. There were beads of sweat all over his face, and he looked as though each stride were painful. Again Susannah had an uneasy feeling and a grudging admiration for her stepbrother.

For the next hour Ladd drilled the men, leading them through a catalog of exercises designed to build muscles and self-respect. At the end Sam came over from the rail, where he had been watching, and made a short speech. "Brothers," he said to the panting, sweating men, "you can be proud of yourselves. When we land in California and defeat the Mexicans in the battle for ownership of California, we'll have you men to thank! But before that there is a reward for everyone! I've been talking to Sister Goodwin and Sister Aldrich, and they've agreed to supervise the making of uniforms for you. Real uniforms, smart and neat." He grinned. "I like the idea so well that from now on I'm going to be training with you."

The men laughed and cheered, for Sam was popular.

"Dis-missed!" cried Ladd, and they left the deck for other duties. Immediately, the women began crowding around Laura Goodwin and Emma Aldrich, everyone eager to have a chance to sew a uniform for one of the men.

Susannah looked about the deck, her eyes sorting through people, trying to single out Sam.

Hat in hand, he was talking with Lucy Eager. Susannah didn't know whether to giggle or to frown at Sister Eager's presence. Lucy was in her thirties, a widow with children, a bit plump but still very attractive. Her hair was black, worn with bangs that always seemed a little too long. Yet the looks she gave up through the screen of her long black lashes and the shining black bangs were fetching. In repose Lucy's looks were plain, yet she gave a total effect of prettiness. Susannah suspected she painted her cheeks, albeit skillfully.

Just now Lucy's raven hair was concealed under her bonnet of moss green, which matched the wool dress trimmed with row after row of narrow dark green braid. She had one small white hand on Sam's sleeve. Susannah went nearer. She heard Lucy's soft, intimate tones plainly.

"Oh, Elder Brannan, I am *so* disappointed that you don't want me to sew your uniform for you. I would do such a careful job of it," she was saying. "How about letting me make just the"—she batted her eyes beneath their double fringe—"just the trousers? I am an expert at setting in pockets, and—"

Sam showed signs of impatience. "I'm very flattered, Sister Eager, and I believe you are competent. However, Sister Goodwin has already promised she'll do my outfit."

Susannah did giggle then. Lucy must be beside herself, she thought, for one thing was obvious: Laura Goodwin, mother of six and herself a very fragile-looking woman, had no ulterior motives in making such an agreement. She would in no way derive the pleasure from it that Lucy was trying to get for herself. Sister Goodwin, if she was a fool at all, was one over her own husband, whose arm she never released when they were promenading on the deck.

Sam raised his hat, ready to replace it on his head. "I'm much obliged to you all the same, Sister Eager." With a bow, he hurried away.

Susannah, smiling to herself, went on down to Flora Humphrey's cabin. Already the women were talking about the way Lucy flirted with Councilor Ward Pell and another man, Ambrose Moses. She had even been so bold one evening after prayers as to take the arm of each, making it a joke, and to walk clear around the deck with them. Actually Susannah liked Lucy personally, and secretly admired her air of unfettered enjoyment of male companionship, but several of the married women were jealous and angry over the attention the men were paying to her. Sooner or later, unless Lucy became more reserved, there would be trouble.

As the women continued to talk, Susannah stepped out into the corridor. Coming toward her was Ann Eliza. Susannah shrank against the wall so that Sam's wife could pass. Smiling, she said, "Good day, Sister Brannan."

Receiving no reply, Susannah stared after her, feeling crushed for no good reason. She envied Ann Eliza Brannan her grace and gentility and her exquisite wardrobe, but the woman had a wretched disposition. Susannah could not understand why. Surely Liza had everything. She was smart, well-dressed, and most importantly, married to Sam Brannan. Perhaps being Episcopalian, Liza simply did not like the Saints—or Susannah.

Still pondering the possibilities, Susannah returned to Flora's cabin and seated herself to do more stitching. She looked at the rough canvas and the palm. Ann Eliza would never do work such as this. It was unlikely that Sam would ever ask it of her.

Chapter Eleven

Throughout the morning, the dark clouds gathered and thickened above until they seemed to be nearly touching the water. The seamen were kept busier than usual, tautening the rigging here, slackening it there, putting on new chafing-gear, "blacking down" or tarring the rigging, recoiling the already perfectly coiled lines that lay on the deck. About the ship was an air of watchfulness, of readying for emergency.

About noon Captain Richardson told Sam Brannan, "We'll be having a little weather soon. Are your people ready? Everything loose should be lashed down."

"I'll send word around," Sam replied. "When do you expect it to start?"

"Oh, any time. Probably not before the first dog watch. But they shouldn't wait to secure objects in their cabins. The glass is dropping, and the mate's rheumatism has him half crippled. I'd go by that as quick as I would the barometer."

While evening prayers were being held on the main deck, a hard rain came up, almost out of nowhere, sweeping like needles across the heads and backs of the Saints. Hurriedly they disbanded and repaired to the large hall below, where they ate meals and sometimes held worship services. There Sam concluded his discourse as though there had been no interruption.

"So you see," he said, "difficulties have their uses. Their mission is not to dishearten. Difficulties are discipline. The good Lord gave us all spunk and gumption; and then He puts difficulties in our paths to make sure we use what he has given us. Brothers and sisters, I want you to remember that. Now let us pray. Dear Lord, we know that in every hard circumstance your eye is upon us. Hear us when we call on you for courage and assistance in time of trouble. Amen.''

Sam raised his head and said quickly, ''We'll forgo the last hymn, so you can get right to your cabins. The boat's starting to rock. I'll remind you again to keep everything battened down. We don't want anyone injured by flying objects. Hurry, now. Praise the Lord.''

From two hundred throats came the reply, ''Praise the Lord!'' Susannah, standing near the back of the room, which was beginning to tip up and down, roused herself from her thoughts. As Sam spoke, she had been recalling a psychic prediction Flora had made the previous day, wondering if she should act upon it.

Her mind made up, she pressed hurriedly toward the center, where Laura Goodwin was standing with her family. ''Oh, Sister Goodwin, please wait a moment!'' Susannah said breathlessly. ''I must tell you something! Be very careful on the companionway, for you are in great danger! Brother Goodwin, please guard her so she doesn't fall!''

Laura Goodwin's soft hazel eyes held great concern as she turned to Susannah. ''Why, sister, have you had a vision?''

''No—but Sister Flora has. Do be careful!''

Isaac Goodwin turned away. ''We are in the hands of the Lord,'' he reminded Susannah.

''Well,'' she retorted, ''God helps those who help themselves, as Elder Brannan just reminded us!''

Isaac glanced back and smiled. ''I thank you, sister.''

Laura, being led away on the strong arm of her husband, also turned back to smile at Susannah and thank her. Then suddenly the ship gave a great shudder and went forward like a bobsled on a downhill run. Perhaps half the Saints were still in the hall. There was a gasp in unison, and as the floor tipped, people fell or sprawled and rolled. Before they could recover, the ship raised its stem, and they were flung back the other way, some sliding halfway across the floor. Along with them slid chairs, tables, and every article of furniture that had not been lashed down. Men shouted useless instructions, and women screamed as they were flung about and battered. The ship rocked violently from one side to the other; no one was able to get steady on his feet before

127

another jolting tilt came and tossed him down again. Prayers were being keened through clenched teeth. It seemed forever before there was a lull.

Susannah, bruised and skinned, pulled herself upright. She sat for a moment, extremely nauseated and uncertain. She had seen Tollie fall and then had seen others roll toward her. Now, with the oil lamps swinging crazily overhead on their bars, and the ship shuddering, threatening to toss them about again, she could not identify Tollie. Nor could she locate Ezra or Prudence.

She tried to get to her feet, holding on to the bulkhead. It was up to her to find Tollie and somehow get her safely back to their cabin. No matter now that Tollie had abandoned Landry. No matter that Susannah still could not forgive her. No matter anything, except that Susannah must keep Landry's unborn child safe.

Susannah stumbled across the floor, taking unexpectedly great steps and losing her balance as the ship lurched again. She did not know that she was screaming, "Tollie! Tollie!" for everyone else was screaming for someone too.

She found Tolerance crushed against a bulkhead with her arms up over her face, and two people trying to collect their scattered wits enough to get off her. Susannah stumbled among them, stepping on someone's hand and hearing the yelp of pain even over her own shrill cries. Then she had her hand on Tollie's shoulder and was shouting into her ear. "Tollie, it's Susannah! Can you walk? Tell me, are you hurt?"

Tollie moaned something, and Susannah bent over to hear her, nearly falling as the ship slid into another trough. Cold sweat trickled down her back. "Tolerance! It's Susannah! Give me your hand! We've got to get you to your bed!" Then the floor rose sharply. Those who were standing upright were flung back down again, but Susannah had a strong grip on Tollie's arm. With her free hand she grabbed the leg of a table secured to the floor, and hung on with all her strength. Tollie seemed unwilling or unable to help herself as the ship reeled in the heavy sea, and was pulled this way and that with only Susannah to keep her in one place. Finally the ship righted itself for a time, and Susannah painfully scrambled up and managed to pull Tollie upright.

Tollie's face was bleeding, but her hands went to her belly. "My poor baby." She sobbed. "He'll die. He'll die, Susannah!"

Susannah's heart thudded uncomfortably against her chest. She didn't know what Tollie meant. Was she about to have the baby?

128

It was much too soon. Susannah gathered her wits. Whatever would be would be, she couldn't change that, but she did have to get Tollie to the cabin. "Stop that!" she commanded harshly. "Come on, move! Quickly! Grab that bulkhead and hang on tight!" She put Tollie's uncertain hand on the projection and they both held on desperately while the ship cavorted and pirouetted again. In this fashion, taking every possible handhold, hanging onto each other through the pitch-black corridors now reeking of bilge, they made their way back to the cabin.

Susannah's imagination was running rampant. The corridors were dark and close, and the odor was fierce. Her skin felt as though it crawled with unseen bugs, and her skirts were heavy and being dragged around her ankles. She closed her eyes against the visions of the rats she had heard spoken about on board. She was gritting her teeth so hard her jaws ached, and her throat hurt from holding back tears of panic. She was taking care of Tollie, but never before in her life had she wanted so badly to have someone take care of her. She didn't want to drown. She didn't want to be beaten and then swallowed by the vicious monster sea.

Around them the other passengers were panicking, or trying not to panic. Susannah could see flashes of pale, taut, terrified faces as all made their way along the corridors. They sloshed through several inches of water that the torrential storm had driven through every aperture in the bucking, tossing ship.

Even down below they could hear the shriek of the wind in the rigging as the ship lay hove-to, flying only her storm suit aloft. They could hear the monumental slosh of water against the hull, hear it rushing over the main deck and running out the washports, hear it splashing in the corridors and cabins betweendecks. The ship bobbed and tossed like a cork in the angry seas, and even the most sturdy passenger was jerked and flung around helplessly.

Susannah's breathing was a whining cry by the time she and Tollie finally made it to their cabin. For once she wanted the comforting presence of her family. They were all going to die tonight, and she didn't want to die alone. She said a quick, fervent prayer, all her mind would allow, as she pushed open the heavy door. The door moved only a few inches, then shut again. Susannah nearly gave up, momentarily succumbing to the numbing fright and exhaustion of her struggle. Then once more she lent her weight and strength to the door. The ship quieted for a

129

moment, and the door opened. But none of her family was inside. Susannah cried out, her hands against her face. Tollie stumbled and bumped her before Susannah once again pulled free of her terror.

In the pitching darkness Susannah could not tell one bunk from another. The floor was littered with articles that had been tossed around. Ezra and Asa had secured their cabin earlier, but not sufficiently, and now oddments of their possessions were flying everywhere. Sodden clothing seemed to reach up and grab hold of her feet, making her fall. Everything, everything seemed to want to pull her down into those cold angry waters forever. "Tollie! Hold on to anything. Get into one of the beds and stay there. I—I'll try to light a lamp." She cried out in pain as something heavy slid over the floor and swept her off her feet. She slammed against a wall, then rolled downhill into something else. Every time she tried to regain her feet, she was pushed back down. Disoriented, fighting terror, she tried to stay in one spot long enough to get her bearings.

She hurt all over. Hardly an inch of her had not been pounded or stabbed by the edge of something sharp and hard, and the storm had only begun. She had never been at sea before. Even the worst storms she could remember hitting the coast of New York had not been like this. How long could it last? Where was her father? Mama? Asa? "Tollie!" she cried, suddenly desperate for the comfort of another human being.

"I'm over here, in the bunk. Susannah, I'm so sick. When will it end?" Tollie moaned, and Susannah could hear the sounds of her nausea.

Susannah, being violently rocked and jerked around, had to swallow again and again to keep from following Tolerance's example. But she couldn't afford to be sick. She couldn't stand being more helpless than she already was, and there was work to be done. Anything loose could injure somebody, and she didn't want any further harm to come to Tollie's baby or herself. But she couldn't see a thing, and couldn't find a rope to tie up something she couldn't see.

After immensely wearing effort she found the matches, sorting through them in the dark until one seemed dry. Afraid it was the only dry match, and that she would lose her chance, she dived for the overhead lamp and with sheer grit hung on long enough to light it.

130

Tollie was lying in her bunk, her complexion green, with a smear of blood across her forehead and one cheek. Her eyes were beseeching.

"Susannah, we're going to die," Tollie moaned. "We're being punished, and we're going to die. My baby—I don't want to die! Please! I don't want—"

Susannah's whole body tightened as Tollie said aloud her own nightmarish thoughts. A frightened anger rose in her. "Stop it, Tollie! Stop it! Don't talk like that! We're not going to die. I'm not ready to die!"

"I'm so sorry, Susannah, so sorry for everything. Please forgive me!"

"Stop it, Tollie! You're not going to die!" Susannah screamed, her hands over her ears.

But Tollie could not stop talking. "I never meant for things to happen the way they did. I wanted to love Landry—I am so sorry, Sus—"

Both girls' heads turned as pounding and scrabbling sounds came at the cabin door. Just as the door was forced open, Susannah came to her senses, and got to her feet. "Papa!"

Ezra, Prudence, and Asa, drenched to the skin, their faces and hands cut and scraped and bruised, staggered into the cabin. The Morrisons all hugged and clung to each other, laughing in relief that at least they were all together on this horrible night. They lashed things down, and sat together huddled for warmth and comfort, waiting for the end of the storm or the end of life.

Morning brought little light and no relief. The gale had increased its ferocity. The ship bucked and twisted worse than ever. It was like being unable to get off a mad wild horse who could not be tamed and whose frenzies seemed only to become deadlier.

By noon they had all been sick once or more. The cabin stank of bilge water, shaken up from below, and of sickness and of nameless musty things that lay waiting for the storm to intensify before crawling up out of the hold and devouring everything on ship.

There was no time to catch one's breath between gusts. Ezra, feeling as helpless and trapped as the others, began intoning prayers, with the rest of the family following. It gave them the feeling of doing something. The storm had gone on so long that

131

irrational thoughts were beginning to seem like good sense. Ezra hated to think of the number of times he considered throwing himself overboard so the gnawing, constant sickness would stop. How often had he thought that they would not survive it anyway, so it was better to choose one's own time. His voice rose, and he looked upward, seeking the God who seemed to have abandoned them. He began to speak verses of the Book of Mormon he remembered, of Christ showing himself unto the lost tribes of Israel.

Almost as if it were Satan's voice, Satan's defiance of their prayers to God, the gale blew down from the north, and around from the east, and the shuddering vessel lay helpless in the troughs of the waves, sometimes rolling over almost onto the side of her hull before lumbering to right herself and rolling to the opposite side. The lightning flashed, and the thunderclouds clapped together with a deafening roar and echo. The storm went on and on with no end in sight, and Ezra raised his voice still higher and screamed his prayers to God.

During the second night everyone was exhausted and dozing, in spite of the constant need to cling to some stable object. Susannah fell into a deep sleep that lasted only moments. She raised her head and looked about the dark room, expecting to see some dreadful thing moving. There was nothing to see. The nothingness was almost more frightening than the something she had feared. Gingerly she lay back down, staring up at the hammock, unable to sleep again, her mind filled with worry and longing for Landry. Susannah finally slept again and woke as the storm renewed its vigor.

By evening of the third day all were hungry, even though weak and dizzy from the surging of the waves and the wind. The ship was shuddering worse now than it had before, making awful cracking sounds each time it dipped its snout and lifted it again.

Ezra had stayed in one place as long as he could stand it. He had been out of the cabin once before, with the intention of going on deck, but he had been driven back with the aid and admonishment of the ship's surgeon. Ezra shuddered as he watched the doctor splinting the leg of a sailor who had fallen from the rigging.

Seeing Captain Richardson, he hurried toward him. "How are we faring, Captain?"

Richardson said, "I'm on my way to meet with Elder Brannan about our situation."

As they spoke the ship plunged stern down into a deep trough, and the two men staggered and flailed their arms for balance.

Sam was already at Captain Richardson's quarters, which, like the rest of the ship, were cramped, wet, and smelly. The men looked pale and haggard, the captain most of all, for he had had no sleep during the past three days.

Richardson wasted no words. "Brother Brannan, we aren't going to make it. I don't know how else to tell you. The *Brooklyn* can't take much more of this strain. Hear her wracking? One of these waves is going to break her right in two."

"Is there any way our people can help your crewmen?" Sam asked.

"It isn't with the crew I need help. It is the ship herself. She's taken a brutal pounding. I expect her to break up at any time. I think you'd better tell your people."

"Must they be told so soon, Captain?" Sam asked quietly.

Richardson's red-rimmed eyes glared angrily at Sam. "Hell, yes! What do you think I am, man, a miracle worker?"

Sam did not rise immediately, but a surprising transformation took place. The weariness had left his handsome face. He actually smiled. "We are a people of miracles, Captain. We'll tell the passengers of our peril. And we'll leave the rest up to the Almighty."

Sam called a prayer meeting in the hall. Wearing their wet nightclothes, carrying sleeping children, the Saints moved down the uneasy corridors to their meeting with God Almighty.

Susannah went with her family, her mind crowded with wishes and regrets. This was like the final stop in the long journey of her life—too short a journey, she realized painfully. There were so many things she wanted to do and see. She sniffed a little at the unfairness of having everything taken from her in the midst of a desolate ocean. She would never again breathe in the heated air of a sunny summer day, or lie lazily back in the grass looking up at puffy clouds, filled with marvelous dreams. She'd never share secrets with Landry again, or see California. She would never know the beauty of being loved by a man, one special man. Tears came as she thought of Sam. She'd never know Samuel Brannan.

Susannah had never been a fervent supplicant before God. Her prayers had always been routine, or occasional breathlessly desperate requests when she wanted some childish thing or had gotten herself into trouble. But tonight she had everything to pray for. Only God stood between her and nothing.

Sam stood in front, at his usual place. His voice was even, calming, but still perfectly audible even in the back. "Brothers and sisters we are, as never before in our lives, in the awesome presence of God. God the Father, having created the world to reveal His glory and His supreme goodness to mankind, reveals them nowhere more clearly than at sea. And being the poor creatures we are, we need reminders of His power and His glory. We are His people. We are His Saints on a mission for Him. Now, raise your voices, men and women of God! Beg Him for your safe deliverance from the destructive force of this storm! Renew your spirits in His goodness, His mercy! Renew your vows to give Him your lives, your hearts, the sweat of your brows, your souls! Renew your mission to serve Him in all ways, even though that may be dying for Him in this black and stormy sea. If God means that we shall go down tonight, we'll go down with His name on our lips. But if, in His mercy and goodness, He saves us, it will be for His glory. Pray with me, brothers and sisters, let us give the Lord our thanks and our love, for His will shall be done!"

The voices of the Saints rose in prayer, and Susannah thought it sounded like the most beautiful hymn she had ever heard. No one looked around at his neighbor; all eyes were heavenward, or downcast. All the voices rang with a sincerity that Susannah hadn't known before. The feeling of love that filled the room lent her a warmth that went far into her bones.

As the Saints prayed, Sam moved among them, joining his voice first to one group then another. Then he came to Susannah. He stood beside her, his sleeve touching hers as they kept their heads bowed, and then with a surge of joy looked up. Susannah shivered with happiness. This was the most intimate moment she'd known. As long as she lived she'd never forget this night of prayer, or this moment of prayer with Sam. Presently he moved on, but not before he had touched her hand and looked at her with love and what she took to be an unspoken promise.

Toward morning the prayers died down. The Saints were wavering with exhaustion. Sam sent all but twenty back to their cabins, leaving the twenty to keep the words of man rising to God with His praise. The others were to rest, and be ready to take their turn in an unending vigil.

Susannah was so tired the words got confused and tangled. She knew that much of what she had been saying for the past hour made no sense at all, but she kept on trying. Sam had selected her as part of the first shift, although the rest of her family went to the cabin. At the end of her time she made her way cautiously through the corridors. She stopped for a moment near the hatch, taking in a gust of air that smelled fresh. She closed her eyes, and breathed deeply. When she opened them, Sam was standing no more than a foot away, his eyes warm on her. He drew her with him over to the darker shadows of the bulkhead.

"Tonight is a night for enlightenment, my little Susannah." He put his arms around her, holding her tight against his lean body. "I've resisted being near you ever since the first time I saw you at meeting. I've denied every feeling I have had for you, and called it good sense, but tonight it merely seems foolish."

"Oh, Sam," she murmured, her heart fluttering with hope. "I—"

"No, don't speak. I want to tell you all that is in my heart. The captain says the ship may break apart. If she does, there will be no hope of rescue. Tonight as we were praying, I was thinking of all those treasures of life that I might never again know, and those I wanted but have not taken for myself."

She waited, her eyes searching his in the darkness, bursting to ask, *What? What?*

"I want first to tell you that I love you." As tears started in her eyes he added, "And second, to promise you that if we live, I will make you mine."

Susannah's arms went up around his neck. He bent his comely head and their lips met, hot with longing, giving with no questions asked in the face of death. She looked at him, her eyes wet with tears.

Susannah pressed her lips to Sam's once more. If God let them live, she would belong to Sam Brannan. Married or not, it would not matter. She would belong to Sam, in all the ways that a woman could belong to a man on earth. "Sam, I love you too," she said, not as she had dreamed of saying it, but urgently, while there was yet time.

He smiled bleakly. "I will not forget that. Now I must go. The others need me. They have already begun the vigil, and I must be with them. God keep you safe, my love." He held her close for another moment, kissed her hair, then unsteadily bumped away down the corridor.

The ship was still tipping, and as Sam entered the prayer hall, people were still being thrown from their feet. Moans of pain could be heard along with the inspiringly lyrical voices of the Saints.

By dawn the hall had filled up once again with the Saints in prayer en masse. They had made it through the night. Suffused with grace and the love of God, spirits began to rise. Presently a high, clear voice rose above the prayer, and began to sing the Mormon hymn:

> The spirit of God like a fire is burning!
> The latter-day glory begins to come forth;
> The visions and blessings of old are returning . . .

Others joined in. They finished the song and started another. The *Brooklyn* still pitched and bucked in a vicious sea, but she did not break apart. The Saints kept up their steady prayer and song of love and praise. People began to look at one another, smiles on their faces, relief in their eyes. The storm had appreciably stilled. The ship still rocked, but the bucking and pitching that had caused it to creak at every seam had ceased. Then a man's voice began, "We're going to California." After the laughter died, the others sang the song and many more of the rollicking tunes they knew. Even before Captain Richardson ordered the hatches opened and came down to tell them they were saved, they knew it. As one, still singing the patriotic ballad, "The Liberty Song," they climbed the companionway and assembled on the main deck.

"Praise the Lord God!" rang to the heavens. Men and women hugged each other and shook hands as though meeting again after a prolonged absence. Laughter and happy chatter made a hum that overpowered the rumbling sea. There was still a heavy ground swell, with the turbid water lacing over and under itself. The skies were still gray, but growing lighter as they watched. The drenched seamen were putting matters in order preparatory to hoisting sail, working quickly under the bawled orders from the officer of the watch. As the passengers knelt, and each in his own way gave thanks for their blessing, the morning sun sent out a beam from a cloud, glittered on the wet deck, and touched them all with welcome light.

Chapter Twelve

The storm ended on a Wednesday. Nearly every passenger and crewman had been seasick, and most were wan and dehydrated. Once the seas had ceased to curl over the taffrail, the Negro cook who had hired on for the voyage served lunch—for each person, half a pound of salt beef and some ship's biscuits. There were complaints, for it did not look like appetizing fare to follow such a debilitating experience. But the cook stood firm. To their surprise, within a short time they began to feel much improved, and even recommended it as a treatment.

Susannah should have been happy, loving Sam and knowing that he felt the same toward her. She wondered when he would keep his promise, but in those first busy days after the storm, even she knew that the time was not right. In the next few days, though, she was seized with a great depression, an intangible dread. She knew she needed to discuss it with someone who cared about her—and Sam was her spiritual leader.

Susannah, feeling exposed and embarrassed, glanced around his tiny office. In the dim light from the swinging lamp she saw two chairs and a small table. They took up most of the floor space. Her eyes went to Sam's.

He stood with his back against the door. His eyes were hooded, his cheeks flushed, his expression one she had never seen on a man before. He did not hold out his arms in invitation, merely gave a soft command: "Susannah, come to me."

She wanted to obey him, wanted to do whatever he asked, but

caution intervened. "Elder Philips knows we're in here. What if . . ."

Sam showed no sign of concern. He smiled and said again, "Come."

Susannah, her mouth softly open, went into his arms. His lips met hers gently and tenderly. Then he drew back, his eyes reading hers. "Do you truly love me, Susannah?"

It was as if Susannah's whole body had turned to water—rippling, sparkling, rushing through her veins, making her head light. Her reply was joyous and instantaneous. "Oh, yes, Sam, I do love you!"

He murmured huskily, "Susannah! Oh, God—God—" His mouth claimed hers again, and she could feel his teeth against her own. His tongue slid against hers, and it was unbearably thrilling, not just to be kissed by him, but to be kissed in this electrifying way. She responded, tasting the warm cleanness of his mouth, wanting the sensation to intensify until . . .

She pressed herself against him, his arms like iron bands around her, feeling the hard pressure of his chest against her soft, full breasts, highly aware of the heat of his body and of his male scent in her nostrils. Deep down in some secret part of herself Susannah could feel a tight, cool little bud beginning to unfold, grow warm, grow moist, open to love and desire. Its pleasurable warmth tingled throughout her entire body.

She stood on tiptoe, straining upward against him, wanting to mingle her heat with his. And for a long moment they touched, his hands under the roundness of her hips, fusing them together, their greedy mouths taking, taking.

With no warning, he wrenched away from her, so that she staggered against the wall. He turned and stood with his back to her, his shoulders heaving, his breath coming in ragged gasps.

Susannah's eyes were wide with astonishment and disappointment. "Why did you do that?" she asked, her own breath catching.

He ran shaking fingers over his mouth and through his hair. He looked at her, looked away, and looked back again. He made a helpless gesture with his hand. "You're still an innocent. You don't know what this will—you don't realize what you're inviting."

"But we were loving each other and—"

"And this loving leads to more, my dear—much more. And we will have it, you and I. But not here. Not now."

139

Susannah nodded numbly. She didn't know exactly of what he spoke, but she, too, knew there was more, much more that never in her life had she experienced. Without volition she put her hands out for him to take. He took a step back. "We—we came here because you—you wished my counsel," he said in a formal, stilted voice. "Please sit down."

She hesitated, not sure if she had done something to offend him or if he felt passions so strong that he must use every tactic to keep her from him.

His hand on her shoulder was harsher than any hand she had ever felt. He moved her from where she stood, immobile, and forced her into a chair. He said, "I did not mean to hurt you, Susannah. Will you forgive me?" When she nodded, blinking back tears, he went on. "This is not the place for us. I was a fool to let it begin here. If you were to be caught, we would both be ruined. Do you understand that?"

She shook her head. "We were just embracing. People do court—what is so wrong with that?"

Sam ran his hands through his hair again, unsure of what to say. "I haven't spoken with your father, nor with my wife. Under the circumstances we might be accused of something other than courting. You must take my word, Susannah. There will be a time and place for us. I will see to it. But until then, do not let your love show in your eyes, for both our sakes."

"I'll try."

"I know you have questions, and so have I, dear one. But please, right now, we must compose ourselves and look like parishioner and counselor. Please now, tell me what is making you unhappy."

She looked helplessly at him, still enthralled by his embrace, and crushed by his sudden avoidance of her. "I don't think I can now, I—"

"Try. For me, please, Susannah, you must try."

Hesitantly she began. "I don't know exactly. I'm afraid something is going to happen, but I don't know what. I was so frightened until I saw you."

"But nothing has happened, and it won't," he said. "You are reacting to the fear you felt during the storm." He was smiling at her easily, as though he were meeting her on deck, as though she were any of his other parishioners. She found it very hard to understand or to accept his lightning changes from hot to cool.

She had never supposed such behavior was a part of love. She looked hard at him for some sign that he really did love her.

"All right," he went on easily, "you're not satisfied. Are you reacting to the separation from the other members of your family?"

"Perhaps."

"Your . . . Sister Tolerance is expecting a child. Is she doing well?"

"Yes." A very small whisper arose in her mind, and immediately she hushed it.

He seemed to remember something. "What about your brother in New York?"

Her suddenly terrified eyes met his. "Landry," she whispered. Susannah hunched in her chair, rubbing her cold hands together.

"Calm yourself. Tell me exactly what you feel."

She blew her nose, and gasped in air, and blurted, "It was as if he was being stabbed."

He sat back in his chair and considered the problem. "You fear for his life?"

"Perhaps it is his soul, and not his life? He is damned as an apostate—damned to Hell," she said dully.

"That's the view of the Church—actually the view of Bishop Waterman. But supposing it is not the view of the Lord. Just suppose now. If in the eyes of the Lord all men who worship Him are entitled to salvation, then your brother is *not* damned. Have I made sense to you?"

She raised drowned eyes to him, and smiled shakily. "Oh, yes! A lot of sense! Oh, thank you!"

He smiled and, reaching into his breast pocket, took out his handkerchief and dried her tears. "I trust you are discreet enough not to repeat my interpretation to anyone?"

Hurriedly Susannah grasped his hand, raised it to her mouth, and kissed the palm. "Never!" she assured. "You sound a great deal like Landry! Sam, I didn't know you felt this way. I just wish Landry had the same—"

"Discretion," he said with amusement.

"Yes, I suppose that is what it is."

"But, my dear, before you take it too much to heart, I do not always feel this way. Sometimes I can see the opposing view, I just don't usually put it into words with which to hang myself." He patted her hand in an absentminded professional way. "Pray for your brother, Susannah. Now you should go, sweetheart. Elder Phillips is waiting.''

As she passed Sister Lucy Eager's cabin, she heard a woman's laugh, full and confident and teasing, and a man's rumbling reply. Though no words were distinguishable, there was no mistaking the generally intimate tone of the transaction behind the door. It was being whispered now that Sister Lucy had three men on her string—Brother Moses, Councilor Pell, and Orrin Smith. The men all were married, and all had numerous children. In meeting Sister Smith sat tight-lipped and apart from her good-looking husband. Rumor had it that they were not even speaking, because of the widow Eager.

Susannah flushed as she remembered herself and Sam embracing and made a note of the sounds that could be heard outside a cabin. She was relieved that she and Sam had kept their voices low.

On Friday, the Nichols child died. He had not been able to recover from the rigors of the storm. His funeral was held on deck, while the warm tropical sun beat down, the sails held full, and the ship plowed her placid furrow through tranquil seas. Sam's rich voice was thick with emotion as he spoke of the life of an innocent child. Sister Nichols stared back at Sam, tears in her eyes, and hope, a true wanting to believe that her baby would remain safe in eternity waiting for her. Still a cry of loss escaped her lips as the small bundle sewn in sailcloth was slipped over the rail into the Atlantic.

Before many days had passed the Saints realized that God had not spared all of them. Old man Ellis Ensign, whose weakness of the heart had occasionally caused him to fall unconscious where he stood, simply stopped breathing. The baby of Brother and Sister Robbins died. Another week and the Fowler infant was dead. The following day Eliza Ensign died of the lung disease that had slowly consumed her.

The day after Eliza's funeral was a Sunday, the eighth of March. Susannah and Ezra stood by the rail, looking out across the water, breathing in the humid warmth of the Doldrums. It was the first time since the voyage had begun that Susannah had just enjoyed being with her father. In the aftermath of the storm, in her gratitude at being spared, Susannah had apologized to her family for her obstinancy. She was glad she had, for no matter how wrong she thought them to be, she loved them.

Ezra turned to look at some young girls flirting with sailors. With amusement in his eyes he nudged Susannah. "Why aren't you over there making a spectacle of yourself?"

Susannah laughed and said saucily, "I'm after bigger fish, Papa."

Ezra chuckled. His Susannah was something special. The movement of the water caught his eye and lulled him to silence. Finally, getting sleepy, he stood straighter and said, "We are to be called to a business meeting. Elder Brannan told me of it today."

"What is it about?" Susannah asked, alert to any news of Sam.

Ezra spoke in a low tone. "He told me in the strictest confidence, mind, Susannah."

"Papa, you know I don't gossip," she said, and grinned. "I just listen and remember."

Ezra howled with laughter. "By God, you should have been my son!"

Susannah looked away, a frown on her face.

"Susannah, I meant nothing by my remark. I just wanted you to know how much I enjoy talking to you about things I don't often discuss with women. I . . ."

"I know," Susannah said before he could go on. "But we can't talk about your son. I've apologized to you, and we've made our peace, but I still long for Landry, and I believe in his goodness."

Ezra's eyes were deeply sad. He stared out at the water. "Do you think I do not long for him also? No matter what he has done I cannot forget that once he was my son. I'd do anything, give anything if I could, to change what happened—but I cannot. I can only accept, and have faith that God's will be done."

Susannah's eyes showed hope. "Do you mean that, Papa? Would you really like to see Landry given another chance?"

"How could you doubt it? But it is not to be. We must learn to live with that."

But his daughter was not to be put off so easily. "But supposing there were a way for him to plead his case? Supposing Elder Brannan reinstated him . . . is that what you would wish in your deepest heart?"

Ezra kissed her on the forehead. "Ah, my sunny Susannah, always the optimist, always seeing the silver lining. Yes, my dear child, in my deepest heart, I would rejoice if Landry could be brought back to us—and to God.''

Susannah's smile was bright, her eyes glistened with tears. "Then there will be a way, Papa. I am certain of it.''

Early in March the *Brooklyn* crossed the Equator. After having been at sea and in close quarters for a month, the Saints welcomed this wonderful reason to celebrate. All who had musical instruments brought them on deck. The Saints laughed and sang and danced, and crowned Sam Brannan King Neptune. In an atmosphere of revelry and jollity, it was only minutes before the Sons of Neptune took to playing pranks on the passengers. It was a night designed to cause trouble, but fortunately they ran into nasty weather before anyone went too far.

Squalls were frequent at this latitude, and the Saints got accustomed to having their drills and their promenades interrupted by wind and rain.

During one of these squalls, Mrs. Jonathan Cade went into labor. The Saints greeted and christened their newest member Atlantic Cade. Again there was much celebrating and good feeling among the passengers.

Sam took advantage of the mood to call his meeting. Ezra arose early the next morning to go. Sam brought the group to order and got right to business. He was not one to mince words.

Sam was a man who had learned young the power of his own mind and determination. He had been but a boy when he decided his father had caned him for the last time, and had moved to Painesville, Ohio, with his sister Mary Ann and her husband. There he decided to become a printer, and vowed he would own his own paper. From that time on Samuel Brannan was on the move. This morning he stood at the front of the meeting hall and looked out at his people. His brown eyes snapped, his voice boomed to the back of the hall.

"When it was decided the Saints were to found a new settlement west, I went to Brigham Young and said, Brother Brigham, give me a hundred good men, and I'll take California for the Lord. He believed me, because he knew I could do it. And I will do it!''

Ezra believed him. Asa believed him. Most of the Saints in the room believed him. Some didn't like him, and others didn't trust his ambition, but they believed him. The one thing a man could say about Sam Brannan was that you could slow him down, but you couldn't stop him. It would take killing for that.

After much discussion they decided on the particulars of the Mormon company. They would form a single company to pay the debts of the voyage and to make preparations for Church members who were migrating overland. For the next three years all would give the proceeds of their labor to a common fund from which all were to live. Those who refused to obey the laws were to be expelled. If all the Saints broke their covenant, the common property was to pass first to the elders, then if they fell from grace, to the First Elder.

Samuel Brannan was the First Elder, titular head of the political entity. The newly founded company was named Samuel Brannan and Company.

Sam was pleased at the end of the meeting. "I knew I was right! Now I can tell Brother Brigham that I will not only take California, but have it ready for him to walk into. He'll believe he's found the lost garden!" He raised his clenched fist and the men whooped approval.

In the days that followed, life aboard the *Brooklyn* lost its temporary gaiety and became very tedious. But there was always Lucy Eager. The ship was rocking with indignant cries for action. Elder Bickle, universally acknowledged as lacking in passionate parts, had caught the widow and Councilor Pell in a flagrant embrace.

Sam was bombarded by opinions regarding Sister Lucy and her swains. The storm at sea had been weak compared to the storm of words poured upon him regarding the Widow Eager. In the end he spoke with the three men and the widow, warning them that their constant flirting was unsuitable. Sister Lucy looked as if she would cry as Sam escorted her out of his office.

After he closed his door again, he sat down staring broodingly into space. Restless after a time, he rearranged his storage space. It made him feel better, and when he returned to the main deck, he was softly singing, ". . . he fell in love with a nice young girl, her name was Barbary Allen . . ." Sam had a bounce to his step as he walked the passageways of the ship. Though he wanted to go directly to her, he had to move in a circuitous route so all would *know* he was about Church business. But his thoughts were on Susannah.

It was dark down in the cargo space once Susannah had put out her candle—dark and musty. Down this deep in the ship, the swishing sounds of the waters were very plain. There were other sounds. She leaned against a wall and waited, chilly and frightened. Though this meeting had sounded romantic and intriguing earlier, it was anything but that now. If she had to remain alone down here much longer, she would go out of her head. Then the sound for which she had been listening came. She shrank back into her niche, eyes wide, heart pounding while she held her breath, listening to the footsteps. It was all she could do not to cry out. She waited, and finally Sam said in a normal voice, "Is someone in here?"

In a shaking whisper she replied, "I'm here—to your right, against the wall."

He struck a match, and with a flood of relief she stumbled into his arms. "Oh, Sam. I'm so . . ." Her words were cut off by his lips, and his strong and secure embrace. After a moment he released her and led her through a maze of tools and vehicles and bags of seed. He led her up a step, and when he lit another match, she found they were standing in the bed of a wagon. He had laid a tarpaulin across the narrow center for them to sit on, but it was impossibly crowded, so at Sam's suggestion Susannah gingerly lay down, pushing herself as far to one side as the space would allow. When Sam lowered himself beside her, their bodies were touching. Against her breast she could feel the warmth of his; against her thighs there was the muscular length of his.

His hand ran slowly down her arm and back up, making little shivers of warmth trickle across her. She reached out to touch him. Under her fingertips she felt the prickly texture of his frock coat. His lips, open and warm, softly caressed her forehead. They lay without speaking for a while, touching each other, kissing briefly. Here in the cozy dark it did not seem wrong for her hands to reach inside his coat, to feel the silky texture of his shirt and feel his heart thudding under her caress. And when he began to open the buttons down the front of her dress, that, too, seemed all right. He was kissing her more now, and when all the buttons had been undone, his lips moved down to the ritual cut mark over the left breast of her "garment," that essential piece of Mormon clothing which was never wholly removed without a fresh one being drawn on at the same time.

His tongue moved through the cut mark to touch the bare flesh

146

of her breast. To Susannah the moist warmth was like a brand, and she drew a sharp breath and shrank from him.

Sam let out a deep breath, and laid his head on her breast. He was silent for a moment, and when he did speak, his voice was gentle and tender. "You have never lain with a man before, Susannah."

She was quiet, and he knew she didn't know what to say. "Do you know what it means to lie with a man?"

"Tollie has talked a little of it," she said hesitantly. "I know it means to marry."

There was a momentary pause, then his fingers trailed down her throat and sought the cut mark again. His fingers brushed her nipple, making it spring up rosy and warm and tight. He stroked it softly. She was such a desirable young woman, he mused to himself. He was unaccustomed to such strong and contradictory feelings. So much of his driving force and his time was taken up with the accomplishment of his vast dreams that he often neglected personal pleasures, like the love of a warm and innocent woman such as Susannah.

He smiled in the darkness as he ran his hand over the smooth, soft skin of her breast. She still thought in terms of marriage as the end of all love, even as she tempted him with her body and the promise in her eyes. He thought of her too often as *his* Susannah, but he had no right to that thought, because he could never be her Sam. He already belonged to his ambitions and objectives.

As much as the confined space would allow he moved away from her, and reluctantly took his hand from her breast. "I cannot marry you. My life is with the new colony . . . I'd like to say that isn't so, that I am the kind of man who could give you what you wish of a man, but I cannot." He was silent for a moment, listening to the catch in Susannah's breathing, and wondering why he was being so honest with her. He wanted her so badly his body ached with longing, and after he finished with his soul baring, it was likely she'd never again meet him like this.

Her voice shook when she spoke. "Do you love me at all, Sam? I thought . . . I thought that if a man . . . if a man . . ."

"You thought that if a man wanted to make love to a woman, he was in love with her and would stay by her side forever," he said for her.

On a stifled sob, she agreed.

He hadn't known it was possible, but somehow this girl had wormed her way into his heart, and he did love her. As he listened to the sounds of her purest dreams of love shattering, something in him opened up and hurt with her and for her.

"I do love you, Susannah; I love you very much."

"But not enough to marry me," Susannah cried. "Oh, Sam, what else is there? How can you say you love me and that you don't want me in the same breath?"

"Oh, my darling one, I have never said that I don't want you. I want you. I want you with all my being."

"Is it your wife then? Do you love her so much that there is no room for me? Please tell me, Sam. I need to know."

He lay quietly, his hands at his sides. "It's not my wife, Susannah. Whatever I once felt for her, she has worn away with her sharp tongue and her suspicious accusations."

"Why don't you divorce her, Sam? That is a terrible life for you. Why couldn't I make you happy as she does not? I wouldn't be sharp-tongued, nor would I . . . I don't think I'd be suspicious."

Sam laughed lightly. "You would be a gift of the gods to a man, Susannah, but that, my dear, is not for me. Even though Liza and I no longer get along well, we suit each other. She cares for my home and my child, and except for her waspish ways, she leaves me to my mission. I will give to Liza the prominence in the world she craves, and she will leave me free to do what I am driven to do. She does not divert my passions, Susannah."

"And I do?"

"You could," he said quietly.

Susannah cried, burying her head against his chest. "I don't want to be without you, Sam. Why did you let me love you and then tell me this? What can I do?"

Sam took a deep breath. He had gone this far, he might as well say it all, and allow fate to decide whether or not he would possess Susannah Morrison. "We can part, or we could love each other fully as man and woman without marriage, Susannah. We would belong to each other in a very special way."

Susannah grasped him immediately, but he held her away. "I want you to think carefully on this, Susannah. Do not tempt me further today, for I have no wish to resist you, and won't much longer. I want you to be certain in your own mind and heart if you come to me." He sat up in the bed of the wagon, and began

148

straightening her clothes, buttoning her bodice. "And now I'm taking you back to your family."

"But when will I see you again? Sam . . . ."

He put his fingers on her lips to silence her, then helped her to her feet. He walked her along the corridors. Near her cabin, as two Saints came toward them, he nodded and gave her a word of fatherly advice.

Susannah couldn't bear to go inside and talk to her family as if nothing had happened tonight. She longed for a place where she could be alone. Above all else she wanted her old bedroom back, the lacy window curtains, the predictability of everyday life. Since Landry had gotten into trouble, nothing was certain. Her whole life had become a series of changes and disappointments. She understood nothing, except that she wanted Sam to love her. He was different from other people, and even if he was too busy and too dedicated to be her husband, he would love her. He did love her.

Turning from the door of the cabin, she forced down tears and went on deck to stare at the dark sea. A bittersweet warmth was deep within her. Sam loved her so much he dared not marry her, for she might distract him from his mission. For a long time she dreamed about what that meant, and when she went to her cabin, her decision was made.

Sam Brannan was an unusual man. He would be a leader always, and he would accomplish things other men would never attempt. It required a special woman to deal with such a man, and Susannah knew that somehow she was that woman. She had a capacity for love that could touch a great man.

Tollie was already asleep when Susannah crept into the bunk. She lay awake for a long time envisioning herself with Sam. She pictured Sam talking to his people, and teaching them how to build a colony, and in the background was she, silently proud, encouraging, ready to take care of him when he completed his daily work. She fell asleep during an imaginary conversation with him as he asked her opinions on the future of the Saints.

It was nearly a week before Sam arranged to meet her in the hold again, and Susannah lived her life alternating between ecstasy and despair as she waited. When the night finally came, she was bursting with the desire to be all he could ever want in a woman, and to be the helpmeet a man such as he deserved. She now saw Sam as a hero, alone and unprotected while he did great deeds for more ordinary mortals. That evening, remembering well the tight quarters of the wagon bed, she took particular care with her dress, making sure it was attractive but simple. She went to the hold too soon in her eagerness, and again had a long wait in the dark, dank corridor. As soon as she heard Sam's step, her heart began to beat so hard she was certain he could hear it. He came to stand a foot from her, his candle held so she could see his face, and he could see hers. His eyes held the question.

Susannah's answer came with a happy smile, as she threw her arms around his neck. "You know what I have decided, Sam Brannan! It could be nothing but yes . . . yes, I am yours," she said more softly. "I will always be yours."

"Ah." He held her close, a surge of warmth coursing through him. It was so seldom another human being touched him as Susannah could that he found the feelings frightening and exciting. Trembling nearly as much as she, he led her to the wagon bed. They lay together, talking softly, touching leisurely, learning each other's bodies. Sam reveled in the feel of her skin. She was an amazement to him. He hadn't known he could love or be loved like this. It seemed a wonder that this untried maiden could reach through all his distractions and touch him so intimately.

To Susannah it was such a novel sensation, the warmth of another's flesh touching hers, that she could not imagine why her heart should pound so, nor why there seemed to be butterflies in her stomach. Hesitantly she put her hand on Sam's chest, brushing the heavy hair that covered it. How different his muscle and bone felt from hers . . . how much heavier and stronger . . . how capable of giving pleasure . . .

He began kissing her mouth lightly, then her throat, leaving little warmths where he touched her, then her breasts. The feel of his lips and tongue on her nipples, teasing them, kissing them, created in Susannah a spreading heat. She remembered it from the other time Sam had kissed her, that feeling of wishing to open like a flower to the sun, to extend her being to accept his.

He went on kissing her, planting soft caresses across her belly and down onto her thighs. His hand rubbed her lightly, teasingly, along her side, along her belly, then slowly down to shift the position of her leg. His fingertips rubbed with a gossamer touch inside her thighs.

Susannah lay still, hardly breathing, so absorbed in the caresses he was giving her that she no longer felt any faint apprehension.

He began kissing her mouth fully, his tongue sliding along hers as his fingers caressed her again and again.

Susannah knew nothing of men and their bodies and their way with a woman, but nature soon instructs the innocent. She knew what he was about to do, knew what that part of him was for, knew that, strange as it seemed, it was amazingly right that his long, warm soft-hardness should come into her as it did. She gasped and her eyes went wide at the flash of pain. But he went on kissing her, his tongue moving in and out of her mouth, that other part of him moving in that same sensuous fashion within her.

She curved her body to him, feeling the driving heat building up in herself. Her breath grew short. A great craving and anxiety filled her, and she began to move to meet Sam's hard thrusts. Then the throbbing began, hers, his, and they moaned together with the soaring immensity of the relief.

At last he relaxed onto her, both of them drenched in sweat. Susannah, half crushed with his weight, gave a breathless little laugh, and Sam, chuckling too, kissed her once more.

"Oh, Sam, I feel like a different person. That was like a divine miracle, only it happened to us."

He kissed her and took his weight off her. For a few moments they lay facing each other, keeping the feeling of closeness and belonging. Then, as they noticed the chill, they fumbled for their clothes and put them back on. When they were dressed, Sam lit a match and looked around carefully to make sure they had not left traces. Susannah watched him. Already he was changing back to the Sam Brannan who led the Mormons to their New Zion. She was already losing him.

The transition from such closeness to the coolness of Sam's public life was jolting for Susannah. Though she understood it intellectually, it was painful to realize that until the next occasion he took time from his divine mission, he would treat her like any of the other Saints. All of his love and all of her own had to be kept inside, when all she wanted was to be close to him and share his every thought and deed.

She stood in the dark near him, clutching her shawl around herself, trying to get control. She was a part of him now. How was she to walk into her father's cabin and be the same Susannah she had been before?

Then his arms found her, and drew her again into his reassuring embrace. "Surely you are not sad, my angel?" he asked tenderly.

"How could I not be sad, Sam? I have been loved, and I want to be with you always and cannot."

He held her and kissed her, his lips warm and firm against hers. "But you have my love. That is always with you."

They turned to go, finding their way through the cluttered hold to the companionway. He was a step farther removed from her, she could feel it. Finally he said, "You know this is our secret, and ours alone?"

She did know. What they had done was surely sacred and had been done under the eyes of God, but it must not be told. She answered, "I wish to share this with no one but yourself."

He hesitated, holding her by the arm. "You will not make love with anyone else? Promise me, Susannah?" Then swiftly, his fingers came across her lips. "I withdraw that. I have no right to ask. This is what love can do to a man—make him forget his senses. Forgive me."

With all her heart she wanted to promise herself to him alone. But the distance of his public self made her silent. There was great pain in being so close to him, and then so far removed immediately after. She didn't trust her voice. A terrible storm of emotions threatened to make her burst into tears at any moment.

His fingers tipped her chin up to meet his kiss, and she was thankful for the blanketing darkness. He said, "Again I must ask you, please, not to catch my eye in public. Even though I am an ordinary man, the others look up to me, and must continue to think I am a step better in my control and discipline, or they would not listen to me. School yourself to hide your emotions, my dear, so that your radiant face does not give you away. Anyway, I want that radiance all for myself. I love you, Susannah."

"I'll try to be careful," she said in a whisper.

"I'll go ahead. If anyone is in sight, I'll come back down. Otherwise, wait only a few seconds and follow me. Godspeed, my love." Quickly he kissed her, and she waited until she no longer heard his footsteps in the companionway before following him.

She slipped quietly into the cabin. Good fortune was with her, for no one woke up, and she was able to slip into her bunk unobserved. She lay awake, her body still tuned and sensitive to the loving with Sam, and her heart already aware of the separation that had begun. She held her silence, but tears of happiness and of sadness rolled off her cheeks onto her pillow.

Sam Brannan went out on the main deck. Relaxed and reflective in a deck chair, he bit off the end of a cigar and lit it. The cool night air flowed past him. Around him were peaceful sounds of a ship under full sail in fine weather—the creaking of the blocks, the shrilling of the wind in the rigging, the susurrus of the ocean washing past the hull.

He took an occasional puff on his cigar and let his unfocused gaze linger on the starlit water. He had intended to review his duties for tomorrow, to plan his prayer meeting, to think of an encouraging speech to prepare the Saints for the monumental work that would be required once they reached California. He began thinking of how he could instill his own faith in his people, but images of Susannah Morrison intruded.

His gaze became dreamier, and he relaxed into his thoughts. The thing was done, the passionate encounter he had at first fought against, and then at last had schemed to bring about. He had broken his marriage vows to begin a love affair that could have none but a disastrous end. He had challenged disaster for ambition many times, but this was the first for himself. He had conquered, but in so doing had made himself captive. He hadn't bargained for the hold Susannah was capable of having on him.

But the night glittered silver with stars; his body was sated, at peace for the time being; and God in his heaven knew what the end would be.

Part IV

Part IV

Chapter Thirteen

The McKays had begun their trek across the country with three wagons and the family carriage. It became quickly apparent that the carriage would never make the journey, and that they would be far better off in the large, lumbering Conestoga they used for sleeping.

Sean had brought the carriage thinking to make his womenfolk more comfortable. Now he gave his wife a sheepish smile. "I knew it all the while, but I guess I was hoping it would stand up to the road. What do they call us fools? Greenhorns?"

Mary patted his arm and smiled back at him. "Nonsense, I know my man. You just wanted to get it as far as Independence so you could sell it for a better price. You can't fool me, Sean McKay, some dandy out there will pay you double what you'd have gotten at home."

Mud-spattered and wet, the Donner group of twelve wagons and one carriage approached Independence, Missouri. The river was running high, too high for the many travelers to cross. As a result the town of Independence was cluttered with a tent community on its outskirts. As far as the McKays could see the tents stretched out, and from a goodly distance the sounds of livestock could be heard as they were set to grazing on every available patch of grass.

Fiona and Coleen entertained themselves on the gray, rainy May afternoon by counting tents. Fiona craned her neck, her hands on her mother's shoulders as she tried to see farther.

"That is very uncomfortable, Fiona—I wish you would find another pillar to lean on," Mary complained.

"Don't bother your mother!" Sean yelled from the side of the wagon where he was walking with the oxen.

"But I can't see beyond the first few tiers," Fiona said.

"How many have you counted?" Coleen asked. "I've gotten to twelve hundred."

"You're taller than I am!"

"But that is only about half!" Coleen said with some concern. She called to her father, "Papa, all these people aren't waiting to cross the river, are they?"

Sean dropped back a few steps to talk. He let out a long breath. "I expect they are, darlin'. You saw what it was like at the Mississippi. We had to wait for it to go down before we could cross—I suppose it won't be any better here. All the rivers are high this year—too much rain." To dramatize his point he took off his hat and shook water from the brim.

For the first time Mary paid close attention to the tents the girls had been counting. Her eyes grew wide. "Goodness, Sean, how long do you think it will take for us to cross? Everywhere I look there are tents!"

Sean shrugged. "Not much we can do about it. We'll just have to make ourselves as comfortable as we can, pray for the rain to let up, find a place for the livestock to graze—and wait our turn to cross."

"Thank God Tamsen and I thought to bring a good supply of interesting books," Mary sighed. "I think I would go mad cooped up in a smelly, wet tent for days on end with nothing to do."

Coleen had begun to think of other aspects of the enforced delay. "There are a lot of people. Maybe we'll meet some nice ones who will join our group."

Fiona's green eyes twinkled. "Some nice *young unmarried* ones, you mean."

"Fiona, you're impossible. That's not what I said at all! Mama, will you tell her to stop interpreting everything I say as if I am on a great hunt for a man! It's embarrassing—and she doesn't know a thing about it," Coleen said in superior tones.

"Your sister does have a point, Fiona. You do tend to harp on it a bit, and it is not a becoming habit you've acquired."

158

"Oh, Mama, I'm just teasing and she knows it. Anyway it's the truth."

"And an unbecoming habit," Mary repeated.

With a pretty pout, and a venomous glance at Coleen, Fiona subsided into silence.

Though the city of tents had been visible for some miles, it was nearly supper time before the McKays pulled their wagons into the community. Sean, walking at the side of the oxen, had the best view of the land, and tried to spot a place that did not have standing water on the surface. It was no mean task, as the spring rains had been heavy, and for weeks travelers had been coming into Independence, making mush of the grass as their wagons and livestock trampled it.

By the time the tent was unpacked and set up and the bedrolls unpacked, it was long past supper time, and everyone was tired. Mary was about to announce that they would manage for that day with dried meat and fruit, when a large, broad-faced woman opened the tent flap, and stuck her head and shoulders inside. "Hello there! I seen you folks ride in, and thought you might be wantin' a bit of hot food already fixed."

"Come in," Mary said, smiling nervously as she glanced quickly around and realized she had no place to ask the woman to sit. Sean hadn't unpacked the camp stools yet, and she didn't even have anything to offer the woman to eat or drink.

The woman watched the play of expressions on Mary's face. She waved a big friendly hand at Mary. "Ah, don't worry about bein' polite—we all feel all thumbs when we first camp in the mud, but we're all in the same puddle! Oh, for goodness' sake, I forgot to introduce myself. I'm Jane Pardee. I been in this mess many times—that's how I knew you'd be wantin' hot food." Jane thrust her hand out to be shaken just as a man might.

Tentatively, and for the first time in her life, Mary put forth her hand to shake the hand of another woman. "I'm Mary McKay, and these are my daughters, Coleen and Fiona, Mrs. Pardee."

The girls dutifully greeted the woman, neither of them knowing what to make of her. As quickly as courtesy allowed, they occupied themselves with setting out the steaming dinner Mrs. Pardee had brought, always keeping an eye on her, enjoying and being amused by her gregariousness.

Jane moved farther into the tent, looked around approvingly, then flopped down on one of the cots Sean had set up. "At least it is dry—won't stay that way for long, mind you, but you'll have tonight, and perhaps tomorrow, free of the stink of mildew and other foul things."

Mary was speechless. Her mind and mouth worked furiously in the attempt to find something suitable to say in response.

Jane burst into laughter, slapping her leg in sheer glee. "You're mighty new to all this, aren't you, Mary McKay?"

"Well, yes, I am, but . . ."

"Why, you're just going to have to loosen up a bit—take it as it comes and not let it worry you. I saw that fancy wagon that came in with you, but believe me, even that will give way to the rigors of the road and the weather. All any of us has really got on a trek like yours is each other. It's a whole lot better to learn from the start to laugh a little, share what you have with others, and accept the discomforts as . . . well, just accept them. You haven't seen anything yet! Wait till the flies begin to follow you in the heat of summer!"

"Ugh!" Coleen said, making a face, which caused Jane to laugh again.

"How do you know so much about the trail?" Fiona asked.

Jane came as close to blushing as anyone would ever see her. "Oh, sweet child, I've been across this land as many times as most trappers—" Suddenly she burst into laughter. "And for the same reason. My husbands keep dying on me, so I got to go get me a fresh one from time to time."

Mary, Coleen, and Fiona gave up trying to fit Jane into a proper social mold and laughed with her. "How many husbands have you had?" Mary asked, nearly strangling at the idea that she could ask so brazen a question of a stranger.

"Well, now—I think it's three. Mr. Pardee was number three, and now I'm huntin' for number four."

They all sat down on the cots, sipped at the hot tea, and nibbled at the corncakes and raisin cookies.

Jane continued, "Now, Mr. Pardee was as good a man as you'll ever find, but he just wasn't suited to the rigors of life out West. The poor man coughed himself to death, an' there wasn't a thing could be done for him."

She was still chattering on about Mr. Pardee and occasionally telling a story about husband one or two, when Sean came into the tent. "Mary—" he called as he pulled back the tent flap, then stopped abruptly when he saw Jane.

Mary's eyes twinkled as she introduced him. Without the slightest effort to be discreet, Jane looked him up and down and sideways, then gave Mary an approving nod. "My, my, what a *fine* man!" She chuckled happily, and shook his hand. "Well, Mary, if you ever want to sell him, let me know. It'd save me a trip across the country. I best be getting back to my own tent now. My son'll be wanting his supper, and you two most likely want a little time to yourselves as well."

"Oh, don't hurry off," Mary said quickly, and got a hard pinch from Sean, who hadn't yet recovered his powers of speech.

"Oh, I'll be around. You can't get rid of Jane Pardee," she said cheerfully.

"We'll be very busy in the next few days," Sean said. "I've got to find a bullwhacker to replace one who left me."

Jane sat down again. "Do you now? It happens my son—the one waitin' for his supper—" She looked over at Mary. "He's really my stepson, Mr. Campbell's boy. Campbell was number two."

Fiona giggled. "What happened to him?"

"Oh, the poor thing! He got caught in a rock slide in the mountains hunting for gold. Didn't find enough dust to fill a tooth."

"More of the rigors," Fiona said, laughing.

"Mrs. Pardee!" Sean said, his voice deep and filled with all the authority he could muster.

"Yes! Sorry, Mr. McKay, I got distracted. As I was saying, my son Brian is with me, and could use the work heading home. No one knows the territory better, and you'd be in good hands. I'll just send him over first thing in the morning." Before Sean could refuse, she was on her feet again and headed for the tent flap. "Goodnight now, enjoy a dry night in here—it may be the only one you get."

The McKay women chorused their goodbyes, and Jane was gone, leaving the tent quiet and empty-feeling.

"Blessed heaven!" Sean breathed. "*What* was that? Where did that woman come from? Mary, don't you let her near here again."

"Papa!" Fiona cried.

"Oh, Sean, don't be a bear. She is very nice. You'll get to liking her too."

"Holy God, woman, she wants to buy me! Didn't you hear her? I think she damn well meant it—and she wants to foist her daft son on me as well!"

"Papa, don't be so unreasonable," Coleen said with a smile. "She is just a little brash in the way she talks, but she doesn't mean anything bad by it. Her son might be the very person you need to guide us the rest of the way. After all, you said yourself that once we cross the Missouri we are out of the United States, and we know almost nothing about what lies beyond. Mrs. Pardee's son knows all of that."

"And he'll probably want to buy your mother—or one of you girls!"

"Oh, Papa, you're funny. She wouldn't do that." Fiona giggled. She went over to her father, leaning against him as his arm went around her. "Mrs. Pardee is really nice—she's just a little . . . different than us, but maybe that's the way people are in the West."

Sean grumbled deep in his throat, but he was smiling when he said, "I certainly hope not." He poked a finger into the stew she had brought. "But she cooks pretty good."

Sean was feeling a little more kindly toward Jane Pardee when he went to bed that night with a stomach full of good food—but not kindly enough to want to hire her son. Thinking to outsmart her, Sean was awake and ready to leave the family tent by six o'clock. He didn't manage ten steps before he heard Jane's voice. "Whooo-eee, Mr. McKay! Mr. McKay!"

Sean winced, but turned around and managed a pleasant smile. "Good morning, Mrs. Pardee. I thank you for the supper. It was very good."

"Why, you're welcome!" Jane beamed, then got to her main interest. "Did you forget I was bringing Brian around to meet you?"

Sean looked with some curiosity at the tall, lean young man standing beside Jane. Brian Campbell was over six feet tall, with sandy hair and an openly handsome, friendly face. He was nothing at all like his stepmother. He was quiet. Sean stood staring at him, not moving.

Brian grinned and put his hand out for Sean to shake. "Ma told me you're needing a good bullwhacker, Mr. McKay. I hope

162

you don't think me boastful if I say I'd be a good man for you. I've been across the mountains before, and I know the territory. I'll do a good job for you, sir.''

"Well! I'll just let you two men get on with your business,'' Jane said heartily. "I'll have a little visit with Mary. I can give her a few tips for the trail.''

Without thinking, Sean began to walk, assuming correctly that Brian would keep pace with him. They went down to the water's edge. The thick mud sucked hard at their boots. Both men watched as water filled in the depressions their feet had left.

After a long, comfortable silence, Brian said, "My ma means well, Mr. McKay. She's a little loud, and she can't help but say whatever pops into her head, but she's got a heart bigger than all the West. You won't find any better.''

Sean chuckled. "I'm beginning to recognize that, but she sure did give me a start yesterday. I'm going to take her word on one thing though—she said I wouldn't find a better bullwhacker than you, and I agree. The two of you are very complimentary about each other. For you, she's the best, and for her, you are. I like that—it says more about a man than anything else I can think of.'' He looked up at Brian and smiled. "If you're willing, I'd like you to hire on with us.''

Brian returned the smile, and put out his hand again. "Yes, sir, I'd be proud!''

Sean spun around and headed back toward the group of tents. "Come on, Mary ought to have breakfast going, and I want you to meet my family. It's best you know all of us before we set out.''

Brian had to duck his head inside the tent, which was no hardship, for as soon as he had entered and been introduced to Sean's three women, he had become painfully shy and self-conscious. It was more comfortable for him to have an excuse to keep his head down, and not have to deal directly with the very beautiful eyes of Coleen McKay.

Coleen had come to life the moment she had been introduced to Brian. A becoming color had crept into her cheeks and remained there. Her eyes sparkled and danced with an awareness of him, and of herself in his eyes. She knew he was uncomfortable, but she couldn't help it that her eyes constantly sought one more look at this tall, broad-shouldered, quiet man.

Mary set out the food on a makeshift table, and they all

crowded around it. Coleen looked on with pleasure and a little amazement at the amount of food this slender man was consuming. She watched as one egg was followed by a second, third, and fourth. Mary and Fiona kept moving back and forth between the cookfire outside and the table, bringing one platter after another of steaming hot food. It all disappeared, and as the platters emptied, the talk became more congenial, and the atmosphere relaxed. Jane, however, could no longer get a rise out of Sean with her blunt humor and was disappointed. Her spirits soon rose, though, when she saw Brian dare look directly at Coleen.

She looked at her son, then at Coleen. She gave Mary a mighty nudge, and nodded at the two, who were now engrossed in each other's gaze. Mary took a deep breath, wondering how Sean was going to take this turn of events—if it developed. With the speed of maternal instinct, she also thought ahead to the many weeks and months of confined travel across the country. She took another deep breath and let it out slowly.

Jane reached over and squeezed her arm. "It'll be all right. My Brian is an honorable man."

Mary managed a weak smile. "If this is the beginning, will mere honor carry them through?" She got up and began gathering dishes.

Coleen, too, got to her feet. "I'll get the water, Mama."

Brian sprang to his feet, forgetting the top of the tent. "I'll get it for you, Miss McKay—it'd be my pleas . . ." his voice trailed off as the main tent pole swayed. He eased himself down, putting the pole back in place as best he could.

Sean, with a stern look, watched the whole process. "The first thing you can do is find the supplies we'll need to raise this tent by half a foot. I don't fancy having canvas in my soup every time you jump to your feet, Brian."

Brian's face turned bright pink. With a muttered, "Yes, sir," he cautiously backed out of the tent, gathered up the water pails, and waited for Coleen to join him.

Both Mary and Sean left the tent soon after. Mary went with Jane to meet some of the other women, and Sean went to town to sell his carriage and see if he could purchase a copy of Lansford Hastings's book, *The Emigrant's Guide*, or Fremont's *Report, with Maps*. It hadn't taken him long to figure out that this business of traveling across the country was a complicated thing, and he wanted to be as prepared as he could be.

Once in Independence, Sean found that he was not the only man who wanted guidance from an expert. He also met several men so determined that they would allow nothing to deter them from heading West. As Sean rummaged through a dry goods store, he noticed a small, nice-looking man who seemed to be moving wherever he moved. From time to time Sean looked up and saw the man's large, benevolent eyes meeting his. The man smiled tentatively. "Charles Stanton," he said. "I'm waiting to cross the river—same with you?"

Sean nodded.

"I had a business in Chicago, but I lost it," Stanton volunteered, seemingly determined to befriend Sean. "Now, I'm going to seek my fortune at the very edge of this continent."

Sean looked at him then. "That's a little extreme, isn't it? Couldn't you have started over in Chicago?"

Charles Stanton smiled. "I expect I could, but I'm done with Chicago. There are no good memories for me there. If a man can't begin anew with good memories, then he'd better start in a place with none. Anyway, if I started over there, I'd never leave. I would never see what lies beyond these plains, would I?"

"I don't know," Sean said.

"Well, it seems to me a man must follow his dreams every now and then. There's not much to life, if we don't take a chance now and then. You're doing the same thing, aren't you, Mr. . . ."

"McKay," Sean said. "Sean McKay. I wouldn't call my emigration the fulfillment of a dream. It's more that I had no choice."

"You couldn't have started over again where you came from?"

Sean hadn't really given it much thought. Now he said, "Not and kept my pride. It is time to move on."

Charles Stanton broke into a warm smile. "That's the way it is with me, Sean. Perhaps we shall travel together and have a quiet drink on a pleasant night on the road?"

Sean finally shook the man's hand. "I'm sure we will, Charles. It's a long trek, and there'll be many nights a man could relish some company."

The ferry had begun to take people across the Missouri, but the hundreds of families and the cattle and other livestock with them made it a slow and tedious process. A few enterprising men

165

of the area had quickly managed to produce other ferries, and for a fee took families across, but still the wait was a long one. With nothing to do but watch the slow process of the ferries taking people across the swollen river, those left behind made friends with each other. Few of them were experienced travelers, and all of them were eager for any piece of information that would warn them of what was ahead. Around the nightly campfires Sean sat with several other men discussing Hastings's book, and trying to glean enough information to aid him in deciding whether the McKay family would do better settling in Oregon or California. Brian, of course, was a perpetual salesman for California. He wanted the McKays as near to him as possible.

On one of these pleasant nights Sean met another Irishman. To his great disappointment, he did not like Patrick Breen. When he returned to his tent that night, he complained bitterly to Mary. "He's the worst sort of Irishman, holding to himself as though everyone was out to take from him."

"Sean, don't give him a thought—he no doubt has had a difficult time of it in the old country. Give him time, he'll thaw out. I've known a few people who thought of you as standoffish until they got to know you."

Sean thought briefly of the effort Charles Stanton had had to put forth just to talk with him, and nearly relented. At the last moment he thought better of it. "No. Patrick Breen is not like me. He's a miserly potato eater, and no more. We won't have any society with the Breen family, Mary. I have decided."

Mary gave her agreement, and was pleased for the opportunity to obey Sean so completely. Had she not shared his opinion, she would never have done so, but she didn't much care for the Breens herself, and she certainly did not like their teen-age son, who was bold and rough and too often could be caught ogling Fiona in a way Mary detested.

The McKays felt quite differently about two other families they had met, however. Both of them liked the young Eddys, Eleanor and William, and Amanda and William McCutcheon. McCutcheon was a giant of a man, and very proud of his young pregnant wife. William Eddy was quite a trapper, and even now was always setting traps to gather fresh meat. Both he and his wife had a ready smile, and a willingness to share whatever they had. The McKays had no reservation left when they saw the Eddys with their children, little Jimmy and a baby daughter. The three families expressed a desire to travel together, at least for a time.

"We'll convince you to head for California before the roads part, Sean," William Eddy said as he took a mouthful of succulent rabbit meat.

Sean laughed. "I wouldn't be at all surprised, you're a persuasive man—but you have your work cut out for you. I'm not one for buying a pig in a poke."

"Neither am I," big McCutcheon said quickly. "And as you can see, I've got good reason for being picky." He glanced at his wife sitting outside their tent. "This Hastings fellow's new pass will cut off considerable time from the journey. Why, we'll be settled and working on another child by the time you ever see Oregon, Sean."

Sean raised his eyebrows and took some time tamping tobacco into his pipe. "I've been reading his book. It does sound like a much shorter route, but what do you know about the man?"

Stanton said, "I heard Hastings has taken several wagon trains through the mountain pass. He even went through there after the snows came—and that is supposed to be quite a feat. It must be a good route."

Sean puffed on his pipe, his mind ranging far into the future. "It would be nice to settle in a new home soon."

"Well then? Hastings offers us the opportunity to do just that, and what's more, I've heard he'll personally escort a train through the pass. The Donner brothers are going with Hastings. Aren't you traveling with them?"

Sean nodded. "We have been, but not with any formal agreement. We happened to start out at the same time, going in the same direction, so we traveled together."

Eddy laughed. "That's the way it is with most of us. I don't think there's one whole train in the whole passel of us here."

"Who knows who we'll end up with—maybe we'll all be together the whole way," Stanton said, passing around his jug.

167

Chapter Fourteen

The McKays crossed the Missouri River on May 12, 1846. Once across, with their wagons and livestock assembled again, the entire family stood at the bank of the river and looked back at the city of tents that lay at the outskirts of Independence.

"This may be the last time we ever see the United States," Mary said sadly.

"Why didn't we think of that before?" Fiona asked. Easy tears shone in her green eyes. "What country will we be in?"

None of them knew.

They climbed back into the wagons with mixed feelings. They were truly on their way west now, with all they had known before in Ireland and in Illinois far behind them. That was a small part of themselves lost forever, except in memory. Before them were the vast expanses of prairie, and what lay unseen beyond those swaying golden carpets of grass and flowers. That was exciting.

With uncertain little smiles exchanged among them, the McKays pulled their wagons into line with the others already on the road heading west. As the day progressed, more and more wagons came across the Missouri, and added their number to the train. Five hundred wagons traveled together in no particular order, with no particular division to designate a formal train.

It was comforting to know that behind them someplace in the long line of wagons were the Eddys and the McCutcheons and Charles Stanton. Sean found that he felt better knowing he had friends, and Mary's only sorrow was that Jane Pardee was not in the train. Jane would not leave Independence for another week. By then the McKays would be far away. She missed Jane and trusted Jane's ability to deal with anything that came her way.

When they camped for the night, Sean, Brian, and several other men headed straight for the stream. Amid quiet, friendly talk of a tiring day of travel, the men put their fishing lines into the stream and brought forth fresh dinner.

The young people quickly discovered they had in their number an entertainer who was always willing to let down the back of his wagon for a stage. Patrick Dolan was a genial man, a good story teller, and could easily be persuaded to dance an Irish jig for the amusement of his audience. He also had a very creditable singing voice, which he liked to display. Fiona wanted to go to Dolan's wagon simply because she liked the entertainment. Coleen, however, was grateful to Patrick Dolan primarily because it gave her and Brian a time and place to be together.

Night after night Patrick Dolan amused his young friends and himself with music and dance. Before too long he had others performing as well. It got to be quite a gay routine. As Mary watched her two daughters walk in the direction of Dolan's wagon in the company of Brian, she pushed her curling hair back from her face. "It's a blessing we have someone like Mr. Dolan for the young people," she said to Sean. "I had no idea how tiring traveling day after day could be. I have seen so many hills and clouds and miles of grassland that I am dreaming about them."

"Is it that hard on you, Mary?"

She put her head on his shoulder. "I didn't mean that, Sean. It is tiresome, that is all. You don't think about how boring the miles can become until they all begin to look like the one that has gone before. I am happy that the girls have something pleasant to do in the evenings. It gives them something to look forward to at the end of the day."

"And what have you to look forward to, my Mary?"

She smiled and snuggled closer to him. "There might be other advantages to the girls being occupied, Sean."

He glanced at the empty wagon, then back at his wife. He kissed her lightly on the forehead, and before he knew it his hand was moving gently along her arm, down to her waist. "It's a quiet, lovely night," he said.

"Ummm, a night when a woman such as I looks forward to what only you can give me, Sean."

His eyes shone a brilliant blue. A slow smile was on his lips as he got up, his arm around her. "Come with me, Mary," he said, his eyes constantly on her. Together they moved toward the wagon.

They moved carefully in the adequate, but limited space of the wagon. Their cot was covered with a spread Mary had crocheted herself, and though she had given up many niceties on this journey, the welcoming prettiness of her bed was not one of them. She sat down on the bed, her shawl falling from her shoulders.

Sean's eyes were dark with love. His Mary was a beautiful woman. He knelt, his fingers working the buttons of her bodice. Gently, almost reverently, his fingers spread across the soft skin of her chest. Her breasts were well rounded and fit his hands perfectly. His lips touched her flesh at the top of her petticoat. Sean deftly slipped the straps over her shoulders, his mouth teasing her nipples.

Mary opened the front of his shirt, caressing and teasing as she undressed him. "You've a handsome body for a man of forty," she said.

"So have you," he whispered, "made just for a man of forty."

They giggled, deliciously naughty together. They soon lay naked, comfortable under the covers, holding, petting, caressing each other. The cares of the trail were forgotten, the outside world shut out, and all that Mary and Sean knew was each other and what would make the other happiest. Somehow they knew that this night there would be no interruptions, and they had all the time they needed for loving and being loved.

Sean's lips found Mary's, and his tongue gently slid along hers while his hand fondled her, bringing her slowly to the peak of passion before he entered her. Then Mary stiffened and put her hand tight on his shoulder for a moment. He stopped what he was doing, tense and anxious. "What—" he began.

"Sh—sh," Mary said reassuringly. "Don't stop now, my Sean. Just kiss me and love me—and listen. It's a song made for us."

It was Patrick Dolan, whose clear Irish tenor rang out on the still air. And Sean began kissing and caressing Mary again, while into their hearts crept the words of an Irish song that, to them, was as old as time:

> No, the heart that has truly loved never forgets
> But as truly loves on to the close
> As the sunflower turns on her god when he sets
> The same look that she turned when he rose . . .

He mounted her, and she lifted herself to meet him and link their hearts and their bodies in a passion for each other that both knew would never die. He would always be her god, she the sunflower turned toward him.

Afterwards they cuddled, Mary's hand absently rubbing Sean's neck and touching his hair. They were warm and sleepy and comfortable, mellow and contented.

Sean and Mary were half asleep when they heard their daughters return to the wagon. Fiona whispered to Coleen, "Shh, Mama and Papa are already asleep. They won't even know we were late, if we're quiet."

Sean and Mary looked at each other in the darkness, and Mary buried her face against his chest to muffle the laughter that bubbled in her.

When they got out on the road again the following morning, Sean had a distinct swagger to his walk, and Mary sang as she straightened their belongings in the swaying, jiggling wagon.

Several evenings later when they camped for the night, William Eddy came by the tent, and pointed out a nearby hill to Sean. "Who do you suppose those folks are? McCutcheon and I have been wondering if they are alone by design, or just haven't the gumption to join us. Think we ought to go up there and say something to them?"

Sean looked over at the small hill on which several people had set up camp. Compared to the long string of wagons he was traveling with, the group looked small and lonely, almost forlorn, but he shook his head. "Why not wait and see what they do?"

Eddy nodded agreement. "That's pretty much what McCutcheon and I concluded, but we wanted a few other opinions. Reed says he thinks they'll come down of their own accord." He shrugged, greeted Mary and the girls, then went back to his own wagon.

171

As usual, Patrick Dolan let down the back of his wagon, and those who had musical instruments gathered round. Because of the location of the stream, more people than usual joined the group. Sean and Uncle George Donner and some of the younger boys built a huge bonfire. With their knitting and fancywork in hand, many of the women sat near the fire.

Most everyone had forgotten the campers on the distant hill, until five strangers walked up to the bonfire. William Eddy, James Reed, and Sean stood near to each other, watching as George Donner greeted the strangers. James Reed had a deep furrowed frown on his face. He said under his breath to the others, "They are pretty heavily armed to come visiting."

Each of the men had a pistol, knife, or both with him, but William Eddy said, "They don't know us any better than we know them, and they are in a small party. Let's not jump to conclusions."

As the man talked and speculated about the newcomers, Uncle George brought them over and introduced them. "Mr. and Mrs. Wolfinger, Mr. and Mrs. Keseberg and their infant, and Old Man Hardkoop," he said, smiling, then added, "They'd like to join our train."

Wolfinger, a richly dressed man, bared his teeth in a smile that did not reach his eyes. "I hope there is no objection."

James Frazier Reed did not smile at all. "What's your destination?"

"California," Keseberg said quickly.

Reed continued to look hard at these newcomers. He was torn between accepting them as persons of substance, as their clothing indicated, or following an instinctive wariness of them. He knew quality cloth when he saw it, and Wolfinger had it on his back. He was also reasonably certain that the jewelry Mrs. Wolfinger wore in showy abundance was genuine, and yet—it was an odd display of wealth on a cross-country trek. Mentally he shrugged. The Germans were always a strange lot. Who could ever know why they did the things they did? He locked eyes with Louis Keseberg. "We are not actually a train. It just happened that we gathered because we all crossed the Missouri together. I don't suppose there is anyone to say you can or cannot join it. It's up to you."

Keseberg was not at all intimidated by the hard stare of Reed.

His small opaque eyes were steady and appraising on the taller man. A smile drew his thin lips taut against yellow teeth. "We will join, Mr. Reed. Companionship is always advisable on a long journey, wouldn't you say?"

Reed didn't answer. He looked away, his eyes seeking Sean. "Goodnight, McKay, I'll see you tomorrow." Shoulders bent he headed back to his huge house-wagon.

His mother-in-law was an old woman who had been unwell throughout the trip. His wife, Margaret, feared this would be the last night of her mother's life. He wanted to be at her side. The Reeds spent that night on their knees, their heads bent in prayer for the old woman. Just before dawn she died.

With the help of his teamster Milt Elliot, Reed built a coffin. By the time the sun had brightened the sky, it was hot, and the men dug her grave. The long line of wagons remained motionless as they waited for Milt and a gunsmith named Denton to cut her tombstone. It was midday before the Reeds had said their final goodbyes to the old woman and returned to their wagons to begin their journey again.

The Germans brought their wagons into line with the others, and little more thought was given to them. They were quiet for the most part, socializing mostly among themselves, sipping beer in their rest periods, and talking in their native tongue. They became a sizeable group when the Spitzer and Reinhardt wagons joined the train. While the Germans occasioned little comment, many of the train members were not comfortable with them. Mrs. Keseberg in particular seemed strange, jumping when her husband spoke, servile to him, like a dog whipped too often, and nervously hushing baby Ada. Sean avoided them whenever he could, and asked that Mary and his daughters have as little to do with them as possible.

"What is it you do not like about them, Sean?" Mary asked.

He shook his head. "I can't give you a reasonable answer, Mary. I do not trust them, but I can't say why."

"That's not very fair, Papa," Fiona said. "You've always told us to give any man a chance until he has proven himself unworthy."

"There are times the best advice does not hold true, Fiona," her mother said. "I want you to listen to Papa. Be polite, but do not become overly friendly with the Germans."

Fiona looked at her father, her great green eyes full of questions.

Sean hugged her to him. "For every rule, my darling, there is an exception, and sometimes a man can only follow his instincts. This time I feel in my gut that these are people we are best kept away from. Trust me, Fiona, for my instinct is all I have to guide you by this time."

Coleen had been quiet throughout the conversation. Now she said, "Brian has said much the same thing to me. I think he plans to tell you of his feelings, Papa. Has he mentioned the argument he had with Mr. Keseberg?"

"No! What happened?" Sean asked.

"Brian had to stop him from entering the sacred ground at the Sioux burial perch a ways back."

Sean frowned and muttered a curse under his breath. "I knew those Germans would cause trouble. I've got to talk with Brian and Uncle George right away . . . this could mean real trouble for the whole train."

That evening when the wagon train camped at the Big Blue River, Sean immediately went in search of George Donner. Tamsen told him George was inspecting the train. With an impatient shrug Sean strode after him.

George Donner walked out from the main camp, looking over the activities of those people with whom he was traveling and whom he was just beginning to think of as friends. George liked cohesiveness and wanted to look upon these people as an extended family—at least as long as the journey lasted.

He changed his direction when he saw Louis Keseberg, Gus Spitzer, and Joseph Reinhardt sitting together, talking and laughing. As he neared, he noticed a distinctive buffalo robe on Keseberg's lap. Hoping he was wrong, he asked in a harsher fashion than was his custom, "Whose robe is that?"

Keseberg's eyes held a cold arrogance for this snooping Illinois farmer. "What business is it of yours? It's on my lap—in my possession."

Donner did not back down. He dared not. "Tell me—where did you get that robe?"

"I found it, discarded, a ways back. Does that satisfy you, or have you more prying questions?"

Donner's face grew ashen. He muttered a curse, then wheeled and ran back to the wagons, shouting, "Reed! Reed! McKay! Jake!"

174

James Reed was the first to respond. It was not like George Donner to be excited. "What is it, Uncle George?"

Breathless now, George panted, "The Germans . . . Keseberg! He robbed the Sioux burial perch! He's got a robe . . . and other things. He'll have the Indians after us. We may be done in."

"How do you know this?" Reed asked, not really needing an answer. He was stalling for time. He didn't seem able to take in the enormity of the danger Keseberg had placed them in.

"Get the others! We must hold council, decide what must be done," Donner said.

As they spoke, others gathered near the Reed wagon. Denton, big McCutcheon, Eddy, Sean, Brian, Milt Elliot, Mason, and others all talked at once, offering opinions. Mason, the most extreme, demanded the Germans be hanged. Other cooler heads determined to replace the objects, and the next day hold a trial for Keseberg. Whatever punishment they decided would be meted out then.

"First, we protect ourselves from the Indians," Reed said. "Perhaps it will not be noticed if everything is replaced. They may never know . . ." At the looks of doubt he saw, he added, "Well, there are birds of prey . . . They might have trifled with the items, shifted them. How are the Indians to know it was one of us?"

Finally they all agreed, and with Keseberg flanked by two armed men, the small party rode back to the burial site. There was an eerie early dawn light when they arrived. Rings of skulls marked the cardinal points of the burial site. In the middle was a scaffold of painted poles. Resting on top of it was the corpse. Dark winged buzzards circled. Others perched warily in nearby trees, waiting. Keseberg entered the area again, and replaced all those things he had stolen two days before.

It was nightfall by the time the party returned to the wagon campsite. Late though it was, and as tired as the returning men were, they held their trial. Master Mason presented the case against Keseberg, and George Donner was the judge.

Mason said loudly, "All groups of people, even a wagon train, must abide by law to protect the many. We who travel in this train have agreed by mutual consent to abide by the laws of the United States. It's our protection. We want no trouble, but this man has endangered us all. He, by his vile action, has placed every man, woman, and child under threat of retaliation by the Indians. We are open to murder—rape—attack by night, because of Louis Keseberg's theft! A man who would endanger all his fellows deserves no mercy. We should offer no mercy!''

Before George Donner could say anything, Keseberg stood up. Arrogant as always, he strode to the center of his ring of accusers. ''What crime did I commit? You dare sit in judgment of me! What crime? I took from a dead man! Does he accuse me—ask for the return of his goods? I took only what I could use. It did not belong to you! No law applies, you fools—there is no law in the territories!'' He spun on his heel so he could see all those in the circle. He had a smile on his face, his hands were out as though he explained the simplest of truths to the stupidest of men. ''Hah? Law? No law. You have no right to judge me! None! I have done nothing.''

Disgusted, George Donner kicked aside the box he had been using for his seat. McCutcheon tied Keseberg's hands behind his back and kept him under guard, taking him back to his wagon.

The men gathered round a fire. Mason continued to insist, ''We should hang him. Let the Indians see that we have given them the man who desecrated their burial bier.''

''Did you hear him?'' Eddy cried. ''He shows no sign of remorse. The man thinks he is above the law.''

''I think it is custom to send the man out of camp without arms or meat to make his way as best he can—or to die,'' George Donner said.

Jake Donner raised his head. ''I'd prefer that. Let God decide if he will live or die.''

''What about his wife? She'll have to go on without him—not knowing if he will ever return,'' Charles Stanton said mildly.

''He should have been thinking of his wife when he risked bringing the Indians down on all of us,'' Sean said. ''There's not another man here who would endanger his family or the others of this train for the sake of a buffalo robe.''

They decided to drive Keseberg from the camp. Some still thought he was getting off easy. The men sat as they were, still talking, still venting their anger and fear. George Donner got up and left to tell McCutcheon. As he walked to the wagon, several of Keseberg's German friends begged for the man's release.

Uncomfortable, George Donner said, ''We have no choice—we

must protect the train. He is responsible for what has happened to him, not us."

Big Mac brought Keseberg into the group of men. Keseberg was jerked onto his horse, his hands tied behind him. He looked down on his captors, his back straight, his eyes filled with disdain. He was taken a goodly distance from the camp. At the last his hands were released, and he was turned out on the prairie without food, water, or weapons.

In the morning the wagon train broke free of the tight circle they had formed the night before, and they strung themselves out along the road leading to Ash Hollow. On the way they camped at the Platte River. Fiona was hanging out of the wagon as far as she dared. She had seen buffalo many times as they traveled, but here they were bathing in the river, undisturbed by the strange creatures that rumbled along the path with their canvas tops flapping in the breeze.

Sean, too, felt a sense of peace when they made this camp. "Mary, take a minute and look around."

He heard Mary's lilting laugh. "Fiona's doing enough looking for both of us."

They set up the camp quickly, and the women and children climbed out of the wagons, eager to stretch and walk through the cool grass and to talk with their neighbors. Children squirmed out of wagons and ran to play in the tall grass near the edge of camp. Shouts of laughter and the sharp-pitched voices of mothers rang out.

Sean and Brian herded the cattle into the field nearby, then came back eagerly as they smelled the odor of their dinner cooking.

Just as the camp population had settled in for a peaceful June night on the prairie, a trill of alarm went through them. Straight-backed and proud, a group of Pawnee swaggered into the area. Fiona ran to her father's side, clinging to his arm. Coleen sought the comfort of Brian. The braves' faces were smeared with paint. Their heads were shaved except for a scalp lock to which they had tied a red-dyed deer tail. Every brave carried a rifle. They stood together, gesturing with the rifles.

"What do they want?" Coleen whispered fearfully to Brian. They all looked to Brian for information about the Indians. "Will they kill us?"

177

Brian squeezed her arm reassuringly. "No. The Pawnee are proud hunters. They want to show off their shooting skills."

Coleen's grip tightened on his arm. "Don't leave me alone!"

He smiled down at her, his eyes warm. "You'll come to no harm."

Each in his turn, a brave moved in the grass, placing on himself a full wolf pelt that covered him from head to toe. "That is to make the buffalo ignore him and think that he is a wolf come to scavenge," Brian told the McKays in a low voice.

"Does it work?" Fiona asked. "They really don't look like men anymore, do they?"

"Watch them, and you will have the best answer of all," Brian said.

Fiona watched the brave now in the field. Stealthily, what appeared to be a wolf crept toward the grazing buffalo. Crouched down, the brave waited for his moment, then shot with unerring accuracy. The buffalo fell to the ground and was lost from view in the engulfing, swaying grass. When the display of marksmanship was over, nine or ten buffalo had been killed.

The next day the train was on the move again, and finally reached the edge of the muddy marsh they had been traveling through all day. The last week in June they managed about twenty miles a day, and came to the stony ground around Scotts Bluff. The rocky terrain soon informed them how much of a beating their wagons had taken. Mrs. Murphey's wagon was so badly warped that it left a trail of flour behind it. Wagon spokes had split. Many of the wagons were sagging so badly that their freight was falling from the beds, or they were scraping the rocks in the trail. Will Eddy had used the last of his meat and needed to hunt.

When they reached the river, they planned to camp for several days to make repairs and replenish supplies.

Jacob Donner removed a heavy linen chest and placed it at the side of the road. When George tried to comfort his brother, Jake looked at him with tired eyes and shrugged sadly, saying, "It's just too damned heavy. It's the first of my possessions I'll leave behind, George, but bless me, I doubt it'll be my last. My wagons are going to pieces on this trail."

George rubbed his chin. "Well, you're not alone. Even Reed is having trouble."

Reed and Milt had the wagon propped up as they tightened the wheels, and replaced a rear axle. On the ground at the side of the wagon the Donners saw boxes. The Reeds, too, were reducing weight.

The McKays faced the same problem. Sean eyed the chest containing Mary's mother's linens. "No!" she cried. "I'll walk before I let that be left behind."

"Mary, darling, something must come out. The wagon is warping—soon we'll look like Lavinia Murphey with all our stuffings falling out as we go." Sean was crushed by the look of sorrow on Mary's face. He hugged her, and kissed each eye before a tear could fall. She was tired. All of them were tired, and only now were they beginning to realize how rigorous a journey this was. "Think on it, Mary love. We'll be here for a bit, so you take your time and choose something you wouldn't mind so much doing without."

"I thought you said we had to secure the freight better—don't we have to do that?"

Sean shrugged. "I thought we'd be going right on, but we're staying here for a bit. There is time." He moved with her to the side of the wagon and pointed to the green pasture outside the wagon circle. The children were playing in the stream, splashing and wrestling with each other. On the grassy banks and in the fields adults had spread out blankets to bask in the sun. "No one seems to be in a hurry."

Mary touched Sean's arm. His eyes followed hers. Without saying anything to each other, they watched Brian and Coleen wandering off together, not touching, not even looking into each other's eyes. Yet about them was a unity, a rightness that seemed to pull them together. Yes, thought Mary, we shall soon be gaining a son. And, Sean thought heavily, I shall be related to Jane Pardee.

"Shall we walk along the river?" Brian asked.

Coleen looked up and smiled. "I know I'll be safe anywhere with you."

Brian blushed, but could think of no reply. They passed the meadow and the place the children were playing, following a narrow animal trail upstream to a low hill. It was a fine and private place, they discovered when they got up on it, with green

179

bushes screening them from the company now some distance away, and a view across a little valley with the stream glittering below them in the sun. Brian took off his hat and threw it gaily into a clump of waxy pinkish pipsissewa, and flopped down on his back among the long grasses and meadow flowers.

Hesitantly Coleen sat down beside him, hiding her tense expectancy by reaching around her and gathering a little nosegay, wrapping the stems with grass. She held it off and looked at it, she twirled it in her fingers, she sniffed it. Brian seemed to be paying no attention to her. He was far away, his eyes shut and an upward curve to his pleasant mouth. Gently, she tickled his face with her bouquet. "Come back, Brian, wherever you are," she teased.

He opened his eyes and turned his head to look at her. "I never left you, Coleen," he said softly. "And God willing, I will never leave you."

His gaze on her was so steady, so sweet and compelling, that Coleen drew a quick breath and bent over him, her lips parted, and kissed him. She felt his quick response, the fitting of his mouth to hers, and the speeding up of her own pulse. But he did not reach out for her. She drew away, humiliated by her own forwardness, feeling rejected in spite of what he had just said to her.

"Coleen," he said lazily. He patted the grass, still smiling a little. "Come lie with your head on my shoulder."

At first she refused, unsure of his intentions, afraid of seeming like an easy woman. But he held out his arms, and she went to him. They lay together as he had said, with his lips kissing her forehead or her hair occasionally. It was loving, it was innocent, it was a time Coleen knew she would never forget.

Brian, perhaps to distract himself from less pure thoughts, began pointing out shapes he saw in the clouds. Eagerly Coleen joined in, seeing different objects from what he saw. But all the time she felt his arm close around under her, his long lanky body next to hers. Around them was the sun-warmed clean meadow, above them the limitless azure sky. After a while they quieted, and Brian seemed to be asleep again. Coleen, content to feel him close by, closed her eyes.

They woke a few minutes later, looking at each other with surprise and pleasure. Then Brian's face changed. He turned his

180

body toward hers and pulled her against him to hold her and kiss her for a long passionate moment. Then he said, "We must go, Coleen." He rose, holding out his hand to help her up. Plainly he had not intended to kiss her again, but Coleen willed him to, and they stood in the sunshine locked in embrace.

She put her head on his shoulder. "Oh, Brian," she whispered. "I never want this to end."

His work-toughened hands stroked her hair. "And it will not, if your answer is yes. Is it yes, Coleen? Will you stay with me always?"

She raised her shining eyes to his. "I will stay with you forever," she promised.

They returned to the campsite. When Mary McKay looked up from her cooking fire, she saw them walking together, their arms around each other, their faces radiant. She looked at Sean and slowly he shook his head. Then after a little while he grinned at his wife.

With most of the people relaxing, some of them tinkering with their wagons, cursing over the lack of tools, and a few beginning to worry both about weight on their wagons and the speed with which they were using their food supplies, no one was thinking of Louis Keseberg. So when he rode into camp in broad daylight everyone was stunned.

George watched open-mouthed as the bedraggled, sunburned man rode in, then slumped to the ground, reins still in his hand. He stood mute, watching Keseberg stumble to his feet and try to speak. Under the tan, the tall blond German had a pallor. His coat hung on him now, and his neck looked scrawny in his collar. Finally awakened to action, Uncle George jumped forward and caught the man before he fell again. He took him to his own wagon, where Tamsen was quick to bring food and drink.

"Go easy with this," Uncle George advised, and placed a cup to his lips.

Tamsen, knowing he could tolerate little, gave him a biscuit with additional warnings not to eat it too fast.

Word of Keseberg's return ran through the camp. Soon a ring of men stood watching him eat. James Reed came close and stared openly. Exhausted and starved as he was, Keseberg had not lost his arrogance. With a sneer he looked up at Reed. "Why do you gawk at me? Have you never seen a man eat before? Are you amused?"

Reed looked away from him in disgust. He said to Uncle George, "He has no business here. Send him away. His punishment was justly set by all of us in agreement."

Donner took Reed aside. "Must we be so harsh? How can we send him away again? And what of his wife? She needs him."

Sean and Brian and several others joined the hushed conversation. Sean said, "I don't trust the man, and by God, I don't like him."

"But there may be another side to it. The journey is harder than we thought," George argued. "His supplies are nearly as great as yours, James. And his wife is afraid to let us even borrow tools without his consent. Now that he is here, we can bargain with him for some supplies and the use of his tools in return for letting him stay."

"We can manage without his aid," Sean said.

"I agree. Why should we bargain with him?" Denton asked.

"Can't we be sensible?" George asked in exasperation. "We need his supplies. What good does it do us if he's gone? Shall we lose the use of needed tools, because we cling to the exercise of punishment?"

"I won't have the man here if he's armed," James Reed said, weakening.

"Big Mac has Keseberg's guns locked up. They can stay there," Donner agreed. He looked at the other faces. Each man was weighing the advantages gained by allowing Keseberg to remain against their dislike and distrust of him. Slowly, George's view prevailed. Donner would bargain with Keseberg.

Knowing he would have his way, Keseberg had the nerve to strike his own best bargain. "I'll give you use of my equipment, *if* I have guarantee of payment for those tools lost or broken," he said boldly.

George Donner, always an honorable man, sometimes to a fault, agreed. Louis Keseberg was once more a part of the wagon train.

They remained camped for a few days, completing makeshift repairs. Soon they felt rested and ready to go on. They moved on their way to Fort Barnard, where they could do more extensive repairs on the wagons and replenish their supplies.

The twenty miles they traveled each day took them past rivers, and ponds, small lakes, and vast open pastures. There were no homes, no huts, no sign of civilization except the comforting evidence that another train was somewhere ahead of them.

But it was beautiful, and Fiona loved it. She breathed, almost in awe, "This is the West!"

Brian Campbell smiled, and started to correct her, but thought better and remained silent. She would find out for herself in time.

Part V

Chapter Fifteen

During April the *Brooklyn* sailed on her solitary way across the undulating waters. When there was rain, all on board set out buckets and tubs to catch the precious fresh water. Then they could enjoy the luxury of a good bath and even do laundry. For all great Neptune's ocean around them, saltwater was unsuitable for these uses.

The ship rolled heavily when the wind was almost aft; but most of the passengers had become accustomed to a floor that might fall away as one's foot went down, and had naturally acquired the rolling gait of the sailors. On good days, with every stitch of canvas straining full, the ship made one hundred and fifty miles or more.

The loneliness of the voyage seemed greater for having bypassed Rio de Janeiro. So when on a fine day in April the cry of "Sail ho!" came from aloft, word went through the ship like wildfire. Susannah, Flora, Mary, and the tentmakers dropped their chores and crowded on deck with the other passengers. They gathered along the rail, watching the taut sails of a rapidly approaching ship. As it neared, the crewmen on both ships worked busily at the sails to slow their progress. Soon the two vessels stood head-on, their bows majestically dipping and rising like dancers in a dream ballet.

Susannah smiled at Laura Goodwin, who had come to stand beside her. They commented excitedly on the clean lines of the other ship, and noticed how the bows rose, dripping bright streams of briny water.

"Isn't it strange how much more beautiful this seems just because there are other human beings involved?" Laura mused.

Captain Richardson hailed the other ship through his speaking trumpet. "Ship ahoy!"

"Hul-lo-oh!" came the reply.

"What ship is that, pray?" Even when the name was obvious, it was a question he always asked.

"The brig *Rosie Finch* out of Melbourne, bound for Boston. What ship is that, and whither bound?"

"The ship *Brooklyn* from New York, bound to California, sixty-two days out." Then, at a few words from Sam, Richardson added, "We carry two hundred and thirty-eight members of the Church of Jesus Christ of Latter-Day Saints, Samuel Brannan, leader, to settle California."

A new voice, in a roaring brogue, replied jovially, "We carry six good Irish Catholics to settle the rest of the United States!"

Shouts of laughter came from both ships, and after a few more exchanges they went on their way, everyone waving and smiling until it was no longer worthwhile.

The next day they slipped along the coast of Uruguay, nearing the mouth of the River LaPlata. The passengers had been told that in this area came *Pamperos*, violent gales from the southwest. Ezra kept a wary eye to the sky. Usually preceded by lightning, the *Pamperos* often destroyed ships in the river, and then hurled their might many leagues out into the Atlantic.

"I think the length of the voyage is telling on me," Ezra said to Tollie. "On an evening like this it isn't likely we'd have a storm, but here I stand alert to any sound and jumpy as a toad."

Tollie sat in a lounge chair, her hands shielding her eyes. "I feel so lazy and warm," she said with a smile. "Don't talk of storms. I couldn't bestir myself to go to the cabin." She had grown quite large in the past few weeks, and was inclined to get herself settled and remain there. Ezra glanced affectionately at her.

Since that one romantic afternoon, Tollie had resumed her status as protected young woman with Ezra. That was wrong for a husband and wife. He didn't know if he was being considerate to Tolerance, or cowardly. Meanwhile Tolerance swelled and Ezra burned for her.

Thinking of this, Ezra smiled, caressing her absentmindedly until one of the crewmen hurried by.

In the southwest he saw black clouds, monstrously angry-looking in the sweetly roseate skies of evening. Lightning flashed, so far away he was not sure they had seen it. But instantly he heard the boatswain's hoarse cry down the companionway: "Al-ll ha-ands ahoy!" Feet thudded as the sailors fell out to obey the rapidly shouted orders to reduce canvas. Men fled like monkeys up the ratlines.

Ezra and Tolerance knew that such a radical reduction of sail signaled danger. Tollie managed to move quite quickly as Ezra gave her his hand. She went ahead of him to the cabin, where he left her before going to the assembly hall to watch from the portholes.

A broad mist, capped with black clouds, was coming toward the *Brooklyn*. Strangely, beyond the mysterious mist, the sky kept its gentle rosiness. Abruptly the ship rocked as the *Pampero's* force hit. Ezra could hear the hailstones and rain clatter on deck. He cringed, imagining what those hailstones could do to a man's face. For sometime the ship ran like a wild thing before the wind, the waters flying past the portholes, obscuring Ezra's view.

Then, as quickly as it had come up, the *Pampero* blew itself out. The *Brooklyn* slowed its mad flight. The sun set in a normal way, and Ezra realized he had been clasping his hands so tightly they now hurt when he relaxed. It was a strange wind, he thought, and was glad the River LaPlata and its *Pamperos* were behind him.

One day at sunrise the lookout called "Land ho!" and the Morrisons hurried from their cabin to be among those who would see. Off their larboard side at the edge of the world, a series of blue humps seemed to drift on the water. Those were the Falkland Islands, they were told, lying to the east and somewhat north of the Strait of Magellan. By midday the islands had vanished. The ship sailed steadily southeast along the coast of Patagonia and Tierra del Fuego. At sunset land was visible again, this time on the starboard bow. It was known as Staten Land. Once past it, they would head into Drake's Passage between the tip of South America and Antarctica. They would be making the dangerous voyage around Cape Horn.

The weather had grown cold now, though it was mid-April and

in New York it would be spring. They were still north of the limits of sea ice, but the breath of the Antarctic carried a convincing chill. There was no heat aboard, but Susannah and Sam had found their own way of creating warmth.

Susannah had not grown accustomed to, or comfortable with, her dual life with Sam. She still felt hurt and abandoned each time he left her, and elated when they were together. Their times together were filled with warmth and intimacy. But the times away from each other—at least for Susannah, who had no cause other than Sam—were misery.

Susannah was becoming an accomplished actress during those times of separation. Because she needed an excuse to disappear for periods of time when she was with Sam, she began to establish a precedent. Often she told Prudence she was visiting a girl friend, and did, so that if questions arose, no explanations would be necessary. And in the privacy of her cabin, when she could get privacy, she practiced an expression of cool uncaring. She smiled into the mirror, imagining Sam close by, and letting all her love show in her eyes. Then she pretended his wife had come into view, and she made her eyes blank, still keeping the smile on her lips. She practiced ways of talking, clever things to say, gestures that would convey indifference. She knew she was successful, for Flora and Mary thought she was a rather aloof, perhaps unhappy girl. She wasn't too pleased with the unhappy part, but it was better than having them guess what she was really about.

On a cold night, after prayers, when Susannah was supposed to be visiting Clarissa Ambrose, she stood shivering, waiting for Sam in another cubbyhole they had discovered. They had two or three places in the ship now, none so safe as the wagonbed in the hold. But Sam, exercising caution in incautious circumstances, had not wanted them to meet in the same place or at the same time. Sometimes Susannah suspected it was a game of intrigue with him, each risk heightening his pleasure, each meeting increasing the danger of discovery.

Sam took longer getting there than she had grown to expect from him. She was about to peer out from her hiding place and then leave, when he arrived.

Instantly he took her into his arms, crushing her to him with a longing that mirrored her own. "My little love," he said, rocking with her. "How I have wanted to be with you today! I thought the darkness would never fall."

"You have only to ask, and I would come to you anytime, my darling," she said. Her hands were all over his body, feeling the hard muscles under his fine clothing, seeking and finding the reassurance that he desired her. At the same time his lips burned a path down her throat and onto her breast through the warm challis of her dress. She arched toward him, wanting to keep the delicious contact of her lower body with his, and wanting to feel his kisses on her bare flesh.

With practiced fingers he undid several of her buttons, so that his mouth could find her breasts and he could take her nipples between his lips and rouse them, making her breasts grow firm in the heat of her desire.

They held each other lovingly, their mouths touching and teasing, murmuring endearments, while they moved slowly against each other. Then their tempo increased and teasing was forgotten. Susannah heard the tiny straining sound Sam made deep in his throat. To her it was as quickening as an animal growl. She responded by pressing closer, and together they reached an enviable bliss.

Afterwards they stayed locked together, holding each other and touching. Finally their breathing returned to normal, and their legs ceased trembling, and the heat that had possessed them cooled. They adjusted their clothing, then tried to find a comfortable way to sit near each other and talk. Susannah loved these times after making love, when Sam would sit near her, relaxed and easy, and just talk about his days, his dreams, and his feelings. The intimacy between them in these quiet times, as much as the lovemaking, made her believe she really was an important part of his busy life.

They had talked only a short time, when she sensed a difference in him. Automatically, her body tensed. She had no idea what he was leading up to, but she knew she wasn't going to like it.

His voice was tense. "Susannah, we are going to sail around the Horn, and—" He paused for a moment, then put his arms around her and held her close. "The demands on my time are going to increase. That always happens when people are unsure or frightened."

Susannah shut her eyes, and held fast to him. "Sam, don't say what I think you are going to say, please! I need to be with you!"

"I have no choice. We must stop meeting—for a while." She raised her head from his shoulder, but he pressed it back down. "We have been lucky, Susannah, but during this time of hazard, I dare not risk discovery. The people need me, and I must be there for them. You understand that, don't you, little love?"

"I understand that we love each other, and that we need each other, and give strength to each other. I don't want to be without you. It means so much to me."

He kissed her forehead. She could hear him swallow. "It's everything," he said at last. "It will be hell without you. But I must see to the Saints."

"And there is no way I can change your mind?" she asked softly.

His lips found hers in an ardent kiss. "If I could do as I liked without regard to duty, Susannah, I'd spend my life with you. I'd make love to you now—again—and tomorrow and all the tomorrows, but I can't do that right now. Try to be patient, sweetheart. And—go on loving me. Help me, Susannah."

Her arms pulled him tighter. "I will. I do love you, Sam, you know that. If I didn't I wouldn't have trouble being patient. But I can't understand why you will leave me, and not see me, if you really love me. I thought loving meant wanting to be with someone."

"It does, Susannah, and I want to be near you every minute, but it cannot be—not now."

Sam held her and she argued with him, knowing that no matter what she said nothing was going to change. He kissed her one last time, and she said, "I'll wait, Sam. I'll come whenever you say."

After that, Susannah didn't change her habits. She might be seeing Sam again, and she wanted to be prepared. So she visited friends and maintained what independence she could from her family.

Her carefully perfected mask of aloofness served her well during this painful time. She felt blow after blow of loneliness and doubt. It was easy to believe that Sam cared nothing for her. He was always busy, and seemed to have time for everyone but her. His manner toward her was, if anything, overhearty. It was almost as if he had to force himself to be pleasant to her. When he greeted her, his pressure on her hand was quickly released, so quickly she had to fight to keep surprise and disappointment from her eyes. Without being obvious to others, he even avoided her sometimes. It was almost beyond bearing. It took all her strength and faith to believe he still loved her and would one day be with her again.

One of the few things that aided her faith in him was that the passengers were indeed more demanding of Sam's time. They had heard plenty about the perils of rounding the Horn, about icebergs miles long and wide, about the graybeards, the huge breaking seas that prevailed in the locality, and about the sudden storms that could send a ship backward. Before any disaster struck, they had begun asking for the Lord's protection. For everything they needed Sam's direction, reassurance, and guidance.

They were surprised, then, by a cold calm day when albatrosses by the hundreds floated like white, peaceful blobs on the heaving gray waters, one moment silhouetted against the sky, the next completely hidden in the troughs of the swells. They watched the Cape pigeons, and the small dark petrels fluttering and hopping over the waves, their little webbed feet pattering as though on land. With their sturdy hooked bills the petrels probed the water for shrimp and plankton. Frequently they uttered their mournful cries, leading some of the Saints to claim that disaster lay ahead.

That evening remained fine, and many of the passengers strolled on deck after prayer meeting. Susannah felt miserable to the point of nausea as she watched Sam, arm in arm with Ann Eliza, talking to a group of Saints. They were all laughing, and Sam seemed to be making a concerted effort to keep his wife happy, and to show to all that he was a happily married man. Susannah turned away, glad of the darkness that hid the quick tears she could not hold back.

Then as she watched the sea, a great heavy, wet fog rolled across the water, stretching up to hide the heavens. In a few minutes it was difficult to see from one end of the ship to the other. Most of the passengers went below, to the familiar darkness.

It was an eerie and unsafe time to be on deck, and after a long

193

roll of the ship, Susannah decided to go below. She groped her way in the fog, jumping when a large shape loomed before her. She ran hard into him, and he put his arms out to steady her. There was no doubting the strength of that embrace, and her heart quickened with gladness.

Sam's deep, pleasant voice said, "I beg your pardon, sister, didn't mean to run you down. You aren't hurt, I trust?" He had not moved, was still holding her. She wanted nothing so much as to press herself to him and feel his mouth possess hers; but others would surely see, or at least hear.

She pulled away. "I'm tolerable, Brother Brannan, thank you."

"I came seeking you, sister. Your mother sent me with a message." He took her by the arm and was firmly leading her to the companionway. "Sister Tolerance is asking for you. I believe we may be blessed with a new Saint tonight."

Her heart gave a great lurch. Tollie had begun labor! Landry's baby was finally going to be born!

Sam helped her down the companionway. They stopped in the first dark place, and for a moment, in perfect silence, they held each other. Into her ear he whispered, "My love, my love." Susannah felt tears gather in her throat and her heart threaten to break as he pushed her away with firm hands and accompanied her to the door of her cabin.

He said, "Would you like to see if Sister Hannah is here? If she is not, I'll fetch her."

Susannah placed the palm of her hand on his dear cheek for a moment. It burned with warmth, even as her cheeks were. She managed to say, "Thank you, Brother Sam. I'll see." She smiled at him, thankful that it had been he who had come to fetch her. Somehow that gave him a share in this night, and in the birth of this very special baby.

The cabin was crowded, even though Ezra and Asa had been sent out. Prudence was on her knees searching through a trunk for the rags Tolerance had brought for his occasion. Sister Hannah had her arm under Tollie's and was walking her across the room.

"Oh, you're here, Sister Hannah. Brother Brannan offered to get you—I'll tell him it's unnecessary."

But Prudence said, "Here, Susannah, change her wet bed and put these pads under where she'll be lying. I'll send Elder Brannan on his way."

It was better, thought Susannah drearily. Given two seconds in the dark with Sam, she'd spend the night longing for more.

"I'm glad you're here, Susannah," said Tollie, sinking thankfully onto the clean bed. "It began so suddenly! There was warm water everywhere!" Her eyes were wide with fright. "I didn't know what to do. I'm so frightened. What is going to happen to me? Hold my hand. Please! Oh, Susannah, it hurts!" Susannah clutched Tollie's hand as the girl doubled over in pain.

Sister Hannah made a noise deep in her throat. "You've not begun the real pains yet."

Suddenly the ship gave a lurching roll, and everyone scrambled for footing. Tolerance grabbed an upright and held on. This brought on another pain, and she grimaced through it. As soon as the ship righted, Sister Hannah had Tollie's arm. She did not believe in allowing her patients to bear their babies the lazy way. She had Tollie up and walking. It shortened the labor time, she declared. But when the vessel took another long roll and they both lost their balance, Hannah had to give up her heroic idea.

Throughout the long night the vessel washed to and fro in high-running seas, rolling with grim predictability from one side to the other, and throughout the long night Tollie's pains came regularly.

Hannah looked on her with something near disgust and, Susannah realized, worry. "Her pains are too shallow," she said, then sighed. "She's awful narrow. I once had a patient just about this narrow, and she never did have her baby."

Tollie's eyes were circled with deep, dark rings of fatigue. "What—what happened?"

"Died," Sister Hannah said flatly.

Tollie tried to sit up. "Am I going to die?" She began to weep uncontrollably, rolling from one side to the other, digging her fists into her eyes and wailing. "I don't want to die! Susannah! Help me, please!"

Prudence and Susannah took action at the same time. "I never heard of such a thing!" Prudence scolded Sister Hannah. "You must be a numbskull, to say that to a young girl in labor! If that's all the better you can do, you can leave this minute!"

Susannah rushed to kneel by Tollie's bunk, fiercely putting her arms around Tollie and stopping the agonized rolling back and forth. "You are going to have your baby, Tollie. You'll be all right. She's a hateful old woman! Don't listen to her. You're doing just fine. It takes a long time with the first child. Please, believe me, Tollie!"

Sister Hannah flung open the door. "If I ain't wanted, I ain't wanted. But Brother Morrison still owes me three dollars!"

As the door slammed shut, Prudence's and Susannah's eyes met. "Well," Prudence said, swallowing. "We are to do it ourselves."

"And we'll do it better," Susannah said loudly, then lowered her voice, "Mama . . . do you know? I'll help, but . . ."

Prudence threw an eloquent glance at Tollie. "We'll be guided. It's the Lord's will. We'll do whatever He tells us." It occurred to Prudence, as well as Susannah, that if Tollie died, the baby might still live. It was a thought that did not dismay Prudence, though she was ashamed to think it.

Tollie was wailing in Susannah's ear, so Susannah endeavored to calm her, "Hush, now. Hush, Tollie. If you let yourself get upset, it's going to take longer. Calm down, now, pray with me. Shh—shh." By degrees she stopped Tollie's weeping. When the next pain came, Tollie groaned hard with it, and tried to throw off her covers. The next moment she was shivering and clutching for them again.

The pains went on. Prudence and Susannah took turns sitting beside the suffering, frightened girl, holding her hands until their own were sore. Finally Prudence thought of giving her a towel to hold. She was very pale, her blue eyes glazed with pain, her dark hair damp with sweat. With each spasm, she tried not to groan, but did anyway. After a pain she drifted off to exhausted sleep and was awakened by the next.

Susannah, never having borne a child, was now sure she wished never to do so. Tollie looked half dead, yet she seemed to be maintaining her strength somehow. It was obvious the pains were becoming harder and more frequent, but Tollie was doing her job with gallantry. It was only the fear in her eyes, which showed along with the pain, that told Susannah she had not forgotten she was fighting for her own life as well as that of her child's. Susannah closed her eyes, wishing desperately there was something she could do.

The room was cold, yet all three women were perspiring freely. Prudence opened the door, and thin gray light came down the corridor. "They've opened the hatches," she said.

Tollie's eyes moved under her veined eyelids. "Is it morning yet? I don't think I'll die if it's morning."

Susannah put her arms around her. "Yes, it's morning," she said gently.

"He's going to come soon," Tollie said.

"Who?"

"The baby. A boy. I want a boy."

With daybreak began taps on the door. The news had gotten around that little Sister Morrison was in the midst. The women wanted to know how far along Tollie was, could they help, and why wasn't Sister Hannah on hand.

Soon Ezra was at the door, looking unslept and anxious as if it were his own child being born, and indeed it was his first grandchild. Prudence tried to keep him out, but he came in anyway. He took Tollie's hand and held it, and kissed her on the forehead. Tollie responded to his touch, a wan smile curving her lips as though he were someone she loved.

He left after a while and returned with food for Prudence and Susannah. Then two or three women came and milled about, getting underfoot and giving sage advice, such as putting a sharp knife under Tollie's bunk to cut the pain in two. Eventually Prudence put everyone out.

Susannah had been counting Tollie's pains as one of the women had suggested. She turned to Prudence. "She hasn't had one for three minutes. They were a minute apart before that."

Prudence looked at Tollie, breathing shallowly beneath her pile of covers. She pressed her fingers to the vein in Tollie's neck. "Let her rest," she said at last. "The Lord knows best."

They sat on their bunks, looking at each other, at the kerosene lamp swinging in its bracket, at Tollie, who barely lifted the covers with her respiration.

Then at last something began to happen. Tollie woke up from her short nap with a scream that went on and on. Prudence flung back the covers and looked. "At last!" she said. "Praise the Lord! Tolerance, you're on your way! Push, child, push!"

There was little Susannah could do, except to hold Tollie's hands and keep her from rolling out of the narrow bunk. Her pains crowded one upon the other, and with each spasm the dark bloody object between Tollie's legs emerged a little more. Once the little head emerged, Prudence was able to turn the baby, and suddenly there was a child lying on the stained sheet.

Prudence said in awe, "Lord be praised! Look at him, Tolerance! Here is your son!"

Weakly, Tollie held up her arms, and Prudence laid the newborn child face down on his mother's breast.

Chapter Sixteen

The *Brooklyn*'s journey around the Horn took nine days, and during that time the Saints endured every kind of weather the locality offered—dead calm, black fog, and seas so heavy that all the forward part of the ship was underwater and the brine poured in through every possible aperture and threatened to wash everything away. For three days they drove on before a strong gale and frequent squalls of sleet. Then one day they were able to see Cape Horn itself, a dark mass of rocky land like a petrified monster with snow streaking its head.

Tolerance made a slow but steady recovery from her confinement. Her baby son seldom cried except for reason of hunger or being wet. He lay in his tiny hammock slung over Tollie's bunk and either slept or looked around.

When he was a week old, Tollie announced, "His name is Elisha." She thought it suited him, a name with honor and dignity for a tiny male who much resembled his father, and whose path through life, she hoped, would be less beset by the Devil's temptations.

The *Brooklyn* was now well to the west of Cape Horn. Captain Richardson set their course to northward as much as possible. There were still fiercely strong winds from the southwest which kept pressing the brave little vessel in toward the shore of Patagonia. But in a few days the Pacific showed them the reason for her name. They sailed northward at a steady pace through pleasant weather.

Sometimes at night after prayers Susannah went on deck to sit, just to be by herself for a while. She did not think she was made to spend long months aboard a ship, never getting out of her nostrils the smell of dampness that permeated every timber and every piece of fabric over the entire vessel. Nothing ever got bone dry; the air between the decks where they lived was never freshened, and maintained the odors of cooking, of sweat, of seldom-washed bodies and illnesses.

She longed for a shampooing of her hair, for a warm bath in a smooth porcelain tub, for scented powder drifted from a swansdown puff over her shoulders, for gentle perfume between her breasts, for the sensuous feel of dry, smooth silk sliding over her bare flesh. A silk nightgown of peach trimmed in lace that outlined her firm breasts and her slim waist and her slender hips. And lying in a clean wide bed with fresh white sheets ironed smooth. And Sam, lying beside her with his strong arms bared, his warm tender hands caressing her curves from breast to thigh. Sam taking off her gown, burying his face in her clean and sweet-scented hair. Sam's flesh against her flesh, warmth and soft-hardness pressing, mingling—

She started violently as Asa's sardonic tones interrupted. "Whatever it is you're dreaming of, it must be a humdinger." He laughed harshly, and leered at her. "I'd give a dollar to be there too."

She regarded him with irritation, saying acidly, "I don't think you would. I was dreaming of warm water and perfume and soap and dry towels . . ."

Asa sneered knowingly at her and moved on.

Afterwards she wondered just how her face had been looking while she daydreamed of lovemaking with Sam. It was frightening what expressions could reveal. She shivered and got up, heading back to the cabin.

The days assumed an almost monotonous serenity. The ship's bells, which struck every half hour, had become as familiar as a shelf clock back home. The sun beamed daily, and the *Brooklyn* slipped along the coast of Chilean Patagonia. Each morning on the main deck the men performed their military drill. They were far different from the bumbling beginners they had been only weeks before. The uniforms which Liza Brannan had ridiculed lent an air of splendor, authority, and intent.

At the end of April, with water running low, they were nearing the port of Valparaiso, halfway up the coast of Chilean Patagonia, when a strong windstorm came at them from the land. For three days the captain attempted to enter port and was blown out to sea again. Laura Goodwin was making her way belowdeck, holding tight on to the rail. The ship shook violently, and Laura's hands broke free. She flipped over and over down the stairs. Those behind her gasped in helpless amazement. At the foot of the companionway Laura lay sprawled, unable to move. Men scrambled down the steps and, as gently as the ship allowed, picked her up and carried her to her bed. Susannah visited the Goodwin cabin day after day, as did Mary and Flora, but there was never any good news to report. Sister Goodwin lay comatose. The accident was exactly as Flora had predicted. Everyone prayed, but there was no change.

Captain Richardson ran for Juan Fernández, an island group about three hundred miles to the west. It became visible at daylight when it was still twenty leagues away. There one of the islands lay, a high blue hump that had the translucency of a cloud. As the day wore on the color changed to a welcoming green of several shades.

They arrived in harbor soon after sundown, but the winds coming down off the mountains blew strangely, and they could not anchor until midnight.

The next morning was Monday, May 4. The *Brooklyn* had left New York eighty-nine days before, in clear, crisp winter weather. Here it was warm and perfect, with vagrant breezes off the ocean and the pleasant scent of growing vegetation. Above all, it was land! How they all hungered for the feel of it under their feet, the scent of it in their nostrils.

After breakfast Susannah, Asa, and Prudence joined the others who were going exploring. The island was only five miles by fifteen, but they had been warned to stay in groups, for it was possible to become lost in the forested hills.

The voyagers were delighted to be on land. Some of the women took advantage of the fair weather and did laundry. Other passengers stayed on the *Brooklyn*—the elderly and their companions, the new mothers, those otherwise uninterested in seeing land unless it was California. Standing in the stuffy cabin, Ezra Morrison looked at his second wife and smiled tentatively.

Ezra had not been a successful businessman for so many years without being able to recognize the knock of opportunity. He gave Tollie a slow smile that started with his eyes. "Have you any idea how beautiful you are, my dear? And how desirable?"

She started to shake her head, but then his lips touched hers. Tentatively. Testing. Starting something. She felt a little shiver wash over her, tendrils of a feeling.

Now his hands were on both her shoulders, slowly drawing her to him. He caressed her cheek and the side of her throat, absorbing through his fingertips the vitality of her fresh youthfulness.

Slowly he rubbed both hands down her arms, holding his mouth against hers. He took her hands and placed them at his waist, and as he ran his fingers back up her arms, he shoved the sleeves of her nightgown away.

With both arms he encircled her, and he found that her mouth was softly open to his. Her arms held him fast now, and she moved her head to derive the fullest pleasure from his kiss. Only when her fingers began plucking at his buttons did he realize that he was still fully clothed.

He let her go and began to undress. Tollie was watching his every move. He was aware of the seductiveness of removing clothing, so he accomplished it with as much grace as he could. He was throbbing with desire, handsomely aloft, and he made no attempt to conceal that with which nature had so generously endowed him. He was also aware of the precariousness of the situation, so he gently slid off Tollie's nightgown and garment and carried her to her bunk before kissing her again.

Ezra lay crammed in with her, more at ease now that he lay with one leg over her, able to keep himself aroused by the touch of her against him. He was excited, taut with ardor, anxious to unite with her, but wanting her experience with him to be one of pleasure. He stroked her breasts, kissed her nipples sweet with milk. Her free hand moved down his side, and he turned so she could stroke him.

With the searing touch of her fingers, he knew that it was too late, that he had waited too long. Hurriedly he positioned himself over her, but already he was losing his power, and he crumpled on top of her so that he would at least be able to feel her body under him as he disgraced himself. When it was over, with neither of them satisfied, he kissed her again and again, speaking of himself as a fool. He hadn't meant for it to be this way. It wouldn't happen again. It would be all right the next time. And when he kissed Tollie's eyelids, he tasted the salt of her tears. So there was that to tend to also. Had he been a woman, he might have found relief in tears himself.

The baby woke up and whimpered, and Tollie nursed him while Ezra watched. He smiled as he saw her spirits restored so quickly and amazingly by the infant. She was still naked, and he sat on the narrow edge of the bunk and casually ran his fingers along her body until she got gooseflesh and, laughing, made him cover her up.

With little Elisha's stomach full, and his diaper fresh and dry, Tollie washed herself and put on a dress for the first time in weeks. She felt no embarrassment at Ezra's steadfast, hungry gaze, and she was eager to go on deck with him, to be with him.

His failure had not been total, then, for their dismay brought them together in a closeness almost as warm as though they had found rapture and not frustration. Without speaking of it, they knew that they would try again, soon.

So great, in fact, were their expectations that Prudence, returning from the sightseeing tour, read their faces and knew she was no longer the only wife Ezra had.

They stayed on Juan Fernández for five days. Under Sam's guidance they ate fresh fruits and vegetables with their salt beef. And he saw to it that the ship was reprovisioned with barrels of fresh produce and water.

Just before they were to sail, Laura Goodwin died. She was buried on Juan Fernández. At her head a stake marked her resting place. The island priest spoke over her grave, and Sam's eulogy was a warm one, for she had been widely respected and liked.

After the ceremony Sam walked back to the ship beside Susannah. He did not care who saw them or what they thought. Making casual conversation with Susannah, accidentally touching her as they walked, he reflected on the ephemeral quality of earthly life. After one was dead, and gone to heaven, it would not be possible to take another mate. The being was stuck, so to speak, with the choices of Earth forever. And though he cursed himself for his romanticism, Sam knew that Ann Eliza through the infinity of time would never make his heaven worth the striving for.

He intended to do something about that, today. There would never be an opportune time to broach the subject with Ann Eliza. He thought sometimes she was an impossible woman, exaggerating characteristics into faults, picking good deeds to pieces, never letting a contention die peaceably. For all he knew, it was her only way of creating excitement in her life.

He knew she did little all day except sit in the cabin where the air was poor, tend to Sammy, and embroider. When he suggested a promenade, she dressed as if for Fifth Avenue at Easter, but would not go unless it was on his arm. She felt it beneath her to talk to most of the Mormon women, and had no recognition of Sam's work, or the power of his ambition. It placed a nearly impossible burden on their lives together. He spent his days, and many of his nights, tending to the business of the Church. She could never understand that an hour-long casual conversation over cigars might do more toward building a settlement than ten good preachings on Sunday.

In short, his wife did not understand him, and he frequently did not understand his wife. Except for Susannah, who seemed willing and able to make the sacrifices needed to give his ambition full rein, he had had difficulty with his relationships with women. It had been like that when he was married to Harriet Hatch—ah, but that was long over. That was one mistake erased from his record, praise God.

Sam wanted to soften Ann Eliza toward him, so that evening he took special pains to see that the water for her teapot was boiling, and the pot heated first, and the quilted cosy placed over the pot immediately upon filling.

She went through her routine of taking off the cosy and placing her palm full against the pot, as she went about the grand performance of pouring tea.

Sam talked to her in a desultory way, drawing her out until he judged she was in as good a humor as she'd allow herself. Then he said, "Liza, I am thinking of taking a step which will advance my position. One necessary if I am ever to have the prominence of Brigham."

She looked at him, half eager, half suspicious. She was always amenable to change if it would advance her position as well as his. She asked, "What is this step?"

"I am going to take a second wife."

"You are *what*?" she asked with subzero emphasis. Then her voice rose. "You are not going to do any such a thing! I will not be humiliated and laughed at for your ridiculous Mormon notions. Advance your position, indeed! Cater to your base animal soul is more like it. How dare you even suggest such a thing to me? And

204

who is this loose-moraled little chit you thought to foist off on me? Who is she?"

"As usual when you lose your temper, Ann Eliza, your poor breeding begins to show through. Lower your voice, please."

"*My* poor breeding? What about yours? Your father was a drunk who used to beat you black and blue—what kind of breeding do you call that?"

"It at least taught me to remain quiet in a discussion."

"You aren't going to do this to me, Sam Brannan! You've got one wife, and that's all the law allows!"

"I am a Latter-Day Saint. Joseph Smith revealed that—"

"Revealed my foot! An excuse for immorality!" she shouted. "I and my child will be acceptable and respectable by the standards of people who count. I will not live my life within the confines of a group of people the rest of the world does not accept!" She pushed aside her untouched tea. "I want to know who she is."

Sam shrugged. "I don't know. I haven't picked her yet."

"I suppose that means that all these hearty little Mormon tarts have been lifting their skirts for you."

"You can be disgusting," he said, and stood up. He reached for his hat and placed it on his head.

"Where are you going?"

"Out where the air is not so stale. Goodnight, Ann Eliza."

As he left, he heard something crash and tinkle against the door. He supposed it was the teapot. He didn't care, he wanted only to find and be with Susannah. It was a beautiful night, and he was a man who wanted to be with a woman who admired and loved him.

Chapter Seventeen

The Saints bade farewell to the Juan Fernández Islands on Saturday, May 9. The *Brooklyn*'s course was set for the Sandwich Islands. There Sam intended to unload some cargo he had brought, and that would help to pay the remaining expenses of the trip.

The Saints were now more anxious than ever to reach California, and were made even more impatient, when around the sixth of June the *Brooklyn* lay becalmed for almost a week.

Sam Brannan alone welcomed their being becalmed, for it meant he would be busy, attending to quarrels and minor mischief, and each time he got to talk with one of his Saints, he also had the opportunity to encourage practical dreams and ambitions for the new colony. He knew that others, unlike himself, needed encouragement from a leader. It pleased him to be that leader. From his early teens Sam had known he was destined to become a rich and famous man with many accomplishments to his name. Every action he took was aimed toward fulfilling that destiny.

Liza's accusation that his father was a drinker who beat him was true. Thomas Brannan had come to America from his native Ireland when he was twenty. To Tom and his second wife, Sarah Emery, were born Mary Ann, Tom, Dan, and John. When Sam, the youngest, was born in 1820, his sister was thirteen and his father was sixty-five and ailing with bone fever. His mother was timid and indecisive, with the result that, at a very young age, Mary Ann took over the raising of her brothers.

As Sam had told Susannah in one of their conversations, he

was Mary Ann's favorite. When at age twenty-seven she married Alexander Badlam and they moved to Ohio, Sam's mother in a rare assertive act helped him go with the newlyweds. At age fourteen Sam became an unpaid four-year apprentice at the Painesville Press.

By 1837 Sam, Mary Ann, and Alex had become interested in the newly formed religious sect in nearby Kirtland, where Joseph Smith, a dynamic young man claiming to be a prophet was preaching the doctrines of the Church of Latter-Day Saints. That same year Thomas Brannan died and left a comfortable legacy to his children and his widow. Sam bought out the remainder of his apprenticeship and took his first business gamble in real estate. He lost most of his legacy in a land fraud.

By then in his late teens, Sam yielded to wanderlust, supporting himself as a reporter, and then editor. He experienced other business failures, not necessarily his own. Back again in Painesville, he married Harriet Hatch. Sam seemed to have a talent for marrying women with no empathy for his ambition. Harriet, and later Liza, felt that his place was in the home. After a final bitter quarrel, Sam left Harriet, telling her to get a divorce. For himself, Sam accepted a fund-raising assignment for the Saints and went to New York. With the Prophet's brother, William Smith, Sam toured New York and New England, raising funds for the Church, as well as few skirts, and many questions about their utterances in regard to the Church. Because of complaints made against them by Apostle Wilfred Woodruff, Sam and William Smith were dismissed from the Church.

Although privately Sam questioned the Church's value in his own scheme, it affronted his pride to be thus discarded. He got himself reinstated. Soon after, he was placed in charge of the Mormon exodus to the West. In this he saw the golden opportunity of his lifetime, the chance to bring to reality every dream of grandeur and success he had ever had. But it did nothing for his marriage.

And now there was Susannah. He loved her as he could not remember having loved either Harriet or Liza. He wasn't too sure how this love had come upon him. Generally his affairs were lighthearted skirmishes with females as worldly wise as he was. But Susannah had bewitched him. She made him feel ridiculously happy. More than that, she made him desire to be completely honest with her—an unfamiliar vulnerability he did not like in himself. Never to anyone else he had been about to conquer had he mentioned his marital situation. Never before had he had this mad urge to marry one of his lovers. He wanted to be with her. He wanted to know she was his in every sense of the word. Ann Eliza's haranguing only made him want Susannah as his bride all the more.

One morning when Sam could not stand to be away from Susannah any longer, he found her in Flora's cabin, stitching tents. Susannah's face revealed nothing more than friendly interest as he paused in the doorway. After exchanging casual conversation, Sam said, "Sister Morrison, the other day you asked me a theological question I could not answer. I will be in my office after lunch, and would like to speak to you about it."

"Thank you, Elder Brannan, I will be there."

After he had gone, Alma Davis tossed her head and said sneeringly, "His *office*. He's so high-and-mighty, always lording it over the rest of us."

"He *is* the First Elder," Susannah reminded her. "He has to have an office where he can talk to people privately."

Mary Addison's eyes flicked from Alma to Susannah. "And what does he do when you talk privately? Does he pat your hand and say now, now, little girl, Elder will make it all right?"

Susannah laughed, and looked straight at Mary. "If he does, I'll tell you about it."

"He looks at you as if he could eat you," Alma observed.

Susannah's pulse quickened a bit. She was not the only one who must hide her feelings. Sam, too, had to be more cautious. She looked at Alma and shrugged. "That's just his way."

"I don't like any of his ways," Alma declared. "We're crowded into a cabin with six people, and he has twice the room for only three people. If you ask me, he takes privileges that aren't due him."

"Too high-nosed to eat with the Saints," sniffed Mary. "Has to take his meals in his *stateroom*. La dee *dah*! He'd be a sight more use if he were a lot humbler!"

Susannah had been going to defend Sam, but unexpectedly Flora did it for her. "Elder's a good man. He is what he is, and all your venom ain't gonna change him. There ain't another living soul on this ship who could take over his job. You might think on how it'd be if some of the others were in charge."

Flora's tone of finality stopped their barbs, for a while. But

Susannah knew that Mary and Alma were voicing the discontent heard in other conversations. Common people were always jealous of position and privilege. But it also made her see how precarious Sam's position could be. She could well imagine the talk and dissension and attack that would come if it were known that she and Sam loved each other. Today she had gotten a tiny glimpse of people's cruelty, and with what relish they would see him brought down.

Susannah arrived early for their meeting. He apologized for his lateness as though it were his fault she was kept waiting. "And now come to me, my dear," he said softly, holding out his arms. "I have hungered for the touch of you."

"And I for you," Susannah said, going to him. Their lips met, and the fire began as banked gray coals smoldered rosily into life. He held her so hard that she felt the strong muscles of him as though they were imprinted on her forever.

But for once she was apprehensive, even while her veins sang with her burning desire for him. "Sam, people know we're here. We mustn't . . ."

In the dim lamplight his face was flushed, his eyes hooded. He drew away from her, then, as he had done before, he took her by the shoulders and seated her, with their knees touching while he held her hands in his. They simply looked at each other wordlessly, longing to be together. At last he smiled.

"How I love you, Sam," Susannah whispered.

He looked away, a pleased smile on his lips, and she was sure he had blushed. "I have come to a decision, Susannah," he said gravely, his voice too deep, too businesslike to be real. "This will not be an easy matter in the circumstances, but—but I want you as my wife."

Hot tears sprang to Susannah's sapphire-blue eyes. "Oh, Sam," she whispered. "Sam." She drew a breath, feeling a tremulous smile on her lips.

A loud thudding on the door made them jump apart. Sam leapt for the door, jarred and angry. "See here, I'm busy," he began.

He was greeted by an equally angry Captain Richardson. "I must talk to you right now!"

Sam turned to Susannah, his eyes questioning.

Susannah met his gaze, but remembering the complaints she'd just heard from Mary and Alma, she quickly excused herself. As she left, Sam murmured, "We'll meet later, sister."

Richardson pushed into Sam's office and puffed out an agitated blue cloud of cigar smoke. "It's that bitch Lucy Eager again. I caught her and Brother Pell goin' into one of the storerooms a while ago. You got to take some action."

"I know." Sam sighed. "But I don't want to do anything right now."

"In God's name why not? Why give her more time?"

"Because many people like her, and once I take action others are going to take sides. I don't want to split the Church. If we were nearer to California, then the idea of the new settlement and the work to be done would make them pull together. If they divide into factions now, only the Lord knows if I could ever get them to pull together, and we must. We must, or we will not succeed."

"So you're just gonna let the fornicatin' go on."

"No, I hope I can do something without bringing the whole situation into the open."

Sam assembled the widow and all three of her admirers, and Captain Richardson, and as a further witness, Ezra. His tone was harsh. He gave them no chance to utter a word in their own defense. He then asked Ezra to find and assign duties which each was to perform in addition to their regular ones. It was a subdued quartet who left Sam's stateroom and returned to the confinement of their cabins.

Sam did not manage to free himself of duties until after supper. He was waiting in his office when Susannah arrived, and he drew her into his embrace and kissed her lovingly. Still with their bodies pressed close, he said fondly, "And what will be your answer, my little love? Shall I have you for my wife?"

Susannah could hardly think clearly so near to him, but nothing felt right. Deep inside there was a fear and a reluctance she didn't understand. It had something to do with the criticism she'd heard, and her new awareness of his vulnerability to attack, but she didn't know how to express it. She kissed him quickly, then confounded both of them by bursting into tears.

"The prospect can't be that horrible," he teased, while patting her and smoothing her hair. "The captain can marry us tonight, if you'll say yes."

She raised a tear-splashed face. "What of the settlement?" She felt more and more hopeless. Some instinct deep inside warned her that there really was no room in his life for her—at least not as his wife.

Sam smiled at her. "You do understand about my need to succeed, don't you, my little love. How is it that one so young can have so much insight?" He held her close against him, his eyes closed in delight. "But you have not given me an answer. Shall you be my wife yet tonight, Susannah?"

Susannah trembled in his arms, but not from longing as he thought. She did not want to lose him, or bring him to harm; she wanted time. "I love you with all my heart, Sam, but if we marry now, it would cause you trouble with the Saints. Get your settlement started first. Then—will you ask me again?"

Sam laughed in appreciation. She understood his needs and the problems of leadership so well. It fired him all the more to do right by her, and he began to argue with her that they should marry immediately in spite of the added difficulties it would make for him.

Susannah remained dogged in her position, blindly trying to protect him. Only vaguely did she comprehend that the travel-weary Saints were ready to turn their frustration onto him. "You must be free to do what the Lord has asked of you, Sam. I cannot stand in your way—not even if I must give up your dear love for a time."

Sam looked at her, love and annoyance mingling on his features. She was throwing at him all the good thinking he himself had discarded earlier, and there was little point in arguing with her. No matter what he said, it gave him the feeling he was arguing against himself. He sighed and gave in for the moment. "It will be as you say, Susannah. We will not marry at this time, but our time will come."

She smiled up at him, relief crowding the tears in her eyes. "And I shall, at last, have you for my husband, Sam."

Both Sam and Susannah, by silent agreement, began to straighten their clothes. As usual, Sam was ready to leave before Susannah. They stepped out of his small room into the corridor, Susannah still patting at her hair. She was very flustered and wondered if her tears still showed, or if she'd be able to hide the tempest of passion and feelings. In this unguarded frame of mind her eye caught Asa's.

On his features there was a mask of righteous disapproval. He

211

walked with the couple to prayer meeting. In a malicious tone Susannah recognized, Asa said, "I hear that you finally put a stop to Sister Eager's sinfulness, Brother Brannan. You are to be congratulated. Not all are so strong they can outwit the Devil of the Flesh."

Chapter Eighteen

Susannah was among the first to leave the prayer meeting. She moved quickly down the corridor. There was so much for her to think about. She had nearly made it to the cabin, when Asa loomed out of the shadows, grabbing her arm in a hard grip. "Not so fast. I want to talk to you."

"Let go of me! Who do you think you are, handling me like a dock walloper?" She tried to jerk out of his grasp, but could not.

He pulled on her arm and began to drag her with him. "*Ouch!*" she cried as he ran her into a bulkhead. "Asa, stop it right now!" With all her strength she hung on to the bulkhead. Let him tear her in two, she was not going one step farther.

Then suddenly it seemed as if he *would* tear her in two, for he gave her free arm a wrench that nearly pulled it from its socket. She gave an involuntary cry before she lost her hold on the bulkhead. She found herself up against him, his hard hand across her mouth. "If you make one sound, I'm going to throttle you! You're coming with me, and you'll do it quietly."

She was cold and hollow with fright, and even more frightened that she should show it. Asa in a vengeful mood was something to reckon with.

Hastily he pulled her along the corridor to a storeroom, shoved her in it, and came in behind her. The closing of the door had an ominous sound. She could no longer hear noises from outside, and the storeroom was dark as night. This hiding place that would have seemed so vulnerable to prying eyes had she been with Sam now seemed inpenetrable because she was with Asa. No one would rescue her, she knew.

She shrank into as small a space as she could. The room was small, and Asa reached out and found her without trouble. "Keep your hands off me!" she screamed as loud as she could.

"I'll touch you, anywhere I wish, and for as long as I wish. Who is going to stop me?" He placed his hand on her slender neck, his fingers at the back and his thumb on her windpipe. He squeezed, experimentally, and Susannah's terror grew.

She grasped for her failing courage. "Asa, what's the matter with you?"

He laughed, a cold metallic sound in the darkness. "That's what I want to know, Susannah. What's wrong with me? Why am I never your preference? I thought it might be that you like little hidey-holes."

She quaked. "You'd better let me go. If you harm me—I'll tell Papa."

His laugh was brief, indulgent. "Would you, my pretty lamb? What would you tell him? And what do you suppose your papa would do to me? Hmm?" His thumb pressed uncomfortably on her windpipe.

She jerked away from him. "He'd see you punished."

The satirical voice came softly. "But I haven't done anything. Not yet."

"You call this nothing!" Susannah all but screamed at him.

He laughed maliciously, and she became as quiet as she could. An inch at a time she was moving away from him.

"Susannah," he said lingeringly. "I can feel that your warmth has left me. I don't like that. I want to feel you close to me."

She felt him near her, though he was making no sound either. Then his hand was on her shoulder, his arms pulling her against him. He was tremendously strong. He had put one hand behind her head, his fingers entwined in her hair so that she could not turn away, while the other arm wrapped around her, his hand under her hips to snug her against his body. Then his mouth met hers cruelly. She could feel his teeth cutting her lips, and she writhed with revulsion as his tongue invaded her. But this seemed only to excite him, so she stopped all motion, letting him kiss her as he wished without responding.

Accustomed to the hard-muscled fitness of Sam's body, she

realized an astonishing thing. Asa, fat, soft-pudgy Asa, was no longer. In his place was a dangerously compact, well-muscled man. The military drills, the running and exercise, had built Asa into a man well able to force his will on her as he chose. Involuntarily, she shuddered, and he grasped her closer against him.

Abruptly he let her go, and his hands were on her shoulders, shaking her hard. "Damn you, kiss me back! I know you're not the innocent you pretend."

"Let me go!" she cried. She thought he would break her collarbones. He shook her again, making her head flop on her neck, making her feel dizzy and nauseated.

"All right!" she said desperately. "Just stop—I'll do anything!" With all her remaining strength she dug both hands into the flour sack behind her, and bringing both hands up, ground the flour into Asa's eyes.

He cried out and let her go, but she was not quick enough to find the door before he had her again. "You'll regret that, my pretty pet. You will indeed." He shoved her against the wall and held her fast with one arm, as he tried to clear his eyes with his free hand. He was in pain, she could tell from his voice, but he went on. "I saw you with Brother Sam this evening. . . . You will have nothing further to do with him, do you understand? No more little chats by the rail, no more exchanging glances in prayer meeting, no more 'counseling.' "

"You've been spying on me!" she shouted, trembling with fright and anger.

"You'll listen to me, Susannah! He's no good! If I ever see you with him again, I'll ruin him—and you." As she gasped, he tightened his grip on her arms. Her hands were icy, tingling with pain. "Hah. You understand that, don't you? Remember it, Susannah. I mean it." He let her go, and she made a leap, hoping to find the door. She banged into the wall, tripped over an open flour sack, crying out in pain as she fell through the door onto her knees.

Scrambling to her feet, she did not know what to do. Frantically she ran down the corridor. Her first instinct was to tell Sam, but that might cause a terrible row, and she wasn't at all sure Asa would not do exactly what he said and ruin them both. She reversed direction, running toward her cabin. She would tell her father, but Asa would claim he was trying to save her from sin.

Calming somewhat, she realized she could not say or do anything looking as she did. Her skin was red where Asa had manhandled her, her lips were swollen, and her dress was covered with flour. Her father—or anyone—would believe anything Asa wanted to say about her condition. She hurried down the dim corridor, heading for the galley, praying that she would find it empty and that there would be some water she could use to clean herself off before she had to face anyone.

When she was satisfied she looked presentable, she returned to the cabin and went directly to bed. The first person she saw in the morning was Asa. His eyes, boring into hers, were filled with warning and lust. She could sense that he wished she'd give him cause to attack Sam.

Everywhere she went for the next few days, it seemed that Asa was nearby watching her, waiting for her to make some move toward Sam. She thought she would go mad if he didn't stop following her about.

The calm that had possessed the ocean for so many days lifted with a fluttering of sails and a mild jerking as the drowsy ship came awake, and the endless prints of cat's paws were on the water. The breeze soon became a strong wind, which shoved the *Brooklyn* on her zigzag course across the Pacific to the Sandwich Islands.

Tempers aboard cooled as the wind filled the sails, and the constant gossip and minding of others' business slowly came to a halt. Even Asa seemed to ease his vigilance. Susannah knew she would have to take extreme precautions if she were to see Sam, but she was beginning to feel confident again that it was possible.

One hundred thirty-six days out of New York, on June 20, passengers lined the deck, chattering excitedly as the *Brooklyn* sailed up past the stark gray bulk of Diamond Head into the harbor of Honolulu. As soon as the ship neared the island, handsome brown-skinned natives appeared, swimming toward the *Brooklyn* or propelling canoes over waves with great skill and speed.

At the docks the Saints were met by a crowd of missionaries and well-clad natives. In the background waited a number of fine carriages. Sam and Captain Richardson were first ashore, and soon Sam was arranging for lodgings for the passengers.

Susannah and the two Conley daughters were to be lodged at the home of the Kapas. Just before she left with her hosts, Sam walked past and said quickly and quietly, "I'll send a carriage for you at nine o'clock on Wednesday morning." He lifted his hat with a little smile and turned to the next passengers. Susannah shivered with delight and excitement.

That evening the Saints were invited to a luau. With their host families, they began to gather on the beach in the late afternoon. The beat of soft drums filled the air, and sweet-sounding voices singing rhythmic songs of the island people. Little brown-skinned children ran around giggling, chasing each other up and down the sand, flopping casually into the water and swimming in it as though it were their natural element. Older children swam far out and returned, daringly standing on some kind of board and riding the creaming surf until the board stopped in the sand.

Susannah, arriving with the Kapas, the Conley girls and the Kapa daughters, had her first taste of what it might be like to be in Ann Eliza Brannan's position. Sam stood out from the rest—all the rest except the several young and beautiful women with whom he was animatedly talking. Ann Eliza stood at his side, poised and regal. She wore a summer dress of pink linen, expertly fitted to her slender figure, with embroidery in shades of pink at the yoke and hem. In spite of the sullenness of her mouth, Ann Eliza's beauty and grooming always contrived to make Susannah feel at a disadvantage. No matter what Sam's complaints, Ann Eliza gave the appearance of being his perfect hostess. She intimated the Brannans had a class and elegance that perhaps Sam alone would not have managed.

From a lonely place within her that couldn't be measured by feet or yards, Susannah longed to talk with Sam. She needed him. But as she watched him move among the people with Liza on his arm, she tried to imagine herself as his wife and she failed to envision her place. It was a long, disturbing evening for Susannah Morrison.

Church services were held the next morning at the Kawaiahao Church. Sam, as visiting dignitary, had been invited to give the first Mormon sermon preached on Oahu. Susannah took her seat, determined to rid herself of the misgivings of the night before. She'd find her place in his life, starting now. She would be the woman Sam was proud of. Her determination was shattered as

Asa chose to take his seat next to her. Despite her efforts, she paid little attention to Sam's words.

After the services, while everybody was still visiting, a slender light-haired youth came up to Mary Addison and her parents. Susannah watched as the two young people became engrossed in each other. How transparent human beings were when falling in love. It was no wonder Sam had warned her to watch her own expressions. Was it possible she had been as obvious as Mary? Then, suddenly, she wanted to turn away. A bit surprised at her reaction, she realized that she instinctively did not trust the young man.

Susannah was ready when the carriage came for her on Wednesday. She had made the excuse of going shopping and later meeting Ezra. The Kapas sent one of their servants, a girl about Susannah's age, as chaperone and guide.

Susannah was dismayed. Nothing was going right. She had no way to locate Sam and tell him what was wrong. She could not tell the servant to leave her, for that would cause an uproar that would reverberate to Prudence and Papa—and Asa. She did not know what to do.

Once they were in the carriage, the driver headed inland away from the town. Susannah was beginning to be concerned when they had gone some distance and there was no sight of Sam. The maidservant and the driver were chatting in their own tongue, laughing and occasionally glancing at her. Finally she could not stand it anymore. "Where are we going?"

The maid giggled. "The driver says that is all *hoomalimali*, that you are going to meet your *ipo*, your sweetheart." She pointed to the driver and giggled again. "It is all right, for I am meeting mine." Within a few minutes they stopped at a little village, and Sam joined them.

It was a perfect day for runaways—warm, dry, with a pleasant breeze off the sea. The sun shone kindly from the high deep-blue sky, sparkling on the sea, warming the pale sands and the red earth. They soon came to a quiet lagoon, fed by a lazy waterfall, surrounded by shower trees of pink and white and gold, and the omnipresent palms. It was a bit of transplanted paradise.

Leila and Pipikane stripped off their clothing and dived into the inviting water. Susannah stared after them.

Sam, glancing at the two graceful swimmers, smiled impishly. "When in Rome, Susannah?"

She knew then that right or wrong she was not like Pipikane or Leila. Just his mention of bathing nude caused her to blush furiously. She could not swim nude. She finally said, "I can't swim."

"You could," Sam said. "If you weren't wearing all those petticoats."

Then she said more truthfully, "It's my Mormon unbringing."

Sam said nothing, there was little he could say. He led her to a place of concealment down a little hill. There was a shallow clearing, shaded now by the trees, surrounded by small fragrant bushes and vines. He looked around him, took a deep breath, and then his eyes came to rest on Susannah. "I have longed to make love with you in the daylight, Susannah."

Her eyes widened. Involuntarily her hand went to her breast, to still the wild bird that seemed to flutter there.

He took her arms gently, and pulled her toward him. "Come, my darling."

She could barely speak. "I could never . . ."

"No one will see us, I promise you." He caressed her shoulders and back, and still she remained rigid in his arms. "You are afraid, but think, my love, what is it you fear. It is only I, and I want only to look upon your body, which I love as I love you. Is that truly frightening?"

For a moment she closed her eyes, her senses alert to every sound, the sighing of the wind around her, the movement of the ocean, his breathing, the sound of his hands as he began to unbutton her dress. There was a delicious warmth that had begun as he undressed her, and with it there was a dread of what she didn't know—perhaps only the forbidden.

In her mind she could see the easy and natural joy of the natives in their scanty apparel, and she had seen no lust in their eyes, no evidence that the Devil had taken hold of them. Yet would it be the same for her? She didn't know, but she loved this man with all her heart. He took off her dress, and several of her petticoats, and still her eyes were closed.

He kissed her again and again, his lips warm on her cheek and neck. The sun beat down on them, the vision in her closed eyes burning red. She felt a false safety in her closed eyes, yet she realized that in the darkness of the ship she had allowed him to

219

undress her, and she had touched his naked body many times. In her mind and with her fingertips, she already knew this man.

Suddenly she felt free, and laughed. She opened her eyes but did not look down at herself as she stood in her Mormon garment and shoes and stockings. Quickly she took off his coat, undid his cravat—carefully storing his cameo stickpin in it—and unbuttoned his shirt. He shrugged from the shirt and let it fall to the ground. He stood still, and Susannah, gazing at his broad hairy chest and wanting to touch him with her fingers, felt her skin ripple with excitement. They fell to their knees, and were soon lying side by side, devouring each other with eyes, fingers, lips.

Susannah teetered between feeling guilt and pleasure with this new forbidden experience. Broken, partial thoughts of her Church teaching, her family, and the natives she had seen flitted back and forth, only to be interrupted by the sensation of Sam's flesh beneath her fingers. Slowly, the thoughts grew weak and then vanished, leaving her free to grasp this day. She watched him avidly as he covered her body with his, noticing as never before the good shape of her thighs. The naked body was beautiful, she marveled, and she gave way to taking full pleasure in it. She felt with every nerve the heat of him, the lightness of his weight upon her, the way they thrust toward each other. She would always remember the taste of his mouth, the tenseness of his fingers under her hips, pulling her tight to him, and her own astonishment as her legs wrapped around him. Then they were shuddering together, moaning with pleasure as the sky and the trees and the perfumed flowers whirled dizzily around them.

Later as he lay beside her, his hard hands caressed her temples, pushing back the tendrils of curls; caressed her breasts, with their dark nipples still erect; wandered down her hipbones, down to the moistness he had left between her thighs. With slow strokes, he brought her to the peak of delight again, until Susannah could not bear the pleasure and closed her eyes and pressed her cheek against his bare shoulder. Then he showed her what gave him pleasure and she did it, watching the play of expressions on his face. But she wanted him to join her again, and for a third time she felt that soul-shaking rapture. An incredible languor stole over them, and they slept. When they woke, he persuaded her to paddle around in the lagoon. They dressed, watching each other, touching each other again and again, kissing lingeringly.

When Susannah arrived at the Kapas', she claimed fatigue from shopping and retired to her room. For the first time in a long time she had the luxury of being able to dream of herself and Sam in privacy. Her thoughts and feelings could be limitless, and she did not need to hide her expressions, or the happiness that shone from her eyes.

Chapter Nineteen

The respite from ship life ended too soon for most of the Saints, but not for Sam Brannan. While he was enjoying a leisurely time, the rest of the world had continued on its course, and made devastating changes. The United States Navy had gone to war with Mexico over California.

Once the *Brooklyn* had set sail again, Sam began to hope he could find a way of turning to good use this devastating news of United States intervention in his plans. There had to be a way for the Saints to have California! He redoubled his efforts at having the Saints prepared. The decks rang with military drills, and the door to his small office opened and closed so frequently it flapped like the huge canvas sails that propelled the ship.

Even with all his renewed vigor and effort, there was nothing of any truly satisfying worth he could do until the *Brooklyn* landed, and there were always the smaller thorns in one's side to contend with. While in the islands, he had taken a bristling dislike to Mary Addison's fiancé, Henry Harris. Having no reasonable excuse to refuse, he had accepted Henry's passage money and found a bunk for him. So when the Saints had set sail, Henry Harris had been on deck close beside Mary Addison and her parents.

Now, ten days out to sea, Sam was realizing just what kind of liability Henry was. A spoiled mama's boy and chronic complainer, Henry was uninterested in the military drill that the Saints practiced every day. When questioned, Henry had looked at Sam with blank incredulity. "I'm not a Mormon, and even if I were, I'm a gentleman."

Sam's eyes had hardened. "No one aboard this ship is idle."

Henry had accepted his work assignments, but Sam soon found that he was a shirker who never completed anything. He was obstructive, often interrupting Mary Addison at her job of tentmaking, wanting to whisper with her in the corridor, or stroll on deck, or otherwise use his time for leisure activity.

In Sam's eyes there was no time for leisure now. He had been told that there were fewer than a dozen dwellings at Yerba Buena, where they expected to land, so the need for tents was going to be acute. Susannah, Alma, and Flora made tent after tent, sewing with vigor and purpose, aware that the time for their use was near at hand. Sam physically barred the tentmaker's door from Henry.

That same day, the captain sent for Sam. It was the Widow Eager again.

Sam sighed. "I'll talk with the elders and hold a trial within a few days. I thank you for your patience, Alf, I know you gave me as much time as you dared."

The trial was held in the assembly room. Sam served as prosecutor. Henry Harris found his niche within the Mormon community. He was in his glory as defense. Captain Richardson presided. Each side called witnesses. By the end of the trial evidence of misconduct was overwhelming against the now-tearful widow and her men friends. Richardson pronounced them guilty. Sam expelled them from the Church: Lucy Eager, Ambrose Moses, Orrin Smith, and Councilor Ward Pell.

As Sam had predicted, there was more dissension than ever. Lucy Eager had gained an unexpected and potent ally. Henry Harris kept the controversy stirred up, constantly talking to people about the injustice done to the four. Sister Hannah and Mercy Narrowmore took Sister Lucy's part at great risk of being ostracized themselves, for few of the women would openly recognize Lucy or her children.

Sam made a valiant effort to keep the Church from separating. He talked with each family privately, urging them to voice their feelings to him whether favorable or not. Then he learned how many of the Saints resented his privileges, his "fancy living," and what they called high-handed tactics in dealing with his parishioners. But at the end of each session, he urged the communicants to stay with the Church, for soon President Young should be bringing his party to California, and together they could build a mighty organization.

Meantime, he was paying scant attention to Susannah. Except for a warm smile and a few words exchanged in passing, she hardly saw him. She worried that he was looking drawn and tired, and she wanted to give him the special comfort that only she was capable of. But there seemed no place for her. And even Susannah could see the Henry Harris-Lucy Eager alliance was a boiling cauldron of trouble for Sam.

On Friday, July 31, 1846, in choppy seas under gray skies, fog, and mist, the *Brooklyn* entered the great passage of the Golden Gate. Like a shock wave, the message of imminent arrival at Zion coursed through the ship.

Susannah dressed hurriedly in the cramped confines of the cabin. Her eyes danced with excitement. "Oh, Mama, can you believe the voyage is finally over? We're here—at last. Oh, do hurry! I don't want my first sight of Zion to be alone. Come with me."

Prudence didn't even bother to hide her own excitement. She pulled her own dress on and rushed into the corridor with Susannah, leaving Ezra, Asa, and Tollie to see to Elisha and make their own way as best they could. As the two women hurried through the corridors and up the companionways, they greeted other Saints on the same mission. The air of expectancy was electric.

They were startled and a little disoriented as they came up on deck into a thick, blinding fog. It was as though the clouds had fallen from the skies with the deliberate intent of depriving them of their first all-important view of their promised land. Holding onto each other, Prudence and Susannah felt their way to a good position on the deck.

A sailor's voice came out of the mist. "Point Diablo and Horseshoe Bay to larboard." A bit later, "Presidio to starboard."

Susannah, Prudence, and dozens of other Saints stood at the rail, oddly silent and oppressed by the fog, peering around through the drifting mist. Prudence let the tears slide down her face, and she clung to Susannah. The voyage had been so costly to her, and now at the end of it there was nothing. There was no

224

comfortably loving marriage with Ezra left, nor was there a golden city of the Mormons. She couldn't bear to look at the moist haze any longer, but she didn't know what else to do. She cursed the powers that had robbed her of love and peace to bring her to this.

Susannah couldn't allow herself to give up. She strained to make out shapes, but all she could discern were nearby whalers and sloops of war as the *Brooklyn* entered the quiet waters of Yerba Buena Cove. Everything—the ship, the people around her, even the port—was so quiet it was frightening. No one was speaking. All of the Saints clung to the rail as though they could not stand alone and stared into the fog, their faces blank and drained.

Susannah shivered, then took a deep breath as the fog separated. In that brief moment she could see rolling sand knolls stretching toward the steep green hills in the distance. It was almost as if she had been given a promise no one could quite trust, and it was not enough to make up for their dreams of a promised land, or their hopes of a garden of God. The Saints had already been charmed by the golden and green beauty of the Sandwich Islands. California, in their dreams, had to surpass that, yet what they saw was a few Indian rafts made out of reeds. Now and then they could make out a few houses of wood and adobe, and Indian huts of clay built in a dome shape. It was not enough. They could not have suffered so much, given up so much, been so faithful, only to come to this! It couldn't be!

Suddenly, through a hole in the fog, they saw an adobe building, the customs house, with an American flag flapping over it. Sam Brannan saw the flag, and his mouth dropped open. "Damn that rag!" he muttered fiercely. He let out a long sigh and rubbed his forehead with suddenly cold fingers. This was the end, after all their preparation and striving, all the days of pep talks and grandiose promises. There was not going to be a war with the Mexicans. There was going to be no glorious Mormon victory. The United States had beaten the Saints to California.

Sam didn't want to see any more. He just wanted to find a good solid wall somewhere, and dash his head against it until all his pain stopped.

Brother Goodwin, standing beside him, said, "Tell me that ain't a U.S. flag, Brother Sam."

Sam said bitterly, "Tell me we landed in Chicago, Brother Ike." He clapped the other man on the shoulder. "It just wasn't to be, that's all. The Saints weren't meant to have a whole territory of their own." But then his natural optimism reasserted itself. "But we'll develop it! The Navy can't do that. We'll get our hands on every acre we can, and we'll build it up, yes sir! When President Young comes, we'll be ready for him! There's more than one way to skin a cat, Brother Ike. We'll make California the garden spot of America!"

By this time there were several men listening to Sam. At the end they broke out into a cheer. All they had left was Sam, and they wanted him, by magic if necessary, to make California fit their expectations.

There was the creaking of oars, and then a young Naval officer came aboard. Captain Richardson greeted him, and the officer said, "I'm pleased to welcome you to California, territory of the United States of America. You folks'll be the first settlers to come in under the American flag."

"We saw," said Sam heartily, and the men laughed.

Their welcome to California could not have been glummer. It was difficult to keep their hopes up. The fog stayed half the day, making clothing unpleasantly damp and clingy. The Saints went down the gangplank reluctantly, looking around, hoping to find houses where they could lodge. It had rained recently, and the dirt streets were thick with mud. If that were not enough to make them wish for the sea again, the few dwellings they could see were very discouraging. Their disappointment overwhelmed them, and they turned on their leader.

"Well, Brannan," said Ambrose Moses, one of those Sam had expelled from the Church, "Is this what we paid out seventy-five hard-earned dollars to come to? Mud streets and mud houses? Some sonofabitchin' promised land!"

"Your language is offending the ladies," Sam said sternly.

"Don't give a damn if it does. You been lyin' to us all along—"

Mercy Narrowmore chimed in. "I left a good-payin' job back in New York, Elder Brannan. You brought me and my boy here to starve!"

Horace Skinner whined, "I wouldna left the farm if I'da knowed we was gonna hafta live with heathen Injuns an' black Mexicans."

226

Sam was well aware that the young officer was hanging on every complaint. He conjured up a smile and said, "Let every heart be joyful, nor let it be afraid. Brothers and sisters, bow your heads and we shall thank God for guiding us across the perilous seas to this green land of plenty." As he spoke there was a rift in the clouds and watery sunshine broke through. "A sign from God," Sam declared, and began a long prayer.

When he had finished, the officer cleared his throat. "Guess I better tell you folks about these puddles. You want to watch your step, they'll suck you right down and you can't get out. Just follow me." Deftly he skirted a vicious-looking puddle. "Sorry Captain Montgomery had to be gone for a few hours. We'll try to get you all fixed up, though. We don't have too many places. Some of you can camp out in the Old Adobe." He pointed to the abandoned Mexican customs house, a long building whose foundation raised it above the level of the Plaza. There was a porch all along the front, with a rail across one end that became a fence.

"We have tents in which many of our people can live," Sam said. "What's that building?" He pointed to another longish building behind the Old Adobe.

"Just a building. Nothing's in it."

"Then there would be no objection to our using it?"

"Well, no. What'll you use it for?"

"My family and I will live there, and I'll set up my printing press there. I also want to build a flour mill. Our people need to get started with their new life as soon as possible, but we'll need more lodging space."

"Mission Dolores is empty now, but it's three miles away."

Sam put his people to work setting up tents, unloading the ship, and getting wagons ready for use in hauling possessions to the various locations.

Within a few days all the settlers' possessions were unloaded, and account taken of the losses at sea because of rats, vermin, and damp. The losses were noticeable. The livestock were in poor condition, though most had withstood the trip. The cattle were set to grazing with men to watch over them. It was determined that one month's provisions remained, and these were divided equitably.

A milk woman came daily to the adobe of old "English Jack"

227

with bottles of milk hung on an old horse. The bottles were one *real*, twelve and a half cents. The settlers eagerly bought her entire supply for their children.

Ezra and his family went to Mission Dolores. There was plenty of room there, once the filth from nesting birds had been scoured out. The families who lived there were fairly comfortable, but all of them were acutely aware of the labor that was before them. Prudence could not recover from the sense of loneliness and loss she had experienced in the fog when the *Brooklyn* had first arrived. She moved about unpacking their belongings dispiritedly. As always, she was efficient. For too many years she had been the good housekeeper to be otherwise, but her heart wasn't in it. Instead, she daydreamed about the way it used to be when she and Ezra had lived in New York. For Prudence that was life, and this place, even if it was Zion, was only a place where she was forced to be.

Ezra watched her, and felt a pain deep in his heart. He hadn't realized how much of his time and attention Tollie had taken. His Prudence was nearly lost to him. In a rush he wanted to make it up to her, so he began enthusiastically to offer his help with the unpacking. He ran into immediate obstacles: Prudence was not so easy to win over, and Tollie had become jealously possessive of him. She wanted his attention. Prudence, in her eyes, was little more than a servant.

Susannah watched the intricate maneuverings Tollie made with her father, but said nothing. Finally, defeated by Prudence's sad silence, and Tollie's constant demand for attention, Ezra's eyes sought his daughter's. Susannah nearly burst into tears. For so long she had wanted her father to realize what sins he had committed regarding his son and Tollie, and now that Susannah could see the pain and the realization in his eyes, she wanted to hide from it. It was horrible being right.

Sixteen people sheltered in the Old Adobe. There never seemed to be an end to their crowding or discomfort. The voyage had been long, and it now seemed that the effort and time it would take to give them comfort here was endless. There were many complaints about Sam's preemption of the large building, led by Asa, who was in charge of those who had to pitch tents on the damp ground.

Ezra Morrison wasn't a happy man. For the next few days he

tried to find a way of making both Tollie and Prudence feel as though they were the most important part of his life—together. They would have none of it, and finally Ezra turned to matters of the Church to restore his faith in himself. He needed the Lord's work, and much guidance. He went to Sam, asking to be given labor sufficient to keep him busy and away from his household problems. Sam was understanding of his problem and eager to have the help of a man who remained uncritical.

While the *Brooklyn* was being refurbished, Sam and Ezra figured out ways that the Saints could earn enough to finish paying their thousand-dollar debt to Captain Richardson. To Ezra's delight, it was a tricky, troublesome quandary requiring all his attention and concentration. A cargo of lumber would be given the captain in payment. Ezra took it upon himself to organize a party to walk to Sausalito. He sent his crew of Saints off on their mission with instructions to hire a sawmill, then haul, saw, and deliver the logs.

As might have been expected, Ezra received some grumbles. He shrugged dramatically, then said with a sigh, "Pray, my fellows, and you will succeed. We will see how deep our faith is by the success of our mission."

There was little objection they could give to that, and the men set off on foot.

Meantime, those left with the company protected their families and began to find jobs by which to pay the ongoing expenses and establish themselves. Both men and women worked. Idle hands did not rest upon Mormon wrists. The men made adobes, the sun-dried bricks used in building; they dug wells, built houses, and hauled wood. Those who had skills gradually got set up as carpenters, cobblers, cabinetmakers. The women cooked or laundered for the whalers and the men of the Naval command. Susannah and Flora continued to make tents, as any they made could be sold with ease. Yerba Buena was a transient settlement, with sailors, trappers, and wanderers coming and going. Permanent houses were rare.

No one shirked his labors, for time was not on their side. One of the men traded for some jerked beef, which proved to be half-spoiled, and some wheat, which had been thrashed on the ground by oxen. The wheat had to be picked clean of gravel and sand, and washed, but it was usable. Food was in short supply.

The Saints had been in Yerba Buena for a little over a week, and had already made a difference. Now that it was known that settlers had come to the cove, the sleepy little settlement became much more lively. Sam held religious services in the morning now, so that those living at a distance would not have to walk home after dark. Nearly everyone in the locality came to hear him. Living in or near Yerba Buena were several old Spanish families, a few Americans, about a hundred Indians, and seventy officers and men from the Naval warship *Portsmouth*.

Occasionally an entire family from a ranch several miles away arrived in town, hauling in produce or driving livestock to trade or sell. They would stay a day or two, enjoying a brief respite from their habitual isolation. While the women visited acquaintances, the men headed for Jim Brown's tavern to drink, talk, and indulge in male horseplay.

Yerba Buena had no *alcalde*, no mayor, so Washington Bartlett, an officer of the *Portsmouth*, served as such on detached duty. Bartlett's inflated opinion of himself had already suffered numerous pinpricks from Sam's casual humor. Besides, Bartlett didn't care for some stranger landing in the cove and suddenly taking over the leadership of every activity. That those activities had not existed before Sam Brannan's Mormons came to Yerba Buena just the week before, Bartlett chose not to recall. He was determined to take the dandified preacher down a few pegs.

Bartlett, comfortable in the atmosphere of Jim Brown's tavern, spoke to the tallest man in the room, a massive, handsome chap wearing a rough hide jacket and heavy jeans trousers. Slung at his waist was a gunbelt with a revolver in its holster. He and his brother had come into the settlement the evening before, driving several head of cattle, which the Saints eagerly bought. He had drunk enough to be feeling relaxed and carefree.

"Robin." Bartlett elbowed him. "See that Eastern dude over by Cap'n Montgomery?"

The big man turned his head and casually looked over the room. "The Mormon preacher?"

"Yeah, look at him—all that curly hair and that purty black suit. I thought preachers was s'posed to be poor. Ain't that what the Good Book says? Hell, he's prosperity on the hoof, wouldn't you say?"

"What's on your mind, Wash?"

"How about if we mess up his haberdashery just a speck?"

"You want a ruckus with him, start it yourself," Robin said lazily.

Bartlett looked pained. "Nothing so crude. I just meant we should treat him to the Royal California Welcome."

Robin threw back his head and laughed. He slapped Bartlett on the shoulder, giving him a smile, then walked over to Sam, stuck out his hand, and said, "Howdy. I'm Robin Gentry, and I'd like to welcome you to Yerba Buena."

Sam stood up and took Robin Gentry's hand. "Sam Brannan's my name. We're just getting up a hand of poker. Care to join us?"

Robin smiled. His eyes danced with merriment, deviltry, then friendship, but there was also speculation as he sized up Sam Brannan. The man might look the dandy, but Robin was sure there was more to him than appearance. "Thanks a lot, Sam, but as a matter of fact, I just came over to invite you to become a member of our organization."

It was Sam's turn to take a good look at this Californian, and he did, missing none of the contrast between his easy manner and the rough-hewn strength that no amount of clothing could hide. Robin's power showed in his face, the expression in his eyes, his body, his carriage. Sam, too, allowed himself a smile. "What organization is that?"

"The Suitors of Calafia."

Surprise registered on Sam's face, and his eyes held Robin's for a moment. "I'd have to know more about the organization, Mr. Gentry."

"Call me Robin," he said, and straddled a chair. The regulars at Jim Brown's moved closer to watch. They didn't often have visitors worthy of the Royal Welcome. Robin crossed his arms, his eyes steady on Sam. "Calafia was a beautiful queen who used to rule over this land. All her subjects were Amazons. Now, they were the most beautiful and desirable women ever made, but temptresses. They could make a man sweat blood with longing. But do you think they'd give in like any normal woman? No, sir. They wanted to be courted, have a man dancing to their fancy, always promising and hardly ever giving." Suddenly his eyes lit up. "But when they *do* give a man something of themselves, he's a king of kings. He's a mighty man. So a few of us formed an organization to court Calafia and her Amazons."

"The Suitors of Calafia," Sam said, and smiled. "Splendid. I'll join. There's an initiation fee, I suppose?"

"No fee, just a little ceremony. Do you want to join now?"

Sam gave him a sharp look. He was not fooled by this man's apparent friendliness, but no man with Sam's gambling instincts would have passed up such a chance to advance himself in the new territory. Whatever else Robin Gentry was, Sam could tell by the reactions of the other locals that he was a man of some standing and respect in the territory. He replied, "The sooner, the better."

Robin's smile was wide, his light brown eyes gleaming. "Come on, then." He gestured to the others. "The preacher is going to woo Calafia, boys!"

There were yells, laughter, and gibes as the men trooped outside into the bright hot August day. One man yelled, "I'll give him till the count o' thirty-five t'make it. I'm puttin' a *real* on it!"

"Last o' the big spenders," jeered another man. "I got fifty cents American says he don't make it at all!"

The bets flew as the men stood in the morning sunshine outside Brown's Tavern. Their noises and laughter attracted others, nearly the entire population of Yerba Buena, including the women. Susannah and Flora came out of their tent to see what was going on, and Susannah saw Sam, a smile on his face, standing at the center of the crowd. Beside him was a man whose good looks, height, and breadth for a moment distracted her from Sam. There were off-duty Naval men in uniform, farmers in their homespun and jackets made of hide. The Mexicans were as always dressed with great elegance, wearing broad-brimmed hats with bright bands around the crown; shirts of silk or figured calico, open to show abundant chest hair (a great embarrassment to the older Mormon women, and a captivating sight for the younger ones); rich waistcoats; long wide velvet trousers. Their shoes were Indian-made, and a good deal ornamented. Around their waists were sashes of the best quality they could afford. Over all they wore a cloak, varying in fabric from dark broadcloth for the well-to-do, to the hand-woven serape for middle-class Mexicans, and an ordinary blanket for the Indians.

Sam was blindfolded, and the betting rose. The coinage, except for that brought by the Mormons, was silver and hides.

Hides were considered worth two dollars. One elegantly dressed Mexican was betting five hides that Sam would reach his goal by the count of seventy-five. A man seemingly trusted by all was holding the bets.

Susannah turned to Flora. The air of anticipation, like that of onlookers at a fistfight, worried her. "Oh, Flora, what are they doing to him?"

Flora chuckled. "Don't you worry none about Elder. He's havin' a good time. Boys'll be boys."

Susannah's attention was drawn again to Robin as he announced, "Ladies and gentlemen! Lend us your ears!"

One man in the audience yelled, "Y'can't have mine, but I'll lend you one o' Abner's!" He tugged at the ear of the man standing next to him, and a small scuffle ensued, while the others laughed.

"Ladies and gentlemen, we welcome you to Yerba Buena, and in honor of the occasion, we are going to initiate Preacher Brannan into the Ancient Organization of the Suitors of Calafia!" Cheers and yells went up. "We're giving him the Royal California Welcome! Now we've got the preacher blindfolded—can you see, Sam? No? Well, then, what you have to do, preacher, is head straight for that post in the Plaza. The sooner you get there, the quicker somebody's going to win his bet. Turn him around, boys, and start counting!"

Several men spun Sam around until he was reeling, then they let him go. Drunkenly, he staggered for the first few steps until he ran into one of the crowd. Everyone laughed and cheered as Sam bowed low in apology. Then he set out again to reach the post. Around him they were counting, ". . . twelve, thirteen, fourteen . . ."

He walked several feet more, then with great confidence took a long step right into a slimy clay pool where the men had been mixing clay and water to make bricks. In a trice he was lying flat on his face in the mud. When he struggled to his feet, laughing heartily, smeared with the thin mud from head to feet, there were cheers amid the taunts. With one mud-covered hand, he wiped more mud out of his mouth and nose, then staggered through the pool to the post, which stood just beyond. When he ran into the post, he clutched it, then jerked off his blindfold and bowed again.

"Boys," he said heartily, "Sam Brannan is one of Calafia's favored! And if my fellow suitors will come to Brown's, I'll buy each and every one a drink!" He threw the muddy blindfold into the air. "Calafia, my darling, you are mine!"

Chapter Twenty

Susannah and Flora returned to work, but Susannah was clumsy. She kept remembering the cheers, and the crowd surging toward Sam, the men slapping him on the back and wiping the mud off him and onto each other until they were all generously smeared. But Susannah's rage focused on the big man who had laughed and had the best time of all. He had been so confident and condescending, as if he cared not at all for who Sam was.

After she had painfully stabbed herself for the fourth time, she leaped up in exasperation. "If I don't get out for a while, I'm going to lose my mind!" she declared. "I've got to go for a walk!"

Flora smiled. "Sure, honey. Just take your time."

Loud rude noises of male enjoyment floated from the tavern through the hot air. The breeze off the cove attracted Susannah, so she walked quickly toward an unused beach. Maybe if she stood and watched the water and the sea birds for a while, she would calm down.

But that was not to be. Beyond a dune in her chosen spot stood a man, arms folded, his back to her, gazing at the lapping waves. Then Susannah's eyes widened. A tall man—very tall—very wide across the shoulders, bigger than the others . . . She drew in a quick breath, and walked up behind him quietly.

Even in her anger she noticed he had changed his clothing. He was dressed in fringed buckskin, tanned and beautifully beaded with Indian designs. On his head was the broad-brimmed felt sombrero that the Mexicans wore. His boots were of dark brown leather, elegantly tooled. Around his waist was a gunbelt. She thought resentfully, even from the back he has power and presence. Well, I'll take him down a peg.

When she was a step behind him, he turned toward her. Startled, she lashed out at him. "I certainly hope you are gratified! Of all the childish, undignified—"

He had whipped off the sombrero, revealing thick black hair as straight as an Indian's. His skin was dark-tanned; his smile showed even white teeth. In his light brown eyes was a sparkle of merriment, as well as little flames of admiration. "Did I startle you? Or were you trying to startle me?"

Susannah, heedless, raged on. "I don't know what you think you accomplished with that disgraceful display, but you ought to be ashamed!"

He looked bewildered. "Disgraceful? Ashamed? That doesn't sound like me. Miss, all I did was turn my head when you thought you were sneaking up on me. If that's disgraceful, I'm a Digger Indian."

"I don't care what or who you are, what you did to Elder Brannan was humiliating!"

"Ah," he said, and grinned. "You've got the wrong man, then."

Her eyes raked his long length, from his glossy black hair lifting in the breeze, down the beaded buckskin jacket to the tips of his boots. She said scathingly, "It would be hard to mistake *you*!"

"Nevertheless, you have," he said patiently. "I'm Cameron Gentry. And you, miss, are?"

"I'm a Saint"—her blood boiled as she saw his eyebrows raise in amusement—"who is exceedingly angry at you! By what right do you lure strangers out into the plaza, and blindfold them, and make them wallow in mud before the entire village?"

Comprehension flickered across Cameron Gentry's face. He said reasonably, "I'm sure Elder Brannan wasn't so damaged that he can't clean up."

"And that's another thing! A good suit, ruined! And you made a fool of a decent man who—"

"Your husband, I presume?"

Susannah's mouth dropped open. She could feel the hard blush sweeping her skin scarlet. "No! He's my—our—First Elder, the head of the Church here."

"And you've got a case on him, is that not a fact?"

Susannah, driven beyond good sense by her anger and frustration, drew back her hand to slap the tall man's face. But he caught her wrists with ease, and before she knew it he was holding her tightly, inches away from his muscular body. She raised her face to his—and looked up and up. For the first time she realized how much taller, how much more powerful, he was than she. She felt a little thrill of fear, and tried to jerk away. "If you don't let me go, I'll scream. I'll bring the entire village down here!"

"Oh, hold still," he said, annoyed. "Listen to me, for I'm losing my sense of humor. And look me in the eye. There, that's better. I am telling you that I'm not responsible for any of those murderous acts with which you have charged me. I was not even present when your boyfriend muddied himself."

She jerked against his strong, hard hands again. "Oh, you contemptible liar!" she raged. "Let me go, you coward!"

He said grimly, "It will be my pleasure—when I'm ready. First, I have a tip for you. When in California, do as the Californians do. Don't try to change us, especially with harsh words and slaps to the face. You'll only make enemies. And I've heard enough talk about Mormons to know you don't need enemies, you need friends."

"Thank you for your valuable advice," she said icily.

"One thing more. A beautiful young woman like you doesn't need to throw herself away on a married man."

He let go her wrists. She gasped, appalled that he saw through her so easily. Scorching with humiliation, her ears burning, she drew the shreds of her dignity about her—and ran down the beach away from him.

Susannah was gasping with a stitch in her side when she finally stopped. She flung herself facedown, with several sand dunes between herself and the man, and tried to cry away her self-anger and mortification. But tears refused to come. She was too out of breath, too shaken.

But he deserved to be insulted! she argued to herself. He—he made Sam fall into the mud! He *was* there—I saw him with my own eyes. He knows all about the Saints, even that Sam is married, and that I . . . If my love is so obvious to a stranger, how could I keep it secret from Asa?

She sat up, unable to bear the bombardment of thoughts. She was terribly angry for making such a fool of herself. What could she have been thinking of? Well, clearly she was thinking of Sam.

"My Sam," she whispered; but before the words flew away on the sea breeze she knew they were not true. Sam Brannan would never be hers. He would never belong to any woman. She would always love him, and never entirely understand him.

Yet what was this strange feeling she had for Cameron Gentry? A few months ago she would have labeled it love. She pictured herself on a high hill in the sunshine where no one else could climb, with Cameron Gentry standing over her, his fists at his sides, the fringed buckskin straining over his broad shoulders . . . And then he wasn't standing, but kneeling by her, his pleasantly modeled mouth warm on her body, kissing her wherever he wished . . .

Susannah shook her head. The dream was as real as the sand she was sitting on. She must not do that, must not think of a comely black-haired, brown-eyed man looking down at her from his great height and desiring her. Only a wanton woman could have the same feeling for two men.

Yet she knew she was changing. She needed a man in her life, to love her and to love.

She also needed the courage of her convictions. If she was going to help her brother get to California, she had better make some preparations. The *Brooklyn* would not remain in Yerba Buena Cove much longer. When the ship sailed, Susannah wanted to send something to Landry.

She rose and shook the sand from her skirts. She set out quickly toward the harbor, noting with dismay that the sun had slid into afternoon. She prayed to be spared another meeting with Cameron Gentry today.

In a way she was, although she glimpsed Sam and the man who was unmistakably Cameron staggering down the rough street together arm in arm, singing hideously off-key. Cameron had changed clothes again and was wearing his mud-stained garments. Strange, she thought.

The *Brooklyn* lay at anchor, looking sprightly with her new paint gleaming in the sunlight. Captain Richardson was on the main deck. "Anything I can do for you today, sister?"

238

"How soon do you sail for New York?"

"Three or four days, soon as the lumber's ready."

She smiled up at him brightly. "I am preparing a birthday present for my brother, and I would like you to take it to him. I'm sure I can have everything ready by the day after tomorrow."

Susannah left Captain Richardson with her mind buzzing as she tried to think how she would manage to accomplish her great plan before the *Brooklyn* sailed. She was going to persuade Sam to lend her the money to bring Landry to California.

He was seated on the dock, in earnest conversation with the big man. With courage conceived of desperation, Susannah approached Sam and asked courteously to speak with him. She ignored his companion, who stared at her frankly as though he had never seen her before. Which, she thought savagely, was the way she wished it were.

Sam was tipsy, but even thus, he had admirable control of his body and his manners. He said, "Excuse us, please, Brother Gentry. Susannah, my dear, shall we stroll around? My head is a little bit stuffy." He was still mud-caked, though at some point he had evidently washed his face. Noticing her glances at him, he added, "It has been quite a busy day."

But the day was fleeing, so Susannah came quickly to the point: "It isn't right that Landry should never see his son. I can't stand watching Tollie and my father acting as though Landry Morrison never existed. Elisha *can't* grow up never even knowing who his father is!"

"I can understand your feelings, Susannah, but I am not certain you should do anything. Brother Ezra will provide a good home for Elisha, and I am sure he will act as a father to the boy. You might cause—"

"But Elisha is *Landry's* son!" Susannah said, almost desperately. "I want to send passage money to him so he can be with his son—and Tollie too."

"Where would you get a sum of money like that?" Sam asked.

Susannah hesitated. "That is why I wanted to see you. I thought you'd lend me the money."

Sam rubbed the side of his face. "I'm sorry, Susannah, I couldn't give you the money even if I wanted to. Everything I own is committed to the organization of this community."

Susannah was crestfallen. She knew Sam well enough now to

239

detect the subtle sound of disapproval in his voice. "But you wouldn't give it to me anyway—is that what you're really saying?"

"If Landry feels about his wife and son as you believe he does, then he will find his own way out here."

"But—"

"No, Susannah, you cannot make another person want something as much as you do. If Landry does care, he must make his own way."

Susannah left Sam feeling distinctly blue and downhearted. Sam had not understood. Nobody understood Landry the way she did. Of course he could make it to California himself! He cared very much, she knew. She just wanted to do everything she could for him, to help him help himself.

Papa. Papa had that much money, and more. She smiled as she thought of it. She knew that her father still grieved over Landry, wishing in his heart that Landry were near him once more. Papa, with his kind heart and guilty conscience, might give her the money. Or perhaps she would just borrow it anyway. When he found out, he might not even say anything. He would simply be glad to have his son back. He had as much as told her so on shipboard.

Walking home to the Mission that evening, Susannah was so abstracted that Ezra commented on it. "Oh, it's nothing, Papa," she assured him, taking his arm companionably. "I guess you saw Elder Brannan receiving the Royal California Welcome."

Ezra chuckled. "Sam Brannan made us proud today. He made many new friends for the Saints through his good sportsmanship. In fact, late this afternoon several of the Saints and their families were invited to a party at one of the largest ranches in this locality. After the Brannans, the Morrisons were the first invited."

Susannah clasped her hands in delight. "A party! It's been such a long time! Oh, Papa! When? Where?"

"Tomorrow afternoon and evening, at the Gentry ranch. Cameron Gentry himself asked me."

Her pleasure was cut as swiftly as by a knife. Frantically she tried to think of some reason why she would be unable to attend. She felt tears spurt into her eyes from disappointment at being offered an enjoyment she must refuse.

Ezra went on, oblivious to his daughter's turmoil. "I accepted immediately for your sake, Susannah. I know how hard you have been working for our community for months now. It's time you had some fun."

There was no way out of it. Ezra too needed some fun. The Morrison household was fraught with tension. Susannah had to attend the party. Somehow—she did not know how—she would avoid Cameron Gentry.

Susannah managed a bright smile and the appropriate response. Ezra patted her hand fondly, pleased that he had been presented with the means to make his daughter happy for a few hours.

Susannah, now having committed herself to an occasion which she would gladly have traded for the chance to walk on hot coals, next began her campaign for the sake of Landry. "How Landry would have liked this!" she said enthusiastically.

"Yes, Landry likes having a good time," her father said evenly. It was the first time Landry's name had been mentioned since they had come to Yerba Buena.

"Oh, Papa, how do you suppose he is? Do you suppose he is well? You don't think the Danites have harmed him, do you?"

"Susannah, your brother is a man grown, and able to fend for himself. Your worrying from across a continent will make no difference in his fate."

"In his fate! But that's what I do worry about! He's all alone there, with no one to love him—he is so vulnerable—" Her voice broke.

"We are all vulnerable," Ezra said.

His tone of finality made it clear she should drop the subject, but she could not. "Don't you ever miss him, Papa? Don't you wish you could see him?"

"I dare not," he replied simply.

She said no more. She had the assurance she needed. Her father still loved Landry and missed him. He, too, would gain when Landry was back with the family again. And she would do whatever was necessary to see that that became a reality.

Susannah had a difficult time choosing the dress she would wear to the Gentry ranch. She was barely able to keep her mind on anything. Time was running very short, and she had not been able to get to Ezra's tithe box. It had to be tonight, or it would be too late.

And here, in the midst of her concern, Prudence had told her more about the Gentrys. It seemed that they were very important,

241

a wealthy and well-respected family in California. The ranch was supposed to be vast, and the house was not a tent or lean-to as Susannah had supposed, thinking it would be similar to the other makeshift dwellings around Yerba Buena, but a large, elegant Spanish adobe house. Prudence, with her Eastern orientation, said "mansion."

Tollie was as flighty as a butterfly, even going so far as to make an unwelcome confession to Susannah: "I could almost wish I was unmarried and not the mother of a child. The Gentry men are not married, and from all I hear, Mr. and Mrs. Gentry are very anxious for their sons to find suitable wives and settle down to raising more little Gentrys. Can't you imagine how exciting it would be if you were a member of a family like that? Just think of having the heir to one of California's first family fortunes!"

Why, she's nothing but a gold digger! Susannah thought. She tightened her lips, against the angry desire to remind Tollie she had already had two husbands.

But the information changed Susannah's whole outlook on the evening. Sam would be there, and if the Gentrys were that important, they would be doubly important to him. She would have to be at her best. Even though Ann Eliza would undoubtedly be there, clothed elegantly and given a chance to show off her manners, Susannah would also be representing the Mormon community to the Gentrys, and what she did and said would also reflect on Sam. She had already behaved badly with that Gentry man. She would have to make up for that, and then impress the whole family favorably.

She had nearly every gown she owned out of her chest before she finally selected a cream-colored silk with black velvet insets that enhanced her coloring and accentuated her trim figure. She even managed to find a fan, which she convinced herself looked Spanish. She took great care with her hair, turning each curl gently near her face.

Though Asa's suspicious little eyes told her she looked particularly beautiful that evening, she didn't need to be told. It was one of those wonderful nights when she *knew* how beautiful she was.

Ezra was not sure when they crossed over from open range onto Gentry land, but it hardly mattered. The ranch was so vast that Susannah lost track of the time and miles that passed before the house came into view. She judged it had taken them well over two hours to reach the house from the point at which she had seen a signpost with "Gentry" on it. They must be exceedingly wealthy. She felt a little trill of uncertainty. Whoever the Gentrys were, she had already insulted one of them. So for Sam's sake, and for that of the rest of the Saints, she would have to be more charming than ever before in her life.

The two-story ranch house was unlike any other dwelling Susannah had ever seen. It was a dazzling pinkish white in the sun, its stucco and adobe fresh and smooth. Red tile was on the roof. In front of the house was an enormous courtyard with fountains and gardens placed around it. The difference in temperature when they entered through the ornate wrought-iron gates into the courtyard was amazing. Susannah had not realized how warm she had been until she felt the cool breeze and smelled the delicate fragrance of the flowers blooming in the gardens.

Carl and Rowena Gentry met them at the door. Rowena Gentry was pleasant and dignified, tall for a woman, with silver threads in her black hair, and a delightful rosiness across her cheeks over a leathery outdoor tan. She said graciously, "Come in, and welcome. It's so good to meet new friends!"

Carl Gentry, though Susannah judged him to be in his forties, did not strike her as an older man. There was a youthful masculinity about him that she found exciting. He was not as muscularly massive as Cameron, but his eyes were the same changeable light brown, his mouth as attractive. His big hand engulfed Susannah's, and after a thoughtful hesitation he reached out his free arm and gave her a warm hug. He said to his wife, "Looks like Sarah, don't she?"

"Our oldest daughter," said Rowena, smiling. "Yes, she does."

The Morrisons were ushered into a large room, furnished with a casual combination of heavy, rich mahogany furniture, lush Oriental rugs, wrought-iron ornamentation, tile floors, and velvet draperies. Animal skins were hung on the walls and strewn over couches and chairs. The house had that air of vitality and contentment found in the homes of openly loving families. With a pang, Susannah realized that that feeling had been missing from her home ever since Landry had been forced out and Tollie invited in to take his place.

The Gentrys chatted with them awhile, then went to greet newly arriving guests. The Morrisons joined Sam Brannan, Captain Montgomery, Washington Bartlett, and several people Susannah did not know. Ann Eliza, she noted, was holding court at a slight distance from her husband's admirers.

Sam came up and shook Ezra's hand. "Prospects are looking good," he said in a low tone. "I've already sounded out Robin Gentry and he is interested in our offer."

"I'm relieved to hear that," Ezra admitted. "There is plenty of room for competition in this big new country. I cannot imagine them turning down a lucrative exchange, for it will involve a good many head of cattle to feed us while we establish our own herds."

"With their bulls," Sam added.

"Perhaps if they don't want to lend them, they might consider selling one or two."

Susannah glanced at her father. She knew him well. The look on his face told her he was questioning where the money was going to come from. She felt a little tremor as she thought of what she'd be doing later this evening, but it was all for Landry, she reminded herself. She was in such deep thought that she nearly missed the quick, intimate look of appreciation Sam gave her. She knew he wanted to be with her, and she smiled at him, her eyes agreeing, but she knew it wouldn't happen. Sam would be busy, involved with his transactions, and she—she had work of her own to do here at the Gentry ranch.

The men went on talking, and Susannah joined the women who sat chatting eagerly among themselves. Then, restless, she got up and strolled about the room, examining the paintings and the statues, eavesdropping on bits and pieces of conversation she could hear as she passed groups of men. Captain Montgomery was saying, "San Francisco is among the best harbors to bring a ship, but for some reason it has always been passed by. I have always thought it to be one of the mysteries of life why this area did not grow. I know of other ports, with bays not nearly so inviting, that are now thriving cities."

"Well, Captain," Sam replied, "we fully intend to correct that oversight. I'm willing to wager that San Francisco Bay will be a humming port in less than five years."

Montgomery laughed. "It would help if Yerba Buena were more than a city of tents."

Susannah sighed to herself and walked on.

"I sincerely hope that sigh does not mean you are bored, Miss Morrison," said a deep voice behind her.

Susannah turned quickly—and looked up. Her heart nearly failed her as she recognized Cameron Gentry. He was dressed tonight in a nutmeg-brown frock coat and finely checked trousers. He smiled down at her, evidently quite free of unpleasant recollections.

Now was the time. Susannah took courage. "Oh, Mr. Gentry! I hadn't seen you before. Please, I do want to apologize for my behavior yesterday. I had no right to criticize you as I did. It was very shrewish of me."

He gave her a lazy smile. "I would never have guessed you could be shrewish."

She nearly blushed. "Either you are being very kind to me, or you are making fun of me again." She looked up at him through her long, thick lashes. "I am offering you a sincere apology."

"You don't owe me one," he said, his eyes now gleaming with amusement. "Although I might have enjoyed being the one to whom you were, ah, shrewish."

"But of course it was you!" Susannah said, with puzzlement and a trace of anger. Couldn't this man ever do anything but play stupid childish games? "I don't understand your sense of humor, and I'm not so much a fool that I don't know to whom I am talking!"

"It's only a joke, but it *is* a joke," said a voice behind her.

She turned again—and there were two Cameron Gentrys. Except that this one wore a frock coat of pale gray-blue, with dark trousers and a finely embroidered waistcoat of silk grosgrain. She glanced wildly from one to the other, her mouth open in surprise. "But you're—and he's—who are you, anyway?"

The brothers laughed, answering at the same time, "I'm Robin—he's Cameron," and "He's Robin—I'm Cameron."

She was still amazed to see two grown men so nearly identical. She stammered, "But which one did I—which one have I already met?"

Robin pointed, laughing. "Him. He always throws ladies into an uproar."

"But who—which one of you—got Sa—Elder Brannan all muddy?"

It was Cameron's turn. "That was Robin. Every time he's off having fun, I'm somewhere else transacting dull business."

245

"Was that you on the beach yesterday?"

"Yes," Cameron admitted, his smile widening. He put his big warm hand on her shoulder. "Never mind, Susannah," he said cheerfully. "Lots of people get us mixed up."

She smiled up at him gratefully. Observing the small tableau, Robin said, "If you'll excuse me, Miss Morrison, I'll leave you two to become better acquainted."

"Come," said Cameron, offering his arm. "Let's go to the barbecue pit before the others. I have it on the best authority that supper will be announced in the next few minutes. It will give us a chance to talk, and I'll convince you that Californians are sterling people."

Susannah smiled. Perhaps he was not such an irresponsible and wild man as she had first thought.

He was looking toward another group of men with a strange, intense look in his eyes. "Who is that?" he asked bluntly.

She followed his gaze. "Oh, that's Asa, my stepbrother."

Cameron made a noise deep in his throat. "He doesn't look at you as a brother would."

Susannah unconsciously moved a little closer to him. "He's not my brother, really." She shivered. "I don't think I want to talk about Asa."

Cameron said nothing, but he continued watching Asa.

Cameron got food for both of them and took Susannah to sit at a table near a large-leafed tree. Tables were set out everywhere, with crisp white tablecloths on each. Susannah had never seen anything quite like this. She had never been to a supper where everyone ate outside. She liked it. "It is very nice of your family to invite us here, and make us feel so welcome."

He looked at her, and the devilish grin that had set her off yesterday appeared on his lips and in his eyes. "Oh, we have our reasons."

"Reasons? You mean all the talk of building Yerba Buena into a city of importance?"

"Oh, that can be done anytime. No, I meant something a little more important than that. You see, we Gentrys have to look to the future. My parents want Robin and me to get on with the Gentry line, so we thought we'd look over a few of you girls. Sam has assured me that if we like you we can check your teeth tomorrow."

246

"What are you talking about?" Susannah sputtered. "Check my teeth—like some kind of horse?"

"Well, only if I like you well enough."

She stood up, trembling so hard her curls shook, then she burst into laughter. "I would not put anything past you. Nothing! I'm not even sure you're who you say!"

"Believe me, I'm Cameron."

She looked into his face. His eyes sparkled with understanding and tenderness; his smile was pleasant. She could not tear her gaze away, for it seemed as though something important was passing between them, and she thought, I could trust this man to the end of the world. Susannah became suddenly aware that other guests were watching them. He did too. He said, "Shall we walk in the garden?"

So they passed an enjoyable evening, with talk, games, dancing, and merriment. When it was time to say goodbye, Cameron kissed her hand and smiled into her eyes. Susannah had the feeling of having been given something she had wanted for a long time, and then being bereft of it. Then she saw Sam's face, a little sad as he watched them, and she withdrew her hand from Cameron's. She chided herself, I already have one love. I'm getting as greedy as Tollie.

On the way home she said little, studiously ignoring one or two pointed remarks made by Asa. She was dreaming of Cameron and the pleasant way he was with her, and hoping she had done her part to further the cause of the Saints with the Gentry family. She realized that she had barely thought of Sam all night, and she had not remembered to praise the possibilities of Yerba Buena as a seaport. As a helpmeet she was a dismal failure. Ann Eliza was much more skillful in advancing her husband's desires than Susannah was. Maybe that was why he no longer spoke of marriage—indeed, he made no point to speak to her alone at all anymore. He had danced with her only twice and had wasted that time in telling her of two or three transactions he was on the verge of making. Now, sitting up half asleep, she had forgotten what he'd said.

It was well after midnight when they arrived home. As Ezra and Asa went round to the stables to unhitch and care for the horse, Susannah realized that she had almost forgotten her mission for tonight. She had to get the money for Landry and take it to Captain Richardson in the morning. There was no more time.

She had heard Asa tell Ezra that the *Brooklyn* would sail tomorrow evening. Her heart sank as she tried to think how she could manage her plan with everyone together.

It was less difficult than she had feared. The other families living at the Mission heard them return and wanted to know what had happened at the Gentry ranch. So Ezra, Prudence, and Tollie went visiting, and Susannah pleaded fatigue. Within minutes, Susannah was alone in their quarters. Quickly, fearing that someone might return, she went to the box where Ezra kept his tithe money. Nervous that the coins would make a noise, and not knowing how much there was, she took them all.

Chapter Twenty-One

Susannah, afraid that the heavy bag of money she planned to fasten around her waist was going to alter her walk so much that others would notice, feigned illness and remained in bed long after the family had gotten up and prepared for their day. Then, an hour after everyone had gone, she rose and ate her breakfast, telling Prudence that she believed she was better and would go to work after all. For some minutes Prudence objected to her walking alone, but finally agreed that the road between the old mission and the village was enough used that there was little danger. But Prudence warned, "Don't think I'm going to defend you with Papa if he finds out!"

Susannah was nearly out the door. She looked back and smiled. "I won't ask, Mama! See you this evening."

The morning was hot, and Susannah had never before noticed how long the three miles were. She trudged along, the bag of money cumbersomely hidden under her skirt, every step seeming harder than the last. She tried holding the bag up with her hand, but it was impossible to get a firm grip on it. She stopped behind a bush and retied everything. That helped, but her progress was still slow.

She had gone perhaps a quarter mile farther when she looked up and saw someone walking toward her. She tried to make her walk brisker, because she didn't want it to be obvious that she was hiding something. She kept her eyes straight ahead and walked with evident purpose. She had never been alone before in this wilderness, and she was very far from help.

The man approaching was Asa. Terrified, she darted a few steps to her left, then stopped still, realizing she had no place to hide. Asa was going to harm her in a way she would never forget.

He drew abreast of her without speaking. He was hard and muscular and coldly determined. Susannah could not help watching his eyes. His gaze flickered across her face, lingered on her breasts, and then . . . moved to her hips.

She tried bravado. "Well, Asa, is there something wrong with me?"

"We'll see," he answered, and matter-of-factly reached out for her. Susannah tried to dodge, but in seconds he had jerked her skirts up and located the bag of money. "What's this?" he said in surprise.

Susannah was twisting, turning to get away from him, revolted by the touch of his hands. She cried, "Don't touch me! I'll tell Papa! Let me alone!"

Asa laughed sarcastically. He grabbed her wrists and held them with one hand while with the other he held up the bag. He looked into her eyes, and deliberately let the bag drop. It hit her painfully on the leg, and she grunted. "I don't think you will, Susannah. I'm sure that money belongs to Papa, and you will not tell him anything. Nor," he leered, "will I."

She backed away from him, her eyes wide, her throat too dry to speak.

He said with soft menace, "You won't escape me this time, Susannah. I've longed for you for years, and today I'm going to have you." His hand touched the side of her neck. She stood still, pale, terrified but courageous, her eyes never leaving his. "You know how strong I am, don't you? You know I'm going to possess you, right here on the ground like the wanton you are. But I'll be generous. I'll give you a choice. You can either submit to me, or I'll take you by force. Which shall it be?"

Frantically, Susannah looked down the curving path. No one was near. She cried, "I'll never submit to you! You are disgusting, Asa Radburn!"

He smiled thinly. "Then we'll do it my way." With an ease learned in his endless military maneuvers, he threw Susannah to the ground and at once lay on top of her. Susannah screamed, and began kicking and squirming. His hand came over her mouth and nose, and she could hardly breathe. Frantically, she struggled, biting, screaming when she could get breath. She turned her head from side to side, writhing away from him, hitting at him with her fists.

Then Asa grabbed and held both her hands together with one hand, while he fumbled with the buttons on his trousers.

Suddenly there was the thunder of hoofbeats, and Asa looked up long enough for Susannah to jerk away from him. Then, incredibly, he stood up and ran away a few steps before he turned and stood still, waiting. Susannah also scrambled up to run. The mounted man was larger and could be an even greater danger. Worse, he could be one of Asa's hard-bitten military friends who would require his turn with her.

Too frightened to look at her next attacker, and desperate in panic, Susannah ran awkwardly and slowly, the bag of money bumping her legs. She stumbled down the middle of the rutted road, screaming at the top of her lungs, her hair wild, tears streaming from her eyes.

Behind Susannah the horseman pulled his mount to a stop and vaulted from the saddle. Running a few steps, he came to Asa. Asa, his fists cocked, landed a blow in the horseman's stomach. He staggered, and the two men began to grapple in the road. The horseman, recovering quickly, hit Asa in the jaw. As Asa's arm came out in a hard clout toward his head, the horseman lifted Asa off his feet with an uppercut that threw him to the sandy earth. Next the horseman reached down and hauled Asa up by his coat, smashing one more blow to his face. Slowly Asa toppled unconscious to the ground. The horseman stood a moment, thumbs hooked in his belt, waiting to see if the other man would move. Asa lay limp and sprawled, barely breathing.

Susannah turned, stifling her scream with her hands. She had only seconds. She wanted to run, but could not. The horse moved, and Susannah's petrified mind sprang to life again. She ran for the horse, and struggled for what seemed an endless time to mount it. She finally managed to get herself seated and gave the horse a kick in the flanks. From behind she heard a low whistle, and docilely, the horse turned and walked slowly to the horseman.

When she saw him standing patiently in the road, she recog-

251

nized him at once. Quiet in action and movement, he reached up
to help her dismount. "Are you all right, Susannah?"

Susannah felt the blood drain from her, and she nearly fell into
his arms, her vision swimming and growing dark. "Mr. Gentry,"
she murmured, letting him support her full weight. She was
trembling all over. She raised her eyes to his, and again nearly
fainted with relief. All she saw there was compassion and
tenderness. She burst into tears. It was all too much. She covered
her face with her hands, and turned her back to him.

Cameron's big, gentle hands were on her arms, turning her
around to face him, pressing her hot face against his chest,
holding her securely against the muscular hardness of his body.
Then, as she calmed slightly, he moved away from her, still
supporting her but withdrawing to a less intimate distance. "Are
you feeling a little more steady, Susannah? If you're better, I'll
see you home."

Susannah tensed. "No," she said too quickly and too firmly.
"I mean, I must go to the village. I have an important errand,
and Flora will be expecting me to work. I must go to the
village!" When he still looked puzzled and undecided, she added,
"I make tents—for the Mormons. Our people still have great
need for them."

"I don't expect your family realized that here you should not
venture out without an escort or a *dueña*—not even to make
Mormon tents."

She said falteringly, "I—I was—I thought I was ill this morning,
and—I thought it would be all right!"

He was pensive for several seconds, then he asked, "Susannah,
is there anything else I should know about this situation?"

His face held only gentleness and sympathy. Susannah looked
away, deeply shamed that she should be lying to this kind man.
She remembered her feeling of the night before, that she could
trust him to the end of time. So, beginning slowly, she told him
everything: about Landry and the Church, about Papa's missing
Landry, about Asa.

Cameron's eyes were on her, with an occasional glance at Asa,
who was beginning to move his head and groan a bit. He said,
"Might Asa try to harm you again?"

"He—he might. Oh, Cameron, don't get mixed up in this.
This is a Morrison family affair."

"It was," he pointed out grimly, "until I got off my horse. Now, I think Sam Brannan should handle the rest of it."

"Sam . . ." she whispered, then all her defenses crumbled. Yes, Sam should know about this. Sam would tell Papa, and other elders, and they would take steps to punish Asa. She began to cry. It was all her fault, lying about being sick . . . being late . . . involving a stranger in private affairs.

Cameron's arms reached out. He put her head against his buckskin jacket and stroked her hair until she stopped crying. When she was done, he tenderly dried the tears that glistened on her lashes.

They left Asa where he lay, fully conscious but not getting up. Susannah looked back at a bend and saw him walking with quick strides toward the mission. She thought sourly that Prudence would bind up her little boy's wounds.

Mounted snugly behind Cameron, her arms wrapped around his wide body, Susannah was able for a few minutes to pretend that all was well, that Papa would not be angry, that Asa had not tried to rape her.

When Cameron helped her dismount outside Flora's tent, he smiled a little and said, "Don't go about alone anymore, Susannah. Promise me."

"I promise. Cameron . . . thank you."

She watched him ride off toward Sam's house, then she ducked into Flora's tent.

Asa marched toward the mission. He gingerly touched his swollen lips and the bruised side of his jaw. Assured that his jaw was not broken, Asa continued to feel the injury, causing it to pain him more and to heighten the cold, ruthless rage that flowed through him. He would see that Susannah paid for this rejection and the hundreds of others he had suffered over the years he had been part of the Morrison family.

He walked into the Mission, shoved past Prudence with a muttered growl at her cry of alarm, and went to his room. There he looked into a small looking glass, and saw, with approval, the damage done his face. He left again, taking one of the horses Ezra had recently bought from the Gentrys, and rode with all haste to Sam Brannan's quarters.

"Brannan," he called, deliberately not using the title of respect.

With a scowl, Sam came out from behind his printing press, which he was cleaning and checking for travel damage. "Good

253

God, man, sit down." Sam took a deep breath. Cameron Gentry had already been to see him, but had not indicated the condition in which he had left Asa.

Asa couldn't keep a hard, crooked smile from his lips. "I caught Susannah with her lover—on the road to town. When I tried to protect her, the bastard beat me within an inch of my life."

"Do you know the man?" Sam asked.

"Oh, yes, I know him, and so do you. It was Cameron Gentry. I knew the first time I saw the Gentry brothers they were not to be trusted—and now I have proof."

"What proof?" Sam asked cautiously. "Be certain of what you say, Asa. These are very serious charges you're making against your sister—and Mr. Gentry."

"Should I see her soul in Hell rather than tell you of her danger?"

"I didn't say that. I am cautioning you to be certain of what you say. Speaking in anger on a matter as serious as this will do no one good."

"I was there! Susannah stole money from Papa, and then went to meet that Gentry fellow. I saw her! I tried to save her, and who's to say I didn't!"

"Cameron Gentry for one," Sam said coolly. "He was just here—a few minutes before you came. He told me of the same incident, but it was quite a different telling."

"Then he lied! He's a Gentile. He has no need to tell the truth." Asa moved in his chair, then got up and began to pace. His anger was towering, out of control again. "I have come to you as the leader of our group. I want action taken immediately! You bring Susannah before a court of elders!"

"And the charge will be?" Sam asked.

"Fornication with a Gentile—and theft of her father's money."

"All right," Sam said mildly. "And we will also have a trial of Asa Radburn for assault and attempted rape, shall we?"

Asa was so angry he couldn't speak for a moment. He lunged forward, bringing himself up short only inches from Sam. "You think I don't know about you and Susannah! You holier-than-thou hypocrite! You have no right to lead us! You're not even a true Saint! And now all those fools who've been following you here are going to know it! We'll see who they listen to after this, *Elder* Brannan!"

"You defy me in this manner!" Sam raged back at him. "You won't get away with it, Asa. By the power given to me by President Young, you are no longer a member of this Church. You are driven from the ranks of the Saints, and I command you to leave this settlement!"

Asa laughed in his face. "You can't drive me out of the Church, Brannan. You are the damnedest apostate of them all. You can't do anything to me, but I will leave the settlement after I've talked with Papa. I'll be going to President Young. I think he'll be mighty interested to hear what I've got to say about you." Before Sam could reply, Asa turned and left the building.

Susannah spent little time with Flora. She begged time to do an errand, picked up a packet she had put together the day before, and went quickly to the *Brooklyn*. Captain Richardson let her use one of the cabins for privacy, and quietly she poured the coins into her lap and counted them. There was more than twice what Landry would need for passage and incidentals. Pensively, she returned Landry's portion to the bag and sewed it together on the end, then made another bag to enclose that. The money should reach Landry in less than a year. It had to! After all she had risked, she had to succeed now!

She made a third bag and sewed the remaining coins in it tightly, fastening this bag to her garment. She would return the money to the tithe box as soon as she could.

She gave Richardson the package with Landry's name and former address on it, then she left. She no longer felt good about her deed. All kinds of doubts were now coming to her that she hadn't paid attention to before. Landry might not even be in New York by now. She began to cry again. What would Papa do when he found out what she had done?

Susannah longed for Sam and his understanding, but he had not understood her in this. Worse, by now Sam would know about Asa, and that meant more trouble. She had never felt so alone and unprotected in her life.

She worked as efficiently as she could that afternoon, wanting to make up for lost time, even though the events of the day had left her shaken and nervous. In midafternoon Sam came to the tent. With a terse greeting to Flora, he asked Susannah to come with him.

When they were well away from listening ears, he said in a

low voice, "There is much trouble afoot, Susannah. I came to you as soon as I could."

Susannah looked down. "Cameron has told you what happened."

"He has, but I had another visitor. Asa has accused you of immoral conduct with Cameron, and—"

"No! He couldn't! Sam, he—"

"I know what he has done, but that does not stop him from spreading his lies. His story is that he tried to protect you from the advances of Cameron, and then discovered that you had stolen money from your father."

Susannah was breathless. "He's lying! He tried to force me— just as he did on shipboard." Immediately she wished she had told Sam of that incident when it had happened, for now he demanded a full explanation, and all she wanted was to ask him what he would do about Asa.

"I'm afraid I may not be able to do anything," Sam told her at last. "I took it upon myself to excommunicate him, but he was quick to point out that I couldn't, and he claims he is going to President Young with his accusations against you—and me."

Her face ashen, Susannah asked, "Against you? Oh, Sam, what have I done? All this is my fault—he hates me so much. What should I do?"

"There will be an investigation. Cameron will back you up. We'll talk to Ezra and see if we can placate him, and do all we can to discredit Asa. At the moment, the more pressing matter is your father. He will surely be looking for you. Asa will have gone to him by now. I think it best if you are here with me when he confronts you."

She shivered. It had seemed almost like a lark, borrowing the money from Papa, doing for Landry what Papa dared not do but what would make him happy—and now this.

She had not long to wait. She sat in the small office Sam had built within his temporary home, while Ezra and Sam talked briefly in the parlor. Then the door opened, and her father stood there.

He was looking pale and disheveled, and he seemed to shrink when he saw her. He had his hat in his hand, and he kept turning it little by little as they talked. He said slowly, "I am told that a fair sum of money is missing from my tithe box. Did you know this, Susannah?"

She whispered, "Yes, Papa."

"Do you know how it came to be missing?"

"I—I borrowed it—just temporarily—just a loan, Papa, I—"

"What was your purpose for this money?"

She raised her head. "I sent some of it to—to Landry."

"Some of it—to Landry." Strange how he seemed unlike himself, dear, assured Papa who always knew the solutions. "How much? And what for?"

She named the sum and told him what for.

His eyes dwelt on her face sadly. He lifted his shoulders in a deep sigh. "And the rest?"

"I—I have it here." Susannah started to lift her skirt, then remembered Sam. "I'll give it back to you, Papa—" She rose to come toward him, but without moving, he seemed to hold her off away from him. She stopped halfway, baffled.

Ezra seemed to have gotten back in control of himself. He said in an icy voice, "I don't want it back. You stole it from me; enjoy it if you can."

"But I didn't *steal* it! I didn't take it for myself—" Something was going on, some undercurrent flowed here that Susannah could not grasp. "Oh, Papa, I am sorry! I thought you'd be pleased if I brought Landry back to you."

Ezra's hat fell unheeded to the floor. His hands shot out and grabbed her shoulders. Roughly he shook her. "You are sorry! You rob the Church and say I'd be pleased! Money meant for God's work—" He let go as Sam pulled him away from her, then Ezra jerked away from Sam. He said, "My God. My daughter! Why? Why did you do this evil deed?"

Susannah's head was whirling sickeningly; her neck felt strange. She cried out, "Papa, forgive me! I love him so! I wanted to help him—both of you!"

Ezra's voice was thunderous in the small room. "Help him? Help an apostate? A minion of Satan? You have robbed the Church to help a spineless creature who has joined the legions of Hell?" When she could not answer, he went on. "If thy eye offend thee, pluck it out! You were my eye, Susannah, my heart—but you are now dead to us. Do you understand? You are dead! You are no longer a daughter of mine! I have no daughter!"

"Papa!" she screamed, and reached for him, for his face had gone an ugly deep red, then suddenly become stark white. Ezra pointed toward the door and repeated in a strangled voice, "I have no daughter. I have cast her out."

Sam said urgently, "Brother Morrison, let me get you to a couch—"

Ezra flailed his arms, brushing Sam away as if he were a horde of flies. He said, "You are my witness! She is no longer a Morrison—she can no longer offend me." He spoke the last words in a whisper. Then Ezra bent over and picked up his hat and walked out of Sam's house.

Susannah, too stunned to weep, asked Sam piteously, "What shall I do? Where shall I go?"

For an instant on his face she glimpsed his self-interest, then it was replaced with concern for her, his warm brown eyes filled with love for her. "Why—you shall stay here tonight, my little love. Then—then we shall see."

She reached out and touched his cheek, stricken by the swift insight that Sam, too, might abandon her. She thought of the things that, one after another, had conspired to part them: Sam's ambition and his commitment to Ann Eliza; Landry's being left behind in New York and her fears for him; her meeting Cameron and Robin Gentry. And now this. Nothing would ever be the same between them after this. He might still love her or he might not; but he could not shelter her. He was, after all, a man of the Church.

She looked at his hand, dear and strong and brown, holding hers against his face. That hand knew her, knew the intimate contours of her body better than she knew them herself. She didn't want to lose him too. A tear ran silently down her cheek. She looked away from him and said, "Is there no place you could hide me?"

"*Hide* you? My foolish Susannah, of course not. You will be perfectly welcome in my home."

Ann Eliza, who had missed little of the altercation going on in her parlor, was displeased to have a visitor; but her mother, Mrs. Corwin, was amiability itself, offering Susannah a cup of fresh hot tea. Sam explained hurriedly that Susannah had been involved in a family row and had come to the Church for shelter.

Ann Eliza said bitterly, "I suppose that means you'll be expected to feed and care for her for months, which really means you expect *me* to do so for her, since you will be ever so busy visiting with her squabbling family and mending their differences."

Sam said quietly, "Ann Eliza, there is a strong possibility she may be in danger. A man attempted to take her life this morning. I would certainly expect Mormon hospitality to shelter her until this matter is settled.''

Ann Eliza's dark eyes flashed with determination. "Not a moment past seven o'clock this evening, and that is my final word.''

Sam flushed but said nothing.

Susannah felt ill. She did not like what she saw of Sam in the presence of his wife. Where was his leadership, his decisiveness? Where, for that matter, was the love he had declared for Susannah? Before this spiteful female standing here with her hands on her hips, everything of value and durability seemed to melt away.

The room seemed to be spinning. She said, "I'm feeling a little faint. May I sit . . .''

Sam took her arm and led her to a large soft chair, obviously one of the comforts Liza had insisted on bringing with her aboard ship, and for which the Saints had criticized Sam. "You will be all right, sister," he said solicitously. "I must leave to attend to business. Mother Corwin will stay with you, and all the doors are locked.''

She held her hand out to him. "Thank you for everything, Elder Brannan.''

He smiled. "I'll speak to your father, and we'll get things right again.''

"Of course." She gave him her smile for the last time, knowing that there was nothing he could do to put things right for her. In the end he would choose the Church, his rise in it, and his ambitions. Once more she was alone.

But Sam was not as easily fooled as she had thought. As he left he said, "Mother Corwin, on no account is she to leave." His eyes rested for a long moment on Ann Eliza. "Nor is anyone to take her from here.''

Fanny Corwin grinned. "I'll see to her, Sam'l.''

Ann Eliza left the room, slamming the door. With hopeless eyes Susannah watched Sam go. She would leave as soon as she could, for she recognized the truth of his position, which he had not yet accepted. She sat quietly for a while, her eyes closed. Then she said, "Sister Corwin, I'm feeling much better now. While everyone is away, I'd like to speak with a—a woman friend. I believe I could stay at her home, and not bother your family at all.''

"That ain't what son Sam'l said. He wants you here." The old lady sat for a moment, her eyes bright on Susannah. "Where would you have a woman friend that wa'n't in the Church?"

Susannah didn't bother to try to defend her lie. She said, "But you know your daughter dislikes me. I don't want to cause contention between Sa—Elder Brannan and his wife."

Mrs. Corwin's bright eyes gleamed. "If there's contention, sister, it ain't you that caused it. No, you keep your seat. By evening it'll be Eliza askin' you to visit longer. Sam'll have her all talked round to it. You'll see."

Susannah didn't know what to say. She hadn't the strength to argue, but she'd get up in a few minutes. She went over everything that had happened this morning, unable to get the memories out of her mind. For the first time, however, she remembered the determination in Asa's eyes. She remembered his threat against Sam aboard ship. Her memories turned nightmarish. She thought about Sam's warning to Mrs. Corwin that she should not leave, nor should anyone be allowed to take her from his house. She knew he had been thinking of Asa. Susannah rose abruptly, bringing back the dizziness. "Mrs. Corwin, I daren't stay here. People saw me come in. I honestly am in danger! My stepbrother—"

The older woman's lip curled. "Brother Asa? I know all about him. Wouldn't want him after *me*! Sister, if you'll trust me, I'll hide you for a few days. I'll tell all who come that you skited away."

Susannah looked at her for a few moments. "Why should you want to help me? No one but me will thank you."

Mrs. Corwin made a sour face. "Pshaw! What's it matter to me? I do what I want, and maybe I don't like seein' everyone linin' up against one woman no matter what she done."

Susannah smiled wanly. Mrs. Corwin's suggestion appealed to her, and so did her reasoning. She did not want to get Sam into trouble with the elders, and this way he would not be able to tell them anything, nor would he have to lie to protect her. She followed Mrs. Corwin through several rooms of the old building to a small room tucked behind another one.

Mrs. Corwin said, "I'll bring you a blanket, some water and some food."

"You won't be telling Brother Sam—"

Mrs. Corwin turned knowledgeable eyes on her. "I'll tell him when he needs to know. You'll be safe here, if you'll just stay."

Susannah made no promises. It was her intention to slip out and seek help when it became dark enough. She had thought of Cameron Gentry when she was remembering the look in Asa's eyes. Cameron would help her. But later, after dinner, there was a lot of noise in the building—men's feet tramping, voices talking. Susannah lay on her blanket on the creaky floor and tried to make no sound. They were hunting for her. If they found her, God help her—and God help Sam.

Sam Brannan was hunting for her as frantically as the other men, for he had left her safe, and now she was gone. His mother-in-law had been so upset she had cried. He wanted to find her, preferably when she was alone, so he could spirit her away from Yerba Buena. He wanted to tell her that he had managed to persuade Ezra to keep the story of the tithe money within his own family, even to the point of speaking against Asa. But if the elders found Susannah first, Sam would have to respond to Asa's claims, and perhaps still have to excommunicate her. Then Sam thought of Asa. If he had her, nothing that happened to her would be bearable. He shivered, feeling a cold, hard knot in his stomach.

The search was called off at dark. Then the elders came to Sam, Ezra among them. They were much confused, for rumors had been spread about Asa Radburn having stolen money and trying to blame Susannah, and about Asa having a go at Sister Susannah and then running away. Some had heard that Asa and Ezra had had hard words. Others had heard that Cameron Gentry had attacked Susannah and stolen money. The rumors were many and varied. What they heard made no sense, and they wanted the truth of it.

"None of the rumors are true," Sam said, then admitted, "Asa Radburn did come to see me. I'm sure you've all noticed how militaristic he has become in recent months. He told me he disapproves of the way we've been handling military activities here, and that he believes he will be happier under President Young's leadership."

"Good," said Elder Phillips. "Never could stand the son of a bitch."

Sam went on, "Unfortunately, Radburn could not leave without trying to do harm, first to a young lady and then to her reputation. I have the word of a Gentile that Radburn attempted

261

to assault her. Fortunately the gentleman happened along in time to rescue her. The young lady is Sister Susannah. She may be in hiding somewhere, or Radburn may have captured her.'' Sam allowed the buzz of comment to die down before he proceeded. ''When I taxed Radburn with this vicious attempt, he denied it, naturally. It was then that he accused his victim of having stolen money from her father—and other things.''

''Why, he oughta be strung up!'' cried Elder Glover.

''We should have been searching for Brother Radburn too,'' Elder Bickle said.

''Brother Ezra, you got anything to say to all this?'' said Ike Goodwin.

Ezra cleared his throat. Grief and worry lined his face. He said carefully, ''I can account for all the money which I brought with me to California. I drove Asa from my sight and my house.''

Sam let out a long, quiet breath of relief. So Ezra was going to keep his mouth shut. Maybe—just maybe—he would not be forced to excommunicate Susannah. If Ezra had come this far, perhaps he'd go a little farther. Perhaps it would be so far as allowing Susannah to return to the family.

''Where's Radburn now?'' asked Elder Phillips.

''I think it's safe to assume he is on his way to President Young,'' Sam said. ''The only question is whether Sister Susannah—'' In spite of himself, his voice broke.

''We'll go on looking,'' Ike Goodwin assured him.

''When we find her, we ought to have her up for questioning,'' Elder Bickle said.

Like wildfire, spread over the Mormon community the news of the disappearance of Elder Morrison's daughter, and of his stepson. Ran away together, the gossips whispered. Over the next few days a thorough search was made of all buildings in the locality, and all swampy places. All members were questioned as to anything they had seen on the day of the disappearance. A few had seen Sam take Susannah to his dwelling, and had seen Sam sometime later leave the premises. But no one had seen Susannah afterwards.

On Friday, Fanny Corwin told Sam where he could find Susannah. Sitting silently in the little room, her heart faint with loneliness, Susannah heard Sam's beloved footsteps. She sprang up to meet him—and drew back. What if she were mistaken?

What if it were not Sam? What if she had been betrayed after all? What if it were Asa?

She shrank back into a corner, foolishly holding her blanket around her as if to make herself invisible. Then he spoke: "Don't be afraid. It's me—Sam."

The door opened, and with a little cry she flung herself into his arms. For long moments they stood holding each other, rocking back and forth, his hands stroking her hair, his lips bringing life to her cheeks, her eyelids, her chin, and at last her mouth.

"You don't despise me," she said, breathless with relief and joy.

Tears flowed down his cheeks as freely as they did down hers. He held her and muttered incoherent things that told her of his love and fears and his gladness at having found her. He was speaking thickly though he had cleared his throat twice. "My dear, my dear, what a blessing it is to find you safe. I was so mortally afraid for you."

She sobbed out, "I never knew that being safe could be so dreadful! I wanted to come to you—but Sister Corwin—"

"She saved you, my love, never forget that. I could never have convinced anyone that I didn't know where you were. But we can stop worrying now. I have some arrangements to complete, then we'll get you out of here. Can you be silent for a little while longer, sweetheart?"

She was shaking against him like an aspen. "I—I don't know. Now that you're here, I don't think I can be without you."

But something in her voice must have reassured him, for he said, "The Gentry brothers are in town. I told them of your plight, and they agreed to take you to their ranch. You will be a guest of their family for a while. Then, perhaps, Ezra will have softened enough to make amends with you."

Susannah gave a queer strangled sound, half laugh, half sob. It looked almost as if fate itself was handing her over to Cameron Gentry. But for now, all she could think of was losing Sam, Sam who had taken care of her when she so needed it, Sam who had loved her enough not to turn his back on her. She cried out, "But how will we see each other?" Then realizing how much she was asking of him, she said, "I'm sorry—I know that isn't possible—we must not be together anymore, but I—"

He placed his fingers over her lips. "Listen to me, Susannah, for we have very little time. If you and I remain apart, there is still some hope that you will not be excommunicated. Your father may relent. Meantime, you will be safe, and we will have gained some time.''

Susannah said nothing, but she knew she would never again be with him. Their moment had come the night he had asked her to marry him on shipboard, and now it was gone. Sam Brannan meant to rise in the Church, and she would only be a millstone around his neck.

Sam hugged her close to him. ''I'll come back for you as soon as I can.''

It was near midnight when he returned. Again she heard the footsteps and was unsure who was approaching. Again he spoke to her, and she flew into his arms. But he was anxious to leave. He had brought her a long gray hooded cloak. He placed it around her, then held her for a last embrace.

They moved rapidly, silently, keeping close to the buildings, constantly looking around. It seemed a very long journey, those few blocks from Sam's dwelling on Clay Street to a little hut where the Gentrys were waiting.

Outside the door, Sam knocked twice. The door opened into blackness. A hand reached out and pulled Susannah inside. The door closed noiselessly, leaving her on one side and Sam on the other. There was a strong smell in the hut, one she recognized as whiskey. She could see nothing, hear nothing, except the breathing of a man.

Susannah felt a wave of panic. She had to get out of here. She fumbled for the doorknob. Then she was unnerved, for her groping hand touched a man's trousers. She gasped, and stepped backward.

The man chuckled. A match flickered. The candle flame leapt, and in its light she saw Cameron—or was it Robin? They looked and moved so alike, and since whoever it was had on an embroidered Mexican shirt she had never seen before, she was not sure which man it was. Even after she saw that they both were there, she was still uncertain and uneasy. One of them was drunk.

The nearest one, she decided, had to be Robin. He towered over her, looking down unsmiling at her in her mussed gray lawn dress with the burgundy sash. In his dark-fringed eyes there was a sardonic flicker.

He said softly, "Good evening, Miss Morrison. How pleasant it is to see you again."

He made her feel as though she had just been thrown against a wall. Sam had removed her from his protection and handed her over to two men, the one scarcely able to move without stumbling, the other who mocked her. Tears came to her eyes. Nobody cared for her. Nobody cared what happened to her. She would be better off on her own.

Robin's eyes flashed with knowledge, and a smile came to his lips as he blocked her way to the door. "Don't tell me you are afraid of the Gentry brothers—an adventuress like you?"

Her head snapped up, the tears scurrying down her cheeks. "You're a cruel man, Robin Gentry, but you don't scare me," she declared. "I was misled. I was told you would conduct me—" She stopped, unable to remember just what Sam had said. She had just assumed, because she trusted him . . .

Robin laughed. "You want not only rescuing, but gullibility as well, Miss Morrison. Did you think everyone would just assume your complete innocence—no questions, no doubts?"

Cameron was standing there looking at her, and she looked from one man to the other. Cameron said, "We'll do what we can, Susannah." His voice, slurred, sounded unfamiliar. She knew that men sometimes got drunk, sometimes without meaning to, but she did not know this Cameron. She nearly dissolved in tears.

Robin said crisply, "That isn't necessary, Miss Morrison. We'd better get going. We'll have to make a night and day trip out of one that should be done in a few hours, just so we can present you to our parents as halfway respectable."

Susannah looked at him with hurt eyes. "I don't mind going on. I don't want to inconvenience you further."

Robin said gruffly, "Well, it's a little awkward waking my parents in the middle of the night. We'll arrive tomorrow." Almost as if he were embarrassed by his considerateness, he said to Cameron, "Ready?"

As the two men gathered their belongings, Susannah stood listlessly. She tried not to look at Robin, massive and hostile. She supposed she'd have to get used to his attitude. It was no more comforting to look at Cameron. She felt overwhelmed between the two of them.

She clutched her cloak tighter about her, shivering beside the door. In a few minutes she would be stepping out of Sam's life, perhaps forever. He was the last link she had to her life as it had been. She nearly burst into tears again as she wondered what would follow.

Robin stood in front of her. "What's your version of the reason why Sam's getting you out of town?"

Susannah hesitated, not knowing how much Cameron had told him, or how he had interpreted it. She said, "It's a family matter—Papa and . . . Asa."

"Her Cerberus," Cameron said grandly.

"The three-headed dog who guarded the entrance to Hades. Fitting," Robin said.

Susannah shuddered, feeling tears scald her eyes. "Asa's—I'm terrified of him. He'd stop at nothing—"

"I told you all that, Rob. C'mon, let's ride."

Robin's face became cold and hard. "Take my word, Miss Morrison, we do understand Asa, and your fear of him. What we—I—don't quite understand is your talent for being in the midst of trouble."

Susannah felt the caustic bite of the man's way with her, but nonetheless she felt safe with him.

Robin glanced at Susannah as she placed bacon in the skillet, and found the mixings for biscuits in his bag. "I haven't the patience with this sort of thing that you have, Cam." He drew in a breath. "Trouble doesn't just fall out of the sky. A man—or woman—has got to invite it. Why couldn't she have been direct and honest in the first place?"

Cameron made a rude sound. "I think you're going to have a hard time finding a woman like the one you think you want. I've never met one yet who thought or acted the way you wish."

"I'll find her," Robin declared.

They ate, cleaned up the camping area, and started off again for the ranch house. Robin seemed to be in a better mood, but for the most part it was to Cameron he spoke. He turned his biting humor on his twin, teasing him about the effect of two whiskeys on his head. Occasionally he would shoot a relatively innocent comment or question in Susannah's direction. Two or three times she tried to justify her position in the matter of the tithe money, but it was hard to convince either Cameron or Robin she had not done wrong when they did not present any arguments against her.

266

Though neither man showed any emotion, they seemed closed to her, maddeningly uncommenting. An outsider, she felt the weight of their disapproval. She fumed inwardly because they did not understand. How could they possibly? These were large, rough men who lived by a severe frontier code. They were nothing like her, or like other men she knew.

Chapter Twenty-Two

The following morning began crisply warm and fresh, grew sultry, and now the cold sea wind blowing across the Gentry wheat fields was bringing in wisps of fog. It was a hard wind at times, whipping up showers of sand and earth and chaff and pelting it like sleet against the faces of the three riders. Finally they came out of the wheat fields and began crossing thick green pasture lands. Susannah saw several head of cattle a distance away from them. She stared at them, thinking that these were the cattle the Saints had been bargaining with the Gentrys to purchase. Everything reminded her of the past.

When the ranch house came into view, no more than toy-size in the distance, Susannah could feel her heart begin to beat heavily with trepidation. She had met Mr. and Mrs. Gentry only a few evenings before, and now she would be their houseguest. If Cameron and Robin had judged her harshly for taking money from Papa, then what would they tell their parents? And what would the parents think of her? What would they do?

And if they wouldn't have her, then where would she go?

As they neared the house they were welcomed, raucously, by a large tricolor Collie dog, who came barking joyously out from under a bush. Robin's smile was full and genuine for the first time that day. He reined in his horse, calling out, "Ho, Macushla!" The dog leaped on her hind legs, barking piercingly. Man and dog met on the ground, and Robin petted and ruffled her tangled pelt, while she leaped around him, licking his face and hands and ears.

Cameron turned around to catch Susannah's eye. "Guess Robin can't be all bad, if the dog likes him," he said, grinning.

Susannah was afraid of large dogs. "Does he bite?"

She sat on the horse, half afraid to dismount until Cameron, laughing, came to assist her. Then Cameron was presenting her to his parents, saying, "Mother, Dad, you remember Susannah Morrison. I've brought her to visit for a while."

There was a minor silence, which Rowena quickly filled by saying, "We're always delighted to have company, Susannah. We hope you'll make yourself at home here, and be happy during your stay with us."

Susannah was relieved that she had been welcomed into the Gentry home without questions about the peculiarities of her arrival with the two men and without a chaperone. No one commented on her mussed appearance, no judgment or disapproval was registered in the eyes of either Rowena or Carl.

Carl Gentry, a naturally friendly man, looked at her as he had the first time, then said, "Well, she still looks like Sarah." The tension was broken as everyone laughed.

"Could she borrow a dress of somebody's?" Cameron asked. "We left in sort of a hurry, and Sam Brannan said he'd get her trunks to us."

Rowena smiled. "Of course. Susannah, why don't you come with me? We have a room for you—and you're about the same size as Sarah . . ."

As his wife took Susannah up the ornate stairs to the second floor, Carl Gentry looked from one tall son to the other. "Now what the hell is going on here? Cameron, is this your doing? What's that girl running from?"

"The law, Dad," Robin said sourly.

"Christ, Robin, will you shut up," said Cameron tiredly. Briefly, and as unbiasedly as possible, Cameron told his father what had happened, adding, "Old man Morrison's going crazy, not knowing where his girl is. Sam said her father refused to take back any of the money left over, but gave it to her. And he knew Sam would shelter her, so yesterday he brought her clothes to Sam's office and said they were to be donated to the needy. It's a funny situation, Dad. From what Sam said, and what Susannah told me, I've concluded that if it weren't for the Church, none of this would have happened. That brother would have come west with them instead of being thrown out. But Ezra Morrison's a staunch Church man, so he's doing what he has to do."

"The damn fool," grunted Carl. "Well, we'll shelter his girl for a while, until there's been some attempt to settle things."

Rowena ushered Susannah into a large bedroom. There was a clothespress, ornately carved and black varnished; there were two chests and a small table and a pair of comfortable armchairs. At the center of one wall was placed a large ornate bed. The coverlets and pillowcases were made of royal blue satin, and trimmed with wide, costly lace. On the table lay a buckskin bag partly open with coins spilling out of it.

"Somebody's forgotten his purse," said Susannah, with a quick irrational fear that she was being tested.

"No, child, that's just a California custom," Rowena said. "We often have guests who might need some cash to see them on their journey. They are invited to take whatever they need, without thought of repayment."

Susannah reflected that, had she known that earlier, she would not be in her present trouble. She murmured, "How considerate! In the East we would never think of that."

Rowena opened the armoire. "You are to feel free to try on any of the dresses, and to wear any you choose. Ah, here's Maria with hot water. Lunch will be ready soon, perhaps half an hour. If you need anything, comb, brush—they are in the chests. And Maria will stay to help you."

Susannah murmured her thanks, feeling overwhelmed by the attention. As quickly as possible she washed the grime of the trail from her skin. She selected a simple calico dress, and Maria buttoned her up the back and helped with her hair. It would be so easy for her to feel at home here. All she longed for was a chance to begin again, a chance to be a new person, to have a new and clean life.

Susannah was as prepared as she could be for whatever the Gentrys would have to say about what she had done. When she emerged from her room to discover that the elder Gentrys knew everything, and did not judge her, she wasn't sure if she felt puzzlement, or relief, or hope.

"Mind you," said Carl, "we'd rather have had your company under better circumstances, but we're not going to pry."

"I'm very grateful for everything," said Susannah with a humility she felt deeply.

Susannah settled into the Gentry routine quickly and easily. For the first few days she rested and got to know her way about the house and grounds. She spent a great deal of time in the lush, cool courtyard, and slowly became friends with Macushla. That was a feat of which she was very proud, and she did a little showing off to Robin, Cameron, and their parents.

Several days after she had arrived, Robin rode in late one evening. After dinner, when the family was sitting outside chatting, the men smoking cigars, and the women talking of plans for the following day, Robin said, "You Saints seem to take great pleasure in doing each other in. There is more trouble among the ranks. Sam is on trial."

Susannah listened with alarm as Robin told them what he had heard and seen. Sam was in a great deal of trouble. She tried not to show her concern, unsuccessfully. There was nothing she could do to help Sam, but her own problem had added to his. As she listened, she tried to recall everything she could about the disagreements that had begun aboard the *Brooklyn*, and all that she could remember of Henry Harris.

Henry Harris was, at best, a malcontent. He had boarded the *Brooklyn* with empty pockets. Now that he was in California and saw what hard work would be necessary to make his fortune, Henry urgently desired to transport himself and the now Mary Addison Harris back to civilization and the rich life. Meantime Henry kept busy minding other people's business. At every chance he reintroduced the resentments attendant on Lucy Eager's trial. As Sam had predicted and feared, each time the topic was discussed, the Church was split a little more.

In telling his parents of the matter, Robin had mentioned that Sam's opponents had forced a hearing by the Naval commander, Captain Montgomery, to judge Sam's actions. Susannah remembered that when it had been held, there was considerable testimony, with Sister Lucy's adherents speaking fervently in her favor. Henry Harris had once again made himself prominent and a thorn in Sam's side. But Montgomery had pronounced Sam's actions as fair and just to all.

The hearing should have been the end of it, but as Susannah knew well, it had not been. The talk continued, the sides continued to exist, and each felt it was justified in fighting for what it believed.

Most of what Robin had told the family this evening, Susannah had known, but Robin had had a bit more to say that disturbed Susannah greatly, for in it she was a contributor, no matter how unwilling or innocent. As Robin sat back and described the trial, which he had attended out of curiosity, Susannah tried hard to control her distress.

The division between the Saints had become an issue in itself, and had placed Sam in the middle. Anything that could be used against him, was. The problem within the ranks of the Morrison family, and the fact that Susannah had last been seen with Sam as he took her to his house, had given the Lucy Eager defenders plenty to talk about and even more to hint at. Henry Harris had a good deal to say to anyone who would listen. The factions got into wild and heated disagreements over Sam's handling of all Mormon affairs.

As an opportunity to equalize matters, the situation was hand-tailored for Henry Harris. Adherents were at his side encouraging him every step of the way, and planting ideas in the fertile slime of Henry's mind. He had numerous grievances against Sam Brannan: the persecution of Sister Lucy; the hearing at which Montgomery had so artificially upheld the Church and Sam against an innocent little lady; Sam's recent excommunication of Mary's father and two other men; and now Sam's failure to take immediate action against a probable thief and apostate. Implying that Sam was the greatest sinner of all, Henry decided to seek justice. In Henry's limited view that meant getting his and Mary's transport money east from the Church, while flinging the mighty Sam Brannan to the ground.

Henry Harris brought suit against Sam for the money belonging to the Church, charging him with misuse of community funds and requiring that those funds be distributed among the Church members—including Harris.

Washington Bartlett, the pompous Naval officer serving as *alcalde*, was in charge of the trial, which was the first court session in California convened under the American flag. It would be a trial by jury.

The lawyer for the plaintiffs was Mr. Hyde. Colonel C. W. Russell acted as Sam's attorney. There was testimony that Sam must be guilty as charged, since when the company had left New York City they had money, and now they had none. Attempts were made—and quickly squelched—to bring fresh accusations against Sam regarding the Widow Eager and her beaus. Finally Sam had been brought to the stand.

Sam had looked haggard. His face was drawn and pale, his eyes were dulled from lack of sleep. Undoubtedly Sam was worried over the trial and the pesky Henry Harris, but Susannah knew there was far more. Sam was concerned for her, even though he knew she was safe. He was exhausted from fighting the battles within the Church, and contending with the rancor within his own household. He was haunted by a feeling of failure, no matter what he thought about. He had introduced Susannah to love, but it had been love without marriage. He had embarked on the great undertaking of establishing the New Zion for the Saints, but that had become mired in argument, divisiveness, and contention.

Colonel C. W. Russell had a great deal of confidence in Sam. He'd said, "Brother Brannan, we'll be able to save some time here if you'll answer one question first. Will you look at the jury and tell them one thing, remembering you're under oath?"

"Yes, I will," Sam replied.

"Are you innocent or guilty of the charges against you?"

The expression on Sam's face was calm, somber, and earnest. He spoke to the jury, every one of them a member of the Church, as he might alone in his counseling chambers. "I am innocent," he said, then gave his brilliant, confident smile, as though he were defending them instead of himself, and he added, "And we'll prove it."

The spectators broke into applause, which Bartlett stopped with repeated blows of a small silver gavel. "We'll have no demonstrations," he said severely, and they rustled into silence.

Colonel Russell began again. "Brother Brannan, will you tell the jury how funds were accumulated with which to pay for the outfitting of the ship *Brooklyn*?"

"Certainly. I have brought my account book, if I may refer to it. While we were still in New York, I received in tithes, personal donations, and fares of passage . . ." He named the sums, giving specifics, reading long lists of items purchased and now belonging to the community as a whole, as Russell requested. "You see that the amounts which came into the Church are less than the amounts which had to be spent for the ship, and supplies after we got here. That left us unable to pay Captain Richardson."

"The company owed the captain a thousand dollars at the end of the voyage?"

"Yes. A work crew felled and milled timber. Captain Richardson agreed to take cargo as payment."

Russell paced back and forth. "So, if I may sum up, a contract was made aboard the *Brooklyn* for the purpose of paying for the voyage, providing necessities upon arrival in California, and making preparations for the arrival of President Brigham Young and his group. The contract was to last a period of three years, during which time you were to handle the funds. Have you used any of this company money for your own benefit?"

"None. I have provided for my family out of my own funds. However, I am doing everything within my authority to keep any portion of the common funds from falling into the wrong hands."

"What do you mean by that? You may answer freely."

Sam smiled tightly. "Henry Harris is a youth who boarded the *Brooklyn* in the Sandwich Islands without a penny, his fare having been paid by his father. Mr. Harris—as he is not a member of the Latter-Day Saints, I do not think of him as a brother, though don't think of him as Mister either." There was an appreciative ripple of sound from the spectators. "*Henry* wants to line his empty pockets with Saint's hard-earned silver pieces. Many of the brethren can testify that Henry is too lazy to work. Give him a shovel, and within seconds he gets *blisters*. He has not gotten around to joining the Church he wishes to rob—"

"Objection!" shouted lawyer Hyde.

"Sustained," said Bartlett. "Rephrase that, Brannan."

"Henry has not gotten around to joining the Church whose money he wishes to share. Nor has he ever contributed a penny to it. But this rash youth believes he should get a share, just like all the Saints who have worked and prayed and endured persecution for their faith, who have suffered the perils and discomforts of a long sea voyage that they might be here. Would it not be an offense against these worthy brethren and sisters, yea, an offense against God, to turn over one penny of this sacred fund to this lazy boy? I submit, brethren, that Henry Harris is being spiteful. Aboard the *Brooklyn* he poked his nose into an affair which was never his concern, and the entire story of which he never did witness—that of Sister Eager."

Sam let the murmurs in the courtroom begin to rise, and Bartlett reach for his gavel, before Sam stopped them all with a triumphant shout. "That affair has been settled for most of us! It would now be water under the bridge if it were not for one raw youth who keeps the waters going slowly in a circle. What I suggest is that Henry is *peeved*. He is *miffed*. He rankles with ill humor because he lost his case, not once, but twice. Henry is taking his childish petulance out on the Church of Latter-Day Saints. He is trying to extort a share of *our* money to pay himself back for his embarrassment."

Sam looked earnestly at the jury. "Brethren, we have a contract to fulfill. All of us. Together. I have given full disclosure of all funds paid in to me and paid out by me. You know where the money is which belongs to Samuel Brannan and Company. You know how much there is, and what it will be used for."

Colonel Russell looked at Sam for a moment, then at Bartlett. He said nothing, but sat down.

Into the silence Bartlett said, "Cross-examine, Mr. Hyde?"

Lawyer Hyde said, "No, your honor."

There was a murmur of surprise, with Henry Harris's voice loudest in protest. Bartlett pounded his gavel, then said, "It is the finding of this court that the charges are not substantiated. Charges dismissed."

Henry Harris gasped indignantly, his face grew red. He turned angrily on his lawyer.

Sam, in a flush of relief, shouted out that he would buy drinks for all.

As far as Robin was concerned, that was the end of the episode, but Susannah was not so certain. She had learned a great deal in the last year, and one of her hard lessons had been that once trouble found you, it held on and on. She was frightened and worried for Sam. He had given up so much for his ambitions, she didn't think she could bear it if he did not succeed. She, herself, had been one of his sacrifices to that grand ambition. He had to succeed. His accomplishments had to surpass his losses— and hers.

Part VI

Part VI

Chapter Twenty-Three

The McKay family celebrated the Fourth of July, 1846, in Fort Laramie. The wagon train had arrived the day before at the clay and brick fort on the Platte River. Clean, rippling Laramie Creek glistened in the sun beyond the fort. It was a lazy, peaceful oasis after a long trek. Sioux Indians lounged at the walls of the fort, their dogs trotting importantly through the long grass. Alder trees offered shade and an inviting place to hang freshly laundered clothes.

Mary, Coleen, and Fiona joined the other women at the creek, splashing the water over themselves as they scrubbed the dust and sweat of many miles from their clothing.

Fiona sat on a rock, her shoes off, her stockinged feet dangling in the water. With a quick, speculative look at her mother, she bent and peeled the wet stockings from her legs. "It's so hot, Mama, and they need to be washed too," she said, giving her mother a spectacular smile. Before Mary could say anything, her auburn-haired daughter had hopped off the rock and was in the stream, wading, sliding on the rocks, and splashing Coleen.

Elitha Donner soon followed, and within minutes Virginia Reed was barefooted and in the stream too.

Mary gave Margaret Reed an apologetic smile, saying, "I suppose I should have stopped her, but to be honest, Margaret, I wish I had the courage to join her."

Margaret smiled politely at Mary, but continued her slow walk to the water's edge. She called Virginia to her. The two of them talked in hushed tones, then after a look back at her friends, Virginia climbed up the gentle bank, stepping from stone to grass.

Fiona watched as Margaret and Virginia walked away. She went over to where her mother still scrubbed, rubbing the clothes against a sunlit rock. "I'm sorry, Mama. I've done it again, haven't I?"

"I wouldn't give it too much thought, Fiona," Mary said without looking up from her work. "Margaret is still trying to maintain a standard that may not be entirely appropriate on the trail, but she and Mr. Reed have some grand plans."

"And I made it seem that we are not worthy of them."

Now Mary looked up, her own gray eyes locking with the deep green eyes of her daughter. "*Seeming* is not the same as being, young lady. There is nothing wrong in taking a little pleasure from the bounty God gives life. Now, let me be, I've got work to finish."

Tamsen Donner seemed to be as busy as Mary, her head bent over her scrubbing, but she was smiling. She said nothing when her own children all ran barefooted into the stream, splashing and screaming with laughter and the shock of the cold water on them.

For the most part the members of the wagon train were in a festive mood and glad for the few hours they had to relax. They had a feast of roasted fresh meat for supper the evening of the Fourth. For a time it was just a pleasant evening with a bit of talk, a little song, and a good deal of laughter, but as the sun disappeared, and light faded into darkness, the talk turned to a discussion of the route to be taken.

George Donner was soft-spoken, but firm. "My brother and I are going to take Hastings's route."

"But what about the warnings the trapper back at Fort Barnard gave us?" Denton asked. "Clymer didn't have one damned good thing to say about the cutoff or the man."

"Does any one of us know Hastings?" Sean asked.

"We know that he will meet us at Fort Bridger and lead us over his trail," George Donner said. "That is enough for me. We save time, and if it were so bad a route, the man would not be willing to travel it himself."

Uncle Jake Donner bestirred himself, saying, "Those of you who want to take the tried Fort Hall trail will have plenty of others to accompany you. The choice is open to you." The older man got to his feet, taking some time to straighten his back and knees, then he raised a hand. "That is my last word for the evening, gentlemen. We can argue some more in the morning."

Sean, too, walked back to his wagon with Mary. If the Donners were going to leave off the conversation, he knew little or nothing would be decided tonight, though the deference shown the Donners was something he didn't understand. Without needing to say anything, Mary and Sean walked past the wagon and out past the fort to the stream.

"It won't be long before we walk out under a more western sky than this, Sean, and the stars above will be shining on our own home. We will be at our destination by the end of summer, won't we?"

"If we go with the Donners to California . . ." he said, then took a deep breath, held it a moment, and let it out slowly. "The time is here, Mary. We must decide if we are to live in California or Oregon."

"You are giving serious thought to California, aren't you, Sean?"

"I am. But I have misgivings. That trapper the men were talking about—Jim Clymer—had little good to say of it. He talked of fog and cold mists . . . but then the others say that it is a place of long growing seasons and vast lands a man can have for little more than the asking. And then I worry a little about the leadership of the Donners. I can't see them as men strong enough or experienced enough to lead us, yet everyone turns to them."

"Don't you like Uncle George and Uncle Jake?" Mary asked.

Sean brought her hand to his lips and kissed it. "I like them very much, but that is not the same as judging them to be leaders. I don't care a tinker's dam for James Reed, but honestly, Mary, I think he'd be a more able leader if anyone could stand his overbearing ways and constant bragging."

With the Reeds brought to mind, Mary told Sean of the small incident the day before at the stream. "Margaret is a snob. I shouldn't admit it, even to you," she said, "but I wouldn't be at all sorry to see her brought down a peg or two. There are days when she hauls out all that china and good crystal for a meal on the trail when I feel like flying over to that wagon like a banshee and smashing every blessed piece of it!"

Sean laughed, softly at first, then harder as he pictured his

281

wife causing chaos in the Reed wagon. "When you decide you are ready, let me know, my love, and I will go with you."

Mary leaned her head on his shoulder, and they stood quietly listening to the rush of water. "Ahhh, Sean, I am glad we are ourselves."

The next morning, with wagons repaired and freight readjusted and secured, the train was back on the road. They struggled up the Continental Divide, everyone's attention on the difficulty of keeping oxen and wagons in line. On July 17, a horseman came upon them. With a smile and a flourish, he gave them an open letter to all travelers: "At the Headwaters of the Sweetwater: To all California Emigrants now on the road." The wagons slowed to a stop, and all gathered round for the news. The United States was at war with Mexico over the very land they hoped to call their own. Sean felt a warm spot inside his chest. He had never much liked the idea of being outside United States territory. This meant he would still be a citizen, for he never considered the possibility that the United States wouldn't win.

The letter also stated that travelers should band in large parties to protect themselves from possible attack by Mexicans. It gave information of a new and better route that had just recently been explored. They were urged to take the road south to Fort Bridger where the writer himself would guide them through. The letter was signed by twenty-year-old Lansford W. Hastings. It seemed to confirm everything they had heard about him—at least the good, reassuring things.

They traveled for nearly a week before they came to a huge rock that was something of a tourist attraction they had all heard about. Independence Rock had carved on its hulking side the names of hundreds of others who had traveled this way.

"Papa! Add our name, please," Fiona begged.

"And yours, Brian," Coleen said, then blushed a bit, because she had wanted to say he should add her name and his.

Sean started to protest that there wasn't time, but the other wagons were stopping and children were already swarming all around the rock, pointing out names and trying to carve their own.

Sean managed to give in with some grace, and even enjoyed the tedious process of carving the McKay name in the stone. Coleen watched as Brian placed their names on it as well. Then he showed her where his own father had many years before carved his name. "I was only five years old then," he said. He looked away for a moment, his eyes far off. "We'll come to a barren stretch of ground soon. Somewhere along that stretch we buried my mother . . . I was six when Dad married Jane."

Coleen looked down at her feet. She hardly knew what to say. There was still much she didn't know about this man she loved, so she said simply, "I'm sorry, Brian. I can't imagine what it would be like if I lost my mother . . . especially out here . . . away from everything and everyone."

Brian looked at her. He ran his hand along the side of her cheek. "Death is something you learn to accept out here, Collie. You are coming to live in a tough land."

She looked up at him, a small cone of fear in her eyes.

He smiled, then said, "I don't mean to frighten you, but it does no good to go blindly. Think of how you were when you first began this journey. The day of labor you put in today that you could not have withstood at the beginning. Look at Margaret Reed. I have heard others call her an invalid, yet she seems to grow stronger as we go. But there are others who grow weaker, and before we reach California, this train will see death."

Coleen walked a few steps from him, then looked back longingly. "I don't like to think about things like that."

Brian was instantly contrite. In two long-legged strides he was by her side, with her hand firmly held in his. "You won't need to. I'll do the thinking on things like that. All you need to think about is taking care of me, and raising half a dozen young-uns."

The warm light returned to Coleen's eyes. "Have you talked to Papa yet?"

"No. I've been looking for the right time," Brian admitted. "I'm not so sure he's going to want a bullwhacker for a son-in-law." Brian grinned mischievously at her. "I thought I might wait until we got a little closer to home so I could tell him—or show him—that I'm a man of substance."

Coleen sighed. "The end of summer."

The train traveled along the Sweetwater. The ground was level and barren. Those in the wagons sweltered in the heat, but found that preferable to walking for long hours with the sun blistering down on their heads. Brian and Coleen both kept a lookout for his mother's grave, but had no real expectation of finding it. Time, wind, and errant wagons would have obliterated her marker.

The miles seemed longer with no trees to break up the wide

expanses of open land. In whatever direction Coleen looked, she saw only the sky coming down abruptly to meet the flat empty land. The willow trees near the Little Sandy Creek were a welcome sight. It was like greeting old and dear friends who had been absent too long. Other parties had left the sandy bank trampled and boggy, but no one minded. It was good to feel the coolness of tree shade and smell the freshness of greenery and water.

Sean looked at the tracks dug into the mud and sand. This was the last camp he would make before he had to decide if he would go on with the Donners or follow those deep ruts of the train that had come before and taken the trail to Oregon.

Others in the group were also debating the question of what trail to take, but this time Sean wanted solitude. He wanted to confer only with himself and quietly mull over the considerations he thought important. He wanted to be settled in their new home as quickly as possible, and that argued for Hastings's Cut-Off. Jim Clymer had been to California and back and had little good to report; that argued against the cut-off. Coleen, though she hadn't told him in so many words, wanted to marry Brian, and Brian Campbell was a Californian through and through. That weighted his feelings toward going with the Donners. Neither he nor Mary wanted to come clear across the continent to have their family separated, and Coleen would go where Brian went—California.

Sean walked slowly, the camp falling farther and farther behind him. Without realizing he did so, he walked along after the wagon ruts heading for Oregon. About a mile up the road he turned back. When he returned to his wagon, Fiona, Coleen, Mary, and Brian all looked at him with eyes filled with expectancy, waiting for his word. "I've just returned from Oregon," he said with a laugh. "I think we ought to try California. We'll go with the Donners."

Fiona jumped up and threw her arms around her father's neck, planting kisses on his cheek.

"The choice need not be the Donners or Oregon, sir," Brian said. "We could take the Fort Hall route to California."

"I considered that," Sean said. "But if we are going to California, it makes sense to go by the shortest route. The sooner we get there, the better I'll like it."

Before they broke camp and parted with those families who

284

had made other choices, the group held a meeting and officially elected George Donner the leader of the party. Though James Reed tried to remind everyone that he was a major part of this expedition by calling it the Reed-Donner Party, almost everyone outside his family called it the Donner Party.

With a great deal of eagerness and anticipation, the newly formed party headed for Fort Bridger, where they would meet their guide, Lansford Hastings. Once he was with them to lead them over the mountains, they would feel secure. Most of the party had heard of Fort Bridger, named after the man who wanted to make it a major trading post for emigrants coming west. Their expectations soared.

After a dry and dusty week-long journey they came upon a weathered and rickety rail fence, the only sign of civilization to indicate they had arrived at the fort. There was a store, a smokehouse, some stables, but no sign of Jim Bridger, who had gone to trade with the Indians, and no sign of Lansford Hastings.

Bridger's partner, Vasquez, did what he could to welcome the party and calm their misgivings. It was to his advantage to ease their minds, for Fort Bridger was not well located for business. Those who took the Greenwood route did not come near enough the fort to do business there, but those who took the Hastings route would pass right through the fort. Vasquez was anxious to accommodate these people and to encourage them to take Hastings's route. "It'll cut near three hundred and fifty miles off your way," he said with certainty, then took a breath, eyes skyward. "Some claim it's nearer four hundred miles."

"But what is the terrain like?" Paddy Breen asked with a scowl. "If this trail's so damned good, why don't more take it?"

"Not many know of it, mister. These are big mountains—takes a fellow a time to find the right way to go," Vasquez said with a slow smile. "But there's nothing ahead to give you pause. The trail's mostly firm and easy to follow. You just get yourself rested up here a bit, then light out after Hastings, who's gone ahead with another train. You won't have any trouble." He looked up at Brian and winked. "Even you greenhorns can find your way."

Paddy Breen grumbled, walking away, but the saved three hundred and fifty miles loomed large in his mind, as it did in everyone's. It was a boresome, bone-wearying task to walk twelve or more miles a day beside oxen shouting, Gee! Haw! or Whoa!

until the dust in a man's throat was thicker than it was on the ground. Three hundred and fifty miles translated into nearly a month's rest at the end of the journey. That was almost as good as the promise of heaven.

Bridger sold supplies at the price he chose to name, made bad whiskey, and offered a blacksmith's shop. There was water for pasturage at the bottom where the Black Fork divided into several channels.

With as much dispatch as possible Brian and Sean set their cattle to grazing, unyoked the oxen, and set to repairing the wagons. Without taking time to rest, the two men reset the wheels and assured themselves that the axles were in good condition. Sean debated for a time over replacing the canvas, as it was tattered and bleached almost white. After weighing the cost against the need, he gave in. Fiona, Coleen, and Mary helped fit the new canvas on the family wagon, and set to repairing the others, patching them with pieces from the old canvas.

Somehow the whiskey, the opportunity to rest, the repeated assurances of an easy trail, and plenty of grass and water lulled all of them into taking a few days to rest at the fort. The Donner Party camped there for four days, then set out again on the thirty-first of July. They had only gone a short distance before coming to a fork in the road. The old road led off; to their left were the fresher tracks of the party Hastings was leading over the mountains. After some minutes of indecision, they turned the wagons left and followed after Hastings.

They had gone only a few miles before Sean was noting how much more difficult the trail had become. The terrain was mountainous, and the labor imposed on him and Brian was telling. They came to a spot where the track ran down a narrow ravine. At Sean's call, Mary, Fiona, and Coleen got out of the wagon and walked behind, watching warily as Brian and Sean locked the wheels at the top of the descent. The wagons skidded and slithered down the ravine, rocking and shuddering dangerously. By the end of the day Sean judged they had traveled no more than twelve miles.

The promised saving of three hundred and fifty miles by this route looked more and more like a gift from heaven. Only Brian expressed doubt. Sean chewed on a chunk of beef. "A mountain is a mountain. How much different can the other route be?"

286

Brian shrugged. "If this is the worst of Hastings's Cut-Off, it will be an advantage, but—"

"Well, we can always take heart that there's a group in front of us, and they are on the move. If they can get through, we can too." Sean laughed shortly. "Course, if we find them alongside the trail, then we may have to do a bit of worrying."

Brian laughed too. "I can't argue with that. Hastings must know what he's about . . . they haven't turned back or stopped."

They saw strange things as they traveled. Fiona stared openmouthed and slightly revolted by a stream so laden with minerals that it gurgled past them like a thin river of blood.

Four days out of Fort Bridger they came into the valley of the Bear River. Encouraged that they were making fairly good progress in mountainous terrain, and aware that Hastings was not too far ahead of them, they forded the Bear River and crossed the next ridge. From there they followed a westward running creek that led them around red rock cliffs. The sound of the wagon wheels on the stone surface echoed and re-echoed in a deafening, endless noise. Sean shook his head, trying to shake away the ringing. He gratefully took pieces of soft wool from Mary and put them in his ears. It helped, but did not stop the annoying noise.

The red cliffs opened into an enormous canyon. All of them were awestruck as they looked at the menacing, towering red cliffs. By day's end they came out of the canyon to a stream flowing northwest, the Red Fork of the Weber River, according to their maps.

Taking a moment, Sean and Brian looked at the maps in their book, and smiled in relief. Sean's finger traced the Weber River right to the Great Salt Lake. Both of them thought of the Great Salt Lake as a milestone. With renewed vigor, Sean led his rumbling wagons in line, following the wheel tracks the Hastings party had left to guide them. Four miles down the trail they came to the river crossing and stopped, for on a bush was a letter. Hastings warned them that the route below Weber canyon was very bad. "I fear my own party may not get through." He suggested that the party send a messenger ahead to get him and he'd return and guide them across by a better and shorter route.

August 6, James Reed, six-foot-six McCutcheon, and small Charles Stanton set out in search of Hastings. The others camped as they had been instructed, and grumbled about Hastings.

287

"What kind of man is he?" Paddy Breen asked. "We've followed him and now he says we can't get through?"

"He'll come back to guide us," George Donner said placidly.

"And if he don't we're in a bad spot," Eddy said, stating the obvious, annoyed with Paddy Breen's constant carping.

Sean remained silent. He wasn't sure what to believe. What he did know was that it was too late to turn back.

Five days after the men had left, Reed returned alone to the camp. He had very little good news to report, and Hastings was not with him. In an effort not to alarm the others, Reed boasted a bit. "We've got some rough terrain to pass through, it is true. The canyon is so narrow there's barely space for the wagon wheels between the rock ledge and the river, but we can make it."

"Is it a clear road?" Brian asked.

"Not entirely," Reed said. "There are boulders that must be moved or gone over. If we do as well as Hastings, the best we can expect is slow going. His group made only about a mile and a half per day."

"Is he going to keep his word and guide us?" Uncle Billy Graves asked.

"He has shown me the route. I have it well in mind. I can guide the train."

"He lied again!" Graves shouted. "Why should we believe him if he never does what he says? There probably is no pass."

"There is!" Reed cried, hands up for quiet. "I have seen it. He took me to the top of a peak and showed me the route we must take."

Finally someone asked, "Where are McCutcheon and Stanton?"

"They could not get horses to replace their worn mounts. They are following me afoot. I bought this horse from the Hastings party and came ahead to give you the news as quickly as possible so that we could be on our way. The sooner started, the sooner we are out of this piece of bad trail."

Working their way through the canyon was backbreaking labor. The wagons moved so slowly that progress was measured in yards rather than miles. To cross boulders too large to roll the wagons over, the men piled brush and rock to form a hill that allowed the wheels to roll.

Sean and Brian worked doggedly, the thought that once out of the canyon it would be easier placed in their minds like a carrot

288

of encouragement. But the canyon itself offered spirit-crushing obstacles. The wagons had to be lifted up over the spurs of the mountain. The men rigged windlasses at the top to hoist them. Sean and Brian once again spiked the wagon wheels, then ran heavy ropes from axle to ribs to the pulleys. Slowly the freight-laden wagons were pulled to the top of the spurs. The animals were hoisted up in a sling, their legs pawing wildly in the air as they swung in terror.

The McKay women sat on rocks, their necks craned as they watched the process. As the men hoisted the bay that Reed had purchased, the animal twisted, his forelegs groping madly for something solid. They watched in helpless horror as the sling began to slip, and the horse, more frantic and terrified than ever, fell free, twisting until he smashed on the hard rock at the foot of the canyon.

Fiona's eyes were like saucers, then suddenly she grabbed for her mother, burying her face in Mary's shoulder as she sobbed and cried hysterically.

Mary comforted her daughter, but her eyes remained riveted on the compelling, revolting remains of the horse. She fought waves of nausea, but could not seem to tear her gaze away. They had gone through rough terrain before, and had suffered long, difficult days, but this was the first time Mary McKay felt frightened about the journey. Somehow that dead animal seemed to be an omen, and she couldn't shake the feeling of sick fright that had settled on her.

Sean ran up to her. "Mary, Mary, look away!" he cried, and blocked her view. "You can't let this upset you, my love. It is to be expected that we will lose animals on the way—remember Reed had to replace two of his oxen at Fort Bridger because they drank bad water? Well, there you see, it's really no different, except that this was—was so bloody."

Mary swallowed hard. Sean was upset enough; she didn't want him to know what she was thinking. With a great effort to still her roiling stomach, and keep the fear and horror from her eyes, she nodded.

The trail, once they had managed to get out of the canyon, offered nothing better. Because there was little choice left, and no chance of going back, the Donner train followed Reed's trail as it had been pointed out to him from a mountain top with vague sweeping gestures by Hastings. The trail had to be cleared. Day after day the men cut down aspen, alder, and willow, many of the trees twice as tall as Reed's towering house wagon. Sean and Brian moved like old men at the end of the day, and neither could hide the knife-like pains that shot through their backs and shoulders after a day of cutting trees, hauling lumber, and then coaxing oxen and wagons over the rough, stump-strewn terrain.

Mary's feeling of unease grew as night after night she and Coleen tended to the men's hands. Sean's hands looked like raw meat. In addition to the trees, there was brush that had to be cleared—a tangle of wild rose, berries, and other vines that all seemed to be covered with thorns. The men's hands were cut to ribbons. Everything they touched was smeared with blood. Mary took to always keeping a jug of fresh water, bandages, and salves handy, and insisted Sean and Brian allow her and Coleen to treat them several times a day.

Tempers were as raw as the men's hands. None of the men had any reserve left for polite consideration. To make matters worse, some members of the party were not working at all. At almost any time Wolfinger could be seen strolling with his wife in his snow-white shirt. Others took to taking time off to sit and rest and watch while the others bent double with the labor and the excruciating pain in their hands, backs, and arms. A night's rest did not heal the damage a day's work caused. Each evening Mary worried, and Sean staggered to their cot too tired to do anything but fall into what was more of a stupor than restful sleep.

Chapter Twenty-Four

Once out of the Bossman Creek area, they went up a side canyon. Their hearts sank as ahead of them they saw a mountain higher than anything they had had to cross before. It took them six days to climb, and reaching the top did not offer relief. The descent was so steep they would have to spike the wheels of the wagons yet again, and coax the vehicles down the incline, holding them back all the way. To make matters worse, there was a ravine so steep and deep that lumber and brush had to be cut to fill it in before the wagons could cross.

Once more Sean and Brian took up their picks and axes and went to work cutting trees much larger and older than the willows and alders they had cut before. "By God, if we ever get back to civilization, I am going to buy a bottle of whiskey, lie on a feather bed, and get roaring drunk," Sean grumbled.

With a semblance of trail cleared, the men began the precarious and dangerous process of easing the wagons down. Several wagons had gone down, and Sean's stood behind the last of the Reed wagons. He helped spike the wheels on Reed's wagon, then began to man the ropes that helped the oxen. Paddy Breen and young Billy Graves manned other ropes. Billy screamed as his rope scorched through his hands and broke free. With taut lines holding only one side of the wagon, the vehicle tilted, righted, and then rolled to its side with a thump. The men scrambled down the mountainside as quickly as they could, Reed leading. The wagon was not too badly damaged, and with the aid of props six men were able to heave the wagon upright again. Slowly they let the wagon down the rest of the incline.

Sean held his breath as his wagon went down the mountain, its new canvas top being torn by the tree branches. It was a sorry sight, but it rumbled down the mountain intact. When they camped, Mary and his girls would do what they could to patch the torn spots and make the canvas whole again.

They finally made camp in a clearing. Mary massaged Sean's back and shoulders until her own arms and back were tired and aching from the effort. Though they were worried about food supplies—for several families were running low—Mary cooked the most nourishing meal she could provide for her men, which included Brian. She wasn't certain just when the family had begun to think of him as one of their family, but all of them did.

As Sean properly appreciated the stewed beef and peas Mary had fixed, Stanton and McCutcheon finally arrived, staggering back into camp. Amanda McCutcheon handed her infant daughter to Fiona and ran across the camp to her husband, helping him back to their wagon.

Fiona tried to comfort the squalling Harriet as she watched George and Tamsen Donner bring Charles Stanton to their wagon. Walking slowly, Fiona reached the McCutcheon wagon in time to see Amanda provide her husband with a steaming bowl of broth.

He said, "We damn near starved." Then between mouthfuls added, "We were lost in the mountains. God! It is a brutal tangle up there—everything looks the same. A man can walk the same path ten times and not know it."

Fiona handed the baby back to Amanda and asked, "Is the way any easier ahead?"

Mac wiped his mouth with the back of his hand. "I wish I could say it is, but there's another mountain range—and the desert beyond."

Patrick Dolan stopped for a moment, listening to what Mac said, then went on, spreading the bits of news as he went. In minutes the whole camp was in uproar, the men milling about near McCutcheon's wagon.

"It's too damn much! We can't go over another mountain!"

"Reed," Paddy Breen screamed, "this is your fault! You said you knew the route and by God we followed you!"

"He never knew the way!" Keseberg added coldly. "It is the

292

pride of swine that makes him boast of knowledge he doesn't have. If we follow him we will never get out of these mountains!''

"Who in hell is to stop you from finding your own way, Keseberg?" Sean asked, his jaw jutted out, his eyes burning with anger at the arrogant German.

Keseberg laughed in Sean's face. The Irishman squared his shoulders, his chest out, fists doubled up as he took two purposeful steps toward Keseberg. Before the German could react, Brian threw himself at Sean and held both his arms at his side. "Get that fool out of here!" Brian yelled. Young Billy Graves came to help restrain Sean, and Mac scrambled to his feet. "Go back to your wagon, Keseberg," he said, standing at his full height, towering over the German.

With a sneer for Sean, Keseberg turned and walked slowly to his wagon.

"That goddamned son of a bitch!" Sean said, still struggling to free his arms from Brian and Billy.

Brian pulled Sean back to his wagon and told Mary briefly what had happened. "I'll go back to the others—they're near panic over this. There may be more short tempers." Giving Sean and Mary a stern look, he added, "You keep him here, Mary. Sean—"

"I'd like to kill the bas—" Sean swallowed the word, then said glumly, "I'll stay put. You might as well tell them there's not a damned thing we can do but go on."

The next morning they did go on. For five days they struggled clearing six miles of road, cutting timber, hacking through brush and wild rose and serviceberry, digging paths down side hills, and rolling out boulders. They frequently had to stop to fill in low spots to cross creeks and rivulets. On the night of the fifth day they camped and discussed what they should do. Reed said, "The canyon narrows up ahead. I'm not sure we can get the wagons through."

Instead of following the narrow route, they crossed to the other side of the creek and hoisted wagons, animals and human beings up the three-hundred-foot sheer north wall of the canyon. Everyone made it safely, and that night they camped on the vast open expanse of Salt Lake Valley. But it was not a happy camp. Brian ate slowly, his mind troubled. "We are moving too slowly, Sean, but I don't know how in God's name we could have gone any faster."

"I can tell you how! If those damned Germans and a few others I could name would do their share, we'd have gone a hell of a lot faster!"

"Sean, your language, please," said Mary.

"If a little bad language is the worst you have to contend with, Mary, I bow to you. You might do better to talk to the wives of these man and get them nagging. We were supposed to save three hundred miles or more by this route, but by heaven we are moving a mile a day and losing time. You heard Brian, we've got to move faster."

"What could happen if we don't hasten, Brian?" Coleen asked.

Brian began to speak, then hesitated. Finally he smiled. "It's hard to tell—most likely we'll make the mountains in plenty of time."

"But what could happen?" she insisted.

"We don't want to get caught by snow—the passes close up mighty fast if there is a storm."

"But it's still summer! It won't snow for a long time," said Fiona.

"It's the end of August, Fiona, and we have a long way to travel. It snows a lot earlier in the mountains than it does nearer the coast."

"Oh, I think we are all so tired we are borrowing trouble," Mary said. "Fiona is right—it is still summer, and we will make better time now. Look around you, the land is fairly level again. We will make up lost time."

Traveling the next day was a dream compared to what they had been through. There were no thickets, the land was firm, and the wagons moved easily over the surface. Even the river fords presented no serious obstacles. Near evening they came upon the tracks of the Hastings wagons again and followed them northward to the lake. They covered more distance that day than they had covered in the preceding ten days. They camped that night with a feeling of accomplishment they hadn't felt for a long time.

On August 29, the going got rougher again. They rounded the point of a mountain close to a lake, the wagons jolting along one after the other. Just as they thought they had made it with no difficulty, one of Reed's wagons broke an axle, and all progress was stopped by the crippled vehicle. Sean and several other men set out to find timber they could use to make the repairs. Hours later, Sean came back sweaty and out of sorts. "Fifteen bloody miles we went to get this," he said, and dumped his load of timber at Reed's feet. Milt Elliot popped his head around the wagon he was working on and said, "But we thank you profusely, Sean."

Sean grinned, waggled his hand at him, and headed for Mary and comfort or whatever type of soothing she'd offer him.

"Yours is not the only bad news we've had today," Mary said. "Tamsen has been nursing Luke Halloran all day. She thinks he is dying. His lungs are very bad."

Coleen shivered. "He's been coughing all day. It is so awful—he can't stop. I don't know how Mrs. Donner can stand sitting with him all the time."

Once Reed's wagon was repaired they set out again, not daring to camp and waste what was left of this day. They kept the wagons rolling until eight o'clock that evening, and they reached Black Rock, where Reed had found Hastings and his party three weeks before. By the time they had camped, Luke Halloran was dead.

On August 30, they moved their camp, but out of deference to the dead, they didn't travel. Someone offered planks from their wagon to make a coffin for Halloran. They buried him next to John Hargrave, a man from the Hastings party who had died at the same place.

Nothing was easy for the group these days. When Uncle Billy Graves, Paddy Breen, and a couple of other men discovered that Halloran had left all his money and other belongings to George Donner, they began to fight, not believing the Donners.

"How're we to know he wanted you to have it?" Uncle Billy said, his mouth turned down.

"I ain't takin' your word for it, Donner, unless you got some proof," said Breen. "I been lied to an' deceived since we started out on this trek. No reason to think you got righteous overnight."

"Especially not when there's money involved," Uncle Billy added.

George Donner dutifully produced a scrap of paper on which Luke Halloran had written his wishes for the disposal of his property.

Without grace, Uncle Billy and Paddy Breen backed down, but it didn't stop them from demanding to know just what Halloran had left the family who had nursed him since they left Missouri.

When it was discovered there was over a thousand dollars in silver, as well as clothing and a few keepsakes, the grumbling and complaining began again. There was little or no trust or cooperation left among the people who called themselves the Donner Party. As surely as night was falling, they were splintering, breaking up into individual families who happened to be traveling the same route, but who had no cohesion or concern for each other. Those few who had not become so embittered tried to stay together. Sean made an effort to keep his wagon near the Donners' wagons, or those of the McCutcheons or the Eddys.

"Some of these folk are worse than a pit of vipers," he said to Mary.

They set out again on August 31, and traveled in a great arc around the edge of a dry lake. As the sun was setting they camped at a place they called Twenty Wells, for there were strange-looking holes like wells in the ground. The wells, ranging from six feet to nine feet in diameter, were filled to the brim with cold, clear water. Yet none of them ever overflowed. Entranced by the curiosity, Fiona, Brian, and Coleen watched one of them for nearly an hour, taking water from it, watching it fill to the top, but never spill over. Brian went back to the wagon and got a rope. He weighted it and dropped it into the well. All seventy feet of the rope went into the water, but did not reach bottom.

Fiona had a half smile on her lips, bemusement in her eyes. "I didn't know there were such strange things. I've seen streams of blood, springs that bubble and steam, and now this. Look, Brian, the ground around them isn't at all wet—it isn't even moist. How can that be?"

Brian shrugged, his eyes still on the cold, clear water. "I don't know, but one thing you learn real fast out here is that nature is full of tricks no man could ever dream up. I've never seen anything like this before, though."

Then, with one of her quick changes of subject and mood, Fiona asked, "Are you and Coleen going to get married?"

"Fiona!" her sister howled. "You mustn't ask questions like that!"

"Why not? I want to know the answer—and I want to know if I get to be in the wedding party."

"She has a point," Brian said, and put his arm around Coleen, pulling her against him. "Are we going to get married?"

"Oh, Fiona! Now you've—"

"Why don't you say something, Coleen?"

Coleen's face was so red by now that Brian and Fiona began to laugh and tease her mercilessly until she couldn't speak at all. Finally Brian, still hugging her, said to Fiona, "We're getting married."

When they left the place of Twenty Wells, the wagon train traveled almost due south around the point of a range of hills. The lake fell far behind them. As they moved along this track, the concern for water became prominent in their thoughts. They came upon a sparkling stream and eagerly went to replenish supplies, but the water was so salty they couldn't drink it. For the first time it was brought strongly home to them that the presence of water did not always mean relief.

From the salty stream they traveled across a long expanse of arid plain. To their left they could see barren hills in the distance. All day long they were reminded over and over how dry, how barren, how sterile land could be without water. The white bleached bones of animals lying stark in the sun made them think of their own fragility. They came upon a meadow with good water that night and were more thankful for it than any of them could have expressed. The McKays remembered to thank God for their evening meal that night.

They also remembered to thank Him for giving them so vivid an understanding of the importance of being prepared for the long, dry drive they would have ahead of them. "It will be no more than thirty-five or forty miles," Sean said to Brian, "but I think we should cut enough grass to last three, maybe four days. These wagons are pretty battered. We could break down, and lose time."

Brian agreed, and the two men set to work cutting grass and filling every receptacle they had with extra water.

For thirty-six hours the Donner Party allowed the oxen to rest and saw to the supplying of their wagons. The women cooked food to last the dry passage, for on the open, barren desert there would be no chance of finding fuel for a fire.

For all their preparation, none of the party was prepared for what lay ahead of them. With the Donners in the lead, the party set off, following Hastings's trail across an open valley. Ahead of them was a range of rough hills. With their eyes on the hills, Brian and Sean trudged in the hot sun beside the oxen. As they

297

came nearer, it began to dawn on them that the hills rose steeply, nearly a thousand feet upward toward a pass.

With no choice, and not having the energy to give vent to their frustration and anger, they prodded the oxen up the hills to the pass. Below them stretched yet another plain, more barren and drier than the one before it. Far in the distance they could see where it ended at the foot of volcanic hills. There would be no water; no relief from the heat or the burning sun.

As Sean forced his beasts forward over the volcanic hills, his heart sank when he gazed below at a perfectly flat plain. There was no sage to break the horrible dazzling sheen of white salt. With all his heart he wanted to turn back, and couldn't. It took all his willpower to take the first step onto the salty, eye-paining, sunstruck surface.

They had to stop on the desert that night, and discovered it was piercingly cold, after sundown. Though Sean had chastised Mary for packing their winter clothing, and had teased her about it on every hot day, he was mighty grateful for her foresight now. The whole family stayed huddled together that night for warmth and comfort. The desert made them feel small and forgotten by God. They needed one another's touch just to get through the night.

The next day dunes alternated with flat level spaces. The wagons bearing lighter loads, and those oxen that were in better condition, pulled ahead of the heavier wagons. The train began to stretch out, straggling for over a mile or two. It was hard to tell. As Sean walked along, he could see many men marching single file in front of him. He couldn't recognize any of them as his fellow travelers. He stopped, trying to distinguish who they were. The column of men stopped with him. They moved when he did, stopped when he did, until he realized it was an illusion caused by the heat and brilliance of the salt desert. He gave a shudder. Sean had always sneered a bit at those who spoke of the Devil as though he were a real person, but now he wasn't so sure. It felt to him that the Devil's scorching footsteps dogged him at every turn.

The oxen were in very bad condition. No matter how much water Brian and Sean dared give them, it was not enough. The beasts missed their step in the soft surface, and stumbled with exhaustion, heat, and thirst. The men did little better. Even after placing a flattened bullet in his mouth to prevent it from feeling dry—a trick Brian had told him of—Sean felt as though his insides had long ago turned to dust. Unable to trust his sight, or his mind, Sean stumbled on, nearly hanging on to the oxen to keep him upright, ignoring the lakes that appeared magically on the desert. They taunted him, frightened him, brought a lonely, tormented rage to live inside him. Part of the time he was irrationally fearful that this was Hell and the Devil would have him captive forever, and other times he cursed God for having done this to him.

That other people suffered with him meant little to Sean. This was a lonely ordeal despite the company. The water buckets were getting low—too low not to cause an added fear—and the lack of water caused a virulent selfishness in all of them. No one wanted to give another man a sip of his water for fear of the moment when none would be left. Irrational hatred ran rampant through the train. Someone had lied to them, saying this was a mere forty-mile stretch, and now they had the horrible sense that it had been a deliberate lie. Someone—anyone—everyone—wanted them to suffer and die.

Sunday morning dawned, the fourth day of their desert march, and still they were on the flat, blinding white expanse of salt and sand. James Reed volunteered to go ahead to the mountains they saw in the distance, and find the first watering place. He mounted Glaucus, his favorite mare, and quickly passed other emigrants who had made better time. None of them fared well. Several families had been forced to abandon wagons. The oxen had been driven ahead in search of water. Reed rode for thirty miles before he found water, and already it was growing dark, and his horse was spent. A few train members were already there with their cattle when he arrived. Will Eddy had arrived with his cattle about ten that morning, and had spent the day resting himself and his oxen. Reed gave himself only an hour respite, then started back with Eddy. Eddy carried a bucket of water, hoping that he might revive one of his oxen, which could not make the trek to water.

The sights Reed passed on the way back were far worse than those he had seen the evening before. Cattle frenzied by the need for water, and blinded by the glare, charged wildly about. Men who did not even note his presence doggedly drove their cattle to water. Women and children staggered alone across the desert. Others Reed found terrified and huddling in abandoned wagons, unable to move or help themselves.

It wasn't until Tuesday that all of the party managed to reach water, and even then the ordeal wasn't over. Nine yoke of oxen were missing, and many of the cattle had wandered off, crazed and searching for water. The men went back to the desert looking for their animals. Without the oxen the wagons could not be drawn, and without the cattle their supply of food was seriously diminished. When final count was taken, the emigrants discovered that thirty-six head of working oxen were lost. Some had died on the desert, but some were simply lost in their blind search for water, and the men, despite their efforts, could not find them.

The mere finding of water did not cure all that ailed the Donner Party. Men and women alike were near despair, feeling betrayed and filled with resentment. Even the usually friendly William Eddy openly cursed Lansford Hastings. They had been betrayed in mind and spirit, and none of them seemed to have the resiliency to recover from it. Without Lansford Hastings there to castigate and punish, they could not prevent themselves from turning on each other.

It was a discordant group that set out again after they had rested and gathered their belongings from the desert. They saw Indians as they moved along, but these seemed friendly and offered no problem. They traveled through wide treeless valleys, and were fascinated and heartened by the herds of antelope that could be seen clustered wherever they looked. For people who had been eating nothing but beans, bread, and salt pork, fresh steak was a gift from the gods.

The availability of fresh water, fresh meat, and relatively easy travel conditions restored them somewhat, but the distrust of Hastings lingered, and again became prominent as they traveled day after day near the base of a range of hills. All eyes were constantly fixed on the ridges, searching for a pass, but there seemed to be none. Hastings's trail, weeks old, went south across the plain, then it turned north, and for three more days they followed the tracks embedded in the scarred ground. "He's a madman," Sean barked at Brian. "And we're following him! He goes south, then comes back north. Are we fools?"

Brian didn't answer. If Hastings didn't know what he was doing, they were all going to perish out here, and that he didn't want to think of. His life was before him. He shouted at the oxen, pushing them to greater speed.

Others felt the same as Sean, so each day a man took a turn riding ahead and breaking trail. It wasn't a particularly pleasant task, but it was a necessary one, and it helped reestablish a minimum of trust and cooperation in the group. Sean took the lead on Monday, and on Tuesday fell to the rear of the train with a feeling of relief that he was no longer the man out front and responsible for the well-being of all of them.

At last they camped at the mouth of a canyon. It was September 28, long past the time they had thought they would already be in California. They watched with wary interest as stark-naked Indians moved around the edges of their camp, but did not approach. On September 30 they came to a westward-flowing river that they knew to be the Humboldt. They forded it and followed a well-beaten track down the north bank. For the first time in weeks, cries of joy and hoots of triumph could be heard—they had rejoined the main California trail! No more of relying on Hastings's word—this was the real trail, tried and true!

They came to a river that set Sean to smiling nonstop. Sometimes it was called the Odgen, but others called it Mary's River. For him it was Mary's River, and a sign that they would make it to California safe and whole.

While Sean was enjoying a moment of grace, the Indians informed George Donner that the group still had over two hundred miles to travel before it would reach the sink of the Humboldt. That was a lot of miles, and it was late in the season. Uncle George Donner called a meeting and told them of their plight. "The cattle are done in, and some of these oxen aren't going to make it another ten miles if we don't stop and give them rest. Now you've got all the facts—let me hear your suggestions."

With a snort, McCutcheon said, "I don't see what good suggestions are going to do. If we don't have oxen we can't go on, and if we don't have cattle, we'll starve. They gotta rest—so we stop and camp."

Charles Stanton shook his head. "Can't argue with that."

Keseberg said, "I think there is overmuch worry about the lateness of the year. It is warm and clear, and I, for one, could stand a rest."

"That's all the son of a bitch has done while the rest of us worked," Sean muttered under his breath. Keseberg had become the focus of all his bitterness and disillusionment. It saved him from turning ill-humor and disappointment on Brian, Mary, and his daughters.

"It might serve us well to divide into two camps," Eddy offered. "That way we'd have better grazing for the animals."

"I'm all for breaking into two groups," Brian said, "but I've got to take exception to Mr. Keseberg's statement that we don't need to look to the lateness of the season. He doesn't know what these mountains are like in winter—even late fall. I do. Men die in these mountains. Above all, even to the point of losing cattle, we need to keep moving."

The others listened to Brian, asked him a few questions, and Brian answered bluntly. "The mountain passes close with the snow. Don't try thinking of snow like you had back east. This is real snow—higher than a man's head, sometimes twenty or more feet deep in drifts. You can walk out of the mountains and come back later for your possessions, but if we get caught up here, it won't matter how many oxen we have. We won't get through the passes."

The Donner Party kept moving. The Donners, now reduced to five wagons, and the McKays with their three, went ahead. Their oxen were in better shape than some of the others' were, so they traveled faster to move ahead. In the second section were the Reeds, Eddys, Breens, Graveses, Murpheys, and the Germans. While the arrangement gave them advantages, it also gave the impoverished Digger Indians, who lived in squalor throughout the area, more opportunity for silent, quick night raids in which they made off with cattle and other food stuff. The Diggers' weapons were as poor and weak as they were, but they wounded cattle, leaving them to die, and stole anything they could lay hands on.

There was little to be done about the Diggers but to push on as fast as possible. With the terrain offering little problem, and Brian's warning fresh in their minds, the Donner Party was making about twenty miles a day. With hope surging again, Sean remembered the friendly Indians saying the Humboldt sink was about two hundred miles away. At this rate they would be there in a week. Surely the weather wouldn't turn before that. Back home the leaves were just now taking on their bright autumn colors.

Mary, Coleen, and Fiona walked along with Sean, lightening the load the oxen pulled as much as they could. They guarded their food supplies jealously, and already everyone was on short rations. Game was no longer plentiful, and many times Sean cursed his lack of foresight. "We should have taken on a supply when we had the chance."

Brian shook his head. "It wouldn't have helped. If we had taken the time to smoke it, we'd have lost too many days. And without preserving it, it would be rotten now. We're in a race, Sean, and we've got to win with what we have."

"We're making good time, now, aren't we?" Sean asked with misgiving.

Brain smiled at him. "We're doing our best. We're making good time, and if we can keep it up, we'll make it through before the snow catches us."

The words were comforting, but Sean had noticed that Brian had taken to looking at the sky several times a day, as if he were expecting the first signs of bad weather momentarily.

Chapter Twenty-Five

Around noon on October 5, the train reached the second section of a ridge. It was a high sand hill, covered with rocks at the top. As the wagons stood motionless at the bottom, and the men looked up to the top of the rise, it seemed impossible. This hill was no worse than dozens of others they had clambered over, but it didn't seem right that they should have another hill to climb. Tempers were stretched taut. No one was eager to wait his turn or do the labor that would put this obstacle behind them. Grudgingly they began to double the ox teams and haul the wagons over.

Two of the Graves family's wagons had been taken up the incline this way, when John Snyder couldn't wait any longer. He moved another Graves wagon into third position and started up the hill, using only his own oxen. Next in line was Milt Elliot, driving one of the Reed wagons. With the Murphey family's oxen joined to his own, he started up the hill. Snyder was barely moving, and Elliot pulled his wagon alongside Snyder's to pass. The way was narrower than it first appeared, and the yokes of the oxen got tangled. The lead oxen snorted, their big heads moving from side to side. They were not responding to Elliot's or Snyder's commands. The men shouted at each other. Snyder, unable to control the angry passions that had built up, began to beat the oxen violently over the head. Maniacally, he pummeled them. Reed rushed up the hill screaming his protests.

Snyder turned his fury on the intruder. He spun to face Reed, his whip raised. "Get out of here! Goddamned bastard!" Snyder ran forward, threatening Reed with the whip.

Backing off, Reed said with studied calm, "Easy now, Snyder. Let us help. We'll get the yoke in line—"

Snyder was not to be calmed with a few soft words. He roared at Reed again, his whip in hand, his mouth spewing curses.

Reed's temper snapped. He was not a man to take a beating from anyone, especially not a man of Snyder's caliber. He drew his hunting knife.

Snyder grimaced, flipped the whip over, and held the butt end like a club. Swinging with all his strength, he struck Reed across the head. Blood gushed from the long gash. Reed danced about, dodging the whip butt, then he darted forward and struck with his knife, driving the blade home just below Snyder's collarbone.

Margaret Reed rushed to her husband and got between the two men, and Snyder struck her. Reed and Snyder continued to struggle. Snyder struck Reed twice more. Reed fell to his knees. Groggy and hurt, Reed shook his head and tried to regain his footing.

Snyder walked a way up the hill, then staggered. Young Billy Graves, who had been watching, rushed forward and caught John Snyder, easing him to the ground.

Reed's wife and daughter tried to tend to his wounds, but already he was regretting the incident and wanted to go tend to Snyder. As he got to the top of the hill and bent over Snyder, the man whispered his last words and died.

With unexpected ferocity, Uncle Billy Graves turned on James Reed, pummelling him. When they made camp, the Reed wagon was set a way off from the others. The whole camp was in turmoil. Resentments that had been controlled and held in through so many frustrations were now unleashed and focused on the fight. Fuel was added to the fires of anger because Snyder had been a young man, only twenty, usually cheerful, and popular. Reed, on the other hand, tended to be too pompous, too wealthy, and too willing to expect respect. Many did not like him, and some had a strong dislike for him. To make the dangerous situation even worse, Keseberg saw this as an opportunity to unleash the grudge he had been cherishing over his own banishment months before. With great relish he encouraged the hatred, and stirred up talk of killing Reed. He even jumped into his wagon and propped up the wagon tongue with an ox yoke for the hanging.

William Eddy and Milt Elliot stepped forward and defended Reed. They were the only ones to do so. With Keseberg doing all in his power to force the group to move as a mob and hang the man, Eddy and Milt and Reed stood together, drew their firearms, and held their ground.

Realizing that if something wasn't done quickly, Reed might be hanged, George Donner suggested that he leave the camp and go on ahead.

"No!" Reed bellowed. "I'll not desert my family and leave them to the mercies of merciless people."

"I'll see to your family—you know you can trust me!" Eddy cried.

"You can count on me too," said McCutcheon. "I have no quarrel with your family."

Sean McKay also stood forward. "I'll see to them. They'll come to no harm."

George Donner said, "You must go. You can see we must avoid confrontation. There has been enough blood shed—and you could do us a service by riding ahead. All of us would welcome a man who could bring meat back to us."

Reed said nothing—his pride wouldn't let him—but he nodded. Perhaps as long as the others thought that he would save them with supplies, his family would be safe. It was the best chance he had.

The next morning a grave was dug for John Snyder. He was wrapped in cloth and placed on a board for decency, but there was no longer wood that could be used for anything so luxurious as a coffin. James Reed participated in the burial with the others, his head bowed in prayer as the body was lowered into the ground. The earth was thrown back into the grave, and Reed made to depart the camp. Virginia and her mother and his other children all gathered around him, the sounds of their crying filling the air.

Just the sound of the family's misery seemed to stir others to hatred again. A group of men gathered, then went to George Donner with their final decree. James Reed was to be sent from camp with no firearms. Donner looked at them in amazement. "That's the same as killing him! If that was all you wanted, it would have been kinder to hang him last night."

"He killed a man!" Keseberg said. "He deserves to die!"

Reed, without firearms, mounted Glaucus and rode out of camp. George Donner returned to his wagons which, fortunately for Reed, were still in the lead. Out of sight of the second group, Donner was able to give Reed weapons to defend himself and to hunt for food.

Reed's banishment took from the party a focus for their resentments, but the ill feelings didn't leave with him. Those stayed in the mind and heart of every man and woman traveling west with the Donners, and they were displayed in many petty ways.

The next day as the train got under way again, Eddy and Pike ranged, looking for game. As they were hunting, they were shot at by Indians. On their way back they found a note left by Reed, telling them he had found evidence of a battle with the Indians. The two men rode back to the camp. As all were gathering, they noticed that Old Man Hardkoop was not in camp.

Eddy and Pike asked around for someone who knew of the old man.

Keseberg had brushed them away. "I'm not a governess, for God's sake! What do I know of an old man?"

Eddy and Pike left Keseberg, but were not satisfied with his answer or his attitude. Both had a bad feeling about the old man. They sent a scout to retrace their steps and see if they could find him.

The scout found Hardkoop sitting beside the road, weak and exhausted. He said that Keseberg had put him out of the wagon to walk or die. The old man was returned to Keseberg, who with a smile and not a single word, took Hardkoop back into his wagon.

Animals, people, and wagons were now strained past the point of endurance. The next day Reed's last wagon was abandoned, for it was too heavy for the weakened oxen to pull. Mrs. Reed and the children transferred a few of their belongings to the Graves's wagon. Each family once again became closed in, not wanting to help anyone for fear it would leave them destitute themselves. As they moved along the trail, Eddy came upon Hardkoop again—Keseberg had put him out once more. "Can you take me in your wagon?" the old man asked.

Eddy looked at him. He was at the end of his supplies, and his wagons were in poor condition, but he couldn't look the old man in the eye and say no. "See if you can make it past this sandy stretch," Eddy said. "This is hard going for the animals. Once we're past it, I don't think it would hurt for you to ride."

With an effort, Hardkoop smiled his gratitude. "I'll try," he said. His voice was thin and reedy from exhaustion.

Sean McKay passed Hardkoop as he moved slowly along. "You need to ride, old man?" Sean asked begrudgingly.

Hardkoop shook his head. He kept his eyes ahead on the Eddy wagon. "I'm ridin' with Eddy, soon's we cross this patch."

Sean nodded and turned his attention back to his animals. Everyone forgot Hardkoop until that night when he was not to be found in camp.

William Eddy went from campfire to campfire. "Sean, have you seen the old man?"

"I saw him this morning—he said he'd be riding with you."

Eddy made a face. "I know, damn it. I told him he could, but then I forgot all about him. I just figured he'd be with someone else."

"Try the cattle drovers—if he dropped behind they might have seen him."

The drovers had seen him sitting at the side of the road in the sagebrush. "He was all played out," one man said, "his feet so swelled the skin busted open."

Eddy looked out into the darkness. With his conscience burning him like a brand, he lit a huge fire so that Hardkoop would be able to make his way to join them.

He had not appeared by morning. Margaret Reed and William Eddy went to the Breens to beg the use of a horse to go find the old man. Breen refused. They went to Keseberg to ask if he would find Hardkoop and take him in. Again they were refused. Their last hope was Uncle Billy Graves, the only other man with a horse left. They were met with a burst of anger. "What the hell good is a dying old goat going to do me? I need these horses. You got a lot o' nerve asking me for an animal. Get out of here. You want the old man so bad, you get him."

Milt Elliot, who had overheard, volunteered to go on foot to find Hardkoop. With others listening now, there was an outcry. "We ain't waitin'! We're goin' on, by God!"

"We're going to get caught up in those mountains," Breen said. "We don't have time to waste on him."

Eddy and Milt bent to the will of the others. The country was getting drier all the time, they had less pasturage, and the animals were worn. There were signs of Indian activity around them. They had seen the corpse of one member of the Hastings party who had been taken from his shallow grave, stripped by the Indians and left to the coyotes. Eddy and Elliot were brave men, and considerate ones, but they were not willing to leave themselves alone and on foot if the others wouldn't wait. They broke camp with the others and moved on, leaving Hardkoop to his fate.

The next day Indians ran off with the horses Billy Graves had refused to use in searching for Hardkoop. William Eddy could not suppress a smile, even though it was a dire happening, and meant yet another wagon had to be abandoned.

They kept the train moving, but the Indians continued to be a dangerous nuisance. The sink of the Humboldt wasn't too far now, but grass was scanty, and the water barely fit to drink. The Indians ran off eighteen oxen and a milk cow. The Donner brothers and Wolfinger were the biggest losers, but it was also a grave loss to the entire wagon train. Uncooperative at best, their strength was being dwindled a bit at a time. Each occurrence of misfortune to one of them damaged the chances of all of them.

The Donners were so stripped of oxen that they had to hitch cows to their wagons to keep going. The next night they made camp at a place where the water was in pools surrounded by mud. The water was unwholesome to drink, so it provided more of a cruel temptation than relief. One of Paddy Breen's mares tried to get to the water, and bogged down in the treacherous mud. "Eddy! Help me with this mare!" Breen called to Eddy, who was standing nearby and watching.

William Eddy had the smart of Breen's refusal to look for Hardkoop fresh in his mind. He stared at Breen for a moment, then said, "Remember Hardkoop," and walked deliberately and slowly away.

Breen wrestled with the rope he had gotten around the mare's neck for a time, but the mare soon sank deeper and deeper into the mud, until it finally closed over her head and she smothered.

It was a bad night for the Donner train. Feelings that were already bad grew worse. The list of grievances each man harbored was longer tonight, and fresh. The Indians increased the party's feelings of persecution and frustration. Moving so silently that the campers didn't hear them until it was too late, the Indians shot arrows at the cattle. Fortunately they didn't kill any, but they wounded many.

All were anxious to be on the road again in the morning. On October 12, they began a long, hard drive across a desert plain. Mountains were on their right, and the sink of the Humboldt was ahead of them. It was a difficult drive, made worse by the poor condition of the oxen and the exhaustion and irritability of the men. They reached the sink at midnight. Two oxen had dropped along the way. That night they built a corral for the cattle and placed guards on it. They could afford no more losses to Indians.

Brian took night guard. There was no sound, nothing to indicate the Indians were around. Through sheer willpower he kept his eyes open, and kept watching for a danger that never appeared.

Along with the other guards, he went to the camp for breakfast the next morning. Brian hadn't taken the first bite before he heard the bellow of a wounded beast. Indians appeared from everywhere; arrows were thick in the air. Twenty-one head of cattle were wounded, and had to be slaughtered. The men cut a few steaks to be used before they spoiled.

George Donner announced later that the train had lost a hundred cattle to the desert Indians. It was a loss they couldn't absorb. He had sent Stanton and McCutcheon to Fort Sutter for supplies. Pray God they returned in time.

William Eddy had only one ox left, and so had to abandon his wagon and all his possessions, putting what food he had left into other wagons and proceeding with his family on foot. Wolfinger found himself in the same predicament, with only one ox left. He decided to stay behind to make a cache of his valuables, which he could return to later. Reinhardt and Spitzer stayed with him.

The train moved on. The Reed family, who had been traveling with Eddy for some time, had nearly nothing left of the great wealth of possessions with which they had started. Margaret and Virginia Reed also had the constant worry that James Reed had come to a bad end. They were always searching for signs of his campfires, and worse, they couldn't help looking carefully to see if there was evidence that the Indians had scalped him. When Eddy abandoned his wagon, Margaret Reed took from it only a couple of changes of clothing for herself and each of her four children. Placing these in the Breen wagon, the Reeds themselves traveled with the Donners.

Eddy was in worse shape than the Reeds. His son was only

three years old, and he had an infant daughter. That morning the Eddys had eaten the last of their food except for three pounds of lump sugar, and the Donners could not take everyone in their wagon. Ahead of them lay the long desert stretch from the sink of the Humboldt to the Truckee.

It was now a thinned-out train, only about fifteen wagons remaining, and people were carrying things as they walked to lessen the load pulled by the weak oxen and cattle. One of the Murphey boys trudged along with his family, wearing a copper camp kettle on his head. It was a terribly difficult walk for man and beast alike. In some places the sand and dust were so light and dry that men and animals sank deep into it with every step. In other places the trail crossed ridges of volcanic rock.

When the party finally camped for the night, the Eddy family was still on the desert. Eleanor and William Eddy had eaten nothing all day. Jimmy and the baby had nothing but sugar to suck on. They finally staggered into the camp, only to find that it was a nightmarish place. From a hundred or more holes in the ground, water oozed out hot and bitter. From one of the holes a fountain of steam spewed spasmodically twenty feet into the air. The party took buckets of the hot water and let it cool to lukewarm so they could drink it, despite its bitterness. They would suffer almost anything to quench the awful thirst of the desert.

Tamsen Donner gave Will Eddy a bit of coffee when he came into camp, and he took it to one of the hot pools and prepared it, then gave it to his wife and children. He took none for himself.

There was still twenty miles of desert to cross and the Eddys and others walked in. Eddy was frightened that his children were dying of thirst, and begged Breen, who had a cache of water, to give him just a bit for them.

Breen wasted no words on Eddy or his children. He turned his back and kept on moving across the hot, dry earth.

Eddy asked again, and this time Breen croaked at him, "I need it for my own family! You whine, but you did not take care of your people! Leave me be!"

Eddy's rage broke free. He grabbed for Breen, and shoved him aside. "I'll have that water, by God, and if you stop me, I'll kill you!" He had his hand on his rifle, and his eyes were wild.

Breen stepped aside, and watched with smoldering resentment as Eddy took a small amount of water for his family.

They now traveled at night, avoiding the horrible glare of the sun. Three yoke of oxen failed and died. Near daybreak they saw trees, indicating a river bottom. At last they reached the Truckee, fifty feet wide, with sweet water running clear and pure. There was plenty of grass and wild peas for pasturage, and men and animals had the first ray of hope in months. Sean fell to his knees, pulling handfuls of the grass and putting them to his face. He looked over at the river. "It's the river of heaven," he said.

Mary, Fiona, and Coleen barely looked up. They knelt at the side of the river, scooping handfuls of water to drink, to run over their dry, dusty sunburned faces, and to drink again. With relief came laughter. The dust had turned to mud, and all of them had streaks on their faces. Fiona pointed at her mother. "You look just like those awful Indians!"

Mary laughed, splashed her daughter, then wiped at her face. As Sean completed his own washing and refreshment, she asked, "We will camp here—at least for a little while, won't we?"

"Mama, look," Coleen said. All of them turned to see Eddy making the rounds again, begging the others for food. Both the Graves and the Breen families refused him.

Mary got to her feet, but Eddy had disappeared. It was nearly half an hour later when she saw him again, and he was headed right for their wagon. He had a grim look on his face. "Mr. Eddy," Mary called out, and hurried to meet him. "I tried to catch you before, but you had vanished. Sean and I haven't much left, but we will see your children get something to eat."

It was the first kindness the man had been shown in a long time, and he blinked hard before he thanked her. "Actually, I came by to see if Sean would let me have the use of his rifle for an afternoon. I'm a pretty fair hunter. I'd be glad to bring back whatever I find for you as well."

Sean had been listening. He returned, rifle in hand. "If you'll wait just a moment, Brian said he'd like to go with you. He's not a bad shot himself, and we have no meat either."

The next day Reinhardt and Spitzer caught up with the train, but Wolfinger was not with them. Mrs. Wolfinger, her eyes wide with apprehension, ran up to the two men. "Where is my husband?"

Spitzer put out a hand to her. "The Indians caught us unawares. They poured out of the hills—we didn't even hear them! They came out of nowhere. There was nothing we could do. Your

312

husband was killed right away. They drove us off. We just got away with our lives.''

Mrs. Wolfinger's knees buckled, and Spitzer had to support her. He and Uncle Billy Graves carried her back to her wagon, and some of the women walked with them to help her.

"What happened to all his possessions?" Breen asked.

Reinhardt shrugged. "Whatever there was, the Indians got. They rifled through everything, and then burned the wagons.''

Breen's avaricious little eyes narrowed. "You mean there isn't nothing left of all those jewels and things he had stashed in that wagon?''

"I mean I don't know. I wasn't going to ask them damn redskins if they wanted to give me all them pretties," Reinhardt sneered, walking away.

Paddy wasn't satisfied, and neither was anybody else in camp, but they could do nothing about it now. It was time to move on again. One day's rest was all they dared take. They set out again and for three days toiled up the canyon. The one bright spot was the day seven pack mules and three riders approached them. Charles Stanton, who had gone ahead with McCutcheon, had returned with food and supplies from Sutter's. That night they had flour to bake with, and jerked beef. Those who still had them fired up their Dutch ovens and baked bread. It was a time of brief celebration.

McCutcheon, ill, had stayed behind at Sutter's, but John Sutter had provided Stanton with mules and two vaqueros, Luis and Salvador. Laughing, Stanton said, "We can trust 'em, I've been assured, because they are afraid of Captain Sutter. I believe it. He is a very impressive man, with a very impressive domain. He's got a whole country back there—and it's all his!''

The group around the campfire was livelier that night, for talk centered on Captain Sutter, and Sam Brannan, a man who had led a religious group to California by sea. "They've mostly settled in Yerba Buena, some little town on the coast," Stanton explained, not sure of the location.

"I know those Mormons," Eddy said. "There's a bunch of them in Nauvoo, not too far from where I come from. They are strange folk, but hard workers.''

Lavinia Murphey kept her head down. Others made a few more comments, and she was tempted to admit that she was—or had been—a Mormon. Instead she said, "They aren't forgivin' folk,

313

and they've got a death grip on God. You don't please them, they'll keep the gates of heaven slammed shut against you.''

No one asked how she knew, and she didn't offer information. The talk went on for a time, but all were weary, and soon the fire was low and they slept.

By October 20, they were camped in Truckee Meadows. The weather was cloudy and threatening, and they could see that there was already snow higher in the mountains. But the trail discouraged them. Above Truckee Lake the trail went over cracked and broken domes of granite. Their oxen and cattle were worn and starved. A man could count the ribs of any of the beasts from a hundred feet away. All that was left was skin and bone. The party would have to double- or triple-team to get the wagons over the pass.

That evening as they sat around the campfire they discussed their predicament. Snow had already fallen, and no one knew how much longer really bad weather would hold off. William Pike and his brother-in-law, Will Foster, sat together. Pike was cleaning his pepperbox pistol. From time to time one man would look at the other and make a comment. They got along well, and were glad for the quiet time.

''Somebody get firewood,'' a voice called.

Pike smiled, looking around for the lazy fellow who wanted someone else to go. He handed Foster his gun as he got to his feet. The pistol slipped through Foster's fingers, hit the ground and discharged. Pike barely made a sound. He twisted, his hand reaching up to his back, then he fell to the ground. His wife, Sarah, tried to tend his wound, but an hour later he was dead.

The spirits of the camp sank lower. They buried Pike without coffin, without even a board beneath him, without Reed to pray eloquent words for his soul. As three men dug the grave, the snow fell. The women banded together and mourned. Pike left a widow and two babies. Now William Foster was the only grown man left in the Murphey family.

They continued to camp at Truckee Meadows, but no one felt at ease. They watched the glowering sky, and the gaunt poorly beasts that were to haul them over the mountain pass. It seemed impossible. They remained there for five days, letting the animals rest and eat as much as they could. Then they began to move away from the camp. The Breens went first. They were in the best condition, having hoarded all their food, and having lost the fewest cattle to the Indians. Patrick Dolan, the Keesebergs, the Eddys, Charles Stanton, the Reeds, and the Graveses went with them. The Murphey family made up a second section, and the Donners and McKays brought up the rear.

A day's journey above the meadows, the trail swung to the right, leaving the river, to avoid another canyon. Shortly after that, they crossed another range of mountains. From the top of the range they looked down upon a lush, beautiful valley. Sean and Mary couldn't help being fascinated by the raw beauty of the trail now. They traveled over rolling hills covered with pine and huge trees. On their right loomed the main range of the Sierras.

In the valley below was a cabin that had been built by a group of emigrants who had become winter-bound. Above the cabin was Truckee Lake. From the lake they could see the great wall of the pass that would lead them down from the mountain and to safety. Once they had managed the pass, they would be safe. From the lake to the pass it was about fifty miles. Sean sighed. "It seems longer than all the miles we've already traveled."

Brian managed a short laugh. "But it isn't—thank God."

"Yes, thank God," Mary breathed, and crossed herself.

Fiona shivered, and pulled her coat closer around her. It had turned bitterly cold, and the snow was falling steadily, seeming to keep pace with their slow progress. No one was alarmed, but it kept falling, gently, frigidly.

With a sudden shout, Brian and Sean halted their oxen. In front of them on a steep incline George Donner's wagon broke a front axle. The wagon jolted crazily forward, and Tamsen ran up to it, screaming. Men and women raced to the wagon, rooting through the jumbled household goods, searching for the baby Eliza. Three-year-old Georgia cried out, and her father lifted her free of the tumbled mess. But they couldn't find Eliza, and there was no cry from her to guide them. Frantically, Jake and George, Sean and Brian, pitched goods from the wagon and shoved other things aside. Finally, under bags of goods, they found her unconscious and limp. Tamsen took her into her arms, patting at her face, then shaking the child until she began to breathe and come round.

Tamsen hugged her child, swaying back and forth with her, tears streaming down her face. "Oh, thank God, thank God, my baby, my baby. George—my baby," she sobbed, then began to laugh with relief.

315

Mary, too shaken to speak, turned and threw herself quaking into Sean's arms. "Hold me—just hold me for a minute, please. I'll be all right if you just hold me."

Sean kept his arms around her, but guided her back to their wagon. Fiona and Coleen followed. Both girls' faces were ashen.

Brian helped the brothers cut timber to repair the axle. George did most of the work shaping the wood for the axle. Just as he was nearly finished, his chisel slipped and dug deep into his hand. They were delayed again as Tamsen cleaned and bound the wound.

They were far behind the others, and made camp on October 31 among some trees before they reached the cabin. Snow already was an inch or more deep on the ground, and the cattle had difficulty finding grass. Brian and Sean cut boughs so the cattle could eat those, and Brian used one of the boughs as a broom, cleaning a patch free of snow. It was nowhere near enough, but it was something.

The next morning was still cold, and when they awakened, clouds hung low over the mountain. They couldn't even see the pass. When the weather finally cleared, it was apparent that the pass was solidly covered with snow. They went on, moving slowly along the north side of the lake, sometimes coming so near the edge that they were worried the wagons might slide into the water. The snow was deeper there, and deeper still when the road began to rise to the pass. They reached a point which Brian estimated to be about two and a half or three miles from the pass. The snow was five feet deep. The men and animals were exhausted. Someone found a dead pine filled with pitch and set it afire. The women and children gathered around, trying to warm themselves. Exhaustion was written on every face. Left alone for the moment, the animals moved close to trees and tried to rub their burdens from their backs. The sky was cold lavender. It would be dark soon.

Charles Stanton urged them to make a big push. "I think we can still get through if we go now."

The party was too exhausted to move. They couldn't make a push today.

The Donners made camp in the pines where they had stopped the night before. The McKays camped a bit off, but still some distance from the cabin, which had been taken by the Breens, and a lean-to that had been built onto this by the Kesebergs. Brian made certain that the McKays had a good spot with plenty of fresh water from a small stream that ran near their campsite. He taught them how to build a hut of boughs. They covered it with quilts and other sheets of material and hide that would keep out the wind.

"If we're going to leave soon, why go to so much trouble?" Sean asked, for he was tired, and wanted only to sleep for a while before he faced that pass again.

Brian kept his eyes on his hands as he spoke. "I hope I am wrong, Sean, but I don't believe we are going through that pass tomorrow or any other day until the spring thaw comes."

Sean sat bolt upright. "What do you mean? We can't stay here! We'll starve!" He looked at Mary, then at his daughters huddled together under a comforter. "Or freeze!"

"We can hunt—and fish," Brian muttered, but his voice didn't hold much conviction.

"My God! We've come all this way—for this? No! We can't fail now. We can't!" Sean pleaded with Brian, as though he had a magic that would change things. Brian didn't look up. "Brian? Brian, what will come of these people? How soon will it thaw?"

"If we're lucky—last of March. More'n likely it will be April before the pass clears."

"No!" Sean shouted in protest. "There's not enough food, and there are too many people!"

Brian nodded.

"Is there no way out of this? Can't we do anything?"

"We'll try the pass, Sean. Maybe I'm wrong."

They tried the pass the next day and were driven back again, exhausted. The snow was heavier. None of the McKays had ever seen such drifts as these. A misstep meant disappearing into soft heavy snow and having to be hauled out. They returned to their hut of pine boughs. Sean was heavy with guilt. He looked at Mary, taking both her hands in his. "I have brought us to our death with my foolhardiness, Mary. God forgive me—will you forgive me?"

"Despair will not gain you forgiveness or grace, Sean McKay. We will not die here. Brian, there must be a means of escape. You know these mountains—can we get through the pass?"

"I don't know, but we can try. Perhaps when it is a bit colder, we could get out if we had snowshoes. I could show you how to make them."

"Show us," Mary said firmly. "Girls, gather round. We will be prepared for the day we are to leave. Brian, are you a praying man?"

Brian looked a bit guilty, then grinned. "I am now."

"Good. Ask the Lord to tell you the right day for us to leave. We will trust His word through you."

Part VII

Part VI

Chapter Twenty-Six

As fall came in earnest, Sam Brannan put all his hardships behind him. In October of 1846 he was driving himself hard, and for those who bothered to watch, he put on an astounding display. The Gentry brothers were among those who kept an eye on this Mormon elder, and they liked what he did.

Sam saw himself as a leader, a Saint on a level with Brigham Young, if not above him. He looked around at tiny, sleepy Yerba Buena and saw its prime site, the excellent harbor, the miles of undeveloped surrounding land with abundant prospect not only for growing crops, but also for building houses and businesses. Never one to be reticent, he talked of the fantastic things that would come to pass, but emphasized that he was the only man who could envision what Yerba Buena could become.

Not for other men were the dreams of Samuel Brannan. The others saw hardly as far ahead as next week. Their eyes were on this evening's meal, tomorrow's shoes to be repaired, the next day's worship service; their eyes were on the dailiness of living. Sam Brannan appreciated these concerns, but he looked far beyond to the thousands of new people who would pour into Yerba Buena, to the fine houses that would grace the hills, and the business buildings that would stand stately on wide streets. He saw a courthouse and a town hall, schools, hotels, taverns, shops and stores, even other churches eventually. He saw the bustle of traffic, heard the noises in the streets and the factories, smelled food and smoke and horse manure and the sweat of workingmen and the perfumes of fine ladies. The spectacle was beautiful, and reachable.

Sam could not sit still and wait for anyone to get ahead of him. Ezra Morrison was building a flour mill; Sam built two on Clay Street. Sam performed the first Mormon marriage ceremony in California, sealing Lizzie Winner to Basil Hall. Their wedding party was a grand success, with jollity among the guests, and great quantities of refreshments on hand.

Susannah heard about the wedding through Cameron and Robin, who had been invited. As time passed, and the Mormons continued to exclude Susannah, she realized how isolated she was. During the first weeks of her stay she was very low in spirit. While safe at the Gentry ranch, she was also a captive. For the first time she realized what Sam's dreams would mean to the city, and to her personally. If Sam were wrong about the future of Yerba Buena, then she had no future there, either. But if Sam were right, and Yerba Buena became a thriving city, then new people would come from all over. There would once more be a society she could enter, because it would not be Mormon.

Susannah did well to put her faith in Sam and his dreams, for he was no one to let a day go by if he could fill it with progress. Dr. Elbert C. Jones was a friend of Sam's. Jones, small in stature, was large in heart, and suffering from unrequited love.

Sam could not bear to stand by and see all that passion and energy go to waste. If Elbert Jones couldn't have his true love, then he should have something else. "E.C.," he said heartily, "why don't we start a newspaper together? A great city can't be without a newspaper, so we'd better get a good run on things."

E.C. glanced at the barmaid, who was smiling as she served a table of customers. He sighed. "Sounds good to me, Sam."

"We might need a couple of men to help."

E.C. pointed. "Get Ed Kemble and John Eager. They've got strong backs and uninquiring minds."

Sam chuckled, and hired the two men on the spot. E.C. was the kind of man Sam liked best. When he heard a good idea, there was no need to commiserate over it, chew at it, or pick it over past its time. E.C. agreed, and the deed was done.

In a second-story loft they set up Sam's Washington printing press, which had accompanied him on his travels from New Orleans to Indianapolis to Ohio, thence to New York and California. They began odd-job printing, awaiting the time when

Sam's *California Star* would become the first newspaper in the state.

Ann Eliza Brannan did not fail to notice Sam's preoccupation with business matters. Nor did she fail to notice that she was not the beneficiary of his preoccupations. Ann Eliza, thus neglected, grew peevish.

So at Washington and Stockton streets, Sam began building Ann Eliza a house. Once more he opened himself to criticism. There were complaints from Church members that he was using Mormon labor for personal benefit. Sam had once let such criticism slow him down, but no more. He was hot on the scent of his dream, and nothing was going to distract him, or hinder him—except, perhaps, the liquor to which he turned more frequently.

For a long time the Brannans' was the finest house in town, with two stories, a front and a back porch, and a couple of handsome additions that marched off to the sides. It was surrounded by a whitewashed fence. At the time Ann Eliza was very much pleased with it, but her personal dreams and ambitions outpaced Sam's ability to provide. To build this grand edifice, Sam had had to borrow money. He found himself constantly balancing his own aspirations against the need to appease his wife and her ambitions.

Ann Eliza, the boardinghouse mistress's daughter, was at last at the top of the social ladder, at least in her own eyes. The Brannans were invited everywhere. They danced weekly aboard the *Portsmouth*. When whalers anchored in the cove, Sam and his wife were among the first settlers asked aboard for dining and dancing. When community festivities were organized, it was the Brannans who saw that every detail was perfect, that every socially prominent back was patted tenderly. When the Gentrys entertained, Sam and Ann Eliza were often the center of attraction, if not indeed the guests of honor.

Susannah found these nights almost unbearable, for she was confined to her room, forced to hear the music and laughter, and not able to show her face or participate. Ezra and Tolerance, often without Prudence, came on occasion. Those evenings were filled with long bouts of crying and regret. It was futile for Susannah to tell herself that she'd be attending the next party, where none of the guests would be Saints. With her father nearby, she longed to be reunited with him, but she still needed to remain hidden from the Mormons.

She felt her isolation even more sorely when Cameron and Robin told her of the parties at the magnificent Brannan home, where the handsome looks, wealth, and pleasant manners of the Gentry men made them popular guests. The Brannans' guests included those in positions of great authority: Commodore Stockton; California Governor Richard Mason; and the *alcalde* of Sonoma, Lilburn Boggs, who had traveled with the Donners for a time, and had been Missouri's governor. Sam's gregarious nature had enabled him to find many new friends whom he entertained with relish. However, he did not forget those others whom he considered the backbone of the future of Yerba Buena. E.C. Jones, the Gentrys, Ezra Morrison and his wives, all were wined and dined by Sam Brannan. And by necessity Susannah was excluded from all of it. The one constant fact was that she could not join Mormon society until the furor over Asa's accusations had died down. Susannah remained hidden at the Gentry ranch.

Ann Eliza Brannan, despite her temporary pleasures in the house and the attention she received as first lady of the area, hated California, hated the occasional makeshifts of frontier life. She wanted to return to New York.

While his wife complained, Sam remained busy. Among his other duties, Sam was preparing for the coming of President Brigham Young and his Saints. Upon the *Brooklyn*'s arrival, now over two months ago, Sam had written an extensive report to Brother Brigham. He had taken great pains to describe Yerba Buena's climate, its advantages and many possibilities. He sought Brother Brigham's advice on certain matters, though he knew it was likely he'd have to settle them himself before Young would reply. He had sent the letter east by a man who was going back overland.

That was another thing he had to do—get mail service to Yerba Buena.

Though Sam liked Yerba Buena and the magnificent city it could become, there were two things about it. One, the name was hard to say, at least for Americans. It just didn't sound like the name of a place of import. That would have to be changed. Two, in spite of its favorable location, it was not Zion. It was already too bustling and urban. Zion should be located in a wilderness, lush and green, with sparkling waters, teeming with fish and wildlife, warmed by a golden sun beaming out of pure blue skies. Zion, in other words, was elsewhere.

Sam took three days away from Ann Eliza, and with a few chosen elders went exploring nearby waterways. At the junction of the Stanislaus River and the headwaters of the San Joaquin, they found a land of matchless beauty. The climate was perfect, the soil rich and deep. Wild animals and game birds were in such profusion that they were almost a nuisance. Thousands of elk and antelope and deer grazed in luxurious meadowlands; ducks and geese flew overhead so low they could almost be caught by the feet. In the gleaming river were many varieties of fish and eels. The river provided a convenient waterway to seaports only a few miles away.

"Brethren," said Sam reverently, overwhelmed by God's answer to his prayers. "I believe we have been led to Zion. This is the very Garden of God."

That night Sam could not sleep. He lay wrapped in his blanket, eyes wide to the cold white stars and the glacial moon. He was thinking of Susannah. There was an empty place in the Mormon community where she had been. He began to remember the long sameness of the days aboard the *Brooklyn*. Sometimes he had wished he could go without seeing her face for a while so that he would have a chance to see her from a distance. He had wanted to know if he would miss her. He had wanted to know if he would perceive qualities in her that would not occur to him when she was in his arms. He had wondered if being away from her would point out that he was besotted with a creature formed mainly in his imagination—a distant dream.

Now, to his sorrow, he knew. Whenever Sam let his mind wander from the myriad duties and goals he had set for himself, Susannah was there. She smiled, she moved with her young dignity and grace through the tight web of his days. Lovingly she came into his embrace and lovingly shared herself with him. Of all the women he had ever known, Susannah alone saw him always as hero. And seeing himself through her gaze, he became more.

Sam Brannan had never thought of any woman as essential to his life. He had married because he was expected to, and perhaps because occasionally he tired of pursuing women for a night's pleasure. In his grand scheme the goal and its achievement loomed largest—larger even than himself, certainly larger than women, wife, or family.

And now he found that, in taking Susannah's innocence, he had given her his heart. He yearned for her; he burned for her

325

night after night; his loins went hot with jealousy as he imagined her submitting to the caresses of the Gentry brothers. He wondered, furious, if she made *them* feel stronger, more handsome, better capable of working miracles.

Ashamed of the way his errant thoughts degraded Susannah, Sam fumbled in his satchel for the whiskey bottle. He sipped steadily, damping the memories and the futile desire by building a fire in his gut. But as he finally succumbed to sleep, he had made up his mind. He must see Susannah. He must discover if she was still his.

What he would do about it if she were, he did not know.

Over the next several days Sam was very busy. With company funds he purchased a launch, the *Comet*, and horses and oxen. From his loyal Saints he chose twenty experienced farmers to clear and plant the land of Zion. While they loaded the launch with seeds, food, wagons, and implements, he sought out Ezra.

Ezra was looking hollow-eyed and thin these days. The loss of his daughter had been even more traumatic than that of his son. When he had lost Landry, plans to sail to California had mercifully cushioned the shock. Now that Susannah was gone, he found no satisfactory outlet for the love he had lavished on her, and though he had tried to ignore it, Elisha reminded him too much of Landry. Ezra's whole life, once so rich, seemed barren and unworthwhile. Neither Prudence nor Tolerance could console him. Prudence herself was as low as Ezra was. Tollie had taken Prudence's place, and Ezra didn't know how it had happened or what to do about it.

Sam, knowing himself all that Ezra was suffering, put a comradely hand on Ezra's shoulder. "I have an undertaking for you, Ezra, if you are interested."

Ezra said bleakly, "I shall welcome any extra duties, Sam."

"Soon—in a few weeks—we will need a man who knows the city and business and who is capable of planning the village, the streets, and the workings of commerce for our New Zion of New Hope. Will you be my man?"

"Yes," replied Ezra. They arranged a date when he should leave for the new colony, and discussed general plans.

In a day or two Sam set out for John Sutter's fort near the Sacramento River. He was curious to see it for himself. Sutter had done exactly what Sam planned to do for the Mormons: he

326

had built his own community. And, judging from all Sam heard, it was successful.

On the way to Sutter's, Sam mulled over his various concerns. He was anxious about Brigham Young's bunch of Saints. Things happened to parties going across country. Something might prevent Brigham from bringing the Saints to Sam's freshly established New Hope, God forbid. He prayed that this was just a passing thought.

Well, if New Hope didn't come up to the expectations, then he still had Yerba Buena. That was more to his own liking anyway. A seaport town, with hills on which he'd build a city that would celebrate his name for years to come. Might even call it Brannan City. Sam grinned at the thought, and puffed pensively on his cigar. Regretfully, it didn't ring bells for him. It should be something more Spanish, like—like San Francisco. That was it! Name the town for the bay. People already knew where the bay was. They'd come more readily to a city with a familiar name. Let the bay lend its fame to the city that had none . . . yet.

Satisfied, Sam's thoughts returned to Brigham Young. There ought to be news of him at Sutter's. The Sutter settlement, with New Helvetia as its capital, had been started seven years before, and was now a major trading post for both inhabitants and emigrants. Somebody there would know about a large emigration of Saints, and where they were.

On the way, Sam would stop by the Gentry ranch. He told himself that he wanted to talk with Cameron about coming to *San Francisco* and starting up a business.

San Francisco. Sam threw back his head and laughed exultantly.

Susannah had settled into a routine at the Gentrys'. She missed her family, missed the community of people she had grown up with and their ways of living. With the Gentry family, however, the subject of her past never came up. So she shoved it into a back closet of her mind and closed the door. All she could do now was to go forward into this new life, and make the best of it she could. She still had some of Ezra's money—Cameron was holding it for her until she decided what should be done with it.

Susannah knew now her father had meant for her to have the leftover money, in spite of the way he had told her to keep it. And he had given her clothes to Sam, so that she hadn't had to wear someone else's for very long. Papa still loved her, and she loved him. He would be grateful to her when his son came back to him. When everything was back the way it should have been all along, then Papa would want her to come home.

And she would go—but only for a visit. One thing she had learned was not to trust to love where the Church was concerned. And never again would she place her entire welfare in someone else's hands.

As much as they could, the Gentrys made her a part of their family. So Susannah was given a *dueña*, Doña Felicia. There were two older daughters of the Gentrys, married now, who had grown up under Felicia's all-observant eyes. She would do fine for Susannah.

For Susannah, the constant, watchful attentions of Felicia took some getting used to. It was a raging bore always to have Felicia along when she was with Cameron. She was hardly ever alone with him, and she wanted to be. She quickly realized that he attracted her in a way that both disturbed and thrilled her. She often thought of Sam, but too often lately she had had to make herself think of Sam. Left to its own devices, her mind would wrap itself around Cameron Gentry. She didn't know what to make of him.

As had happened too many times before, she looked up and caught him watching her daydream about him. He'd appeared out of nowhere. Susannah immediately glanced self-consciously at Felicia, but Cameron didn't seem to mind or notice her presence at all. He lounged quietly, gracefully against the stucco pillar of the courtyard wall. The sun beat down on him, making his skin glow more golden than ever. His eyes sparkled, the light brown color also appearing golden in the light. Susannah couldn't handle that deep, penetrating glance. She squirmed, then blushed and was forced to look away from him. Why didn't he say something? What was he doing to her? She began to greet him, then realized she had waited too long and would now sound ridiculous saying "Hello, Cameron." She blushed again, and realized he had made her wait too long. She began to feel angry. How dare he control her with those long, pensive looks of his!

As her eyes gleamed with anger, he smiled slowly, bestirred himself, and sauntered over to sit near her. "You've been out in the sun too long. Your face is red," he said mischievously. "It is the sun, isn't it?"

"Yes," Susannah hissed. "It is the sun. What else could it be?"

He still hadn't taken his eyes off her. Curiosity, appreciation, and speculation were in his gaze. "That's what I was wondering. What else might cause that heightened color?"

Susannah grabbed her skirts and stood up. "You are getting to be just like Robin!"

Cameron shook his head. "No, I'm not. Robin wouldn't ask you if you'd like to take a ride. Would you?"

With a quick pang, Susannah tried to think of Sam. She couldn't get a picture of him. She should not want to ride with this man, but she did. She wanted him to take her out this afternoon, talk to her, touch her. She wanted to be near him. He didn't say much, and all his movements were spare, but he exerted a special force on her. She gave up trying to maintain better judgment and smiled. "Yes, I'd love to go for a ride, but does Felicia have to come with us?"

Cameron could barely keep his mouth straight, but he managed to scowl, and say, "She certainly does. You wouldn't want to be thought improper?"

Susannah considered a moment, then flirted with him a bit. "Of course not, and you wouldn't want that either—would you?"

Cameron, she had discovered happily, was an affectionate man. He frequently put his arm around her, sometimes both arms, looking down and smiling at her from his lovely height. But his embrace could hardly have been more brotherly. She didn't understand his brotherliness, nor did she understand why it bothered her. If she loved Sam so much, she could not possibly feel such a strong attraction to Cameron. She tried again to convince herself it was like having Landry around. Cameron was as dear as Landry, as much fun to share secrets with, and their minds were even more alike than hers and Landry's. Between her and Cameron was a magnetic force that drew them to sit near each other in a group, to seek each other's eyes and approval. Somehow that didn't seem brotherly.

At the height of autumn's warmth the Gentrys gave a *fandango*—Susannah's first. The *fandango* was an informal dancing party Rowena planned ahead. She had sent one of the Mexican boys around to the neighbors with notes of invitation. Neighbors might live ten miles away, but neighbors they were.

As the evening began, Susannah got a surprise. Cameron had told her not to wear one of her best dresses, but would not explain why, just grinned. She had supposed that he was making some joke and she had missed the point. She dressed quite prettily, she thought, in a burnt-orange velvet gown with long fitted sleeves and a becoming lace collar. As she came out of her bedroom door, Cameron sneaked up behind her and cracked an egg on her head. The egg had been blown out beforehand and filled with bits of gold and silver paper, which scattered all through her hair and down into her lace collar and stuck on the velvet fabric.

She squealed in alarm. "What did you do that for?"

Cameron grinned widely, hands on hips. "That's first blood."

"And this is second," said Robin, breaking another egg on her head. This one contained cologne, fortunately a light fragrance.

She did not know whether to laugh or cry. She stood there, covered with sparkles of paper and smelling of somebody's scent, looking in bewilderment from one grinning man to the other. Before she recovered, Robin swung Susannah up onto Cameron's shoulder and, kicking her heels against his chest and giggling in spite of herself, she was carried through the house at an unfamiliar altitude.

They put her down in front of Rowena, who seemed to have decided to wear her old painting clothes, a gold satin gown liberally smeared and streaked with all colors. She was laughing too. "They wouldn't let me warn you, Susannah," she said. "But if you really care about the gown, you'd better go put on something less valuable. Otherwise you'll end the evening like this." She glanced down at herself ruefully.

"I don't understand," said Susannah.

"It's just part of the Royal Californian Welcome," said Robin, starting to grin as he saw that she remembered Sam's mud-wallowing introduction to the state. "We throw a little bit of dye around, break *cascarones* on people's heads, paint faces—a few friendly things like that." He waited, watching her expression closely.

Susannah recalled with mortification how badly she had taken the joke on Sam. This time she'd go along with California ways if it killed her. She lifted her head, her eyes blazing. "I guess I can spare a gown."

Robin's eyes lighted with approval as they met Cameron's.

"Good girl," he said, chuckling. Cameron's eyes on her shone with pride.

"Do I get ammunition too, or am I the only target in this war?" she asked pertly.

"Everybody gets ammunition." Robin picked up a tray of little vials and offered them to her. "Here, have some purple dye. The idea is to—" He ducked, laughing as she flipped some onto his shirt front and his ear. "I see you get the idea." Casually, he wiped his ear with his finger, then lightning quick, smeared a streak down Susannah's face. She flinched, but found herself laughing.

"Where do you get the eggs?" she asked.

"The servants prepare them," Rowena replied. "We try to have a dozen for each guest."

Their conversation was interrupted by a series of Indian whoops from outside.

"Company's here," said Cameron and Robin, both grabbing vials of dye and hurrying toward the hitching racks. The women followed, to see the fun. Carl Gentry was helping a woman down from her carriage, and at the same time she was smearing streaks of red stuff down his cheeks and across his nose. Robin and Cameron had mounted their horses and, laughing wildly, were chasing three well-dressed young men in crazy circles around the yard. When they came back some time later, all five men were oozing several colors of paint and dye and laughing jovially together.

Susannah had completely forgotten that she might be decorated too, and so was unprepared when short little Farley Masters, dripping blue and green from his red whiskers, grabbed her, kissed her, and nuzzled her face and neck. Everyone found it hilarious, so Susannah joined in.

But there must have been something in her face that said how little she liked this idea, for Cameron, smiling, put his arm around her and pretended to hide her behind him. Feeling bolder with his warmth so close to her, she stuck her head out and declared, "I'll get all of you later!"

Everyone who arrived went through the painting ritual. Some were more successful than others at evading first blood, but eventually all were striped, streaked, and spotted.

The dancing was the most fun. There were many dances that Susannah didn't know, but she had plenty of partners willing to

331

teach her. While Cameron took his turn playing the piano, with others playing harmonica, violin, and banjo, Robin danced with her. She had many offers to dance, and took them, before Cameron claimed her again.

"Let's get a drink and sit this one out," he suggested.

They got cool glasses of lemonade made with a dark red California wine, a drink that seemed to both quench the thirst and warm the blood. They walked in the gardens, sipping their drinks, with Cameron's arm around her. After a few moments they were alone, behind some tall-growing plants with harsh-scented red blossoms.

Susannah's heart began to beat faster when Cameron took her glass and set it with his at the base of the plants. When he straightened back up, he said softly, "Come here."

"You come," she said, feeling impish.

He pulled her body against his with a thud, wrapping her so completely in his long-armed embrace that she felt deliciously imprisoned. She put her face against his bare neck, burrowing, and nearly choked as she inhaled his scent.

"You smell a regular treat, Cameron." He was a favorite target of the women, who had to catch him seated or bending over, to douse him with cologne.

"It's just good old California water," he murmured. "Find it in any drainage ditch."

She raised her head, hoping he would kiss her, but his eyes were far away. He was slowly rubbing his hand up and down her side, and that was nice, so she subsided against him with a small sigh of contentment. It would be better if he would kiss her, and make love to her, but he never seemed to want that. Vaguely, she wondered something, so she asked, "What do you think of when you are holding me?"

He drew away just enough to look down at her. "Things. Like how soft and shiny your hair is . . . like what smooth skin you have . . . and how good it feels with you here. Nothing startling. What do you think of?"

"Oh . . . how strong you are, and how clean you always smell, and what a fine person you are . . . and how I . . ."

"How you what?" he asked lazily, his lips against her forehead.

Had she answered, she would have revealed too much. But the foliage parted suddenly, and two of Robin's friends were upon them, squirting dye and breaking *cascarones* on their heads,

332

cackling in glee. Cameron tried to shield Susannah, but finally let her go with a rueful smile. The two youths picked her up in a quickly formed hand chair and bore her back to the party. Someone else there poured wine over the threesome, in spite of which they went on dancing.

Later the wild music stopped, and Carl and Rowena invited their guests to wash up. Some time after that everyone emerged from bedrooms, faces clean, coiffures repaired, clothes changed, and smelling less violently of several colognes.

The dancing began with a waltz, led by Carl and Rowena, Cameron and Susannah, and Robin with a svelte blonde, Merrily Watts. This was a time of the most courtly behavior, in exaggerated contrast to the obstreperous revelry with which the evening had begun. There was no snatching a young lady from the arms of her partner, no careful planning before pouncing upon a hapless victim with paint or scent. Gentlemen bowed before ladies to request each dance; the ladies were at their most captivating.

The supper began about midnight. There was cold chicken and roast beef, quail and squirrel and hummingbird, salads of fruits and of vegetables, cakes and puddings, and various dainty sweetmeats. The supper was washed down with generous libations of champagne and a native port wine of which Carl Gentry seemed very proud. Everyone drank astonishing quantities, including Susannah, who did not understand when Cameron put his hand over her glass, indicating that she was not to be served any more. She felt like squabbling with him over that, but the words tangled themselves on her tongue and she wound up giggling.

That night when he escorted her to her bedroom, neither one could walk very straight, and they found this hysterically funny. They exaggerated their condition, pretending to bump into the walls, and reaching out for things and missing. At her door they stood looking at each other. She leaned against the door frame; he loomed over her with a big hand on the wall beside her.

He had a way of saying her name, tenderly, ruefully, lovingly, when she had done something idiotic, or something that pleased him, or when he was at a hopeless loss for other words. He said it now, shaking his head with a little smile, drawing out the phrase a bit. "Oh . . . Susannah."

Her reply sounded lonesome, soft and far away. "Kiss me goodnight, please, Cameron."

He leaned toward her, his lips forming the very beginning of a kiss, then just as she might have shut her eyes, he kissed her hair.

She hated herself for pleading, but it would mean so much. "Please . . ."

He was holding her at last, his loins pressed against hers, his hard chest crushing her breasts, the heat of him making her shake with passion. He said, "Not tonight."

She almost asked him again. Just in time, she caught herself. He would think her a loose woman. Cameron wanted only to be her friend. She couldn't think of a satisfactory reply, so after some silence, while she felt the surging of his heart under her cheek, she said, "Thank you for a lovely party."

His eyebrow went up and gave her a knowing smile. Then he let her go and moved away down the corridor.

Chapter Twenty-Seven

On a warm morning late in October Susannah was baking pies, a task she was very good at, and one that the Gentrys appreciated. The sun was big in the sky, and the high-ceilinged kitchen was sweltering even though the windows were open to the breeze. Sweat ran down Susannah's back; her hair was a mass of curls that clung to her pink neck and cheeks; there was flour down her dress. Susannah was as happy as she had ever been. Even with a *dueña* in constant attendance, she was experiencing a kind of freedom she had never known before. For the first time in her life, she was learning to do something both useful and ornamental, and there was a man who would appreciate it when it was done. Maybe two men, for Robin might be back today.

She opened the oven door. "Are they ready to come out yet?" she asked plump Zama, whose artistry with food was praised by every guest who ever came to Agua Clara.

Zama flicked a glance at the amberine meringue on a lemon pie. "Let it get browner in the hollows, Susannah. You know how Señor Cameron likes meringue, *casca* tan. It enhances the flavor."

Rowena was cleaning chickens for the noon meal. "You are surely more patient than I, Susannah. Zama gave up teaching me to cook years ago. I could never wait to get things out of the oven." Rowena Gentry, for all her other pleasing traits, was a terrible cook.

"That is why you have me, Señora." Zama laughed. "With my cooking I feed the body and lift the spirit."

"Ah, *perfecto*!" said Susannah. The meringue was just two shades lighter than Cameron's eyes. She placed the pie on the rack to cool beside others. "I'm going out to the pump and cool off for a minute."

She took the water bucket, which always needed filling, and stepped the short distance to the well. The water here was cool and sweet, and she drank a gourd dipperful before letting the water flow over her arms and hands. She wetted her perspiring face and let it dry in the dry air. While she pumped the bucket full, she gazed over the fields toward the trail that led to Yerba Buena or Sacramento.

A solitary rider was moving down the trail. He was too far away to distinguish, though she shaded her eyes and even tried the telescope trick Sam had taught her, looking through a small hole in her fist. Cameron was in the fields, and it could not be Robin. Nobody sat tall and beautiful in the saddle as the Gentry men. Then the rider disappeared behind a hill, and she knew from experience it would be ten minutes before he would appear again. She picked up the bucket and went back inside.

"A stranger's coming along the trail," she said.

"I'd relish company for a while," said Rowena.

After a few minutes Susannah went outside again, followed by Rowena and Zama. The horseman was much nearer now. Suddenly, with a great lurching of her heart, Susannah knew who it was.

Then he was there, leaping off his horse, arms outstretched toward her. She ran into the welcome refuge of his embrace, laughing, panting, crying, incoherent with ecstasy at seeing him again. Their lips met and clung, their bodies were pressed loins to loins, breast to breast, and all the old emotions sprang once more to life.

"God in heaven, how I have missed you!" he said, drawing back from her to look warmly into her eyes. "I have thought of you every day and every night."

"And I of you," she replied, though now that he was here, she sinkingly realized that something was different between them. Cameron lurked in the back of her mind. That his mother was watching her with Sam disturbed her.

He was still looking at her face. He said quietly, "But there have been some changes, my beautiful one, haven't there?" He pulled her to him again, pressing her face against his breast, and after a while he released her. He said, "Time, you thief."

She clung to his hand, searching his eyes. "I'll never love anyone else the way I love you, Sam," she cried, feeling bewildered and false and a little desperate.

Felicia was hurrying toward them, scowling and scolding. In Felicia's bright eyes Susannah could see just how deeply her impulsive behavior had offended, and she felt frightened. She was standing on a dirt road on a California ranch between her past and her future. She tightened her grip on Sam's hand, but her awareness of Felicia and Rowena was acute. Past and Future—she didn't want to lose either, and yet she knew she could not have both. She looked back at Sam. "I must tell you the Gentrys are strict. We will have almost no chance to be alone, even to speak together."

Sam glanced toward Felicia. "I am still your elder, my dear. I shall be afforded the courtesy of counseling one of my Church members. Do not worry."

Susannah smiled, but the uncomfortable, troubled look was still in her eyes. There were many things she wanted to talk with Sam about, that was true, and the Gentrys were bound to understand that. Most of all, and first, she wanted to know about her family. "Sam, how—"

She was interrupted by a torrent of angry Spanish from Felicia.

To stall off her scolding as long as possible, and perhaps to ease it, Susannah said, "Felicia, this is Elder Samuel Brannan, my—my priest."

Felicia's eyes flashed angrily. "A Mormon *padre?* You, Señor, are a *padre?* What kind of *padre* is it, who takes liberties with my young señorita in the road?" She turned to Susannah. "You must come with me now, Señorita. It is not proper for a young *doncella* to be alone with a man, even her *padre.*"

Susannah was dismayed. She wasn't certain what to do.

Sam said respectfully, "Doña Felicia, you cannot deny Susannah the comfort of her religion. Whether you like me or not, I am her *padre.* Please remember that."

Felicia dipped a curtsey. "As you say, Elder Brannan." Her mouth was a thin line of dislike and disapproval, but Sam and Susannah walked side by side in front of her.

It was strange, thought Susannah, how much more tension was created between them when she knew she could not touch Sam.

337

She looked up at him, and they smiled. They still loved, still desired each other, and it was still just as difficult as on board the *Brooklyn*.

But even that fact was today making Susannah uncomfortable. There was a new factor—her feeling of loyalty and the closeness she shared with Cameron. She didn't know what to call it. It could not be love, she was sure of that. This hungry desire with Sam was love. Cameron had never even kissed her.

"How long will you stay?" she asked.

"I want to talk with Cameron and Robin, so I suppose a night or two. Perhaps we can slip Felicia sleeping powders."

His face showed that he was teasing, partly. But Susannah was surprised to find that she was glad Felicia would be standing guard.

Rowena waited for them on her porch, Macushla by her side. She was polite, and welcomed Sam in a friendly manner, but there was a reserve in her that Susannah didn't fail to note.

Once in the house, Rowena had Sam shown to a room and given fresh water with which to wash. Rowena insisted he have a bite to eat, as lunch was two hours away. Susannah was very nervous. When she was reserved and impersonal in talking to Sam, he watched her behavior with calculating interest. But when she allowed her true feelings to show, and tried to be friendly and share her joy in his presence, she could feel Rowena assessing her relationship with Sam. It brought Susannah down to a level of wishy-washy indecisiveness. She couldn't even decide which pie to offer Sam. Finally, thinking of Cameron's preference, she cut the fruit pie and put a piece for Sam on a handsome china plate.

She was glad she had had the forethought, for the next moment Cameron came in from the fields. He hugged his mother, he hugged her, he put out a friendly hand to Sam. "Good to see you again, Sam. You don't look any the worse for your troubles of late," he said, and laughed, then turned to Susannah. In his eyes she saw the same speculative assessment she had seen in his mother's. She felt she and Sam were naked and exposed, and she was ashamed.

"Any of that pie left for me?"

Susannah, jolted into action, felt herself go pink. "Fruit or lemon meringue?"

"You know what I like," he said curtly, as if he were angry.

338

Her blush flamed deeper and her hand shook. She could feel Sam's eyes on her back as she tried to get the slice of pie centered on the plate.

Cameron smiled tightly at Sam, speculation back in his eyes. He glanced at Susannah's high color and frowned. He dragged his attention back to his guest. "Tell us about Yerba Buena."

Sam had not missed Cameron's unspoken question about Susannah, and he realized Cameron had not meant for him to miss it. Cameron Gentry was a quiet man, but a powerful one. Sam smiled, challenged by the man who had declared himself a rival, and a formidable one. He wondered if Susannah had told Cameron about their relationship, or if Cameron had conclusions of his own. He looked at Susannah now. Then Sam smoothly turned the conversation to matters that would interest and concern Cameron. They were deep in business matters by the time the women went to prepare lunch.

"Cameron, you must come to San Francisco. Join me and make your mark on the city. Men like you and me and your brother must buy up every acre we can. With all my being, I know this city will grow and become a force in this country. In the next few years the price of land will skyrocket. Get in on the ground floor, man. Not only will you be rich in ten years, but the city needs men such as you."

There were many things about Sam that Cameron did not particularly like, not the least of which was his relationship with Susannah. Sam was an opportunist, and Cameron didn't entirely trust that in him, yet on the other hand, he recognized Sam as a true visionary.

Sam was too impatient to wait for Cameron's response. "I've invested ever penny I own, and every penny I've been able to borrow. I have a divine conviction about this. So far, I own two flour mills, a little tavern, the biggest house in town, and the start of a newspaper. Two men are running a tanning business for me. I may sound boastful to you, but I believe in myself, I believe in this territory, and especially this city. But we need a special breed of men to bring the dream to reality."

Cameron raised his eyebrows, and took a deep breath, exhaling slowly. He was thinking of the money and land he and Robin already had in Yer—San Francisco. "I'll talk it over with Robin. You're a convincing man, but as you said, this will take some special men—and thought."

Sam grinned confidently now. "You'll be glad you joined me—after you decide. When I leave here, I'm going to Sutter's Fort. Shall I stop here on my way back so we can ride to San Francisco together?"

Cameron laughed with genuine amusement. "Confident, aren't you?"

Robin arrived home, and Sam started in immediately trying to persuade him to come to San Francisco as well. But Robin was even more closemouthed than his brother. He said flippantly, "Nope, don't want to be tied down, Sam. I walk my own road."

Sam Brannan did not like being thwarted, or lied to, and right now both things were happening. But the look in Robin's eyes reflected a steely will. He would have to bide his time, waiting for Robin to unfold his plans at his own convenience.

For Susannah that evening was incomparable. The Gentrys genuinely liked each other and bantered together in a happy way. She sat quietly, looking from handsome Sam to handsome Cameron and Robin. Being able to watch the three men so close together, Susannah had several strong and conflicting feelings. She really did not know where she belonged. Everything in her life had changed so quickly and so drastically. She looked at Sam, and some of the old feelings flared to life in her, but then she would look at Cameron, and a deep-down longing stirred her.

She barely caught herself in time to keep from shaking her head in sad resignation. How could she feel such longing? Cameron was merely a friend. His tightest embrace had been purest friendship, and he had never kissed her lips at all. If Sam had taught her nothing else, it was that when a man loved a woman, he wanted her in every way it was possible to have her.

At bedtime Robin rose and graciously offered to see Sam to his room. So Susannah said goodnight to him with the others. Rowena was watching, and Cameron moved close and put his hand lightly under her arm. They knew! They all knew! Robin's eyes caught Cameron's, and she realized it was another example of the silent communication between the brothers. She had always known that Robin did not believe that she and Sam were merely elder and parishioner, but now she realized that Cameron too recognized it—and didn't like it.

She turned to follow the others upstairs, but Cameron retained his light pressure on her arm. After the others disappeared into the upper hallway, he led her out into the fragrant courtyard. Susannah, half excited, half frightened, started when Macushla came out from her nest, tail wagging joyously to follow them. Cameron sternly pointed a finger and the dog slunk away.

They walked about the bricked and stuccoed courtyard, enjoying the night air, the scent of flowers, the clean mist of the water from the fountain. Then Cameron said, "Mormons often have more than one wife, don't they?"

Susannah tried to speak, but stumbled over her words. She tried again, and managed only a simple, "Yes."

"Is that why Sam came here today—to talk to you about marriage?"

Susannah's heart was beating against her chest wildly. "No—no, Sam told me about Mama and Papa—and Tollie. He wanted to see you and Robin. He—" she said, and choked, then she went on, "He's my spiritual adviser—my elder."

Cameron laughed bitterly. "And what am I?"

"My—my friend," Susannah gasped out.

"And what if I courted you?"

"I don't know," she said, and wished her pulse were not so frantic. She couldn't think, and was certainly not saying what she wanted to say. "I never thought—"

Again his laugh had an edge to it she didn't understand. With a quick, unexpected move, he brought her behind a heavy cluster of large-leafed plants. He was holding her lightly around the shoulders, their bodies barely touching. Susannah could say nothing. She was aware to her nerve ends of the warmth of him, and of the sudden shift of her thoughts and feelings. She was aware of his bigness and muscularity. His big, strong hands caressed her shoulders gently, almost kneading them as his lips touched her forehead, her cheeks, and the tender pulse spot at her temples. She stood with her face lifted to him, eyes half closed in hungry anticipation.

"Susannah," he said, his voice rough.

Then his long, familiar body curved against hers as his hands slid slowly down her back and he lifted her off the ground and met her mouth with the sweetness of his own. It was marvelous,

341

feeling so light, being held so firmly while his lips ravished hers. Her veins sang with a tumult of joy. She tingled with the thrill of his muscular chest pressing against her breasts, of his lean belly and his pelvis thrust against her in an unashamed revelation of desire.

Gradually he lowered her and she stood on tiptoe, wanting this rush of delight to go on forever. Then the tip of his tongue swept as light as a butterfly across her lips. Involuntarily she drew in a breath, as a throb of passion possessed her. Her head went back, held by his arm. Her mouth opened to him. She could feel his hardness and heat growing, and an answering heat in her own body. Their tongues met and slid along the other slowly, sensuously. All the while, in Susannah's body, tremors of ardent elation rippled back and forth, upwards and downwards.

He stopped kissing her for a moment, as though regretting what he had started. Mesmerized by the dearness of him and forgetting any maidenly reserve, she ran her hand down the pounding pulse at the side of his muscular neck, then inside his open shirt to the hair on his chest, and laid her warm fingers full on his bare breast. He shuddered. She could hear his quickly indrawn breath. For a long delectable moment her fingertips moved with exquisite pleasure over the rigid knot of his nipple. Then she slid her hand out and pressed her palm to his cheek. For so long she had wanted to touch him thus. "Oh, Cameron," she sighed against his skin. She could feel the tremors in his arms around her. With her cheek pressed to his breast, she heard the turbulent racing of his heart. She knew her own would sound the same.

For some time they did not speak, and moved only to increase the intimacy of their contact. He held her as though his arms could never grow tired of her, his chin nestled in her fragrant hair. It was a moment of intense, waiting passion, and yet of contentment with the perfection of their embrace.

Suddenly he picked her up as though she weighed less than a spray of daisies, and carried her to a small alcove in the garden. He lay her down on the moon-dappled ground, and stretched his length beside her. He put his muscular arm under her neck for a pillow. Gently he caressed her hair, her cheek, and with his fingers traced the outline of her lips.

Susannah was wild with wanting him. Her pulse thundered

with desire. Her hands ached to know all the mounds and hollows of his firm, virile body, to realize the hairy roughness of his bare flesh against the silkiness of her own, to have the soft, hard heat of him thrusting into her. She began to tremble, experiencing it all in her mind, her entire being receptive, open, melting with the need to share herself with him in loving.

Cameron was in no hurry, though he too shook with passion. He turned her so that she lay facing him, their bodies tight together. Still leisurely, he began kissing her closed eyelids, her ears, the corners of her mouth. At the neck of her dress, he kissed her throat, his lips moving from side to side on her warm, yielding flesh. The touch of him, the breath of him, roused a sweet aching in her that she knew would never be stilled until they had become one.

He felt the same, she knew. At any moment his strong, gentle hands would move into new territory, and he would stake his claim on her. But she dared not do the same to him. She had been too bold in caressing his breast. Now she must confine her caresses to his hair, his neck, shoulders, arms, and wait for him.

His tongue moved silkenly across her lips, and Susannah responded with a moan of anguish. She moved so that both her arms could be around his back and the fullest embrace become possible. Casually, as though he hardly realized what he was doing, he put a long leg over her body. All her responses were ungoverned now; she pressed closer to him.

His kiss became deeper, more determined, much less loving. She sensed the difference in him, subtle though it was. She squirmed away from him. "Cameron, don't."

"Don't what?" he whispered lazily. "Don't stop?" He ran his fingers down her bare arm, and the simple touch of him tingled the whole way down to her hands. "Do you say 'don't' to Sam?"

Susannah was hardly breathing. A cold, frightening sickness was spreading through her. Her emotions were in a frenzy, wanting him, knowing he wanted her now after all these weeks of what she had assumed to be mere friendship. Yet that cold feeling told her she could not let him take her. Something was horribly wrong.

She said, "Take me back to the house."

"In a few minutes." His hand was gentle, stroking her hair; his thumb moved across her cheek. "Susannah—" He dropped a

343

light kiss on her forehead. "I am not a man who will share his woman with another man—any man."

"Share me?" Susannah said weakly, playing dumb. "But you do. You share me with Robin and Felicia all the time."

"It's too late to protest your innocence, Susannah."

Her startled eyes met his. She was glad that he could not see her blush, or read the humiliation in her eyes.

He went on, "You are a woman who knows the ways of love."

"You think that because I touched your breast," she said, head down.

He made a little sound. "How naive you are in some ways, and so worldly in others. No, I knew long before that. It is in your eyes, and the willingness of your lips, and the anticipation of your embraces."

Susannah tried to move away, but his leg kept her firmly in her place. "It is Sam Brannan," he said without rancor. "Preacher or not, you two have known each other. I don't want you telling me what it was, or is. I'm afraid I have guessed already."

She wanted to deny it, to say there was nothing between her and Sam. But as Cameron had said, she had already told him everything by her actions. She looked at him, her eyes searching his.

Her voice was little more than a whisper. "I have made a terrible mess of things, haven't I? I didn't mean to, you know. Cameron, can you believe that? I never meant—"

He put his finger to her lips, and kissed her gently on the forehead. "I know, Susannah. I do know."

Chapter Twenty-Eight

Sam was eager to be on his way, and was traveling the following morning. Susannah, with Felicia hovering suspiciously nearby, managed to talk with him. They sat decorously apart, having at Felicia's insistence put a small table between them. There was a good deal of constraint on Susannah's part, for she had slept poorly, and had gone over everything that Cameron had said and done. She felt pale and frail today, and very much alone as she struggled to understand what was right and wrong in her life.

There were things she had to find out about Sam and herself. She said, "Sam, when you come back, I want to return to Yerba Buena with you."

He was not quick enough to hide his dismay. He tried; he contrived to look merely surprised as he replied, "My dear, you can't possibly."

She said coolly, "I take it you have dismissed me from the Church?"

He put out a pleading hand. "Susannah, I had no choice. The rumors about your disappearance became vicious. Some people preferred to believe Asa's story. Most of them felt you were a fallen woman and left for that reason." At her angry, mutinous look he added, "The elders made the decision for me."

"So between your ambition and myself as a human being, ambition won as always. I rather expected it would."

"Susannah, you are being unfair. I had no choice, I tell you! You admitted to me yourself that you had taken your father's money. I could not in good conscience condone your actions. We've been through all this before. Let us not spoil precious time in a fruitless quarrel."

"Very well, Sam. Suppose I choose to live in Yerba Beuna?"

He paled with concern. "Surely you are not seriously considering that! Susannah, believe me, I am thinking only of you when I say that no Mormon family would take you in. You could not even support yourself. You have no skills—"

"I can make tents," she said tersely.

"Everyone in town knows the rumors about you. Who is going to trust you? My dear girl, I don't know why you have gotten this idea, but the worst thing you can do is come back where your name has been blackened, and hope to make any sort of life for yourself."

"You have done quite a remarkable job on me in the name of God, Sam Brannan. What won't you sacrifice to your ambition? How can you sit there and tell me I have no means by which to make a living, I cannot return to Yerba Buena for no one will ever trust me, and if they should, the Saints will teach them better. Where do you suggest I go, then? I have no other home. Or have you and the Saints decided the Gentrys—miserable Gentiles that they are—should take care of me for the rest of my life? Or perhaps all you chosen of God would prefer I wander out toward the mountains, so that in your services you can lament an apostate dying at the hand of the Lord?"

Sam stared at her, his mouth open in shock. "My God, Susannah!"

"What is it?" She fought for control of her voice. "Should I be more grateful for what has been done for me? After all, this most certainly *should* lead me onto the right path."

Sam put on his professional face. "You are so bitter. It can only harm you. I know the things I must tell you are harsh things, but I *am* telling you for your own good and protection."

"Aside from allowing the Gentrys to continue to care for me, where do you suggest I go, Sam?"

He leaned forward and spoke to her very confidentially. "My best advice to you is to attract the interest of some eligible young man and make a marriage."

Susannah laughed. "Since you don't *suggest* I go near Yerba Buena, I take it you mean I should marry Robin or Cameron—or perhaps you have a ranch hand in mind for me?"

"Susannah," he said severely, "I am trying to give you my best advice. Your bitterness and sarcasm do nothing to enhance the situation. Both Robin and Cameron seem to treat you with affection. Perhaps one might fall in love—"

She said tightly, "A man fell in love with me once, and I with him. Look how I have benefited. I lost my Church, my family, and my virtue, while the man is rising in his vocation and expects to build a city, a city he does not want me to enter."

His face went dull red. "I do not deserve blame for all that, and you know it. These losses you speak of are not trivial—nevertheless, you have sustained them because of your own actions. Think on that. In each case it was a step you took which led to your present situation."

Her voice rose. "And you had no influence over me!"

Sam said softly, "I did not lie when I said I loved you. Only yesterday you said the same to me. Men and women in love do not always act in the best interests of the loved one. I will not apologize, for I would be insulting you by intimating that my words would restore your former life. Do you wish to leave here?"

Susannah had not entirely understood her own motives for attacking Sam. Certainly she had not expected him to voice the harsh truths he had, nor had she expected her own bitterness. She had not even known it was present until it all slipped out her mouth. She had hoped she could return to Yerba Buena someday, but if Sam were right about the strength of the feeling against her, where would she go, if not there? She couldn't expect to remain here at Agua Clara forever. She had to plan for the day she would leave. She said slowly, "I'm not ready yet. But sometime soon, I may be."

As she hesitated, Sam said, "Don't do anything in haste, Susannah. Give your present circumstances every chance to improve. If later on I can do anything, just ask me."

Later in the day Susannah stood with Rowena, waving good-bye as Cameron rode a distance with Sam. After the men had gone, Susannah wondered nervously if Cameron and Sam would speak of her. She closed her eyes in dismay as she remembered all that Sam had said to her. If he repeated all that to Cameron, or if Cameron decided to ask Sam point-blank what was between Sam and herself, she didn't know what would happen. Sam could influence Cameron in such a way that he would never care for her as someone to marry—and perhaps hereafter would not even want to be her friend. Finally, so uncomfortable she couldn't bear it, she went to her room and lay on her bed staring mindlessly at the wall, awaiting Cameron's return.

She didn't have an opportunity to talk with him until the following day, and by that time she was beginning to understand that Cameron was a man who valued honesty above almost all else. She decided to tell him everything she could about her life with the Latter-Day Saints, and hope that he might be able to understand her and her actions better, even if he had never lived as a Saint.

When she had finished, Cameron sighed. "I find it difficult to believe that your people could actually be as vindictive as you claim. And yet, here you are, and I know the circumstances that brought you here." He shook his head. "Yours are a strange people."

"I am no longer a Saint, Cameron. Before I came here, I lived as I had been taught. I knew nothing else."

Susannah had little hope that he would understand, but as he looked at her, there was warmth and an admiration in his eyes that she had never before seen there. He took her hand and led her to the courtyard. They walked through the gardens, and sat by the fountain. He kept their conversation light, and away from the topic of the Saints or Susannah's transgressions.

A few days before they expected Sam to return, Susannah knew it was time for her to make plans to assure her own future. Cameron had remained friendly to her, but again it seemed a strictly brotherly friendship. If she had learned nothing else, it was that she did not want to be his sister. It left her with little choice. She would maintain his charade, and, like a sister, would ask his assistance in building security for herself. Then she would leave Agua Clara. Perhaps one day she would meet him again, and it would be different between them.

She approached him in private. With a smile she said, "Cameron, I know you have helped me often in the past, but might I turn to you one last time?"

He looked up, his eyebrow raised, a smile already twitching at the corner of his lips. "One last time—so dramatic, Susannah."

She sat a proper distance from him, her hands folded neatly on her lap. "I didn't mean it to be. I have been thinking that it is time for me to see to my future. Sam has told me of the difficulties I will have in trying to establish myself in Yerba Buena—''

"San Francisco," he corrected her.

"Yes, San Francisco. I—I still have Papa's money, and I would like to invest it. Will you guide me?"

The humor was wiped from his face instantly. He had never felt comfortable about that money, and now he was less so. "If you want to do something with the money, why don't you make peace with your father?"

Her mouth fell open. Make peace with Papa? Go to Papa and ask forgiveness when she had taken the money as much for his benefit as hers? She shook her head. "That would be the same as saying I forgive him for everything he has done to Landry and me."

"Yes, it would be."

"But I couldn't . . ."

Cameron's eyes were hard as he said, "Don't you find it a little strange that you claim to love your father, but will not forgive him or see him because of what he has done to you? And you claim not to be in love with Sam Brannan, but behave as though he had no part at all in your plight? Didn't you just tell me a few days ago that Sam excommunicated you? Why do you count that as nothing?"

"It's not the same—I never thought—"

"You Mormons seem to have a habit of not thinking. Forgiveness begins with one person, Susannah. Look—there is a great deal in this situation that was not your fault. But no one seems interested in that. Human beings are *supposed* to forgive each other their trespasses. Isn't that the Christian way? Yet it isn't your way, and you people claim to be Christian. I do not understand the Mormons. You were nearly raped, you were lied about, forced to flee from your own family, dismissed by your Church on the word of your attacker—" He suddenly broke off, shook his head. "I do not understand the Mormon code at all."

"Then why do you encourage me to see Papa?"

"Because it's important to you to be at peace with yourself over this. It's important that you make the effort, even if it fails. It is not the money that counts, Susannah, it's honor."

Susannah hesitated. But she knew that if she thought about it, she would find some excuse never to approach her father. Cameron was right. She said, "Will you take me to see Papa?"

Seeing the little smile and the warm look of admiration in his eyes, she knew what his answer would be. He said her name in a slow, sultry drawl, "Ohhh . . . Susannah."

His smile grew, like the sun coming out after a bad storm.

Chapter Twenty-Nine

Sam Brannan was content only when he had too many things to do. Accordingly, he was content overseeing his many business interests, entertaining distinguished guests, making new business and political contacts, and receiving reports from his settlement of New Hope. Matters there were progressing well. Under Will Stout the men had cleared and fenced 160 acres and planted crops. Ezra and two others had laid out the town and were building roads.

At every opportunity Sam mentioned San Francisco as the new name for Yerba Buena. Even Washington Bartlett, the *alcade*, agreed with the soundness of the idea. But Sam had had no success in convincing Bartlett of the importance of issuing a proclamation of the new name. Sam reminded him there were other communities around the bay, and that others might seize upon the name first. Bartlett, inflated with his authority, stalled.

In October Sam set out for Sutter's one-man empire near the confluence of the American and the Sacramento rivers. He rode up along the Sacramento. A well-worn path led him to a bustle of activity at the ship landing. A launch was being unloaded. Boatmen were shouting and swearing at the near-naked Maidu Indian dock workers. Drivers cracked their whips at their straining teams of horses and oxen as they plodded along, pulling heavily loaded wagons up the incline toward Sutter's Fort. The odor of a tannery close by smote his senses like a hammer blow. Sam introduced himself to a man or two, and chatted awhile. As soon as they heard his name and business, two Indian youths raced each other to get to the fort ahead of him. Sam rode on, past a few dwellings.

The sheer bulk of Sutter's Fort had made Sam stare for a long time with slack-jawed admiration. One man had built that, or caused it to be built: an immense adobe bastion surrounding five acres of land, covered, so he had heard, with buildings. The wall itself was eighteen feet high and thirty inches thick. Cannon were placed at the corners, and also projected ominously through embrasures at the main gate.

The sentry on duty at the gate challenged him, but from within the walls a uniformed Indian infantryman spoke a few words, and Sam was conducted down the well-kept street. His eyes darted right and left, assessing the wealth of Captain Sutter's town. He saw a bakery, a gristmill, a shoemaker's shop, another shop where a black cooper and a helper were making casks. Here were barracks-like buildings, there was a jail. Somewhere nearby was a distillery; his mouth watered at the scent of brandy. He could use a drink right now. But then, he could usually use a drink.

Walking up and down the streets were American soldiers. Having heard that Sutter had his own smartly-trained and uniformed garrison of Indian and Kanaka foot-soldiers and cavalrymen, Sam assumed that the Americans were here now because of the war presently going on between the United States and Mexico. His guide told him, with an eloquent sneer, that the Americans now called the locale Fort Sacramento. Still, there seemed to be a great many people around. Many were emigrants, dusty and weary from months on the Oregon and California trails. Men hurried along, carrying tools or boxes, rolling barrels. Women casually crossed the street, holding a child or two by the hand.

Sam had his first sight of an emigrant train, probably twenty-five wagons. The largest were broad-tired, pulled by four to six oxen, curved upward at both bottom ends. Over a series of high half-hoops was stretched a canvas cover. He learned later that these large wagons would carry eight tons of household goods and freight. Lean, tanned men walking beside the oxen touched them occasionally with their whips, or spoke in easy tones to guide them. Around the wagons scampered children and dogs. Tied to the wagons were crates which held chickens, ducks, and geese. Perched on one crate was a small calico cat that hissed routinely at Sam's horse. Women sat on the wagon seats, their knitting and mending forgotten as they stared at the industrial metropolis that was Sutter's Fort.

John Augustus Sutter, whose calculated fiction of having been a Swiss military captain had made his American life much pleasanter than his European one, was in his early forties. His eyes sparkled; his entire demeanor, though that of a courteous old-school gentleman, was one of enthusiasm. He grasped Sam's hand, exclaiming, "My boy, my boy," in his rich Swiss accent. "Such a delight to haff you visit me. I haff hear of you for so long. Come, come, sit, haff a drink, light a cigar."

Sutter produced glasses, brandy, cigars. Through clouds of blue smoke, as Sutter stroked the head of a large, heavy bulldog, the men became acquainted. Sam managed to relate some of his ambitions for San Francisco, but in time deferred to the much faster-talking Sutter. "And so," said Sutter, winding up a long tale, "after fife years here in America, I come to California. I vas captain in the Royal Swiss Guards, you vill remember, at the court of Charles Tenth, so I am accustomed to command. I personally selected this site for my colony, my empire which I call New Helvetia. I talk to the Mexican governor, Juan Alvarado, and in due time he bestow on me citizenship and forty-nine thousand acres. In return, I build a small fort and keep the Russian and British trappers off the two rivers. Now the Americans haff taken over my property, but this little Mexican var von't last long, and then I shall own it back again." Unexpectedly, he jumped up. "Come. I show you my empire."

Sam quickly finished his brandy, following the swift-moving Sutter outside. Sutter clambered awkwardly onto a mule, proclaiming unnecessarily that he had "neffer learn how to ride good." An entourage formed, consisting of two mounted men, Putzi the bulldog, Sutter's *vaquero* Olympio, and a small bodyguard of uniformed Maidu Indians. Idly Sam wondered if Sutter was always thus accompanied within the walls of his own fort.

They rode out through the gate, Sutter snappily accepting the salute of the sentry, and for an hour or two he pointed out this pasture with cows, that meadow with sheep, the Indians working nearby. "And do you know vhere I get these stock?" Sutter asked rhetorically. He answered himself, "From the Russians. From them I buy Fort Ross, and Bodega, and everything in them for thirty thousand dollars, cash two thousand and the rest in crops, soap, and tallow. It vas two years, vorking all the time,

353

before I get mofed everything here to New Helvetia. I have seventeen hundred cows, nine hundred sheeps, and nine hundred forty horses at the start. I also get fife boats, many tools, some flintlock muskets, and some cannon. The uniforms you see on my soldiers come from Fort Ross. I haff plans for my empire. Come now, ve travel back to the fort and I show you something else."

As they rode along the river, Sutter said confidentially, "Vun feller try to tell me there is gold along this river."

Sam's ears pricked. "Gold? Here on the American River?"

Sutter shrugged. "Alvays fellers are hunting for the easy path to riches. This vas a trapper, Jean Ruelle. He had vorked in gold mines before. In 1843 he find a little bit of gold, and he show me, and he vant me to outfit him so he could find some more gold, farther up the river. Ve vould share, he says. I tell him he must think I am as foolish as he, so he goes back to his trap lines and giffs up on gold. Anyvay, he doesn't talk about it anymore."

All Sam's senses were on the alert now, but he said casually, "One of the Gentrys was telling me that in 1841, a dry diggings in Placerita Canyon yielded about a hundred thousand dollars in gold. Sometimes those veins run for miles."

"If you ask me, I am sorry I open the subject. There is not gold enough around here to blind a gnat." Apologetically he added, "But might be I am wrong."

Sam was preoccupied as Sutter led him past storerooms, and showed him through the workmen's quarters and the barracks where the garrison now lived. Gold, he thought, right here. If there was a little, there might be a lot. Already his mind was busy envisioning the way that a large find of gold would benefit San Francisco—and himself. He scarcely saw the factories and the other shops Sutter took him through.

At the end of the tour they were standing by the corrals, leaning on the fence. Sutter pulled out a pocket flask, courteously wiped off the neck with his sleeve, and handed it to Sam. "Maybe you think I haff some motife in showing you my empire, eh?" His kindly eyes looked slyly at Sam.

"I'm sure you do, John, but I'm more than impressed by your accomplishments in only seven years here. Even with all your workmen, this is overwhelming. I envy you. I only hope I can do the same with San Francisco."

Sutter waved his hand as though shooing flies. "San Francisco, pah! You are the head of the Saints in California now, is so? You can tell your people mofe, and they vill mofe, is so? Vhy not mofe them here, to New Helvetia vhere is a town already? Eh?"

Sam chuckled. In John Sutter he had found a mind remarkably like his own. "They've already begun to settle in San Francisco. We're starting to get a little trade, a whaler now and then, and the ranchers come into town occasionally. I doubt if I could issue an edict that would make them come out here to the wilderness."

"Vilderness!" Sutter's face grew red. "Vilderness, you call it! Vhy, only yesterday ve got three vagon trains coming through. All the time ve are getting mountain men, hunters, trappers. Efen yourself, Sam. Vhy are you here if this is a vilderness?"

Sam was saved from replying by the rapid approach of a gaunt, whiskered, rather wild-eyed man. Sutter said in a low voice, "People call him crazy, but he can do anything, make anything. I vish I haff a dozen vorkmen as crazy as this vun." He turned to welcome the newcomer. "Sam Brannan, this is my employee and friend, James Marshall. Jim has been exploring up the South Fork of the American River." As the men shook hands, Sutter went on, "Haff you find anything yet, Jim?"

Marshall's eyes wavered significantly between Sam and Sutter before he replied. "I think I have, Cap'n. It's about forty-five miles northeast, a little vale the Maidu call Cullumah. Plenty of timber, easy access to the river. This looks ideal to me."

"Fine, fine. Come to dinner this efening and ve talk it over, eh?"

Marshall nodded. "Meantime, Cap'n, I'll get back to makin' the shuttles for those new looms." He strode away, a man with lots to do.

Sutter said, looking after him, "A very valuable man, is Jim. Anything with the hand, he can make—vagons, coaches, plows, spinning vheels. He is ingenious. At present I am needing mills vorse than anything. In a month or so my mechanics vill begin a big gristmill at Natoma, four miles east from here, on the American River. Vhen Jim and I settle on details, he vill take a crew and start building a sawmill at Cullumah. I am needing lumber for my own vork, and I must haff lumber to sell people who are settling in my empire. But now, my new friend Sam, ve vill get down to vhy I vas go glad to haff you visit me. Let us find you first a room. Then ve vatch the garrison drill, then ve haff dinner." He patted his mule apologetically before mounting again. "Katy's saddle is not a right fit for my backside."

Sam was well impressed by the military drill of the Americans. Sutter explained that his own troops were off fighting the war. "They are proud soldiers," Sutter declared. "I train them myself. They are good fighters."

Sam reflected that since Asa had gone, and now that there seemed no necessity for fighting the Mexicans for possession of the territory around San Francisco Bay, his own militia had more or less fallen apart. There was no crime in young San Francisco. Only a few of militaristic bent continued to drill in the Plaza. He should encourage that more, thought Sam. When great numbers of immigrants came, the Saints would need some ready means of control and law enforcement. If they were prepared, the transition from village to city would go smoothly.

When he got back, he'd put Samuel Ladd to work on that again.

"These Indians," he said to Sutter. "How did you tame them, and train them? I've seen them all over your land, doing all sorts of tasks."

"Vell, Sam, they vere not vild to start with. Among themselves they go naked, but they are an intelligent and friendly people. They liff in villages of thirty or forty lodges. They haff a mythology that refers to a creator, to genesis, to immortality and heaven. They are skilled artisans—weavers of cloth, makers of nets and ropes and baskets. Their spearheads and ornaments are creations of beauty. Their diet is more varied than my own."

"Did they approach you, or you them?"

"I leafe little gifts—brown sugar, beads. Vhen they come to see me, I teach them to plow and plant, to vork vood, to tend stock. And"—his eyes twinkled—"I put clothes on them. Many of them are my friends, and my best vorkers. I depend on them, Sam. If I don't got vorkers, my empire vill fall apart. That is vhy I hire anyone who asks for a job. There is plenty of vork here for all."

"Even in San Francisco, we have heard much of your generosity."

"Pshaw, Sam, is good business."

In view of the lavishness of Sutter's domain, Sam had expected his dwelling to be comparable. But John Sutter wasted no money or effort on unimportant things. His large dining room

356

was furnished only with a common pine-plank table surrounded by benches. The food, as Sutter himself had said, was not inventive. Soup, game, bread, cheese, and fruit were served, followed by a tea made from herbs. Brandy and cigars completed the meal. There were only four at table: Sam, Sutter, Marshall, and John Bidwell, Sutter's clerk.

After Marshall had completed his business and left, Sutter said, "Now. Ve talk, Sam Brannan. I vant you to come here. Open up a big store. I haff show you everything. I see your eyes take in much more, and you know what the prospects are here. You haff the flair, you could bring in some Oriental goods, something in the luxury line. Get it off the boats at your San Francisco."

"I appreciate your offer, John—"

"Vait. I am still speaking. Tomorrow you come to my store and vatch the vomen. For business purposes, you understand. Look at their eyes, their hands. For months they haff been on the emigrant trail, valking in the dust and liffing like animals. They hunger, they starve, for the feel of new silks and things nice. So many of them say they had to dump their extra possessions back along the prairie. This fort—this vilderness, if you must—represents their first glimpse of civilization. They vant to be able to look female again. These emigrants haff money. They vill spend if they can find nice goods. I *know* this. They do it all the time. You are a merchant. You vatch. You consider."

"I'm in over my nose right now, John. House and business mortgages, loan payments. In a year, maybe."

Sutter took Sam's upper arm in one hand and squeezed gently. "This is too good a chance to vait for a year. By a year I von't need you. You are the first man I meet who I know could make a success. You haff style, Sam. Borrow the money. Borrow from me, if you vish. But get a store started here now."

Sam said shrewdly, "Why don't you do it, John? Hire some-one to run it for you."

Sutter shrugged. "I don't need. I get plenty business in efery shop inside the fort. I vant some new blood, some competition to keep me in tune. I like you. I vant you get rich too."

Sam stayed for a few days at the fort, and was astonished at the number of emigrant trains which came in, all needing supplies, fresh horses, and advice. Sam directed as many as he could to San Francisco, expanding on its present advantages and its potential.

357

Before he left, he arranged with Sutter to open a store as soon as he could procure merchandise. He was determined to have a plentiful supply.

On October 26, when Sam returned to San Francisco with Cameron, he was pleased to be able to sell Cameron several pieces of land, including one on Montgomery Street several blocks from his own splendid dwelling. There, Cameron said, he was going to build a house. Before he left for Agua Clara, he and Sam had completed arrangements with a reliable carpenter who would do the job.

Sam was pleased. "It's what I'd have built, if Liza hadn't wanted a mansion. You must be going to live there yourself.'

Cameron shrugged. His plans for Susannah were none of Brannan's business. Then he grinned, as if to himself. "Who knows?''

Part VIII

Chapter Thirty

On October 28, a tall hollow-eyed man on foot was conducted to Sutter's office. He swayed as he stood, introducing himself with gentlemanly courtesy. "I am James Frazier Reed, from Springfield, Illinois, sir, and I come on a mission of mercy for my family and my fellow emigrants."

"I am Captain John Augustas Sutter, late of the Royal Swiss Guards at the court of Charles Tenth. Come, sit, haff a drink. I get you some food. John!" His clerk came promptly.

Cautiously, Reed sipped the proffered glass of brandy. His stomach had been so long deprived that he was afraid the liquor might make him sick. He began again. "My family is starving. I've been three weeks afoot, sir—"

"You eat a few spoons hot soup, and you tell me." Reed ate a little, and waited for the roiling of his queasy stomach to subside. Sutter's hand reached for Putzi's head and stroked meditatively. "Aren't you vith your party?"

Reed had finished his soup and now sat unmoving, hoping that the food after so long a fast would stay down. He said, "I was banished, Captain Sutter."

Sutter's eyebrows rose. "Banished, vhy?"

Reed's tired eyes looked infinitely sad, as though he had faced a terrible truth night after night. "I killed a man."

He sat forward in his chair. Strange how such a small quantity of food could make a man feel so elated, as though the world were no longer cruel and loved ones no longer separated. Or was it that, since leaving Margaret and the children, he had had no one to talk with who might understand how he felt about taking a man's life?

Reed began his story. "About a year ago my neighbors, the Donners, decided to come west."

"So you decided too."

"Yes. We had a fair group leaving Springfield, the three families, six adults and sixteen children. Across the county we traveled with various other parties until we reached Fort Bridger in Wyoming. I tell you, Captain, we've had almost nothing but trouble ever since."

Sutter said cautiously, "I haff hear of this Bridger and his partner Vasquez."

"They are the two greatest scalawags and rogues I have ever had the misfortune to trust. And," Reed went on heatedly, "they were in cahoots with a so-called guide named Lansford Hastings, whom I also hold responsible for our present plight."

"Go on, go on," Sutter said impatiently.

"Soon after we left Bridger's on this Hastings Cut-Off, the party elected leaders. George and Jacob Donner were chosen. This group has not pulled together. It has been every family for itself. The Donner men have given us very little guidance." Reed then declared passionately, "*I* could have bound us into a cohesive group so that we all decided as one, all worked as one for the common good."

"Vhy did you not, then?"

"There was some, er, ill will toward me. From the first there were those who resented my affluence. So when I made suggestions, they were not welcomed."

Reed straightened again in his chair, seeming to see for the first time the dish of creamed eggs and fowl which one of Sutter's Indian servants had set on a small table beside him. "You'll excuse me, John, if I stop talking for a while and try to eat?"

"Of course, of course." Sutter nodded.

But Reed, provided with an audience for the first time in weeks, went on talking between bites. "I promised to tell you of the incident for which I was banished from the train."

Sutter refilled their brandy glasses. Reed sipped his brandy and told the story of John Snyder's death. He was visibly shaken when he concluded, saying, "I threw my knife into the river.

362

Still bleeding profusely, I went to Snyder where Billy Graves was cradling his head on the ground. I heard Snyder say to Breen, 'Uncle Patrick, I am dead.' I got in to Snyder, leaning over him, and I said to him, 'John, I am to blame. Forgive me.' And—this is the one thing I can never forget—as I spoke, I bled onto him, and the blood that flowed from both of us was joined on John Snyder's body as he died.''

There was a long silence in the room; each was wrapped in his own thoughts. When Reed continued, his voice was rough. "I was ostracized from that moment. In the end I was banished. But I am returning—for the sake of my family, if not the others.'''

Sutter nodded. "Do you know William McCutcheon is here? Perhaps Mac vill vant to return with you.''

On the morning of Saturday, October 31, James Reed and William McCutcheon left Sutter at Fort Sacramento. With them were two *vaqueros* and twenty-six horses, and provisions for the stranded emigrant train waiting at Truckee Lake for a warm spell that would clear the pass of snow. However, there was no warm spell, and McCutcheon and Reed had to turn back to Sutter's Fort.

Two weeks later Reed was reflecting upon his own idealistic and not wholly practical nature, and the fixes it sometimes got him into. A courier had arrived with letters from Colonel John C. Fremont, now in charge of forces at Monterey. Fremont reported that a large force of Mexicans had repulsed the marines of the frigate *Savannah,* and had taken the towns of Los Angeles and Santa Barbara. Fremont was requesting volunteers to augment his forces so that he could retake Los Angeles.

Reed signed a paper agreeing to serve as a volunteer and recruiter for Fremont. He accepted the lieutenancy of the company which was about to be raised.

As a result of his folly, Reed spent Christmas week 1846 serving as a lieutenant of a motley group of sailors, whalers, and landsmen who were fighting the Mexicans as mounted riflemen. They were presently stuck somewhere just south of Yerba Buena, preparing to march against the enemy.

At first Reed chafed mightily at the delays, but as day succeeded day, he adopted the fatalistic view that what would be would be. He was bolstered in this attitude by meeting up with emigrants he had known while crossing the country and the prairies. It eased his mind to reminisce with them, to speak of Margaret, and Virginia, and Patty and Jimmy and Thomas, sharing with old friends the hard times that by contrast now seemed the essence of normality. He also met others who had been caught in the Big Snow of '44, and it gave him comfort to hear that though they had suffered, they lived to talk about it.

But sitting and talking palled after a few days. What Reed needed was action. His company of thirty-three volunteers marched toward San Francisco and were met by a band of twenty volunteers under the command of two men who looked so much alike he couldn't tell them apart for days. Reed invariably applied the wrong name to the point that it became a joke among the three of them.

It confused commands drastically for a time. Finally Cameron and Robin Gentry took to wearing identifying colors. Robin always had a red bandanna around his neck; Cameron wore a blue one.

Reed found the two worthy companions. Cameron was the strategist, while no one could move men to action as Robin could. They had marched from San Jose almost to San Francisco. As they neared the village, they found the number of Mexicans mounting attacks against them increasing. The entire army of which Reed and the Gentrys were a part was just over a hundred men. The Mexicans numbered they knew not what. They seemed to be everywhere, a fact that meant little to Reed, but to the Gentrys these Mexicans were men who had been their neighbors, and until the Americans had come, people with whom they had lived in peace.

"I thought these people were like the Indians," Reed said in perplexity. "Savages."

Robin gave a curt laugh. "If you plan to settle here, Lieutenant, you'll change your mind soon enough. They are a cultured people—a fine people."

"They why do you fight against them?" Reed asked him. "The army is not organized enough to know what you do."

Robin's eyes narrowed a bit, torn loyalties showing, then he shrugged. "I am an American man," he said simply. His brother agreed.

The three men with their troops advanced against the Mexicans. Their column was composed of roughly organized volunteers, a detachment of marines, and ten seamen with a six-pound cannon pulled by two yoke of oxen. For days their show of force simply made the Mexicans retreat. They could be seen everywhere around the hills of Santa Clara, dressed in their colorful clothing, with bright sashes and capes, and brilliant saddle blankets on their horses. At some point Reed realized that the two tall, powerful men who rode beside him also had brightly colored blankets on their horses, and black straight hair. Robin wasn't above fostering the idea that perhaps they had infiltrated the American army.

Cameron laughed at his brother, but said, with an edge of seriousness, "You'd better watch that tongue, Rob, you're going to get us shot by that trigger-happy Kentuckian."

"Price?" Robin laughed, and glanced over at the man. "He sure does want to shoot something awful bad."

"Yeah, a Mexican—or us, thanks to you."

As they spoke, Price stood near Reed, saying, "Think them two is greaser spies, Lieutenant?"

Reed looked at the lean, hard man who had crossed the prairies with the Donner group. He thought about it for a moment, then said, "No, they are Californians, and I'm learning that the term covers a wide range of people. You keep your sights set on the ones in the hills."

"Well, shit, Lieutenant, them greasers up there don't want to stay still long enough to draw a bead on 'em. What d'ya suppose they're doin'? Leadin' us into a trap?"

Robin sauntered up to the two, his hat pushed back on his head. "Just being here is a trap," he said. "Look at them. No one can outride a Mexican." Then, with a grin, he said, "Except for mine and Cam's, their horses are better than yours, and they know the countryside better. They could have you in a dead-end canyon before you knew what was happening."

"Daa-aaammmmn," Price breathed. "That so, Lieutenant?"

"I expect it is," Reed said grimly. "But don't worry, the seamen are keeping them out of range with grape-shot."

Price shook his head. "Hell of a way to fight a war."

There was shouting and cursing, and the crack of a whip. The cannon had mired down. While several men ran to push the heavy weapon, and some others stood by gaping, the Mexicans galloped toward them.

Robin shouted at Cameron, then punched Price in the ribs. "Wake up, son, you can get a bead on them now."

Finally realizing he was being made fun of, Price spat a respectable wad of tobacco, hoisted his rifle, fired, and nearly knocked a Mexican soldier off his horse. Robin complimented him.

Price scowled. "I missed the sucker—git him next time."

Robin and Cameron both mounted their horses. With a blood-curdling yell, Robin wheeled his horse and started toward the thick of the Mexican charge.

With a shake of his head, Cameron followed, muttering to himself, "If we die, we'll never know which side killed us."

Others in the company fired inexpertly, hitting trees and rocks, causing more danger by richochet than intent. One bullet put a hole in the Mexican flag. Robin and Cameron were in the midst of the Mexicans fighting hand to hand. They maneuvered their horses with the same expertise as did the native Californians, wheeling the beasts to avoid contact, counting on the well-trained animals to respond instantly to their slightest command.

Then, at a command, the Mexican army turned their horses and rode away. The Gentry brothers remained alone on the field. Price hastily loaded for the third time in hopes of getting one last shot. He cried, "Come back and fight like men, you white-livered varmints!"

For the remainder of the day the little column moved on cautiously. Two men had been wounded and were now carried on stretchers. They camped before dark, the men tense and alert for further action. The Mexicans had fought some bloody battles with the Americans lately; this small army wanted a chance to avenge American deaths.

About the time their supper was ready, there came the sound of cantering hoofbeats, and foreign voices raised in a light ribald song detailing the amorous frustrations of a certain *alcalde*.

Every man in the camp scrambled to his feet, rifle or cannon at the ready. Robin and Cameron stationed themselves with the two biggest groups of men, ordering patience. A small group of horsemen bearing a large white flag on a long pole rode into view. "Hold your fire!" ordered Captain Weber. The men relaxed their weapons, and Cameron Gentry walked up to the horsemen. Behind them the Americans stayed at their ready positions.

The Mexican officers dismounted and were met by Weber and Reed. Cameron acted as interpreter for them. "We have come to seek a truce," he said.

"Very well," Weber said, concealing surprise. "On what terms?"

Cameron spoke rapid Spanish, and the Mexicans talked among themselves for a while.

Reed picked at Cameron's sleeve. "What are they asking? What are they talking about? Can you understand them?"

"They are saying that they never really wanted to fight a war, but they didn't like having their ranches plundered by military authorities seeking to feed their troops. They felt they had to do something to show their feelings about this. They want that stopped." He turned as the Mexican leader seemed prepared to talk to Weber and Reed. Through Cameron he said, "We will fix the terms of surrender together."

For some time the men discussed terms and worked out a treaty. Once that was accomplished, the makeshift army disbanded. The volunteers went to their homes, or continued interrupted journeys.

By the time the Gentrys reached Agua Clara, they were told they had fought in the famous battle of Santa Clara. They looked at each other and grinned. "The famous battle of Santa Clara," they said in unison, and had a fine time that evening at supper regaling their family and Susannah with tales of the famous battle.

However, once they had finished making a fitting story out of the dreary little battle, they began to discuss something much more serious. Reed had talked constantly, and his subject most often was his family and the Donner Party trapped in the mountains. "He is going to San Francisco to see if he can raise money and some men to rescue those people," Cameron said. "He kept counting cattle and saying John Sutter told him they would survive on that number."

Robin added, "Just the fact that he keeps worrying about it tells us they are in serious trouble. Poor devil can't face the thought of his family dying up there, but from the sounds of it they aren't going to make it until the thaw. Someone will have to go up there and lead them out."

Carl Gentry scratched his chin. "I take it you are going?"

Cameron hesitated. "I'm not so sure—I wouldn't put money on anyone getting through that pass now, but Robin is all set to leave."

"What good will it do if you can't get through, Robin?" Carl asked gently.

Susannah listened wide-eyed to them. She couldn't imagine snow such as they were discussing. To her snow was a nice white covering of several inches on the ground that allowed one to sled and build shapes. What Cameron and Robin were talking about was a house-height mountain of snow. It was impossible for her to imagine—and frightening.

After some more discussion Robin conceded that they would have to wait for a while. "But I am going to get them out," he affirmed. He got up from the table and walked outside.

His father looked after him for a time, then asked, "What's got him so keyed up about this? What isn't he telling us?"

Cameron glanced down at his hands. "Jane Pardee's stepson is trapped up there with the Donners."

"Brian?" Rowena asked, her hands on her chest. "Oh, poor Jane!"

"Brian knows the mountains," Carl said.

"Reed told us Brian had been bullwhacker for the McKay family. Reed was very impressed by the McKays, and I think Robin is too, even if it is secondhand."

"That doesn't sound like Robin," Susannah offered.

Cameron chuckled and shook his head. "It isn't usually, but Reed dwelt for some time on a McKay girl named Fiona, and she has caught Robin's imagination. Reed said he'd always be haunted by Fiona McKay—apparently he has transmitted that haunting to Robin."

Rowena sighed. "I expect we ought to begin gathering supplies. Once Robin's mind is set, he won't be stopped."

Chapter Thirty-One

With the arrival of January another of Sam Brannan's dreams came true. His first issue of *The California Star* was printed. The dateline was January 9th, 1847. He watched as John Eager justified the type, made sure he had the forms properly locked, and placed them on the bed of the Washington press. Sam stood by with his brayer. When John finished, he inked the type and placed the sheet of newsprint in position. "Ready?" he asked, grinning boyishly.

"Read that over just once more," said E. C. Jones. "Wouldn't surprise me to find a mistake or two."

"We'll run 'er mistakes and all," Sam declared, and spun the wheel. The press plate glided down onto the paper and made a print. Sam took it out, and they all crowded around to look at the first newspaper printed in the territory of California. "Perfect!" said Sam. "Perfect! Now let's see if we can do it twice."

For the next few hours they took turns running off sheets. Of the items printed in the paper, Sam was proudest of one statement: "The price of the *Star* is six dollars per year. But it is a mistake for people to imagine that for the sum named they buy the editor."

Before the next weekly edition came out, John Sutter had sent a messenger to tell Sam of the people stranded in the Sierra Nevada Mountains.

"Damnedest thing I ever heard of, Mr. Brannan," said Hawk Larsen, Sutter's messenger. "These folks were tryin' to cross the

369

Sierras in October—three months back—and they had to halt because a whoppin' deep snowstorm come along. Ever since, they been up there near Truckee Pass, starvin' to death. They can't get out. One snow after another keeps 'em there.''

"They must be nearly out of supplies," said Sam.

"*Been* out," said Hawk. He tapped Sam's arm. "Know what they been eatin'?"

"Boiled hides—twigs and so on?"

"Might be. Mr. Brannan, they been eatin' each other."

Sam took a sharp breath. "*Each other!* My *God!* How long have they been without food? Where are they now? How many of them are known alive?" He picked up pen and paper and began scribbling notes.

"No one knows for sure. Some got as far as Sutter's. The rest of 'em need help bad."

"Look man, sit down. I want you to tell me everything you know about this."

After getting as much information from Larsen as he could, Sam inquired around the village. On page two of the second issue of the *Star* a story appeared, headlined EMIGRANTS IN THE MOUNTAINS. Sam had written, "It is probably not generally known to the people that there is now in the California mountains, in a most distressing situation, a party of emigrants from the United States, who were prevented from crossing the mountains by an early, heavy fall of snow . . ."

At last, three months after he had been banished from the Donner Party, James Reed was in San Francisco. He sought audience with the *alcalde*, Washington Bartlett.

"Umm, yes," said Bartlett. "It happens I've already heard of your plight, Mr. Reed. Captain Sutter sent a messenger a few weeks ago. And only yesterday I received a petition from the citizens of San Jose urging a relief expedition. You understand that we are fighting a war here now, and that our hands are tied so far as a military action?"

Reed's cold hands grasped Bartlett's desk. To have come so far . . . "Isn't there something you can do?" he asked, feeling as though he might faint.

Bartlett continued as though Reed had not spoken. "We may, however, be able to do something personally."

Reed impressed upon Bartlett the seriousness of the situation.

"When I left the party, there were over eighty people, half of them children. Great quantities of supplies will be needed, sir."

"I don't believe there are eighty left now," Bartlett said. "Seems to me some of 'em died."

"Who?" asked Reed in a failing voice.

Though hardly the most sensitive of men, except on his own behalf, Bartlett dimly realized Reed's distress. He said vaguely, "Oh, one or two of the young men, I heard. See here, Reed, what if I called a public meeting for the subscription of funds? We might be able to get up a few hundred that way—maybe get some men to go on an expedition for you."

Reed's face was white. He murmured, "Thank you, sir. Thank you."

As Reed left, Bartlett decided he'd call on two or three influential men and get the first contributions. If he could present a substantial sum to start the public meeting, it might show Sam Brannan a thing or two about political power.

Sam was in his own tavern, enjoying several drinks in the company of friends. He patronized his own bar as often as possible—maybe too often. Or maybe he was just getting so he couldn't drink as much as he used to. He'd heard about men who got that way. But that wasn't happening to Sam Brannan.

It was late when E. C. Jones came in. He walked right to Sam's table. "Sam, I've got to talk to you right away."

Sam smiled and waved a hand. "Pull up a chair, E. C. You're among friends here. No secrets among friends, right, boys?"

E. C. looked close into Sam's face. "Boy, you've got to sober up and listen."

Sam chuckled. "Come on, have a seat with the best heads on the West Coast."

Jones sighed. He said into Sam's ear, "Have you heard about the public meeting? Have you heard about James Reed?"

Sam, who had been leaning back against a wall, let the front legs of his chair down with a thump. "All right, E. C., we'll talk." As he got up, he realized the room was not as steady as usual.

They walked through the chill night. "What's this about a public meeting?" asked Sam.

Jones explained, adding, "Bartlett thinks that if you don't get the news right away, you won't be able to put anything in the

Star till next week's issue. He wants an exclusive for himself on this one. Lucky I happened on Reed and found you.''

"That son of a bitch Bartlett. You know what, Jonesy? I think Bartlett is taking bribes for land. If I find it's true, I'll blow that pompous bastard wide open.''

"Hold your temper, Sam. You can't afford to be his enemy yet.''

They found Reed surrounded by avid listeners in the pleasant surroundings of the Portsmouth House. After introducing himself, Sam put his hand on Reed's arm, gently drawing him away from the crowd. "I'd like to print your story in this week's *Star*. I hope I won't offend you if I offer the hospitality of my home.''

It had been many nights since Reed last slept in a genuine bed. He said, "Thank you, Mr. Brannan. I accept with pleasure.''

E. C. Jones walked with them to the comfortable mansion on Montgomery Street. He joined Sam and Reed in a nourishing late-night supper. Reed was feeling a mighty fatigue, but Sam, on the scent of a story or a business deal, knew no such thing as tiredness. He looked at James Reed with bright, expectant eyes.

At the end of the telling Reed drew a long breath. Sam sensed the facts of the story had been exhausted. Before Reed could speak again, he said, "Jim, you are done in. We'll talk in the morning.'' Sam took his visitor to his bedroom.

When he returned, E. C. Jones yawned hugely. "My God, what a story for the *Star*.''

"Yes, we must do it up brown, E.C. Already I'm thinking of ways to get people to dig down deep in their pockets to help this party. Just between you and me, I'll be gratified if there's anyone left alive up in Truckee Pass.''

"The human mechanism has incredible resilience, Sam. We might be surprised at how *many* survive to tell their stories.''

"We'll need an expedition. There must be a few men here willing to go up in the mountains, even in winter.''

"How about yourself, Sammy?'' Jones asked, with a twinkle in his eye.

Sam chuckled, and put a hand on E.C.'s shoulder. "Goodnight, Jonesy. See you in the morning.''

The public meeting to raise funds to aid the Donner Party was held at the Portsmouth House on the evening of February 3. There were perhaps one hundred and fifty on hand, including the Naval officers, the Gentry men, most of the male Saints, including Ezra, and other residents. No women attended, for this was men's business. Washington Bartlett introduced James Reed, who spoke eloquently of his journey and its hardships. Then, when someone in the audience asked him to speculate on the condition of his family, Reed broke down in choking sobs. Bartlett, to give Reed a chance to pull himself together, read the petition from the people of San Jose urging that military authorities send a relief expedition.

Sam, observing that Reed was recovering, was on his feet. He said, "Fellow citizens of San Francisco—this is a historic occasion. It is the first time that the people of this growing city have been called upon to give in the name of charity. I feel certain that the generous men in this room will offer up much more than a mere *petition*!"

The audience, released from the spectacle of a man's grief which touched upon them all, clapped and cheered. Sam spoke again. "I'll give the first hundred dollars—if every man from San Francisco will contribute something."

"I'll match you, Sam." Robin Gentry stood up.

Cameron raised his hand, and equaled his brother's contribution.

Carl Gentry stood by his sons.

"Yea! San Francisco!" Several of the men yelled, laughing and stamping their feet.

Bartlett waited until the noise had died down. "Thanks for your generosity, gentlemen, even if these aren't the first contributions. Governor Hull has given fifty dollars to start the ball rolling!" Irritably, Bartlett wished the governor had been more openhanded than Brannan and the Gentrys. He slapped a pile of coins down on the table. "And Captain Mervine! And my own contribution! We've got a hundred and fifty to start with—"

"Two fifty, if you count mine," Sam called, and there were chuckles. The rivalry between Sam and Bartlett was a sly joke in the village.

Then Bartlett was surrounded by eager men, all holding out money to give to Reed's fund. Bartlett asked Ezra to act as clerk, to keep track of the names and amounts. Ezra could not look Cameron in the eye as he took his money. He wanted to ask about his daughter, but he couldn't bring himself to do it. Afterwards the men lingered, everyone wanting to talk with Reed, to reassure themselves in some way that they had not sacrificed—as they truly had—in vain.

Sam pounded on the bar with a bottle, riveting attention to himself. "I'll make a promise to every man here," he said. "However much you give, I'll see that it's doubled. If we collect a thousand dollars for the Donner Party, I'll go out on the streets and knock on doors and I'll do my damnedest to collect *another* thousand!" The men cheered. They knew Sam could do it—and would.

Partway through the evening Ezra counted the piles of money; he added up the figures on his sheet of paper. He said, "Brethren, we have contributed seven hundred dollars." He waited until the cheering had died down. Then, with a smile, he added, "Now, Elder Brannan, the rest is up to you."

Sam laughed. "I've made my brags, Brother Ezra, and I'll live up to them. But while we're all here, let's get men signed up to go on that rescue party! San Jose sends around a scroll of paper, but *San Francisco's* going to send men!"

A few volunteers agreed to go. Privately Robin and Cameron told Sam that they had already made plans for an expedition of their own. "We won't be volunteering for this one tonight, Sam, but you can count on us," Robin said.

"Robin figures we know the mountains as well as anybody, except maybe Caleb Greenwood," Cameron added.

Sam couldn't help feeling admiration, even though he'd rather not feel it for Cameron Gentry. Already he had had many occasions to wish Cameron were less of a man, but now he smiled and said graciously, "Then we can rest assured the Donner Party will be brought back to safety." As soon as he could, he turned his attention to lesser men.

The three Gentrys, with their business done, returned to Agua Clara. Cameron was preoccupied as they rode back to the ranch.

"Are you going to talk about it?" Robin finally asked, no longer able to stand his curiosity.

Cameron gave him a vague smile. "I was thinking about Susannah's father. Did you see him?"

"I saw him," Robin said grimly. "But he hasn't done anything to improve things with Susannah—of course, she hasn't either. To my mind, the less a man has to do with the Mormons, the better. They're too strange a lot my taste."

Cameron didn't reply, but as soon as they entered the ranch house, he took Susannah into the courtyard to speak with her. He wasted no time in getting to the point. "Not too long ago you promised me you'd make your peace with your father if I took you to see him. We're going tomorrow."

Susannah looked at him open-mouthed, and had to reach out and grab hold of his arm to prevent him from leaving her there gaping. "Wait! Cameron. Why is there such a hurry? You haven't said a word about this for weeks, and now you are demanding we go tomorrow."

"I saw your father tonight, Susannah."

"How is he?" she asked, a lump in her throat.

"If appearances tell the story, he isn't well. He couldn't even look me in the eye. Shame can do terrible things to a man."

Susannah blinked back tears, then said in a small voice, "I want to see Papa, Cameron, but I'm afraid. Supposing he won't talk to me . . . supposing he won't even greet us? Must it be tomorrow? If we wait a bit longer perhaps he'll be more willing . . ."

"I want you to see him before I leave for the mountains, Susannah. If something should happen to me, you would have your family to return to. At least the groundwork would be set for them to help you."

Again her eyes were wide with apprehension. "Cameron . . . how dangerous is it for you and Robin to go to the mountain pass?"

He looked at her and realized how little she knew about this territory. He shrugged, and smiled. "Dangerous enough," he said mildly. "You never know when a horse will break a leg, or slip—Robin and I could be afoot."

"But—but it . . . it isn't worse than that, is it? I mean . . ."

"We won't die," he finished for her, and wondered if it were the truth.

The next day Cameron took Susannah to San Francisco. She was amazed at the difference a few months had made in the sleepy little place, which had been really more a line of tents than a town. The road was still more of a bog than a pathway, with sucking mud covered by mud-caked planks to give people a fighting chance to cross from one side to the other. But there were people everywhere. Music from many tents mixed and jangled in the ear. Men, not too sober, staggered from one tavern to another. Men with carts loaded with lumber and other goods bustled to and fro from tents and makeshift wooden storefronts.

"Cameron," she breathed. "It is really becoming San Francisco! So fast!"

He smiled, and thought ahead to the day he could bring her here and show her the surprise he had planned for her. He said, "Emigrants are coming in on ships, and some are coming down from Oregon. Next spring when the wagons come over the mountains, there won't be sleeping space for the fleas, there'll be so many people."

"Sam was right about San Francisco," she said absentmindedly.

Cameron sat a little straighter on the buckboard seat. "He's not the only one who has something to do with this city."

Susannah sat still, wishing she could bite back the words she had just said. Meekly, she said, "I'm sorry, Cameron, I didn't mean this was all his doing. It's just that we—I have heard Sam talk about it since our first meeting in New York."

Little more was said until Cameron pulled the wagon up in front of Ezra's home. He got down, and managed to lift Susannah off the buckboard and over a puddle as large and dangerous as a small canal.

Prudence came to the door. Her blond hair was pulled back severely as usual, but it did not have the same look of careful grooming Susannah associated with her. "Mama?" Susannah asked with uncertainty.

Prudence's mouth worked. She looked up at Cameron with gratitude, then tears gushed from her eyes as she held her arms out to Susannah.

As the two women embraced and cried into each other's shoulders, Cameron looked on with the first real hope he had felt regarding the Mormons. He had almost convinced himself that these people were not like others, but now he saw the emotion, and felt the love and relief pouring from both Susannah and Prudence.

Recovering, Prudence released Susannah, wiped her hand across her eyes, and gave a self-conscious laugh. "I'm forgetting my manners—letting you stand here on the steps. Come in, and let me offer you a cup of tea." Impishly, she looked at Susannah. "Hot tea is a regular thing now. Tolerance may go to hell as a result of it." Again Prudence gave her impish smile, then added, "I'm helping her."

The words jarred Susannah. There was a malicious relish in

Prudence's voice that was unfamiliar. She had never known Prudence to be anything but kind. This was not kind.

"I expect you want to see Ezra," she said.

Susannah put her hand on Prudence's arm. "I have come to see Papa, if he will see me, but first I'd like to talk to you."

Prudence smiled at her. "I know what you're thinking, Susannah, and we will talk later—if you still wish it. But first you must see Papa."

Prudence showed Cameron and Susannah into the parlor, then left them while she went to fetch Ezra from his study.

As soon as she left the room, Susannah said to Cameron, "Something is terribly wrong! Mama is never cruel—even in thought. What has happened to her, Cameron?"

He considered whether he should say anything, then decided he would. "It might have something to do with young Mrs. Morrison. She's quite the lady about town."

"Tollie?" Susannah asked in surprise. "She was always so—so religious!"

With a smirk, Cameron said, "I don't think religious is the term most people would apply to her now."

"What do you mean?"

"Let's just say that she and Ann Eliza Brannan have a good deal in common. They're both inflated with the importance of their position."

Susannah shook her head in confusion. "Tollie? I never liked her, because of what she did to Landry, but I never thought—" Susannah broke off as Ezra walked into the room. Apparently Prudence had not told him who his visitors were, for Susannah thought he was going to faint.

His face paled as soon as he saw her, and he grasped at the doorjamb for balance. He tried to draw upon the strength that carried him through the business day, but his voice came out as the weak thread of an old man when he said her name.

"Papa?" Susannah said, and hesitantly got up from her seat. "Will you see me—talk to me?"

Ezra couldn't speak. He let Prudence lead him to a chair near his daughter. Then Prudence turned to Cameron. "I've just made a fresh blueberry pie. Would you like some while it is still hot?"

Without further prompting, Cameron followed Prudence to the kitchen.

Susannah stammered through several false starts, then said, "I

377

didn't know I would cause you such grief, Papa. I thought I was helping.''

Like a dumb animal in pain, Ezra Morrison wagged his head back and forth. In a broken voice he said, "I am to blame. I am to blame for everything.''

"No, Papa! You did what the Church ordered.''

"The Church way is not clear out here, Susannah . . . I fear I suffer from the same failing as Landry—I don't know what is God's way and what is not.''

"Ye shall know them by their fruits—'' Susannah began.

"Rotten! All rotten!'' Ezra groaned in a rasping voice.

Susannah threw her arms around him, no longer caring what he thought of her. He was the father she loved, and he was in terrible pain.

For a long time they sat together, saying little, and that was disjointed. It was nearly half an hour before Ezra was finally capable of talking with any coherency. "I have lost my son, my daughter, and my beloved Prudence,'' he said, staring at a blank wall. "Nothing can ever undo the harm that has been done in the name of God Almighty, and He will condemn us for the blasphemy we have committed.''

"Papa, please—I am here. I forgive you! With all my heart I forgive you, and I love you, Papa! Look at me, please! I love you!''

Ezra's eyes were rheumy as he turned them on her. "You are coming home?''

"In my heart,'' she said cautiously. "I have come home in that way, Papa, for I will always love you and Mama and Landry, but I cannot come back into this house.''

Ezra nodded slowly. "No. It is not a good place to be.''

"But it could be—for you and Mama. You could make it good again, Papa. Landry will come here—I just know he will. Let him see to Tolerance and Elisha. You take care of Mama.''

"Tolerance is my wife,'' Ezra said dully.

Susannah sputtered. "She is—she is—a gold digger! I have heard all about her! Mama is your wife!''

"Mama loathes me now, Susannah, and with good reason. I was a fool—still am.''

"Stop it, Papa! Stop it!'' she cried, putting her hands over her ears. "I won't hear any more of this! Mama! Mama! Come here, please!''

At the sound of Susannah's shrill cry, Prudence ran to the parlor, her heart pounding. Cameron was at her heels.

"Mama!" Susannah said, running to her and dragging her to Ezra. "Tell Papa you love him! Tell him you have always loved him—and always will through eternity! Tell him, Mama!"

Prudence had a glitter in her eye. Ezra had hurt her beyond repair, and she thought now that she could repay him for the myriad slights and insults he had dealt her ever since Tollie had gained precedence over her. Now he was naked, with Susannah laying bare all his and her worst fears.

A sudden wave of compassion washed over her, and was followed quickly by fear. Did she still know how to tell him she loved him? Would she be able to become as vulnerable and naked as he to say it to him? Prudence was trembling all over, and her voice quaked and she said, "I love you, Ezra. With all my heart, all my mind, all my soul, I am yours and always will be."

Ezra got to his feet and embraced his wife. Within minutes Ezra, Prudence, and Susannah were in tears, and Cameron Gentry was wishing he could melt into the woodwork. Ezra and Prudence began to talk quietly, no longer aware that Susannah and Cameron were in the room with them. Susannah backed away and edged toward the door. It was time to leave, but she knew she'd always be welcomed back. There had been no time to talk of it, but Susannah placed a leather pouch filled with her father's coins on the hall table. Smiling she and Cameron stepped out of the front door just as Tollie emerged from Ezra's shiny black coach which he had had sent on a freighter from New York.

Tollie was dressed stylishly in a green velvet suit, and a matching plumed hat sat pertly on her head. She gave Susannah an inquiring look. "What are you doing here?"

Susannah gave her a full smile. "I came to see Mama and Papa. They got married today—for eternity!"

She didn't wait to hear what Tolerance might have said. She took Cameron's arm. When he put his hands around her waist to lift her over the canal-sized puddle, she kissed his cheek. "Thank you!"

Cameron chuckled and his eyes were bright with pleasure, but he didn't miss the knowing look Susannah gave Tollie, who was standing on Ezra's front stoop. Neither had he missed the assessing, invitational look he had gotten from Tolerance Morrison. Cameron was a reserved man, willing to give anyone a chance, but that look had gone a long way toward making him accept some of the other things being said about Tolerance. The second Mrs. Morrison had her flags flying; the message was easy to read. Maybe comparing her to Ann Eliza Brannan wasn't quite fair to Sam's wife. He had to admit to a new curiosity about Landry Morrison. It would be interesting when he arrived—if he arrived.

The next few days in San Francisco were hectic. More men volunteered for rescue parties, and several donated supplies and equipment. One man lent a small schooner, and men were kept busy loading it all day. Sam collected another six hundred dollars, with more promised at the end of the month. The men were ready to sail on the evening of February 5, when John Sutter's launch appeared. He had sent Hawk Larsen with urgent news: William Eddy had made it down the mountain. He had started with a party of seventeen. Two had turned back the first day, and of the others, eight men had died. This left Eddy, a Mr. and Mrs. William Foster, and four women who got back to civilization. One of the women was Mrs. McCutcheon, whose baby had died. There were thirty or forty people still in the mountains.

"*Where* in the mountains?" asked Reed impatiently. "My wife was with them—do you know anything about Mrs. Reed, about my family?"

"Don't think I heard the name called," said Larsen.

"Bet they camped up at Truckee Lake," said another man.

"That's where they are," Larsen replied. "And by the looks o' them that got out, they ain't in too good a shape." He paused, looking at his audience. "I seen 'em. Me'n three other boys went up the trail after Foster an' the women. Looked like skeletons. Feet been froze an' thawed, and they were bleedin'. Fact is, we tracked 'em by Eddy's bloody footprints for six miles to Captain Ritchie's spread."

A little man sidled up to Larsen. In a low voice that Reed wouldn't hear, he asked, "Wasn't you here in Yerba a few weeks back?" When Larsen nodded, the man asked, "Wasn't you the one that said they was eatin' human flesh?"

Larsen's eyes narrowed. "I said that." He looked up at his listeners again. "Ain't no use tryin' to hide nothin', 'cause you'uns'll find out anyhow. These people been eatin' them that died, they're that bad off."

James Reed turned abruptly away, and walked down the street a few paces.

The men digested this news in uneasy silence.

Hawk Larsen said, "There's another rescue party bein' got up at Sutter's Fort. When I left, there was Mr. Glover, an' Sept Moultry, and Joe Sels. Cap'n Sutter sent me after reinforcements. Reckon you boys'll be it."

While the men gathered the last of the supplies, they learned that William McCutcheon's relief efforts had also borne fruit. From Sonoma that evening came old Caleb Greenwood, with news that yet another rescue party had been organized, and that there was additional financing. Horses for the expedition, said Greenwood, were corraled at his camp near Napa Valley.

The San Francisco men did not exactly greet his news with jubilation. Here they had busted themselves to get an expedition going, only to find out they weren't the first after all. Or even the second. Besides, who in hell was Greenwood? Just an old man in an antiquated outfit of tanned buckskin.

Albert Purvis came up about that time with a wheelbarrow loaded with supplies. He and Greenwood called each other bad names, embraced, and batted each other heavily about the shoulders. "You want to listen to this ol' boy," Purvis proclaimed. "He may be eighty-three, an' his eyes ain't as keen as they once was, but nobody can beat him in the woods, or on the plains, or in the mountains. Ain't that a fact, Caleb? He can track, an' trap, an' live on air—why, he's even got a trail named after him—the Greenwood Cut-Off, offa the Oregon Trail. That's the one the Donner Party shoulda' took, beggin' Mr. Reed's pardon. But ol' Caleb here came to Californy with Jedediah Smith, back in '26. Caleb *knows*. You tell us, Caleb. Can we get over the hilltops to Truckee Lake?"

Caleb stood straighter, as befitted an authority on the West. "I b'lieve we can. We're gonna need every man you got, an' every man I got, an' all the horses. We're gonna have t'pack these people out o' the mountains. Most of 'em what ain't dead ain't gonna be able t'walk. It'll take more'n one trip up an' back. So if any o' you'uns are weaklin's jes' go back home to yer mams."

As Greenwood outlined it, it was going to be a heroic effort, not manned entirely by green settlers and ex-city men. As experienced outdoorsmen he mentioned his son Brit, and John Turner, and some hunters he knew. One party would go by schooner.

Greenwood's party—to which Reed attached himself—would cross San Francisco Bay and ride overland. At Napa Valley they would get horses. The two parties would rejoin at the Feather River.

On February 7, when the two parties left, Sam rode out to the Gentry ranch. He told them of the several parties, saying they need not go.

As though Sam were not there, the brother spoke fragmentary thoughts.

"Be April before we can get there, maybe May or June when we get home again."

"Good chance everybody up there will be dead by then."

"Dead or crazy. It'll be some trip back."

The two brother's eyes met, and Sam knew without a word being spoken that the Gentrys were going. He tried anyway. "The need for you to risk yourselves is no longer—"

Cameron interrupted. "I have a few arrangements to make first, Sam, but we're going."

Sam didn't ask what those arrangements were, but he had a good idea. By now the pain of losing Susannah should have lessened, but Sam felt the old familiar sharp jerk at his heartstrings. Had Susannah been his wife, or still his love, he would not have sought her consent or approval for such an expedition. If a man wanted to go, he would do so with or without a woman's encouragement. Yet he envied Cameron the right and pleasure of talking it over with her.

Chapter Thirty-Two

By sunrise on the morning of Monday, February 22, James Reed had two hundred pounds of beef dried and bagged for the journey up into the mountains. William McCutcheon had helped him, keeping the fire going all night to smoke and dry the strips of beef hung over a scaffold. While they had worked, hired Indians had ground wheat in a hand mill.

The past two weeks had both flown and dragged for Reed. Still greatly concerned over his family, he chafed at every delay, every flooded stream his party must dangerously cross. Woodworth was late in arriving with the schooner. Reed and McCutcheon had gone ahead, leaving Caleb Greenwood and the others to keep the rendezvous. The two men arrived at Johnson's ranch, at the foot of the Sierras, on a Sunday. By Monday morning, when Greenwood and his men arrived, still not having seen Woodworth, the party was packed and ready to leave.

There were a dozen, nearly all of them tough mountain men. John Turner, who like Greenwood had come to California with Jed Smith in 1826, was a large, strong man, even larger than McCutcheon. McCutcheon himself, though he no longer had any reason to go, with his wife safe and his child dead, was returning out of his sense of responsibility. Brit Greenwood, Caleb's son, was half Crow Indian.

Reed could hardly wait to start, for there was a strong hope that he might meet his own family on the way.

"A gentleman named Mr. Glover from Sutter's Fort took

seven men up that trail about three weeks ago," said Johnson. "They hadn't been gone but a day or two when a four-day storm broke. But they were in good shape when they left here, so I expect they'll be bringing some people back with them any time."

Reed's expedition left on Monday. By Thursday, with exceptional luck and good weather, they were camped at Mule Springs. The next morning, having left the horses and some supplies with Greenwood, Reed and the remainder of the men went ahead on foot, struggling through the snow. On the second day they met two wan and exhausted men coming down the mountain.

Reed recognized in the older man an upper-class quality like his own. He moved forward with clumsy haste to clasp his hand. "I'm James Reed."

"I am Aquilla Glover, sir. Pleased to make your acquaintance. This valiant youth is Daniel Rhoads, a member of my rescue party. The others are following behind us. I'm sure you'll be happy to hear that Mrs. Margaret Reed was holding her own when we left her, as was young Virginia."

James could not contain his eagerness and dread. "Patty? Thomas? Jimmy?"

"Jimmy is with his mother. I myself took Patty and her brother Thomas back to the lake, and left some food with them."

James Reed's eyes were filled with doubt, and questions.

Glover went on. "Your daughter Patty is the bravest, most gallant child of eight I ever hope to see, Mr. Reed. Whatever you and your wife have done in rearing her, you have made of her an exceptional human being. Many a man I know could take lessons in social acceptance of one's lot from her.

"Your son Thomas walked for two miles—as heroic in his way as Patty. But neither of them could keep up, even with the laggards, and they could not be carried. It was up to me to inform Mrs. Reed that your two children would have to go back, whether or not she went on herself.

"She had a heartbreaking decision to make, especially in her frail condition. But I pointed out to her that she would be of more use to you and the other two children if she allowed the two weakest ones to return. I gave her my word as a gentleman and a Mason that, unless I met you on my way, I would go back for them once I had reached sanctuary."

James Reed took Glover's hand in the secret Masonic handshake.

Nearly overcome with emotion, he said, "I now release you from that promise, Mr. Glover. I am going for my children myself."

"I appreciate your feelings," said Glover. "I shall never forget Patty's farewell words to her mother. She said, 'Well, Mother, if you never see me again, do the best you can.' And on the way back to Truckee Lake she confided that although she felt sure she had seen the last of her mother, she was willing to return to the camp and take care of her little brother."

All the men were silent, gripped by a little girl's courage in the face of death. Glover kept his own silence regarding the rest of the story, reluctant to tell of the shocking reception the Breen family had given the two children. Patrick Breen, who spent most of his days kneeling in prayer for help for his family, swore mightily at Glover and Moultry for burdening him with two more mouths to feed. The last Glover saw of them was Patty with a protective arm around Thomas, who was crying bitterly.

Reed smashed his fist against his knee. "She *will* see her mother again! I will reunite them—or die trying."

The next day's journey seemed longer than any he had made over the previous months, the snow more irksome, the cold and fatigue greater. They camped that night without a sign of the party they hoped to meet. Reed, now that he was so near to his wife, ground his teeth at having to stop. But it gave him the opportunity to prepare a small special treat for his loved ones. Knowing how hungry they would be for fresh bread, he spent most of the night baking bread and sweet cakes.

They met early the next morning. Reed and his party were going through a woods, each footfall breaking through a hard crust on the snow. And suddenly, there in a clearing was the remainder of Glover's party. Its members were strung out in a long line, several burdened with small children in their arms. One woman was weeping as she shuffled along, muttering, *"Mein Ada, mein bebi, mein Kind,"* over and over. James, hearing her words, realized that she must be Mrs. Keseberg, and that her little Ada had died.

His heart flopped sickeningly. He could not recognize Margaret, or Jimmy, or any of the gaunt, ragged, staggering apparitions. God above, weren't they there? Weren't any of them there? He stumbled forward. "Is Mrs. Reed with you? Tell her Mr. Reed is here."

At the sound of his voice, a frail woman, struggling along on the arm of another woman, fell lifeless to the snow. A young girl ran, as best she could in her weakness, to hurl her thin body into Reed's arms. "Father!" cried Virginia. "Oh, thank God you are here! We just kept moving and hoping—"

"Your mother, my child, your mother!" cried Reed, still in an agony of suspense. "Where is she?"

"There. With Eliza. She's only fainted, Fa—"

But James had run to his wife. He bent over her, he scooped her up in strong arms, he covered her thin face with joyous kisses. Margaret Reed regained consciousness, saw his dearly loved eyes searching hers, and she said. "Oh, James . . . at last. Oh, James."

As Reed bent to put her down, suddenly he felt a movement on his leg, much as if a tiny weak animal were smiting him. He looked down and heard five-year-old Jimmy crying, "Don't hurt my mother!"

Laughing with tears sluicing down his cheeks, James picked up his son. "I'm your father, Jimmy!" He felt the boy's arms tighten around him, and Virginia and Margaret clinging to him, and he knew that no matter what might happen from now on, at least part of his world was back in kilter again.

He said eagerly, "I have treats for you all." He gave the sweet cakes and the bread to his family. The others, with their dark-circled dry eyes and their sunken faces, crowded around with pathetic eagerness, and he gave fresh baked bread to them all. Within his chest he could feel the ache of heartbreak, wishing he had more, wishing that it would be safe for these starvelings to eat as much as they could hold.

Jimmy ate all his portion of sweet cake, but stuffed the bread into his coat for later. "Father," he said dully, "we ate Cash."

Reed's eyes widened. Cash had been the Reed family terrier, much beloved as the children's pet.

Margaret said, as though seeking approbation, "We used every bit of him, James—hide, bones, everything. By being very frugal, we had him for an entire week."

He heard again about Patty and Thomas. "They were nearly as strong as we are," Margaret insisted. "It was just that when we were walking in the foot tracks of the one ahead, poor little Thomas had to crawl up over the humps between. But in spite of that, he managed to walk for two miles. Oh, James," she burst out, relieved that at last she could once again turn over responsi-

386

bility to the head of the house, "do you suppose they are being fed anything? Mr. Breen would let them starve—he would."

James put his arm around his wife so that she would not see his face. He said, "Glover left extra food for them, Margaret. Besides, I will be there in another day or two."

"I wish I could go with you!"

James looked at his wife fondly. It occurred to him, as it never had before, that for all her seeming frailty, his wife had an amazing endurance and strength. But he shook his head. "You and the children must get back to civilization as fast as possible. Tell me about the others. Milt Elliott?"

"Milt died, James. He was faithful to the last. As he was going, he reached out a hand to me and said, 'Well, so long, Ma. See you in a better land.' Virginia and I buried him on top of the snow, in that crazy-quilt he liked so well. He was heavy for us, and we were so weak, we had to haul him up there with ropes. We were quite gasping for breath when we finished. No one would help. Virginia covered him with snow. We pretended it was earth."

"Baylis died," said Eliza dreamily. Her eyes were too dry for tears; nonetheless, she seemed to be crying. "Baylis is dead."

Reed put his hand on the serving girl's shoulder. "Yes, I know, Eliza. Your brother was a good man. And you're a good girl. You must help Mrs. Reed in every way you can."

"Baylis," said Eliza blankly, looking off toward the mountains.

Within half an hour Reed had bade his family goodbye, and he and his nine men began the most difficult part of their journey. He felt much better about it than he had before. By afternoon his wife and children would be at the camp at Bear Valley, where he had left men and food. Another two or three days would find them at Mule Springs, where there would be horses. They could move ahead quickly then, and at the lower altitudes find trees, bare dry ground, and green grass. In spite of his gnawing worry about those still in the mountains, Reed was cheered by the hands reaching out to other hands to rescue the small band of survivors of the Donner Party.

Reed's expedition consisted almost entirely of hardy mountain men, but it was Reed who led them now. After some miles they cached food. Brit Greenwood climbed to the top of a tall tree, secured the provisions there and, to keep predators away, smoothly cut off all the branches as he came back down. It would be a simple matter to fell the trees upon their return.

They camped in late afternoon because the snow had become slushy and progress extremely hard. At midnight they pressed on. John Turner led them fearlessly through the night and the crackling cold of the following morning. They camped again when the snow grew soft, but with the temperature falling again, and the wind rising, they moved along. John Turner, looking around where they were and naming concealed landmarks, said, "The snow must be thirty feet deep here, boys."

At a windswept corner they came to the body of John Denton, one of the young bachelors of the Donner Party. He was wrapped in a quilt, seated by the remains of a small fire. James remembered him—he was one of those who had wanted Keseberg hanged. Virginia had said they gave John a quilt and each gave him a scrap of food when they had to leave him behind.

A few hundred feet on, they came to the top of a cabin just beginning to stick out of the greatly melted snow. There was an eerie feeling, not a sound around the whole place.

"Hello-o-o!" James called. "It's James Reed! Hello! Is anyone here?"

After a little while a small, scraggly dark head poked up out of the snow. "Father?" asked the child doubtfully.

"Patty!" Once again the clambering through the snow, once again the glad clasping of a loved child in his embrace. "Thomas! Where is Thomas? Is he here, Patty?"

"He is in bed, Father." Patty, who had been strong for so long, broke down in tears. "He's sleeping—so soundly—so soundly—"

"Show me how to get down there," James commanded. He followed Patty's small body through a snow tunnel. He recoiled at the stench and the swarming vermin and the strangely familiar bones on the floor, but dropped to his knees at the side of Thomas's pallet. The child was a mere skeleton, little bones held together by the parchment-dry skin, bitten all over by body lice and fleas. But he was alive. He was sleeping, he was warm, his breathing shallow yet steady.

Thomas's eyes came open, and he was frightened. "Patty," he whispered.

"I'm right here, Thomas," said Patty in a voice so adult that it cut Reed to the marrow. "'⸱ ⸱er's here, Thomas. We're safe now; Father's here."

Again the weak whisper, the dull eyes seeking his sister. "Is it truly Father?"

"Yes, it is truly I. Thomas, look at me. I'm your father, and I've brought you food." James reached into his pack and brought out one of the sweet cakes for each child.

"Wull, begorrah, you ought to have some o' that for her bennyfactors, seems to me," said Patrick Breen.

Patty whispered, "He wouldn't share, Father. He was cruel to us."

Reed felt an awful anger swarm over him. Had Breen been a healthy man, in full control of his actions, Reed would have whipped him to a pulp. He drew in a deep breath, had to let it out, and drew in another one. He said, "There is food for all, Breen. You'll get your share when the other men come."

"Ye be still high an' mighty, Reed, 'spiten all I done for your brats."

Swiftly James Reed rose, and before he knew it, he had Patrick Breen's coat front in his hand. His fist clenched to hit him. Mrs. Breen scrambled up from the pallet where she lay. Then, with the realization of Breen's feather-lightness, sense returned to him, and he let go. Breen staggered back several steps, eyes wide.

James hung his head. "Forgive me, Patrick. I—I thank you for everything you've done for my children."

"You should," said Breen, and Reed's gorge rose again.

Fortunately big McCutcheon and even bigger John Turner entered the cabin. The Breen family fastened on them, and all were given food. Quickly the men of the expedition found other snow-buried cabins, and sent two of the rescuers to the Donners.

Reed and McCutcheon cut wood, and built up the fire to heat water. With gentle motions, and ample soap, they washed Patty and Thomas, although Patty protested she knew how to wash herself. Then they oiled the children's skin and wrapped them in clean blankets from their own packs. They helped Mrs. Breen wash her children. There were no more clean blankets, so they had to go back to their louse-infested beds. Patty, looking remarkably spry in her cocoon of flannel, motioned to her father to come near.

"*She* shared," she said, pointing to Mrs. Breen. "He didn't know."

"I'll remember that, Patty." James smiled at his daughter.

Thomas, having had a warm, pleasant scrub and a very small serving of beef soup, was content to sleep again. He asked weakly, "Patty, is it truly Father?"

James smiled at his son too. "Yes, Thomas, it's truly Father. In a few days we'll all be together again—the three of us, your mother, Virginia, and Jimmy."

"I do hope Mother has done her best," said Patty, getting drowsy herself. "I advised her to do so."

James looked from one child to the other. Tenderly, he laughed. "Your mother did her best, Patty. And so did you." In a whisper he said again, "And so did you."

Chapter Thirty-Three

With Rowena's and Carl's help, Cameron and Robin prepared for the first step of their rescue mission. They would stop at Sutter's Fort, gather the most recent information, and add to their supplies whatever they thought necessary before heading to the mountain pass. All the Gentrys worked until ten o'clock the night before Cameron and Robin were to leave. Susannah stood beside Rowena doing her share, but her mind was elsewhere.

Cameron had said she would find peace within herself if she forgave her father. How right he was! She felt a warmth and the abiding love that comes when one is part of a family. Even though she was unlikely ever again to live under Ezra's roof, she was his daughter again. She had a sweet smile on her face as she packed food wrapped in oilskin and placed it in the mule packs.

When the supplies were finally ready, and Carl and Rowena retired for the night, Susannah waited for a few minutes alone with Cameron.

The brothers checked packages against lists, then tried every knot and every fastening before they were satisfied all was secured and ready for their departure. Finally Robin bade Susannah goodnight, and Cameron walked with her into the parlor. They had with them only one small oil lamp. The wavery light brought the room eerily to life. Cameron waved the lamp around, both of them marveling at the flashes of red tile, then golden stucco that sprang into life then died out again as the lamp passed. Shadows and flares of color waltzed across the ceiling and down the hall. Susannah laughed. After one more dramatic wave of the lamp, Cameron set it on a table. With one easy move his arms slid around her waist, and they stood facing each other in the loose circle of his arms.

Susannah's hands were on his arms. She looked up into his eyes. "I almost wish we were still playing with the lamplight," she said softly. "As long as we were having fun I didn't have to think about your leaving tomorrow." She looked down and wished he would pull her hard against him. When he didn't, she said in a small voice, "I'll miss you, Cameron."

"How much?"

She looked up quickly to see a devilish humor-filled light in his eyes. The corners of his eyes crinkled, and his lips twitched, wanting to smile.

Susannah felt invaded. Cameron had snuck right into the private place where only she had known how much she cared for him. Uncomfortable now, she squirmed in his embrace.

Still teasing, he lightly kissed her forehead. "If you can't tell me, it must not be very much."

Completely flustered, Susannah blushed wildly, saying, "If it were just a little bit I could tell you easily!"

Cameron laughed and pulled her against him. With a sigh of relief she snuggled against his chest, her arms wrapped tightly around him. It was so much safer here against him than it had been out there all alone with him tramping into that private place of her love before she was ready.

He tilted her head up. His lips were warm, touching the softness of hers. Tantalizing her, he kissed her again and again softly, gently, his lips teasing hers.

Though Sam had taught her to expect more physical expressions of passion, Susannah quivered with a heady feeling of fulfillment she had never known with Sam. Between her and Cameron there crackled an electric desire that both satisfied and created an intense yearning.

Breathless and glowing with his love, she clung to Cameron, wanting always to be in the magic circle he had created for them.

The warmth that had flowed through her that evening remained with her until he had been gone for a day. She had waved goodbye to him, and watched as he and Robin and their pack mules had become dots in the distance. But his presence had still been with her then. That he was going to Sutter's, and then to the mountains had seemed a part of their closeness. Now, a day later, she felt lonely; she was only beginning to realize that they had given to each other a part of themselves that night. Always, now, when he was away from her, a part of herself would be missing too.

She went to her room and cried for her loss as she had never cried before. Rowena, not certain why Susannah was so unhappy, refrained from intruding. Finally she could stand it no more, and went to the girl's bedroom. She knocked at the door, and entered at Susannah's invitation.

"Susannah, I don't mean to pry, dear, but I can't bear to see you so unhappy. Has this to do with your visit with your father—or with Cameron's leaving?"

Susannah couldn't speak at first. Her feelings wouldn't go easily into words. Never before had she known that wanting the presence of another human being could have such awesome power. She was both lifted to the heights of a magical love, and dashed on the rocks of an abysmal loneliness. With eyes lighted with an inner fire, and clouded with tears, Susannah said simply, "I didn't know how much I loved him."

Or what love could do to a person, Rowena thought, but did not say aloud. As she had many times in the past with her own daughters, she took Susannah in her embrace and cradled her against her shoulder, rocking her back and forth, comforting, waiting for a young woman to come upon her own solution.

Susannah sniffed, and began to talk again. "I wish there was something I could do to help him . . . I want to take part in what he does." Susannah dissolved into tears again, then came up for air, saying, "I want to be someone—someone of value to him, and I don't know how."

Rowena sat with her and let her babble on for some time. When Susannah had finally worn herself out, Rowena left so Susannah could take a nap. It wasn't until later that night, after supper, that Susannah thought she might have a solution. She said to Carl and Rowena, "When Sam came here, he and Cameron were talking about Sutter's Fort. They made it seem as though it is a fairly large community—is that so?"

Carl nodded. "Sutter has a busy place up there, and more people coming in all the time. He chose his location well."

"I was thinking I might go there. I can still make tents, and there must be a decent place where I could rent a room. Maybe I could help with the survivors, too. I want so much to participate in what Cameron and Robin are doing . . . Is that a silly idea?"

Carl frowned a bit. "I don't know that it's such a good idea having you on your own at Sutter's."

"Jane Pardee lives there," Rowena said innocently. "With Brian among those lost, she might welcome company, and if Susannah wanted to help with the rescue effort, there would be no one better to guide her than Jane."

"Mmmm," Carl mused. "She'd be safe with Jane."

As Carl concentrated on his food, Rowena looked across the table at Susannah. Smiling, Rowena winked at her, then returned her attention to her husband. "We could send Maria as her *dueña*, and Juan could drive her there. We could spare him for a time, couldn't we?"

Carl Gentry put down his knife and fork. He looked at Susannah for a long moment, then at his wife. Slowly his eyes crinkled and became merry. "By Jove! I'm being railroaded by two of the darnedest experts around."

Rowena began to laugh softly. "I never get away with a thing! But do you agree that Susannah may safely get to Sutter's?"

"I agree."

During the next couple of days Susannah and Rowena packed clothing, and a few additional things Rowena thought Jane would be thankful for. The women talked endlessly, becoming good friends. Finally Susannah was ready to leave. She was outfitted with her guide, her supplies, and young Maria as her *dueña*.

At the last Rowena handed Susannah two letters to Jane Pardee. "This one will introduce you, and the other will give me a chance to gossip a bit with Jane. Be sure to tell her I'm expecting a letter back filled with news of her last trip east, and word of Brian's safe return."

Susannah gave Rowena a quick kiss on the cheek. "I will. I won't forget anything!"

Carl Gentry stuck his face forward for his kiss, then smiled at her. "You take care of yourself—and send messages home so we know how you are."

Carl helped her mount her horse, and then Rowena, caught up in her maternal duties, reminded Susannah to keep warm. "Not all of California is like this. We wouldn't be worried about the people in the mountains if it were. Bundle up, Susannah."

Carl laughed and put his arm around his wife. "Stop fussing,

Rowena. She is anxious to be on her way, Cameron and Robin already have a four-day lead." He gave a signal to Juan, and the small party got under way.

Juan spurred his horse when they left the ranch-house yard, and the little caravan moved along at a smart pace. Susannah was at ease for the first few miles, but thereafter her impatience burst into full flower. She begrudged every rest the horses took, every meal that seemed to take endless time to prepare on the trail. She didn't relax or give Juan and Maria much chance for relaxation until Juan announced that Sutter's was no more than another two hours' ride.

As they neared Sutter's Fort, the traffic increased. Horsemen and occasional wagons passed them on the road, and it was easy to see that there were other trails leading to the rivers, to New Helvetia, and to Sutterville. Susannah's fatigue left her, and she was filled with curiosity. She had expected nothing of Sutter's Fort out here in the wilderness. Now as they passed by it, Susannah could see a large and substantial adobe brick and wood fort. Rising above the high, thick walls, she could see the top of a building. For miles around the fort, which stood at the point where two rivers met, they traveled past Sutter's wheat fields. Even now, this late in the year, there was activity.

To her question, Juan responded, "The Indians work for him. Mr. Sutter has been able to do with the Indians what many other white men have not—he keeps his bargains." Then the dark-skinned man pointed to the horizon. "Out there, farther away than your eyes can see, are his grazing lands."

Juan took them along the road that led away from Sutter's Fort and toward New Helvetia.

Susannah was nearly speechless. Everywhere she looked there were both signs of civilization, and of an incredible wilderness that seemed impenetrable and untamable. She was excited, and sure she had made the right decision.

New Helvetia was a collection of shops, houses, smithies, cattle pens, and wagons, some empty, some loaded with goods. Susannah looked at one of the storefronts. Three wagons crowded in front of it, and several men stood by the door laughing and chatting with those who were unloading the goods. A large sign on the facade announced the owner, who was of some interest to Susannah: C. C. Smith and Co. Charley Smith was Sam's partner. She remembered when Sam had first spoken to her about this

395

store, and now he had done it. She might see him again. She'd like that. There was a part of her that would always belong to Sam, would always care about his welfare. Sam had taught her a great deal, some of it good, and some of it painfully hard to learn.

Sam Brannan's Shirttail Store, as it was popularly known, was left behind. Susannah's thoughts turned to Jane Pardee. She knew little about the woman. Rowena had rather mysteriously warned, "Don't let Jane's way misguide you. She is a very generous, capable woman."

Susannah had no idea what that meant, and now she worried that perhaps Jane wouldn't like her, or want her to stay. She was apprehensive when Juan pulled his horse up in front of a neat house, part log, part clapboard, and dismounted.

Susannah studied the house. Perhaps it would tell her a bit about its owner. It looked as though, in a fit of industry, Mrs. Pardee, or more likely Mr. Pardee, had enlarged the house with whatever was at hand. The two sides did not match, and yet it had a comfortable hominess. It told her little, except that perhaps Mrs. Pardee was given to whims. She took a deep breath, stepped to the front door, and knocked.

Susannah took a step back as the door swung wide, and glanced down at the letter with directions. The woman blocking all the light from the house behind her was enormous—nearly six feet, Susannah judged, trying to compare her with Cameron's height.

"I—I'm Susannah Morrison. I have a letter of introduction—you are Mrs. Pardee? Jane Pardee?"

The huge woman smiled. "I am today. I'll be called something else tomorrow if I can find a man willin'." She burst into raucous laughter.

Susannah stared at her dumbfounded.

"C'mon in and tell me about your letter. C'mon. I won't bite. Y'look like a scairt rabbit, girl."

Susannah glanced almost wistfully at Juan, then lifted her chin and entered the house.

The house was cozy and comfortable. Jane Pardee had a surprising amount of furniture in the front room, and of good quality. Susannah perched on the edge of a settee, her hands folded in her lap. She handed both of Rowena's letters to Jane, then sat back waiting as the older woman read her letter of introduction. Jane's eyes moved quickly, scanning the letter, then

396

she began again, reading slowly, a slight smile on her lips. Susannah couldn't help staring at her. Mrs. Pardee must weigh all of two hundred pounds, she thought, and every ounce was surely muscle. There was nothing about the woman that was soft. She had a broad forehead, well-spread brown eyes, a straight nose, and an unfemininely square jaw, and yet, Susannah admitted, there was something about Jane Pårdee that was all female. She managed to defy all rules of feminine style, and yet to exude femininity.

Jane put the letter on her lap and looked at Susannah, her brown eyes snapping with curiosity. "So, Rowena sent you to me. You want Cameron, do you?"

"She said that!" Susannah blurted.

"I said that. Rowena says you want to help out here. She also says you're a Mormon. That so?"

"I was a Mormon . . . that is, I am no longer a member of the Church."

"Know Sam Brannan?"

Susannah looked down at her hands. "I know him. I came to California aboard the *Brooklyn*."

Jane chuckled. "He calls himself a preacher, and maybe he is, but he sure ain't goin' to heaven by the direct route."

Susannah didn't know what to say to this strange woman, didn't understand her small talk, and couldn't tell if she was pleased or annoyed. "Mrs. Pardee," she said. "I have taken enough of your time. I appreciate your seeing me and reading my letter of introduction, but Juan and Maria are waiting, and I want to find Cameron yet tonight. I thank you for your kindness, and will be on my way."

Jane let out a guffaw loud enough to shake the window glass. "Now don't jump the gun, li'l Eastern gal! Your people are out back gettin' a good hot meal, an' your pack animal an' horses is gettin' fed and rubbed down. If Rowena wants you looked after, I'll look after you, 'cause she's my friend, and a good judge of horseflesh. I was just hopin' to find you an' me could be friends too."

Susannah softened immediately. "I'm sure we can be, Mrs. Pardee, but we've only just met. Given time . . ."

"Maybe I was thinkin' too, you're pretty green to be doin' what you're doin'. The West isn't a gentle place. Sometimes there ain't no time to give. Take those folks your man is goin' to

397

save . . . I don't suppose they ever thought about not havin' any more time. Most likely they thought they'd have all the time they needed to cross the mountains and start a new life." Jane stopped talking and considered Susannah for some time. "The West is a hard place, girl. Don't forget that. It can be a deceivin' place too. Everything's plentiful—too plentiful. Take John Sutter—he's got so much land you can't walk from one end of it to the other in a day. Plenty—land o' plenty. But it takes its toll. John owes everybody money, but that land must be served. Once a stone starts down the mountain, ain't much gonna stop it. Same with your preacher Brannan. And now here you are at my door wantin' to be Cam Gentry's woman. Before you say you want my hospitality, you might give some thought to it."

Jane got up from her chair and beckoned Susannah to follow. They walked through the old part of the house, took a few crooked steps down, and entered the new section. Jane threw open a door. "If you decide to stay here past tomorrow, this will be your room. I ain't runnin' a free show, an' I'm a widder woman, so I'll be lookin' for five dollars a week from you, an' your share o' the chores. There's plenty of them."

Susannah didn't know if she had been welcomed or warned away. She said, "Thank you, Mrs. Pardee. I am certain I'll be staying here, and I would like to find useful work as soon as possible. I would like your advice—about volunteer work—to help the poor refugees."

A sadness entered Jane's eyes, but nothing showed on her usually mobile face. "My boy Brian is with those people."

A new, uncomfortable feeling entered the room. Susannah began to understand Cameron's mission as he did. The refugees had previously been nameless, faceless people for her. They had hardly seemed real to her, and now she was talking to the woman whose stepson was among them. Even though Susannah didn't know Brian, he had become a person to her. Now the bitter cold of the mountains seemed real; she could feel it inside. The fright and loneliness of being trapped was real, and she couldn't help shuddering, thinking of it and the appalling hunger and the hopelessness.

She felt like apologizing to Jane, to everyone for her over-whelming ignorance and thoughtlessness. She was no longer the pampered daughter of Ezra Morrison, or the rebellious, curious young girl who had tried to be Sam Brannan's woman; she loved Cameron Gentry, and she had grown up.

Recovering from her emotion, Jane said, "We'll need help all right. It will get worse before it gets better, especially when those poor wretches are brought down from the mountain. We can use you."

"Have—have you had any word of Brian?"

"Nothing good. Big McCutcheon said Brian left the main group with the McKays. Not a word's been heard, and they haven't shown up at Johnson's ranch, Ritchey's or Sutter's Fort. That means they're lost in one of the passes—or dead."

Susannah felt like crying. "I am sorry, Mrs. Pardee, so sorry."

"Don't give up yet," Jane snapped. "If there's any way on earth to come down from those mountains, my Brian will find it. Like I said, there's plenty to be done, and many hands needed to care for them that do come out. I still say you oughta think on this—I don't expect your life's ever gonna be the same again, if you take it on yourself to stay."

Part IX

Chapter Thirty-Four

The Reeds were reunited on March 4. Shortly after that Cameron and Robin left Fort Sutter and rode to New Helvetia. Still shaken from the sight of the men and women coming down from the mountain pass the day before, they headed for a tavern.

Robin took a swallow of whiskey. Grimacing, he said, "My God, Cam, did you see those people? There's little left to tell they are human."

Cameron pushed down the urge to be sick. He had never been faced with anything like that before. He hadn't been prepared for the physical assault brought on by the sight of women with their hair matted, and filled with filth and vermin, the sight of eyes so sunken and cheeks so hollow they looked like death's heads afoot. It stirred in him a revulsion so deep that it could be expressed only in hatred, yet how did one hate winter storms, still raging so fiercely that they prevented rescue parties from getting through, and how did one hate circumstances with no face, no voice, no personality. He couldn't kill nature. He couldn't blaspheme at the clouds that rode low over the mountains and unloaded their burdens of rain and snow. It gave him no satisfaction to curse the ignorance, the apathy, the poor leadership and poorer judgment that brought the Donner Party to their tragic plight. He swallowed hard, his Adam's apple bobbing uncomfortably against his shirt and the lamb's-wool lining of his coat.

"How long do you think it will be before we can get back to the fort, and be underway?" Robin asked. He was more eager than ever to face the mountains. There were seventeen people left at Truckee Lake, and every day lessened their chances of survival. Robin felt it was the power of himself against nature and the Almighty, grappling with the grasping mountain, and he was going to win.

"We have most of what we need—we'll just have to pick up some climbing gear and a new compass. We should be on our way tomorrow." Cameron took a long drink.

"I wish we could go tonight. Peter Wimmer told me he had heard that Brian had broken off from the Donners and is lost. I'd like to find him."

Cameron's face, already pale, lost more color. "God," he gasped. "I don't know what I expected, Rob, but this is worse than I . . , did you see them?"

"I was right beside you."

"I know—by God, they were hardly people at all!"

"You're not trying to tell me you no longer want to go?"

"No!" Cameron said. "No, I'm just saying that I didn't expect them to look so—to be so . . ." Words failed him, and again he felt ill. After another swallow of his drink he said, "Let's stay at Aunt Jane's tonight. I'd like her to know we'll be searching for Brian. It will ease her mind a mite."

"Yeah," Robin agreed. "We have to find him. He's too good a man to die up there. He knows horses better than most men know their wives—can't lose a man like that."

"Poor Aunt Jane. She doesn't have much luck with her menfolk, does she?"

"Maybe we can change it for her this time," Robin said. "Drink up."

Jane gave Susannah plenty of hot water, and plenty of time for her to luxuriate in a warm bath. While her guest was so occupied, Jane fashioned a small surprise for her. "We've been too dreary around here, Millie," she said to her serving woman. "You get yourself out to the kitchen and see what you can rustle up, and I'm going to visit a spell. If Miss Susannah comes out of her room before I get back, don't say a word about this. Just tell her I got business and will be right back."

She breezed into Sam Brannan's Shirttail Store, calling a cheerful greeting to all. She found Sam in his back room.

"Jane, my dear," he greeted her.

"I've got a friend of yours visiting me. I thought it'd be nice to surprise her, if you've got the time and appetite to have a bite of supper with me tonight, you handsome devil." Jane teased Sam for a bit about being her next husband, and told him of Susannah's arrival.

"So, Susannah is here in New Helvetia—almost in my backyard. You knew that her family came here on the *Brooklyn*?"

"So she said. I thought she'd like to see someone she knows. She's stayin' with me until Cameron Gentry gets back from the mountains, and if you want my opinion, she doesn't know enough about this territory to know what real waitin' is."

Sam grew silent. Cameron Gentry, he thought. It was getting so he could do nothing without hearing the man's name. He should be glad—the Gentrys were the kind of men who could make San Francisco great—but he had never anticipated the effect a rival of that caliber would have on him. He asked for a drink as soon as he entered Jane's house.

Jane handed him a tumbler of his own best whiskey. "I swear, Sam Brannan, you're the hardest drinkin' man I've seen since my first husband."

Sam laughed. "Well, he went to his reward happy, didn't he, Jane?"

"Couldn't say. He drowned in the creek on his way home from the inn."

Susannah came into the front room wearing a simple white blouse and dark blue skirt, having taken her cue from Jane's dress as to what was appropriate here. She had just entered when she noticed Sam at the far end of the room refilling his glass. "Sa—Elder Brannan!" she cried, and after a stunned moment, smiled broadly.

"Now don't you two go startin' all that brother, sister, elder business with me!" Jane said.

"I think Sam and Susannah will do just fine," Sam said, walking across the room to take Susannah in a more than friendly embrace.

He smelled of fresh whiskey, and his lips, appearing chaste on her cheek, held a heat that was a question for later. Susannah quickly returned his kiss and moved away from his embrace. "This is a wonderful surprise, Jane. Thank you." She sat down, aware of Sam's dark, smoldering eyes following her. She couldn't recall ever having been near him when he had been drinking like this. She didn't like the effect it had on him.

"What do you folks say that we have something to eat?" Jane suggested. "You never seem to be hungry, Sam, but I'll bet my guest here is fit to eat a horse and chase its rider."

"I am hungry," Susannah admitted.

"Millie!" Jane yelled without getting up. "How long?"

The smiling servant poked her head into the room. "I got it on the table just as you called, Miss Jane. Come along now, or it'll get cold."

Sam's mood shifted for the better as Jane heaped food on his plate and nagged until he ate it. Susannah sipped at her wine and told him about her reconciliation with Ezra. "I think Papa needed forgiveness even more than I. Sam, why didn't you tell me how bad things had gotten between Mama and Papa?"

"I didn't see that it would serve you well. I am happy you and Ezra saw each other, but I wouldn't have guessed he was willing, Susannah. He has—"

Jane jumped up from her seat to answer the door. Sam and Susannah began to talk earnestly about her father and all that had happened since she had sent the passage money to Landry. She leaned forward, her head only inches from Sam's. "What kind of person has Tolerance become? Has she laid aside all her rigid morality for—"

"Look what the cat drug in," Jane said in her booming voice.

Susannah glanced up, then sat bolt upright, her eyes lighting with flecks of color and warmth. "Cameron!"

Cameron looked from Susannah to Sam and back again. He said nothing. Feeling the temper rise in his brother, Robin stepped forward. "Good evening, Sam. I'm here too, Susannah. No greeting for me?"

"I'm sorry, Robin—this is such a surprise."

"So we saw," Cameron said coolly. "It seems we interrupted something . . ."

"No, not at all. Sam was telling me about Tolerance. Sit down beside me, please."

Cameron smiled but his eyes were cold. "Thanks anyway, but I think I'll stick to my best girl." He took Jane's arm and sat her down, then sat beside her, placing Robin between himself and Susannah. "Got any more of that food for a couple of hungry travelers?" he asked Jane.

Jane called for Millie, and exchanged glances with Robin. It hadn't taken her long to figure out that having Sam Brannan as a surprise guest was not one of her better ideas. She didn't understand the ins and outs of the situation, but she had gotten the message loud and clear that Cameron Gentry didn't like it. She tried to ease the tension that had sprung up. "How about some music? I'll get my fiddle out—and Brian's guitar. You can play that a bit, can't you, Robin?"

"I know where it is, Jane, I'll get it," Robin said. "Cam, you got your harmonica with you?"

Cameron hesitated for a moment, then said, "It's with my gear. You go ahead and start—it may take me some time to find it." He rose quickly from the table, gave Sam a hard look, nodded to Susannah, and left the house.

Jane went over to Robin. "I sure put both feet in it this time."

Robin's eyes were on the door. "I hope not, but you may have, Aunt Jane."

"Think you ought to go after him?"

Robin shook his head. "Not yet. He might really be looking for his mouth organ—or maybe he'll settle down. If he doesn't come back soon, then I'll go find him. It won't be too hard. He'll be at some bar or in some—"

"Never mind," Jane said caustically. "I've got the picture. Well, let's see what we can do to keep Susannah happy. She looks like someone just hit her in the face with a pie. Don't she know what's going on with Cam?"

Robin frowned. "I wish I knew. Sometimes I think she knows just what she's doing, and then . . . I'm not sure. Cam never tells anyone anything. Maybe she doesn't know how badly she's treading on his feet."

"I wish I had known about this before I got so smart surprisin' everybody." Jane sighed.

"How were you to know we were coming? We just decided to stop here for a night's sleep and to tell you we'd be looking for Brian."

Jane squeezed his arm. "Your mother mentioned that you were going to the mountains, but it means a lot that you told me yourself."

"Since so many are headed for the Donner camp, Cam and I figured we'd go after Brian. He's a good mountain man. He's probably got that McKay family holed up somewhere safe waiting for a break in the weather. With a little help he'd get down easily."

"Why do you suppose he left the main group in the first place?" Jane didn't say anything for a few seconds. Robin just looked uncomfortable. Then she said, "You think maybe those stories about flesh-eatin' are true, an' Brian got outta there."

"Could be, Aunt Jane. I've heard the story a lot for it just to be talk. And I keep hearing the name Keseberg over and over. When Cam and I were at Santa Clara, we talked a long while to James Reed. He had dealings with Keseberg—too many of them, and all bad. It could be true. In a way that could be good for us. It may mean they're alive, and like I said, Brian has them holed up somewhere."

"I pray you're right. I met the McKays in Independence. They're a nice sort—good heads on their shoulders—but they didn't know beans about travelin' on the trail." She took a deep breath. "On the other hand, they all seemed willin' to learn. They woulda listened to Brian. If he told them to hike, they woulda hiked."

Robin gave her a hug, pressing her head to his shoulder. "We'll find him, don't you worry."

Jane blustered and sniffed a bit, then shook herself free of emotion. "Let's go join Sam and Susannah. They're gonna think we forgot 'em."

"They'll hold," Robin said. "Are you all right?"

"I'm just fine, and I don't want you gettin' me to cryin' and worryin'. Brian's a good man. He'll be fine too."

"That's the spirit," Robin said, then turned toward the dining room. "You two gonna sit there all night? I can't play unless I've got an audience."

Susannah stood up. "Aren't we going to wait for Cameron?"

"No," Robin said firmly, and plucked at the guitar, tuning it.

In a lower voice, Susannah asked, "Where is he, Robin? What is wrong? Is he angry that I came here?"

"He went out for a bit."

"Please, don't do this to me," Susannah begged. "Was I wrong in coming here? Did I violate some unwritten code?"

"Why did you come?" he asked, his light brown eyes searching her face.

"Why—to be near Cameron. I wanted to help."

"If that's your reason, you didn't do wrong."

"Then why—"

Robin gave her a strange look, half disgust and half pity, that shut her up. "Aunt Jane has a pianoforte. Do you play?"

Swallowing hard, Susannah nodded, turning to the instrument. Dispirited and confused, she went to the keyboard and played, following Robin's lead.

They played for nearly an hour. The only one enjoying himself was Sam. He sat in an overstuffed chair; his bottle in his hand, his dark, passionate eyes unwaveringly on Susannah.

Robin missed none of it, nor did he miss Susannah's lack of response. Her mind was not on Sam. Robin put the guitar down. "I've got to find Cameron. We'll have to get an early start in the morning, and it looks like he went out to do some funmaking."

"Well, Sam, I'm gonna put you out too," Jane said. "Susannah an' I got some tidyin' up to do, and an early breakfast call for these fellows."

Sam nodded, but poured the last of the bottle into his tumbler and lifted it to Jane. "To an interesting evening, my love Mrs. Pardee." There was little left of the Mormon Elder Brannan in the man sitting in the chair. There was merely a man into whose heart ambition had eaten a great void that would never be completely filled.

Robin waited until the glass was drained, then held out his hand. "I'll walk you back to the store, Sam. Cam's most likely there drinking your whiskey while you're up here drinking Aunt Jane's. It's no wonder they say you're one hell of a businessman. You make money no matter where a fellow drinks."

Robin actually did hope that Cameron was at Brannan's store, and he was mildly annoyed when he was told Cameron had gone on to Sutterville.

Robin rode to Sutterville and saw Cameron's horse hitched to the post outside the Wimmers' house. He found his brother in the parlor looking the worse for wear. Robin talked with the Wimmers as long as courtesy demanded, then said, "I'll take Cameron off your hands, Peter. Thanks for the hospitality. Aunt Jane sends her best, Jenny. She'd like you to visit after Brian gets home."

"She must be fit to be tied," Jenny Wimmer said. "She dotes on that boy. You tell her I'll be there, and if there's anything she needs now, let me know. We're never too busy to help a friend."

It took Peter's help to get Cameron seated on his horse. Any hope Robin had of talking to his brother tonight was gone.

Cameron was fit only for sleep, and tomorrow he would not be a pleasant traveling companion. Rarely did Cameron drink too much, and always it happened when he encountered a situation he hated. Robin had been too late, and now all he wanted was to go to sleep himself—and avoid Susannah's hurt eyes and her many, many questions. Anticipating Susannah's confusion, he was in a bad humor himself by the time they got back to Jane's.

Susannah had turned her sorrow on Jane. The two women had talked the entire time Robin was gone, and little by little Jane began to understand the situation. "If I were you, I'd leave him be tonight. You let me wrestle with him."

"But he'll leave early in the morning, and I may never see him again!"

"If I don't miss my guess, Cameron isn't traveling early. You'll see him tomorrow. You got my word. If I gotta tie both of them to the bed, they'll be here tomorrow."

Reluctantly, Susannah agreed. "I guess there isn't anything I can say to him. Whatever I say, even explaining about Sam just makes things worse." She stood up and moved about aimlessly, not wanting to leave. She cleared the table, and then with nothing else to do, went sadly to her room.

She heard the men return. Robin sounded tired and irritable. Susannah discarded her impulse to join them. She got into bed, pulled the quilt over her head, and cried.

Robin advised dumping Cameron into bed and saying nothing until morning. Jane shook her head. "You go to bed. I can manage him, and I've got a few things to say."

Jane poured hot coffee into Cameron. He kept falling asleep, and she kept awakening him and forcing more of the scalding liquid down his throat. "You're killing me!" he howled.

"No more than you deserve," she said. "What the hell do you think you're doin', drinkin' yourself simple-minded?"

"It was that or pound the gizzard out of your dinner guest," Cameron gasped after a long drink of hot coffee. "Why didn't she just stay at the ranch? I'll tell you why," he said quickly. "She thought I'd be in the mountains and none the wiser."

"That ain't what she told me."

"What'd she tell you?"

"That she'd come here to help you."

Cameron looked hopeful for a moment, than made a ghastly face. "She just said that. The first thing she did was find Sam.

410

Don't let her fool you like she did me, Aunt Jane. It was Sam she came to see."

Jane shook her head. "I'm the one who got Sam over here. I didn't know the lay of the land then, Cam. I thought I was doing everyone a good turn. Now that I know how it is with you and Sam, I'll—"

"No!" Cameron held up his hand. "Sam and I get along fine. It's Susannah! She's the trouble. All I wanted to do was take care of her. She seemed so small and . . . and couldn't take care of herself. She was in trouble and . . ."

"Then quit your blubberin', man," Jane said harshly. "Tomorrow you get her set up here and go about your business. By the time you get back you'll know if she's true or not."

This time not even Jane could help. Cameron was asleep. She covered him with a quilt and left him in the overstuffed chair Sam Brannan had occupied earlier in the evening. She walked to her own bedroom sighing. "What a night! Love sure is blind, deaf, and when it's a man, usually drunk."

The following morning, when Robin came down for breakfast, Cameron thanked him, then added, "But it may have caused a delay. I can't leave here until I have Susannah settled."

Robin hadn't slept as well as his brother. Gruffly, he said, "I expected as much. But I'm not waiting long. I'll go without you."

"You're in lousy humor. What bit you?"

"Nothing bit me. I spent the night chasing a jackass."

Cameron, unable to disagree, smiled weakly. He went to Susannah and apologized to her, but did not tell her the whole reason for his behavior. "Robin and I have a lot on our minds—I didn't expect to see you here."

"But why did you act as though you hated seeing me?" she asked. "I thought you'd be happy. I'm going to help Jane nurse and supply the refugees. And—I thought I'd try to find work here."

Cameron said, "You seem eager to get on with your life. I talked to Jane last night—I'd like to help you, if you'll let me."

Susannah looked at him with hope in her eyes. "Do you want to?"

He nodded, smiling. Quite naturally his arm slipped around her waist. They went to the dining room, where Jane and Millie laid out a sumptuous meal.

Jane, Robin, Susannah, and Cameron sat at the table long after breakfast discussing the possibilities for Susannah. At Jane's suggestion, and with Susannah's wholehearted support, the four finally settled upon a shop of some sort.

Susannah said, "I've learned that more and more settlers are coming here. That means there will be houses built—and more people—and more women, and no one to provide nice things for them. Why couldn't I have a shop exclusively for women?"

Cameron listened tolerantly. "From the sparkle in your eyes, you aren't thinking of calico and work bonnets."

"Of course not!" Susannah said with a pretty pout of indignation. "I'm thinking of silks and satins and linens—all the things women love to have and wear for their men."

Both Cameron and Robin laughed. "Your clientele would be small, and for the most part not the sort of women you'd be wanting to do business with," Cameron said. "You are going to have to be more practical."

Jane smiled rather shyly, a rarity for her. "I wouldn't mind havin' me a couple o' fancy gowns. With Mr. Pardee gone, I'll have to be scoutin' around again. Wouldn't hurt to look nice."

Robin looked at the plain, large-boned woman opposite him. She was certainly no beauty, but he could understand how she was able to acquire the seemingly endless supply of husbands. Jane Pardee was the kind of woman a man needed out here. She was kind, most often of good cheer, always with a pleasant or humorous word for everyone, strong as an ox, willing to work, and there was little nonsense about her. He had never thought of her as a woman who would want to bedeck herself in finery before. But she did. He could see that in her sudden and uncharacteristic shyness, the slight blush that tinted her broad, plain face. Perhaps Susannah had a good idea. "Besides the appeal of looking beautiful for your man, Jane, when do you see women having use for such garments, and, I assume, jewelry? You know as well as I that a good portion of a woman's life out here is spent in hard work—not a time when you would be wearing silks and fine linens."

Jane was silent, and Susannah spoke quickly. "You men have been saying that San Francisco will be one of the most important cities in the country. Here at Sutter's there are all kinds of plans afoot to draw people and to accommodate emigrants who will be coming with the spring thaw. People mean society, and society

412

means parties and balls and soirees and musicales. Women should be able to buy new gowns and hats and jewelry in current fashion right here. Why should a woman have to send east for a gown, only to have it arrive six or seven months later and out of style before she has it on her back?''

"How would you prevent that, even if you had a shop?'' Cameron asked.

Susannah wrinkled her nose and made a face at him. "My own seamstresses will make gowns right here. All I need is a Godey's sent by mail.''

Robin raised his eyebrows. "She has a point, Cam.'' He stood up as though the matter was settled, and now they could get on to more important matters.

Cameron was tempted to argue just for the sake of argument, for he still suspected Susannah was here more for Sam than for him. But he nodded agreement.

Cameron made arrangements that day to finance Susannah's venture into the world of commerce. He sent Juan back to Agua Clara with a letter instructing Carl Gentry to make funds available to her, and then spoke to several merchants in and around Fort Sutter and New Helvetia, setting up credit for her.

That night was clear with a bite in the air. Susannah was warm in her cape, but she was hatless. She liked this early spring air that nipped at her face and ears as it brushed through her hair. She was happy. Cameron was at her side, his jealousy quieted; they were once more in harmony; and she liked living in New Helvetia. Here she had found the new beginning of which she'd been deprived when the *Brooklyn* had landed at Yerba Buena. "Cameron, I am so happy. I feel at home here—at peace, and we'll be partners.''

Cameron slipped his arm around her waist and pulled her close to him, so that their every move matched as they walked. He still could not bring himself to feel comfortable with her being here, and even less with her proximity to Sam Brannan. But he looked down at her and lost himself in the beauty and fineness of her features.

Her eyes sparkled, and she had a lovely color in her cheeks. She was a treasure—if only she were truly his. The pressure of his arms tightened, and Susannah turned toward him. They stood in the cold moonlight, and she went on tiptoe to place her warm lips lightly on his. Cameron was light-headed. She might annoy

413

and perplex him, but she was more desirable than ever. His hands moved hungrily on the curves of her waist, and then to her hips. More than anything he wished he had the right to have her in his bed with him, to be able to awaken with her warmth and her sweetness next to him every morning. He didn't want any other man near her. "Susannah . . ." he began, but she seemed to know what he was thinking, and said, "Come back to me soon, Cameron. I will be waiting for you . . . only you."

Chapter Thirty-Five

Sean McKay lay back against a mound of snow, too tired to help the others gather wood to make a fire that might keep them alive for one more night. One more night, he thought. What difference was one more night? They were dying. Slowly, surely, inevitably, they were dying, and one more night wasn't going to change anything. A fire meant one more night of agonizing pain in frozen fingers and toes, one more night of fighting off that peculiarly pleasant sleep from which one wouldn't awaken again.

Angrily he fought the tears that came and joined icicles that had already formed on his scraggly, long beard. He hadn't thought he had enough feeling left in him to cry. They had started out with so much hope, and so many things had gone wrong. What great sin had he committed, that God should have brought this down upon him and his family?

Why hadn't he seen that, even before they had joined the Donner Party at Fort Bridger, the journey had not been going well? There had been no organization to the wagon train from the beginning. It was and always had been a collection of wagons, ever changing, ever breaking up, and then reassembling. But, oh, in the beginning they had looked so beautiful making their way along in the early spring sun. Wagons with their covers flapping, filled to overflowing with children, dogs, pets, and household treasures, beginning their long trek from the farmlands and cities of Ohio, Illinois, Indiana, Missouri. Yes, thought Sean, it had been a bright beginning, full of promise and of hope. It now

415

seemed so long ago, and almost unreal, the stuff of dreams and imaginings.

Sean was lethargic and apathetically sleepy now. Lying as he was against a mound of snow, he felt comfortable. He smiled a bit, his tears leaking from his sore, reddened eyes. He enjoyed remembering what he had been, what his family had been. He had only not to question what had brought them to this fate. He couldn't bear thinking of that, of what mistake it was that had brought them down.

He sobbed audibly, his thin chest racked with a deep cough. Oh, God, he thought, why had the McKays been brought to this? Why could he not suffer alone whatever punishment had to be meted out? He took a deep breath of icy air into his lungs, held it until it was moist and hot, and then exhaled slowly. He was so sleepy, and his hands and feet didn't seem to hurt now. His head slumped heavily onto his chest.

As his last willful act on Earth, he went back to Springfield, to the day he had come into the house and told Mary they had to move on. "Our men have taken Mexico to task, Mary. We're at war, and soon California will be a part of the Union. Both Oregon and California are open to settlers."

Mary had looked over her shoulder laughing, her arms elbow deep in a huge bowl of bread dough. "And, Sean McKay, when and if we take China to task, will we move there too?"

He grinned suddenly. She was in *that* mood! He took a quick glance about to be sure neither Fiona nor Coleen was about. With a clear coast, he dashed across the room and enfolded his laughing wife in a bear hug. He buried his face in the curve of her neck, which smelled of the sweet tang of the lemon she used on her hair. Warmth and desire flowed through him. He was a lucky man. Even after all these years of marriage, he still felt more like her lover than her husband, and yet, she was all wife to him. She was everything.

She laughed again. "I can't knead my bread with you hung on my shoulders like a shawl." She turned in his arms, holding her dough-covered hands out. She rubbed her nose against his.

Unthinking, he took her hand. "Ahh! Mary! Wash your hands! I want to talk with you." He wiped his hand clean on her apron.

Her gray-green eyes sparkled as she gave a tilt to her head and said smartly, "Pour yourself a cup of coffee and I'll be in the parlor with you in a minute."

He tried to make a stand, but did not get a word out.

"Sean!"

"Finish your bread quickly—please." He added, a sheepish leer on his face, "We'll talk upstairs—in the privacy of our bedroom, Mary, my love."

Sean wanted to stay deep in the soft, welcoming past, locked tight in Mary's embrace, but somewhere, somewhere far away, he was being torn from that past. Pieces of his rebuilt memory were splintering and fading away. Pain intruded. His shoulder was being roughly pulled.

"Papa! Papa! Wake up. Papa, please!"

Sean tried to pull away from the intrusive voice. Fiona. His Fiona was trying to drag him away from where he wanted to be. His mind veered away from the present and put her in the past too, where he liked to see her. She was Mary's image at fifteen. Her hair fell about her shoulders in deep auburn waves that caught flashes of fire in the sunlight and framed her lovely face in a halo. Her skin was fair and rich as new cream, and her eyes were a bright green that could rival the deepest emerald when she was happy. And Fiona was nearly always happy.

The pressure on his shoulders wouldn't stop, and the sobbing desperation in Fiona's voice would not allow him to remain comfortable. "Papa! Please, Papa, open your eyes. Don't die! Don't sleep, Papa!"

Sean, with great effort, forced his eyes open, then they flickered closed again. It was so difficult to come back. White. Endless oceans of white snow. He closed his weakened eyes again against the pain of that white glare.

"Papa!"

He was suddenly wide awake. Disoriented, he stared with momentary horror at the frost-encrusted scarecrow before him. He had gone from dream to nightmare. A girl with reddish-brown hair, dull and matted, hanging in frozen clumps from under her hood, stood over him, clawing at his shoulder. Her coat hung like a sack from her wasted frame, and her snowshoed feet looked like stumps, bound as they were with pieces of bark and rags. He began to cry again. His Fiona! He shook his head pathetically. No! His Fiona had the face of an angel, and the body—the body of a healthy woman, like her mother. She could not have become this scarecrow unfit even for his cornfields.

Fiona pulled at her father's shoulders again, trying to make him sit up straight, unsupported by the mound of snow. Her waning strength was fast giving out. As surely as he kept slipping from her grasp, he was going to slip into that welcoming, endless sleep Brian had warned them about. She sank to her knees, her breath coming in short, sharply painful gasps. "Don't give up, Papa. Wake up!"

Too slow-witted from hunger and cold, and too tired to move him without resting first, she considered that she too might stay where she was and let the cold and sleep overcome her along with her father. She thought fleetingly of her mother, of her sister Coleen, of Brian, but the thoughts went nowhere. If help didn't come soon, Coleen, Mama, and Brian would be dead too. But she didn't regret their flight. She would rather die in the snow, than to have stayed behind at the camp with the Graveses, and Kesebergs and Breens.

She had known that the stranded people there had turned slowly, reluctantly to cannibalism. Papa had tried to get them away before his family knew what was happening. But she knew. They all knew. None of the McKays spoke about it, perhaps for fear that once in the open, they, too, might fall prey to it. She wondered if she would have felt differently about it if someone like Patrick Dolan had told her of it rather than Keseberg. Even now she shuddered, remembering the gleam in his eye, the look of pleasure that was on his face when he had seen how ill his talk made her. Louis Keseberg was a sadistic man. If for no reason other than to be away from him, she would prefer to die out here lost in the cold, than to have remained with the rest of the Donner Party.

As the heavy snows had continued, the weight had collapsed the McKay hut, and they had been forced to move onto the lake and beg for shelter. The Breens had been jealously guarding their supply of meat, and would share none. The Murphey cabin was already overflowing with people, but Widow Murphey took in the McKays and Brian. It was there Fiona had been forced into the company of Keseberg, who claimed to be injured, but Fiona doubted the truth of that. He wanted only to preserve his own strength, while others fought the cold and hunger and their own fear of pain and dying to find food and wood to keep them warm. Louis Keseberg lay about, keeping warm and alive on the labors of others. Fiona always had the feeling he watched to see who was most likely to die next to keep him whole for another period of time.

He would be watching her and her father now, if he were around. He would wait, knowing the sorts of thoughts going through her head as she slowly came to the acceptance of death. The knowledge stirred a nearly dead anger in her. Fiona got to her knees, then to her feet, and began to pull at her father's shoulders again. She wouldn't give up. She couldn't, and she wouldn't let him give up either. She put all her weight into her task, managing to sit him upright, then she quickly positioned herself behind him, her back to his. Using her legs to do the heavy work, she rocked against him, keeping him in motion, and bringing him to reluctant wakefulness. "Mama! Coleen! Brian! Help! Mama!"

Three other scarecrows stumbled from the barren trees and scraggly pines, their backs hunched against the biting wind and the burden of wood and twigs they carried.

Mary dropped her bundle and staggered to her husband. She wrapped her arms around him. "Sean McKay, don't you dare give up and leave me!"

Sean put his arm limply around her neck. He would give anything to her, do anything for her, but this time it was not in his power. "No paradise, Mary . . . not here."

"You faithless man!" she scolded, her voice hoarse and rasping from strain and emotion. "You want everything handed to you! Get on your feet, man, and help me build the fire that will keep your family alive for tomorrow. Tomorrow we will get out of the mountains."

Brian, tall and rangy, his sandy hair laden with snow, took one of Sean's arms, and between him and the womenfolk they got Sean to his feet. Mary looked gratefully at Brian, and thanked God for the blessings He gave even in the midst of travail. Had it not been for Brian, her family would have been dead days ago. Brian, with his superior knowledge of the wild, his advice in preparing them to leave the Truckee Lake camp, had hunted for them, taught them to build fire from sodden wood, to boil hides and bark when there was nothing else to eat, and to survive.

Mary kept at Sean's side. He was now moving feebly on his own, but she kept her eye on him constantly. He couldn't leave her. They had gone through too much to die now. They were going to get out of the mountains, though she didn't know how.

Two days before they had slipped out of the Truckee Lake camp, hopeful and expecting to make it over the pass to safety, and then a storm had come, and they had searched for shelter. Some of their carefully considered supplies had been lost, and the world had changed.

They didn't know what direction they had taken in the blizzard, and they no longer had a compass. For days they had been heading toward what seemed to be west, although it was hard to tell where the sun was, with leaden skies spewing snow with such ferocity that one could not keep one's eyes open. But she hadn't given up. No storm lasted forever. One day—perhaps tomorrow, as she had promised Sean—the sun would pop through and guide them west to the pass, to Bear Valley, to safety. She clung to that piece of inevitability. It was all she had. That, and her faith that God had not given them Brian to teach them to survive so long, only to let their lives end here in this wilderness. No, they would get out of the mountains. Brian had seen them through so far, and he would continue to.

She thought of the many times the five of them had shared one small rabbit, barely able to wait for a fire to warm the animal's flesh before they wolfed it down, gnawing at sinew and bones like ravenous animals, saving the skin to boil and eat when they had nothing else.

Mary was thankful, but she still shivered against her newly discovered awareness of her own savagery. She had been appalled to find that all the learned gentility of her life and upbringing fell away in the face of hunger. She had torn apart animals with her bare hands, eating uncooked flesh, savoring the nourishment of still-warm blood. She now knew there was little she was not capable of, and for the safety of her own soul, she would always be thankful that Sean had decreed they were leaving Truckee Lake before she found out what her limits were—or were not.

Brian guided them as they built a platform of sorts on which to make their fire, so that it would not burn through the crust of snow and go out. Hampered as they were by limbs that no longer moved because of the cold and deprivation, and the slowness with which they comprehended even the simplest things, it was laborious, taxing work. Brian, Mary, and Fiona did the bulk of the work, as they had done for the last two days. Brian worried about Sean. If help did not come soon, or if they did not get a break in the weather to find their own way out of the mountains, Sean would not last. Already Brian had seen too many signs that he was failing. And Coleen . . . He didn't like to think of how long Coleen would survive.

He had never been in love before he met Coleen. His stepmother had teased him regularly about the woman who would catch him. She might have had Coleen in mind, for she had always said it would be a sparkling-eyed girl from his own people. She had been a bit off, for Coleen's people were Irish, and his own had Scottish blood, but still, it was the same ancient stock, and the same misty land.

He hadn't believed Jane, for he had been raised in the West, and had no idea that a man could long for his own race without even knowing. But Brian had taken one look at Coleen and known that he would always be a glutton for her talk, her laughter, her company, her love. For a somewhat taciturn man, that was quite a revelation. He had thought, above all else, that he was practical, and here he was planning to marry a vivacious girl straight from the gentle rolling farmland of Illinois, who was in no way prepared for the mountains or the harsh realities of a pioneer territory.

If he were a more thoughtful lover, he knew he would pack her up, as soon as they reached safety, and take her back east to a gentler life. But he wouldn't. He was a Westerner. Somehow, if they made it out of the mountains, he would have to teach her how to live the only way he could.

He wondered if his father had thought the same thing about his mother. If he had, then Brian would have to do a better job than his father had. His mother lived only five years after his birth, and then the trip west had taken its due in the form of an Indian raid. In later years he had seen his stepmother, musket in hand, stand off such raids, but his mother had just been frightened, and the sight of savages paralyzed her rather than spurred her to action. Coleen was like his mother in that respect, but she would have to learn, because he could not lose her.

With the fire built they huddled close to its warmth, keeping vigilant that no one put a foot into the fire, not being able to feel the pain. Coleen lay close to Brian, her head on his chest, his arms wrapped around her. Sean, Mary, and Fiona made a similar embrace next to them, each taking and giving heat and heart to the other.

"Tomorrow, perhaps the sun will show through the clouds," Mary said.

Usually they didn't talk much. It took too much effort, and there was little to say that was not discouraging. Tonight, however, they talked, for they all needed to be strengthened by hope so they could go on. No one said anything about the fire-melted snow that soaked through their coats and fur rugs. No one mentioned the pain and ache in chilled joints, or the frightening knowledge that there were parts of one's own body that no longer had the sense of touch. No one spoke of the moments in the day when they had not been able to see for snow blindness, or the fear that one time that blindness would become permanent. They didn't speak of hunger, or note that there had been nothing at all, not even bark or hide, to eat this night.

"How many days has the storm been?" Fiona asked.

"Seven," Brian said.

"I think it's been six," Coleen said.

"Well, whichever it is, it cannot last much longer. The longest of all of them that I recall was nine days, wasn't it—the one in December?"

"It will end soon—tomorrow," Fiona said, and smiled at her mother. She closed her eyes for a moment and she wondered if that were true. Would tomorrow be the day?

Chapter Thirty-Six

Robin and Cameron arrived back at Sutter's Fort on March 22, 1847, just in time to hear that a rescue party had been formed and was to leave the next day from Johnson's ranch.

"We can't make it in time—not with all these pack animals," Cameron said.

Robin, already tense from the other delays, whirled to face his brother. "If we mount up and leave right now, we can catch up with them by tomorrow night."

Cameron stared at his brother, speculation in his eyes. "What are you so fired up about?"

"Brian's up there," he said curtly.

"Uh-huh," Cameron said, hands on hips, hat tilted rakishly to the back of his head. "All of a sudden you're Brian's best friend. I don't recall you showing so much interest any other time—like when he went hunting for gold and no one heard from him for months. Why no gallant rescue then?"

A look familiar to Cameron came across Robin's face. Cameron watched his brother's expression close, his jaw tighten, and his eyes turn to hard, bright chips of glass. He had seen that look many times as they grew up. Some things never changed. Robin didn't want to talk, perhaps didn't know how to explain what was driving him with such urgency to the mountains. Cameron grinned. "I'm ready to leave. What's keeping you?"

The life came back to Robin's face, and he smiled and punched Cameron's arm playfully. "Mount up! Time's awastin'."

Within the hour they once more had the packs onto the mules, the animals in a fairly orderly line, and were on their way out the huge gates of John Sutter's wilderness fort.

For the first few miles both men rode in silence, both sets of eyes fixed on the snow-covered slopes in the distance. Both men were deep into their own thoughts. Cameron felt as though he were being pushed along by an unseen hand that had suddenly taken control of his previously well-ordered life, causing chaos, confusion, and uncertainty. Though he had no logical objections, he did not like Susannah living and becoming a shopkeeper in New Helvetia. Or perhaps it was that he did not like her closeness to Sam Brannan. He was beginning to realize that Susannah Morrison had a power over him that no other living person could claim. She could stir a passion in him he couldn't contain. Yet every time he thought that passion was returned, Sam Brannan seemed to intrude. He would have to come to terms with Susannah. She was capable of destroying the ordered existence of his world.

Robin's reverie was even less relaxed than his brother's. With each rhythmic jolt of the horse's gait, he expected Cameron to ask him for an explanation for his fevered determination to pursue the rescue party, and he had none, at least none that he knew how to state in words that wouldn't make him sound like a madman, or an adolescent dolt. How did a grown man say that he simply had to do something that would tax him to the ultimate of his physical capacity, or burst with frustration? How did one explain that he simply had to climb the mountain, challenge ice and snow, wind and storm, and emerge victor simply to soothe the longing of his own spirit?

He glanced at Cameron, and was relieved to see the look of intent introspection. It meant no questions. For now there would be no probing into the how and why of Robin Gentry by the one man who might best be able to touch the depths of his twin.

Robin looked again at the man who rode so near to him he could reach out and touch his mount if he chose. They had been born within minutes of each other, and had shared the most intimate of living spaces for nearly nine months, and yet there were differences between them that assured Robin of his own individuality. Cameron had a calmness that Robin was both envious of, and horrified by. Sometimes he would question why he could not be content with the bounties nature or God laid at his feet, and at other times he felt wildly, passionately thankful that

424

he was driven to climb one more mountain, chase one more rainbow, dream one more distant dream. This was one of the times he felt driven.

He knew Cameron had within him the same driving passion. That worried him too, because Cameron kept such a tight rein on his emotions that they exploded from time to time. Perhaps challenging nature, and ultimately himself, was not so bad after all.

Though they remained silent, and immersed in their own thoughts, it was a pleasurable ride to Johnson's ranch for both of them.

"Well, now, y'missed 'em by a day," said the owner cheerfully. He slapped his knee and chuckled. "Can't say as I'm sorry though. Gives me another evenin' o' company. I ain't had so many visitors ever—guess I owe those Donner folks thanks. I sure would like to meet George Donner. Most o' the folks they bring down from there is skin an' bones an' all eat up with frostbite," he said in nonstop monologue. He invited them to sit by the blazing fire that roared in an enormous fireplace in his front room. "Have y'rselves a sit—git warm. Y'wouldn't have any corn likker, would ya?"

"Perchance I have," Robin said jovially, and produced a jug. He took a deep draught, then passed it on to Cameron.

After his turn with the jug, Johnson got up. "Since you got such good fillin's, I think I kin bestir myself to find us three good mugs."

Cameron and Robin left Johnson's at dawn, well fortified by corn whiskey and very little sleep. As closely as they could gather, the rescue party was approximately ten hours ahead of them. Late in the afternoon they began to cross Bear Valley. The faraway mountain began to tease them upward, coming nearer, looming monumental. Sheets of rock rose above them, tantalizingly majestic and appearing deceptively gentle along the grades, and in the passes, cruelly teasing with expanses of snow ten to fifteen feet deep, solid-looking, but treacherous.

Cameron approached the mountain with a look of grim acceptance. Robin's face was flushed with an almost desperate look of challenge.

Cameron said, "We may not be able to get through the pass. Let's make camp. We'll start out again in the morning."

Robin began building a fire, while Cameron unpacked supplies from the mules.

"This isn't just snow—there's a bad storm brewing up there," Cameron said, looking at the leaden, slow-moving clouds over the mountain.

"It doesn't change anything. The Donners and the others are still stranded, and we're still packed and ready to go."

"Are we going to the Donner camp first, Robin, or just search for Brian and the McKays?"

"We don't know where the McKays are," Robin said.

"That's why I'm asking you. I agreed to come on a rescue mission—not a suicide mission. We don't know which direction to take—we could use a little information, and a plan wouldn't hurt."

The campfire was high, and hot now. Robin made a show of being busy with their supper. Finally he knelt back on his haunches, his hands resting on his thighs. "I'm going to find Brian and the McKays. I may never find them—and I may get into trouble myself. But you asked what I had in mind, and that's it. I want you to come with me, but I don't blame you if you've got better sense."

"Jesus Christ!" Cameron muttered, and pulled his bedroll around him.

"Well . . ." Robin prompted.

"I'm the twin of a madman. Get some food into me, and give me a night to think on it."

They awakened to heavy snow on March 28. Cameron arranged and repacked their gear. If this were anyone but his brother, he'd turn back. This whole thing of Robin's was worse than madness—but he kept on packing equipment. Cameron also kept on looking to the sky. His face was covered with cold, sticking flecks of snow that clung to his hair and his two days' growth of beard. If this weather continued—and he was sure this was one of those big, long-lasting mountain snowstorms—these innocent, beautiful flakes would freeze and turn into frost and then icicles. Suddenly he felt Robin's need to succeed grip him. No matter what Robin wanted, the storm might defeat them, but not without a good fight.

They continued to make good time across the valley, but the nearer they came to the mountain the heavier the snow became, and the slower they moved. By the first of April they were near the pass that would take them to Truckee Lake.

The climb was steeper and the footing less certain. Snow had fallen steadily for the last four days, and this day didn't look promising. Sometimes when the wind gusted they couldn't see each other at a distance of twenty feet. Cameron, in the lead, was still astride his horse. Robin had dismounted and was at the rear of the pack, urging the animals up the uncertain inclines, moving them laterally along the most secure ledges. Cameron turned at a shout from Robin. One of the mules had strayed out of line and was buried belly deep in a drift. The mule brayed and struggled. Robin slid across the snow to grab hold of the animal's lead. With harshly barked commands, he dug and pulled and maneuvered until the mule's feet hit solid rock again, and it got back in line.

"Need a breather?" Cameron yelled.

"No, move 'em along. They'll all panic if we don't keep moving."

Cameron urged his horse forward, but the animal was jittery. He took a deep breath and realized that he was just as jittery. They were all in perilous positions. Cameron gave encouraging commands, and the mules moved reluctantly, heads down, puffs of warm air exploding from their nostrils.

Despite the cold and the snow, Cameron was sweating under his heavy leather coat. He looked at the stark white slopes, and the great jagged breaks in the rock that meant the pass. No place to stop for a rest. He heard a shrill, panicky braying and turned sharply in his saddle, giving the rein a sharp jerk. His mount shook his head and began to prance on the precarious outcropping of rock.

Cameron's attention was on his mount, as he soothed the horse, but the animal had already lost his footing. His haunches were bouncing up and down in an effort to gain purchase, his hooves digging frantically at the slick rock. The horse's belly was nearly touching earth as he lost his ground.

Behind him, Cameron heard the wild braying of the mules, and Robin's tension-fraught voice. Cameron's horse fell down on its knees. He dismounted, but slid on the snow, holding on to the horse to regain his footing. He turned just in time to see a mule slide back on its haunches, twist, screaming and pawing the air as it tried to right itself.

Robin lunged for the animal's lead, leaping out of the way just as the mule tumbled heels over pack down the incline. Robin, propelled by the force of his own motion, slid down the slick embankment on his belly.

427

The other mules pranced and pawed, heads back, braying loudly, the whole pack train in danger of beginning the precipitous slide. Then one mule made a powerful lurch forward, forging his own path up the steep mountain. The others followed.

Cameron watched the sudden rush forward, then looked down at his brother lying spread-eagled on the snow-covered ledge below. The mule lay fifty or so yards farther down the mountain, a twisted, still carcass, its pack spilled and strewn. Cameron tied his rope around his saddle horn, then around his waist, and carefully edged toward Robin, clinging to the icy edge of the mountain. He wasn't sure that he, Robin, and the horse would not follow the path of the dead mule. The two men worked well together. Cameron threw the rope within inches of Robin's hand. Moving slowly, cautiously, Robin fixed the rope around his chest, and began inching his way up from the ledge. As aware as Cameron of the jitteriness of the horse, he put as little pressure on the rope as possible, using it only when his own and Cameron's strength was not enough. Forty-five minutes later the two men embraced, and sank breathless and sweating to the snow.

"God," Robin breathed. "That's as close as I want to come."

Cameron didn't trust his voice. They sat, leaning against the rock walls until their breathing slowed and their heartbeats were nearer normal. Finally Cameron said, "There isn't much daylight left, and if we don't find those mules and your horse, we'll have to turn back. All our supplies—"

"What I wouldn't give for a swallow from one of those jugs now," Robin interrupted, getting to his feet. "Their trail shouldn't be too difficult to follow."

The mules, after their initial flight, had slowed down after going through the pass and had wandered off to higher ground. By the time dusk was making purplish shadows on the snow, and blackness outlined the deeper outcroppings of rock, Cameron and Robin could hear the mules, if not see them. They moved steadily toward the sounds. It was near full darkness when they found five of the six mules safely huddled together, and Robin's horse standing head down several feet away. The noisy braying had been due to a tear in one of the mule's feed packs. The mules had been in constant motion, with the others pursuing, so there was a trail of oats quite easy to see on the snow.

They got control of the mules, tied them to a pine, and began salvaging what grain they could, building a fire, and setting up camp for the night. They had lost two mules with their supplies, and most of the grain from the third pack, and had lost their way as well.

"How far off Truckee Lake do you think we are?" Cameron asked, easing himself down into a nest of blankets near the fire.

Robin laid down a waterproof sheet on which he'd make his bed. "We can't be too far. Three or four miles north, I think." He sank down, impatient for the water and beans to make into coffee. "Supposing Brian and the McKays had been driven back from the pass—sort of the reverse of what we were. Mightn't they be somewhere near us?"

Cameron gave a dry laugh. "They might be. Or they might be three miles to the south, or—"

"All right," said Robin. "So I'm grabbing straws, but it is likely they are north or south of the lake, and since we're already north of it, why not look around tomorrow? One thing about people—they always leave evidence behind."

Cameron grunted agreement, then poured coffee and dug the potatoes out of the coals. He tossed three of them to Robin, then went back to his bed. Both men were exhausted and fell asleep after they ate.

Robin was awakened first, and sat straight up, his ear cocked to a sound he couldn't identify as animal or human. The shrill sound came again, and this time Cameron stirred.

"What's that?" he mumbled, sleep-fogged. "Cat?"

"I don't think so. Listen . . . Cam, I would swear that's a voice yelling 'Papa' . . . Listen, there it is again."

Cameron was on his feet, moving toward the sound. Then he turned suddenly to his left, for it now sounded as though it were coming from over there.

Robin moved closer to his brother. "What do you think?"

"Damned if I know for sure. It sounds like a woman's voice. I thought it was coming from over there, but now . . ."

"It's these damned rocks—they bounce sound around and fool you. And it carries on a night like this. That sound could be a couple of miles off, but I say we take a look."

They set out with the horses, and a small amount of food, and one jug of whiskey, another of brandy. They agreed to search the area nearest their camp. Methodically they made a fan-shaped search, moving farther laterally with each sweep away from their camp, stopping periodically, hoping to hear again the plaintive cry of a woman calling Papa. They heard nothing resembling that original eerie sound.

"It must have been a cat yowling after all, or the howl of the storm," Cameron said, staggering with cold and fatigue. "Let's try again in the morning."

Robin agreed, but pulled a red bandanna from his pocket and affixed it to a pine bough. "We'll know where we've been. I sure don't want to retrace our steps."

They returned to camp and fell into an immediate sound sleep wrapped in their blankets near the fire.

Chapter Thirty-Seven

Brian had spent a good deal of time in the mountains, sometimes hunting for sport, sometimes prospecting, chasing after elusive rumors of wealth to be picked up in the mountain streams. He had never found anything, but he had learned about the mountains. He had been lost before, but never in the snow, and never when the skies were so thick he didn't have the sun or the stars to guide him. In other circumstances, he would have stayed put, gathered wood, tried for game, and waited for better weather, but Sean was not going to survive if he wasn't kept moving, and Coleen was slowly succumbing to the mind-numbing lethargy that could spell disaster. He had to hope his instinct was correct, and that he was guiding them south and west, where he thought the lake was, and the pass beyond.

He walked ahead of his small band. Sean was several yards back, being helped by Coleen and Mary. Only Fiona seemed able to keep up with him. He didn't know how she managed. She was as weak as the rest of them, as cold, and as frightened, but she kept going, her green eyes burning with determination, her small round chin set. He wished he had something hopeful to tell her, anything to reward her efforts.

They moved more easily now over level ground, through a copse of pine. Fiona took two quick steps, and clutched Brian's sleeve. She had helped him hunt so often that he obeyed her silent command. He stood still, his ears trained for sound, his eyes scanning the area. The wind had died down, and he neither saw nor heard anything. Then, as a breeze whipped up and made the pines sough, he saw a flash of color. He and Fiona moved forward.

The McKays and Brian had depended on each other so long and through so many hardships that certain patterns had been established. Coleen, Mary, and Sean stopped walking, huddled together, and waited, watching as Fiona and Brian stalked something—some game, perhaps tonight's meal.

Fiona and Brian came out on the far side of the pines, and Fiona stood staring at a red bandanna knotted to one of the lower branches. It nodded and waved with the motion of the tree limb. "Brian," she said hesitantly. "Someone's been here . . . Brian! We must be near the lake—or someone is looking for us."

Brian looked carefully at the bandanna. Its color was still bright, and though it was covered with snow and frost, it obviously hadn't been on the tree for long. "Two days at most I'd guess," he said, and checked the bandanna for tears, marks of any kind that would indicate how long it had been there. The most encouraging sign was that the deeper folds of the bandanna were dry—dry and clean. He tried to restrain the urge to laugh, but couldn't. His rusty voice cracked out across the crisp, cold air. Fiona, with tears in her eyes and her knees nearly buckling under her, joined him.

The unlikely sounds of laughter brought the other three running. "What's happened?" Sean asked, his face white with exertion.

"Fiona, you are all right?" Mary put her arms around her young daughter. "Are you laughing or crying?" she asked, frightened she was seeing the beginning of hysteria. They had to stay united, and strong for each other. They had to.

"Mama," Fiona said, raising her face from Mary's shoulder, where her mother was fiercely cradling her head. "Someone was here. Look—Brian, show her the bandanna. Someone was here and left it tied to the tree!"

Mary stared at the bandanna, tears in her eyes. "We're saved?" she asked, her voice cracking. "Sean, Sean, people have been here . . . we may be saved." She stood helplessly looking at her husband, her eyes filled with gratitude, love, and tears. "I knew we would be—we prayed."

"Mary," Brian said uncomfortably, "I don't want to make you doubt, but these people—or person—may be in trouble too.

432

The bandanna may have been left here in hopes that someone can help the owner.''

"Oh, my God," Coleen moaned. "Will there never be mercy!"

"Hush, now," Mary said, going to Coleen. "We'll have no talk like that. There is always mercy, and it will be ours. We are alive, and we will find our way out of this wilderness. You'll see.''

"And we'll find this man," Fiona said. "Even if he has lost his way, one more added to our group will be another hand to gather wood and hunt. Whatever the bandanna means, Coleen, it is good for us.''

Coleen wiped her eyes, but there was anger there. "You don't know what you're talking about!" she cried. "You're saying stupid things to keep us going one more day, then another and another. There's no end to it! The cold will kill us, or the hunger, or we may die of old age forever lost!''

"Coleen!" Sean cried. Mary reached out to her. Uttering a shrill cry, Coleen hit her mother with her thickly wrapped hand, and with a burst of strength flung herself away. Mary sprawled on her back in the snow. Coleen ran wildly through the pines crying and screaming.

"Coleen! Coleen, come back!" Fiona cried, running, trying to keep pace with Brian in pursuit.

Coleen ran erratically, looking back over her shoulder from time to time. The scarf she had wrapped around her head came loose, and streamed behind her. "Go away! Leave me be!" She hunched over and ran faster, then suddenly disappeared.

Brian's long legs left Fiona far behind. By the time she caught up with him, he was lying flat, digging frantically at a depression. "Call your father quick! She's buried in there! Hurry, Fiona!" He was scooping snow, digging the hole deeper and deeper, and still there was no sign of Coleen or her scarf.

Fiona screamed for her parents. Sean and Mary came running. All of them dug with Brian. "Where did she fall?" Sean asked.

"I don't know exactly!" Brian said with a frightened quiver in his voice. "I saw her go down here—somewhere . . . We must get her out soon, or—''

"Don't say it!" Mary said shrilly. "We'll find her. Blessed Jesus help us, we'll find her!''

Robin and Cameron were moving steadily, slowly away from

the McKays when they heard again the strange animal cries that sounded like a woman. They stopped, looking at each other. "That's no animal, by heaven," Robin said. "I don't know who it is. But I sure as hell am going to find out."

In one accord, the two men turned their horses and moved a few yards, then stopped, hoping for more cries to direct them. This time the noise didn't stop, and they heard more than one voice. "Was that someone laughing?" Cameron asked in bewilderment. "I'm beginning to feel like we're having an hallucination."

"Sounded like laughter to me—a man and a woman."

After that they heard nothing, and moved forward slowly, not wanting to go in the wrong direction. "Come on, whoever you are," Robin said through tight lips. "Make noise. Come on . . . guide me!"

Almost on command, they heard a woman's shrill screaming, and then several others shouting. "That was no laugh!" Robin said, and put his heels into the horse's side. "Leave the mules here."

Cameron tied the mules securely to a pine, then followed after Robin.

A hundred yards farther on he came across tracks, and Robin saw the bandanna he had tied to the tree two nights ago lying on the ground. He followed the tracks, and came upon four people digging in the snow. One of the women cried, "Blessed Jesus help us, we'll find her!" Robin felt fear clutch his throat, the kind of fear that threatened all men. He didn't need to know who was buried in that snow pit; it threatened him as it did all who knew life. He leapt from his horse and ran to join the group who were so intent they did not even notice his arrival.

Soon after Cameron joined. He asked no questions either.

Coleen was blue and limp when they finally uncovered her head.

"Is she alive?" Sean shrilled, his face working grimly. "My baby, is she alive?"

He and Mary were crying and working in unison, pleading with God as they dug deeper.

Cameron caught Robin's eye. "I'm going for the mules, we'll need the supplies."

Only then did the family notice that two strangers had joined them. A girl with emerald eyes that burned like colored flame stared at Robin, and then incongruously smiled at him with a warmth that melted him. "She'll live, I know. You were sent to help us. Thank you." The girl never stopped working, nor did the incandescent glow that seemed to come from her diminish. Robin worked as hard as she, then realized this should not be so. The girl was more than half frozen, probably starving, and yet there glowed from her a vitality the like of which Robin Gentry had never before known. With a power that startled him, he wanted to get this woman out of the snow, warmed, and alive again because this waif of a woman beside him said it should be so. If she said it, he believed it, and he'd work to make it happen.

With the rope from Robin's horse, Brian and Robin pulled Coleen free after they had dug down as far as her shoulders. "Go easy," Robin said, seeing the impatient anxiety on Brian's face. "Slowly does it. We don't want to cave it in again. Eas-ssy!"

Fiona stood by the snow pit watching to see if she'd be needed again. Satisfied that she wasn't, she went alone to gather wood, and began a fire to place her sister by.

With each of them taking a limb they rubbed Coleen's wrists and legs, almost willing life back into her body. Robin stood to the side, wanting to help, but not able to intrude on what was a family effort. As he watched them and felt the love flowing among them, he thought, we've found the McKay family.

As soon as Cameron returned, Robin ran to help bring up the pack mules. From one pack he extracted the brandy jug, and fished around for a small gourd dipper. "Try to get her to drink this. Just put it to her lips and let it trickle down her throat," he said, offering it to the oldest man, but Sean just looked blankly at him. Robin stood, hand outstretched, then he turned to the girl. "This will warm her if she can be made to swallow a little."

Fiona looked at him without speaking, her brilliant green eyes sending shock waves through him. Then she held out her hand for the gourd. "I do not know whether you are real or not. You just appeared."

A mule brayed noisily, and broke the tension. Robin smiled. "Oh, we're real enough. Now, try to give her some of this, and you take some as well. It won't hurt you, it's just brandy. It will warm you."

As Fiona touched Coleen's lips with the brandy, Cameron and Robin were unsure what to do. Of all the reactions they had expected, this had not been among them. "I don't think they know we're really here. Brian doesn't even seem to recognize us,'' Cameron said in amazement. ''What do we do?''

''Give them time to bring the girl around, or see that she cannot be saved, and then we'll just take command. What about starting a big fire and having some supper right now? Real food might bring a startling change.''

It was nearly nightfall before Coleen showed signs of reviving, and the McKays eased their concentrated vigil. Mary McKay was the first after Fiona to pay heed to the strangers. Her eyes were red and running from tears and fatigue. ''You saved my daughter's life, and ours . . . how can I . . .'' She broke down in racking sobs.

Brian, hearing another distressing sound, jumped up and came over to Mary and Cameron and Robin. Only then did he recognize the heavily bearded, heavily clothed men. His gray eyes grew wide, a look of disbelief on his face. ''Cameron . . . Robin . . . surely it isn't you?''

Robin put his hand out and smiled. ''Surely it is. We told Aunt Jane we'd find you and bring you home.''

Brian lurched forward, his arms widespread to embrace both Gentry brothers. When he was able to speak, he said, ''We've been lost for over a week—we left the camp—there were people there who—we couldn't stay . . .''

''We'll have plenty of time to talk once we get to Sutter's. Rest easy now. Let Cam and me do what must be done. Let's get food in you and some warmth.'' Robin led him to the fire that he and Cameron had built. One by one the McKays were seated, waiting like obedient children to be fed. Their eyes were huge and staring as the odors of hot coffee, broth, and roasting potatoes came to them. With the food barely cooked, Cameron made certain no one ate too much or too fast. Even the small amounts they were permitting might not be accepted by the stomachs of starved people.

Almost immediately after eating, the McKays fell into exhausted sleep. Brian tried to remain awake and talk with the Gentrys, but he lasted only a sentence or two, and then his head nodded and the brothers were alone keeping watch through the night.

Both of them wanted to remark on the time they had arrived to find the McKays, and neither of them knew how to say it. Though both Robin and Cameron were men of God, neither of

436

them was familiar or comfortable with expressions of faith. But their advent was too timely to go unnoticed. Cameron shook his head. "Do you feel strange about this? If we'd have come ten minutes later that girl would not be alive." He watched Robin with a mild apprehension, wondering if he was going to receive a cynical reply.

But Robin was staring into the fire, a fixed look of bemusement on his face. "I don't know what to say. Fiona asked me if I were real . . . she thought we were angels sent to help them . . . but damn it, Cam, I've never met people who affected me like—like these do. I'm not sure *they* are real." Robin made a face, making fun of his admission. "Maybe we all died and this is heaven." He looked back to the fire, embarrassed. He wondered what Cameron would think if he knew all the strange feelings he had had that afternoon and night.

Robin hadn't said much about Fiona. He couldn't, without sounding ridiculous. He had the impression of an enchantingly beautiful girl, yet there was not a shred of beauty to be found in that skeletal bag of tied rags and oddments of clothing that lay on the ground across the fire from him. She was haggard and dirty, and emaciated, and on the verge of death, yet somehow she gave him the sense of life at its fullest and most vibrant. He shook his head, his eyes fixed on the leaping flames. She was his reason for coming to the mountains, he decided, then laughed silently at his fancy. She had nothing to do with it, he argued with himself, and then laughed again. *She did*. He knew he would climb any mountain, walk through any snowstorm, fight any man or beast that ever dared harm her. He might have come upon her by accident, but there was something about her that touched him so deeply that from now on her well-being was his well-being.

In the morning the Gentrys prepared another light meal and portioned it out carefully. Sean, now certain that the men were real, and that he and his family would actually get out of the mountains, looked pathetically at Cameron. "Is there no more?" He held out an empty tin plate.

"We'll eat again in a couple of hours. If you eat more now, you'll only throw it up. Drink this." Cameron offered the gourd half full of brandy. "It will help."

Under his breath Robin said, "Go easy—we lost several jugs on that mule that wandered off. We may have a long trip down the mountain."

437

Cameron raised his eyebrows. "We'd better make it a fast trip, because as soon as they realize they can eat again, we are going to have the devil's own time keeping them out of the supplies."

"Can we make it with what we have left?" Robin asked, suddenly unsure.

"How lost are we?" Cameron asked, shrugging. "Maybe we can—maybe not."

"You're cheerful this morning. I'll talk to Brian. He thinks we're his salvation."

"Good. Brian will understand that we're going to have to stay on strict rations. He'll impress that on the McKays."

Robin said certainly, "We won't have trouble with the McKays. If no one else can keep them going on rations, that little daughter will."

"Fiona?" Cameron asked. "She's just a girl."

Robin laughed, but said nothing. Fiona McKay would never be "just a girl."

Cameron and Robin and the scraggly band of four McKays, Brian Campbell, four remaining pack mules, and two horses began the long trek across Bear Valley on April 15, 1847. For the first time since they had been trapped, the McKays believed they would reach California to begin their new life. As they moved steadily toward Johnson's ranch, they passed the Fallon rescue party on their way to Truckee Lake. The two groups stopped only long enough to ask a few questions, to offer congratulations and good luck.

"How was it up there?" Fallon asked Robin. "We heard things was pretty bad." He lowered his voice to a whisper. "They really eatin' each other—maybe helpin' some o' the weaker ones along?"

Robin thought of some of the disjointed statements Brian and the others had made. He shook his head. "I don't know. We never made it to the lake. We were lost in a storm, and Providence led us to these people."

The other man sighed. "Well, there's nothing for it but to see for ourselves. I hope it's just rumor. I'd sure like to bring down some live, healthy people."

Robin nodded, then added, "Live maybe—but not likely healthy." He pulled on the horse's reins and waved. "Good luck to you."

He rejoined his own band, and discovered they had decided to ride to New Helvetia rather than stop at Sutter's Fort. Robin looked at the drooping, bedraggled McKays, then at his brother. It was probably best, if they had the strength. None of them was going to receive appreciable care until they reached Jane's house.

Once out of the mountains, the McKays began to thaw, and were in greater pain than previously. Robin stayed as near Fiona as he could without making his interest too obvious or bold. She sat rigidly and bravely on her mule, but she couldn't keep the pain from her eyes, and she couldn't prevent the tight, pinched look on her face.

When at last they reached Jane's, Robin was nearly as thankful to see her as she was to see them. He had never seen Jane cry or behave in what he thought of as the usual womanly way, but she did now. She nearly swallowed Brian in an embrace, laughing and crying at the same time. But she indulged herself for only a short time, and then she was all business, sorting out people, issuing directives to Millie, and busily assembling her herbs, cures, and folk medicines. Basins of cold water were brought in to ease the thawing of frozen toes and fingers. Soup was soon simmering on her huge old stove. Robin was sent back outside to chop extra firewood.

He complained, grinning, "Don't I get tender loving care?"

"No," Jane said cheerfully, waving him out the door. "There's no solace for heroes, m'dear."

But that wasn't true for all heroes. Cameron had barely opened the door before Susannah had run and flung herself into his arms. Her dark hair was shiny and bouncing with fresh, clean verbena-scented perfume in it. Cameron lifted her off her feet and swung her around. "You're home!" she gasped. "You're safe!" She kissed his cheeks and eyes, squirming and laughing at the roughness of his beard. She helped him off with his coat and stood waiting as each successive layer of clothing, scarves, boots, and hand-wrappings, came off.

Cameron smiled up at her as he worked on his left boot. "You'd better start holding your nose. I'm pretty ripe by now."

Susannah began to protest, but didn't, for she had to release her held breath before she could speak. They both burst out laughing. "I'll draw your bath for you—but I don't want to leave you long enough to bathe . . . perhaps . . ."

"No!" he said quickly, then looked down. "Not with a houseful of people."

Susannah smiled and went after the bathing tub and hot water. She was eager for a quiet night and a quiet, private time when Cameron would tell her all that had happened, and the thoughts he had had while he was gone from her. If they were nearly as filled with longing and desire as hers had been for him, this might be the time all barriers between them would be overcome.

Susannah did not get her quiet time, or private moment with Cameron that evening. Once she had seen to his bath, she didn't have another free moment. Beds were hastily put together, furniture rearranged, special foods prepared for use in the days to come. Small meals were parceled out almost hourly to the emigrants.

As soon as Cameron was washed, Susannah prepared a bath for Robin, and once that had been accomplished, Susannah, Robin, and Cameron were all put to work, under Jane's supervision, washing the McKays' and Brian's hair. Their old clothes were removed and burned. Fresh nightclothes—voluminous gowns of Jane's—were put on everyone, including a loudly protesting Sean. "By God! You'll ruin my manhood putting this pink frippery on me!" he squawked.

"Quiet," Jane said, pushing him into a chair. She tossed a towel over his head and began to rub his hair dry. "I'll not have lice in my house. Either it's naked as you came into the world—or pink frippery. Sit still. There are others yet to have their heads washed and dried."

After the first flurry of activity, which was, in some ways, more strenuous than the trip down the mountain, the McKays and Brian were all tucked into bed, and expected to sleep through the night and most likely through the following day. Jane, Cameron, Susannah, and Robin sat in the kitchen, for there wasn't an empty space anywhere else in the house.

It was then that Robin pointed out, "You don't have space for the whole family here. You haven't left yourself a place to sleep."

"We'll make do," she said firmly. "I can sleep in a chair. Right now, we must guard against fever with these people." She sighed.

"We'll have to move someone," Robin insisted. "You won't

be able to keep up without proper rest." He waited until he saw agreement in her eyes.

"We could take Sean with us and leave the women here," Cameron offered, and received a scowl from his brother.

"I was going to talk with Mrs. McKay in the morning to suggest we take one of the daughters home with us. Mother will be doing the nursing. It will be easier for her to look after a woman."

"Isn't the same true of Aunt Jane?" Cameron asked.

Jane let out a guffaw that set them all chuckling. Robin said, "Mrs. McKay can look after her husband. She's pretty strong. I think Aunt Jane will have an able helper in her soon."

"She is a fighter, isn't she?" Jane said. "I knew I liked the McKays as soon as I met them." She laughed again. "From what Brian says, it's a good thing. Our families will be merging as soon as young Coleen is on her feet again." She lowered her voice. "Truth to tell, I think he picked the wrong one. The little one, Fiona, is much stronger—and I think livelier."

"Then I'll ask Mrs. McKay about Fiona. If Brian and Coleen are to marry, then . . ."

Cameron had known all along what Robin wanted. He glanced at Susannah, her eyes sparkling and avid on him, and he felt what was becoming a familiar rush of desire. He took the snifter Jane offered.

"I propose we all toast each other, particularly the Gentry brothers," she said. "For all time, you men have my gratitude. I wouldn't have my Brian if it weren't for you." She paused, her eyes sparkling. "And next we'll toast my future grandchildren. Think they'll call me Granny Jane?"

Cameron, Robin, and Jane slept in bedrolls on the kitchen floor. Susannah had reluctantly gone alone to her own bed, and Cameron found that with her so near, sleep was difficult even with the aid of brandy and fatigue. Those times he did doze off, it was to dream of her. He could still recall the scent of her hair and skin. He had only to close his eyes to be haunted by the feel of her warm soft lips on his. He spent an uncomfortable night.

Robin didn't sleep much better. He was so anxious to talk with Mary that he kept awakening, thinking it was morning. When at last he heard the sounds of a rooster crowing, he arose, put on coffee, and paced outside until he could decently talk to the woman.

Mary listened quietly and patiently, then, with her hands folded neatly on her lap, her gray-green eyes steady on him, she said, "I have seen how you look at my daughter, Mr. Gentry."

Robin blushed, and began to speak. She held her hand up for silence. "I am not chastising you. I am merely pointing out that I believe you have a special caring for Fiona. I want to know if that is true."

Robin was having difficulty speaking. This was a very direct, if gentle, woman. He wasn't accustomed to that. Nor was he accustomed to having to admit his feelings baldly to a stranger, but he managed a strangled reply. "Yes, it's true, but I would never pose a danger to her, Mrs. McKay. I would protect Fiona with my life."

Mary smiled at him, her eyebrows raised. "I know that, Mr. Gentry. You already have, and I know you would do it again. But Fiona is very weak right now. You know her only in a small way . . ." She looked down, a smile playing on her lips, yet she was very serious. "Your feelings are not likely to remain noble, nor so manageable, when she is more herself. You see, Mr. Gentry, I know my daughters, but I do not know you. Fiona just turned sixteen while we were in the mountains. Even though it might not be fair, should anything, uh, unmaidenly happen to Fiona, my husband would not take into account that Fiona is capable of driving a dead man to drink. Her honor would be upheld . . . and if necessary, avenged."

Robin stared open-mouthed at this frank woman. Had that come from any other woman he knew, including Jane, he would have thought she was warning him away from a loose-moraled daughter for whom he'd be held responsible no matter what. But she wasn't doing that, he was sure of it. She was telling him the plain, honest truth. She had seen his reaction to Fiona even in her starved condition, while she was sick and unattractive, and knew how much greater his feelings would be when Fiona was herself. Robin was nearly shaking with excitement. "I still want to take her to Agua Clara, Mrs. McKay. I want her to be well again, and—and . . ."

Mary laughed, showing a trace of her old cheerful self. "And you want to be there to watch her."

Again he blushed. He wasn't comfortable with this woman who seemed to know his thoughts, pure or otherwise, and also put them into plain language. But it also thrilled him. What kind of family must this be when they were all healthy and full of talk and activity? How did one live with people this natural, and this willing to be open about one's most intimate thoughts and feelings? Stimulated by the McKays, he might never settle down, but he would always desire to climb mountains and challenge nature and himself. He suddenly wished he could rule the world, and it seemed a reasonable wish. Perhaps he would try it.

He must have had as daft a look on his face as his thoughts indicated, he decided later, for Mary went into peals of laughter. "I shall entrust my daughter to you, Mr. Gentry, but beware. You have been forewarned. Take good care of her."

Robin's face nearly broke with the grin that stretched across it. "I will! She'll be well taken care of, and healthy again in no time. And I'll come back here and escort you to Agua Clara to visit her as soon as you are fit."

Mary stood up when he did. She leaned forward and kissed him lightly on the cheek. "You're a good man, Robin Gentry."

Chapter Thirty-Eight

Susannah stood behind the counter of her shop. It still had the smell of newly sawed lumber. One day she'd have real plaster walls with the most fashionable of papers on them, but that would be later. Those walls would be in the shop in San Francisco, and there was much to be accomplished here before she could begin that venture. She had enough on her hands now, dealing with the shippers' agents in Monterey, through whom she supplied this store.

Meantime, she took great pride in her small country store. The counters shone from hours of her own labor as she rubbed wax into the finely sanded surfaces. Her hand now moved automatically across the wood grain, taking pleasure in the smoothness and searching for any remaining rough spot. She was thus engaged when the Gentry brothers entered.

Susannah's eyes lit up. The brothers were so beautiful to look at, and at least in feature, so much alike. She took in their straight dark hair, well-shaped noses, mouths made for smiling, and the green flecks in their light brown eyes, which she knew were like smoldering green fires waiting to be ignited by passion. But there the similarity ended. Robin crossed the floor space of the shop in four predatory steps. Cameron stood still, his eyes taking in the details of the stock on the shelves, the array of brilliant colors, every change since he had been there last. He stood in front of a display of hats Susannah had spent an hour trying to get right.

"Do you like it?" she asked, unable to keep pride from her voice.

"Yes," he said in appreciation. "You are very deft, Susannah. No wonder the ladies buy bonnets."

Susannah smiled. Still excited, she grabbed Cameron's hand and led him to the other side of the shop where an unfinished display case stood. "Look, it's almost done! Peter brought it over last evening." As an afterthought, she looked at Robin, who lounged against the bolts of calico, silk, muslin, and brocade she had stacked on a table. "We're—I'm going to display our fine jewelry here. The case will have glass—beveled glass on the front and top just as they have in the finest New York stores. Sam says the glass should be here soon, a few more weeks. I'll just die if any is broken, or if there isn't enough ordered that I may purchase some. I couldn't stand to wait for another shipment!"

Cameron's eyes were warm on Susannah. He loved to see her happy and excited. He wanted to hold her, but he could not. He could not forget she wasn't his. Sam Brannan's name was always on her lips, and the man was always nearby. He gave her a brotherly hug, then said brightly, "We are here on business. Will you accept the Gentrys as customers, Miss Morrison? We have quite an order to fill."

Susannah's eyes danced mischievously, but behind the teasing there was a deep, heated passion that Robin didn't miss—one that Cameron attributed to a reflection of his own unruly desires, which must be controlled.

"I think I can satisfy your every need," Susannah said in a deep, husky voice, her eyes blazing on Cameron, her hand out for the list he clutched.

Cameron stood dumbfounded, his eyes on her, his mind anywhere but on the list of supplies for Fiona.

Robin plucked the paper from Cameron's hand and gave it to Susannah. "Everything she's likely to need in the way of clothing. You'll know. Several lengths of material suitable for the sort of dresses she'll need once she's up and about again . . . and include some of those Godey designs you're so proud of. Mother and her seamstress will need them. Pick out the necessities that would make a wardrobe you'd like yourself, Susannah. That should do. Mary said they have nothing left."

Susannah was all business now, her eyes flashing down the list, her pencil poised to make additions and deletions.

Robin wandered about the shop, picking up an item here and there. He selected a finely tooled silver and turquoise comb, and an ornately stitched silk shawl. "These, too."

Susannah gave him a look. "These are very expensive . . . and not necessary, Robin. I have others not so—"

"I'll have these," Robin said, and his expression told Susannah his choice had nothing to do with practicality or necessity. "Also send samples of cloth over to Mary and Coleen. Help them select goods for two gowns each, and put it on my account. And send Jane a set of combs—your finest."

"Don't you care to choose them yourself?"

He gave Susannah a hard look. "You can choose them well enough. Cam, I am going over to Smith and Brannan's. I'll meet you there in an hour."

Susannah looked after Robin, her pencil beating a tattoo on the windowsill. "It makes one wonder, doesn't it?" she asked. "Your brother is very generous, especially considering the McKay women are virtual strangers."

Cameron could be as noninformative as his twin. "Yes, he is."

Being a natural tactician, and knowing when retreat was as good as a victory, Susannah turned, smiled brightly, and said, "But not nearly as generous as you! A gown will soon be out of style, but your gift to me is a part of my life and shall go on as long as I need it. Oh, Cameron, do you really like what I have done with the shop? Am I spending the money you gave me wisely? Oh! I haven't shown you my office yet." She led him into the small private room. With a pride-filled smile, she turned and looked at him.

Cameron took her in his arms, for that was what she seemed to want, yet the rich, warm feel of her against him made him angry. He had the awful feeling that he was following a script: Now it is time for Cameron to put his arms around Susannah. Now she will smile up at him and tell him he is wonderful.

Almost on cue, Susannah unwittingly said, "When will we be alone together? It's been so long—I miss you, Cameron."

Knowing he was being unreasonable, he tried to hold his temper. He laughed brittlely, and took a step back from her. He wanted more than anything to take her in his arms and squeeze her so close to him that she would become a part of him. But at the same time he kept hearing Sam Brannan's name repeated over and over. Sam would get glass. Sam had the store down the street. Sam was wonderful, Sam this and that. With his voice barely under control, he said, "I wouldn't have thought you'd have had time to give me a thought. You've been very busy with . . . the shop."

"I have," Susannah said, still chipper, but beginning to sense that not all was well between them. Nothing made sense, but it was threatening, and she felt like fighting. Without cause, she was angry with him. He complicated the simplest of things. A little more cautiously she said, "Every item in this store makes me think of you. I wouldn't be here if it weren't for you. I came here to be near you, Cameron."

"Did you?" he asked, and the control in his voice was gone. The words came out harsh and accusing.

Her heart pounded with the threat in his voice, and the fear and anger that overwhelmed her. Her eyes sparkling, her small jaw jutting out, she said, "What do you mean by that?"

"I asked if you came here to be near me. That's simple enough for you, isn't it?" Cameron said patronizingly, his own eyes brown and green fires.

"Why else would I have come to this Godforsaken place?"

"Why indeed—I thought you said earlier that you loved it here, you felt at home. What happened to that?"

Color leaped to her cheeks. "You're confusing me—you're evading the questions!"

"Well, if you could phrase a question, I might answer it, but all you do is dance around it!"

"Me! I'm not the one. I said very clearly that I came here to be near you, and you attacked me as though I had done something awful! If you don't want me—if you—" Susannah blushed as the idea that he might not want her as she wanted him was driven home. Quick tears sprang to her eyes.

Cameron made a face. "If you can't say what you mean, try tears, is that it, Susannah?"

"Why are you doing this to me?" she screamed, and pounded her small fist on her new desk. "If you don't want—"

"Why did you come here?" Cameron yelled, pushing his face so close to hers he could feel her breath.

"I told you! I told you! Why are you doing this?" she screamed back.

"Because I'm sick to death of you using me to gain what you want!"

"What?!"

"You heard me! You want Sam Brannan, and I'm your easiest way of getting near him."

"Sam! Sam has nothing to do with this!"

Cameron shouted, "He has everything to do with this!"

"Nothing! You leave him out of this."

"You love him!"

"I love *you!*" Susannah screamed, before she had time to think.

Cameron was too angry and too filled with his need to shout at her to have even heard her. "I know what you're up to—you wanted him, and by God, you didn't give a damn who you used or how you used him to get what you wanted. Well, Miss Susannah—no more! I'm getting out!"

"Cameron!" Susannah yelled, pounding on his arms. "I love you! You, you fool! You!" He paused to draw breath and she yelled, "I love you!" She leaped forward and threw her arms around his neck.

"What the hell are you doing?"

She began to laugh. "Getting your attention. Did you hear what I said?"

"Let go!"

"No! Did you hear me?"

"I don't want to hear you!" he growled.

Susannah was laughing hard now, near to tears, but unable to stop the compulsive laughter. She gasped, "I love you—not Sam—*you!* Cameron, kiss me! Do something!"

"What did you say?" he asked hesitantly, his hands on her interlocked hands, trying to remove them from his neck.

"I love you!"

His hands stilled, and he looked into her eyes. Tears streamed down her face, but she was still making laughing sounds. "You love me? Not Sam?"

Susannah nodded, her blue eyes brilliant.

Cameron's hands moved along her arms to her shoulders. "You mean that? Oh my God, Susannah . . ." Then his mouth was on hers, seeking, searching. His lips and tongue filled her with such an overwhelming passion that she almost forgot to breathe. She clung to him, gasping, "Oh, God—oh, Cameron

. . ." as he turned his head away from her. She could feel the hot urgency of his desire for her, and with decision she took his face between her hands and returned his lips to hers. Quivering with intensity, she felt his tongue slide into her mouth, and she accepted it eagerly, meeting it, caressing it with her own.

Holding her with one arm, he reached out and covered her breast with his hand, rubbing her almost too hard, his fingers spread as though to crush her softness. Rapidly she unbuttoned his shirt and pulled out the tails, and ran her fingernails lightly down his chest through the coarse curled hair.

His tongue forced itself farther into her mouth, while his lips seemed to open and close on hers with an expertise she hadn't known he possessed. He undid the buttons of her bodice, and soon her dress lay in a silken pool about her feet. She fumbled at his belt buckle, but in the end he undid it himself. His boots flew across the room, to land in corners, and his trousers crumpled up near them. He jerked the tape on her petticoat, and it floated away.

Naked together now, he laid her on the bare floor and lay beside her. None of their movements were gentle. Both were in the grip of a passion too long denied. He threw one leg over her body and she scarcely noticed the weight of it. His hard palms were one on each side of her face, while his tongue pillaged her mouth. Then his palm rasped down the side of her neck to her shoulder and onto her breast, down her belly to the moistness between her thighs. Still caressing her there, he moved his mouth to her breast, taking her nipple gently between his teeth, nipping, sucking, kissing, teasing.

Susannah shuddered with excitement as she took his hand and pressed it harder against her. With her other hand she groped for his penis. It throbbed in her palm, long and thick and hot.

Cameron could wait no longer, nor could she. She eased him into her, and moaned with pleasure at the sensation of being filled. His hands were under her hips to snug them tight together. They moved in rhythm several times, both giving gasps and whimpers of satisfaction and delight, until they were floating along on the great floodtide of release.

Robin Gentry, having grown impatient waiting for his brother, returned to the store. He opened the door and peered in. He saw no one, but the sounds he heard caused him to back away to the door. With great presence of mind, and a muffled laugh, he picked up the CLOSED sign, placed it in the window of the shop, and stood guard outside at the door.

When two matrons came up to the shop, he smiled pleasantly and said, "I am told Miss Morrison was called away on an emergency. She is to return in about half—no, an hour."

The two women said they hoped the emergency was not one of an unhappy nature, and that all was well with their favorite little shopkeeper.

"I'm certain she'll be just fine," Robin said, with a rakish smile that caused both women to feel ten years younger, and to gain amazing color in their cheeks.

Susannah and Cameron lay still on the floor of the office, spent, sweating, making small, fond, pleased noises of reminiscent approval. With their fingers they stroked each other lightly now, and Cameron's hand came up to push the curls away from Susannah's forehead and her cheeks. Once again he kissed her mouth in that devastating way, and she responded with hers.

Although they had scarcely finished, their passion rose again. She murmured, "Oh, Cameron . . . more . . ."

A chuckle began in his throat, and stopped. "I just did," he said. The corners of his mouth were lifted.

She felt him throb within her again, and she said, giggling and sliding first one thigh and then the other against him, "You just will."

He smiled, astonishingly cocksure. "Maybe I will at that."

This time there was all the time in the world. They made love slowly, leisurely, stopping twice just short of climax, feeling nevertheless an inward flow unlike it only in degree, and waiting for a moment to prolong their excitation.

With great care Susannah moved her legs so that he was straddling her and she held him as tightly as possible within her. Curving his long body to accommodate hers, he kissed her, his mouth nibbling hers. They came simultaneously, explosively. Then they lay drained, weak and smiling together.

Susannah had not realized her eyes were shut until she opened them and caught Cameron's glance. They were too exhausted to laugh, but were content just to smile and make satisfied sounds. With her fingertips Susannah massaged the hard muscles that lay across his shoulder blades. Cameron grunted in gratified surprise. He lay still on her, savoring the novelty of having his wants and desires so pleasurably fulfilled. When she stopped, they went on touching, kissing, murmuring endearments, and caressing each other.

When they grew drowsy, they dozed. Then he came awake with a little start, and smiled into Susannah's eyes, saying, "What a woman!"

Lovingly Susannah licked the salty sweat from his shoulder, and ran her fingernail lightly down his upper arm. She laughed tenderly. "What . . . a . . . man . . ."

Some moments later he said, "Susannah."

"Mm-hmm?"

"Did you mean what you said—that you love me, not Sam?"

"I meant it," she said lazily, content. "How could you doubt me?"

"I had reason . . ." he said, and fell silent for a long time. Then he said, "You and Sam . . . you were his lover, weren't you?"

It was Susannah's time to be quiet. She didn't know what to say. If she told the truth, she could scarcely blame him if he left her; and if she lied, he'd know it, and the result would be the same. She touched his bare shoulder, feeling the smooth texture of his skin, sad that this might be the one and only time she'd ever be with him. She started to speak, then fell silent again. It wasn't fair. She had been but a young girl reaching for the stars when she had met Sam, and she thought she had grasped one when he loved her. But what she had known with Sam was only a glimpse of love. Cameron *was* love. He was a part of her as no other man would ever be. How could she answer him?

"Why must you keep asking me about Sam, Cameron?" she asked in a small voice.

"I must know."

She could hear the sincerity in his voice. She took a deep breath. At least she had had this one day with him. She didn't see that she had any choice. Whatever she answered, the result was going to be the same. He'd leave her. "Yes," she said. "Sam and I were—with each other on the voyage from New York." There was silence. She waited for a few seconds, then could stand it no more. "Do you hate me now?"

Cameron exhaled a long held breath almost in a shudder. He rolled over on his side, propping himself on one elbow. His lips touched hers gently, warmly. He nibbled at her lips, mingling their breath, then he moved back, looking at her, his eyes warm

451

and loving, devouring the sight of her. He said softly, "I love you, Susannah."

"But . . ."

He kissed her again, gently, softly, for a long time.

"This isn't the end?" she asked, still unable to believe that he was not angered by her confession.

"Never an end with us," he said. "Do you suppose they make a cannon that could shoot out the sun? If we're this good in the daylight, just think of the night."

An ecstatic shiver rippled over Susannah's flesh. "This night?"

"Why not this night?" His eyes twinkled; his lips held back a smile.

For a moment she watched him, not sure, then she realized he was teasing.

He said, "Now that you've taken advantage of me, and I've discovered how wonderf—"

She poked him in the ribs. "Vantage even, darling."

Kissing her again, he declared, "I'll always be kicking myself for waiting so long to have you."

"Mmm. Next time, don't wait," she murmured, kissing him back. "I'll always want you, Cameron, I'll never tell you no." Already, again, they felt the flames of passion flickering.

"You haven't said you love me yet. How do I know this isn't mere physical attraction?"

"I have!" she said shrilly. He laughed, and she hoped he'd go on asking, so that she could tell him in detail the ways she loved him.

He said lightly, "Well then, perhaps time will tell." His lips met hers once more, but just as Susannah was going to surrender all her control to passion, he stood up and held out his hand to her. "Time to get back to business, Susannah."

She pouted prettily, refusing to move. "No, I'm ruined already, so why shouldn't I just stay here?"

He grinned down at her. "Please yourself, *mi vida*."

Susannah took a deep breath of well-being. He had called her "my life," his dearest.

Swiftly he had his clothes on and drew on the high boots. "I'd better get going," he said. "See you tonight, Susannah." He headed for the door and had his hand out to lift the latch when Susannah saw Robin standing outside and uttered a horrified shriek. "Cameron, don't!" She ran back for her petticoats before she realized that he had fooled her again. He had no intention of opening the door yet.

"Oh!" she cried, half of her attention on struggling into her clothes, and the other half divided between Cameron and Robin. "How long do you think he's been there? Oh, Cameron, what if—"

Cameron laughed. "He's been guarding us against intrusion."

"He knew!" she squeaked.

"I expect he did," Cameron said, then added with a wry grin, "You know, Robin thought we should have 'talked' a long time ago."

Susannah's face was on fire. "Don't open the door—ever! Don't let him in. I can't face him—he knows!"

Cameron came back to where she was dressing. Since her arms were strained as far as they would go in an effort to button her bodice in the back, he helped her. Then he leaned over and kissed her neck. "He isn't going to be the last to know."

A gust of breath left Susannah. "Who else?"

"Jane Pardee. I'm going to tell her I plan to marry you, and I'll be sleeping in your bedroom from now on—so unless she raises the roof over it, that's the way it will be." Susannah was big-eyed, and seemed to be holding her breath, so he asked, "Regrets?"

"Never," she declared, her eyes shining. "Oh, Cameron, I love you so."

He put out a big hand to cup her head, his thumb stroking the tendrils at her temple. He whispered only, "Thank you, Susannah," but his eyes said all the rest.

Cameron was to think back over that moment many times during the days following Robin's leavetaking. His desire for Susannah grew daily. He wanted her all the time, even when he was not in her presence. And they found a closeness that was enhanced by their new physical intimacy. Cameron loved and wanted her, and at last believed he was the one and only man she loved and desired. But Susannah was not the same young, untried, naive girl she had been when she had fallen in love with Sam. She knew that now she had to find a place for herself in Cameron's daily life. If Sam had done nothing else for her, he had taught her that a woman had to have an importance for a man that went beyond the bedroom.

Even before Cameron recognized them, Susannah was aware of the emotions raging in him. As surely as the sun rose every day, Cameron Gentry's ambition was resurfacing, and soon it would have to be served. From her experience with Sam, Susannah knew there were certain men for whom ambition came before all else. Their ambitions might take different forms, but the drive was present. She could feel that in Cameron. He was very different from Sam, and even different from his twin, who also had that drive, but the ambition was a part of him, and as his wife she'd have to find her place of service to it, or she'd lose him.

Susannah set about in a practical manner to make herself important in Cameron's plans. Since Cameron was not particularly talkative about his ambitions, she had to improvise and try to draw him into the activity of New Helvetia. Above all else Susannah wanted Cameron to be in contact with men of vision. For the rest of April she was busy at her shop, and Cameron met and exchanged views with John Sutter, Peter Wimmer, Sam Brannan, several of the carpenters, and a few mountain men and soldiers who came and went from the fort and New Helvetia.

This time was a turning point for her. She remembered when she had reached that point with Sam. Now she knew he had not been the right man for her, but the knowledge he had given her was proving invaluable.

On May first they were in Jane's kitchen when she said, "Cameron, I would like you to examine my books before I order more goods. Could you come to the shop this afternoon?"

Cameron gave her an odd look. "Are we making appointments now?"

Mary McKay glanced up from the tracing paper she had laid out on the table in order to make a transfer pattern. "You must admit, Cameron, it is almost a necessity. I'm afraid we McKays are a terrible handicap to this household. We'll all be relieved when Sean is well enough to begin hunting for a place of our own. I am sure it won't be long now, and then you kind people can return to your normal routines."

"I'm a guest here too, Mary," replied Cameron. "If your family is a handicap, so am I."

Mary laughed lightly. "A guest perhaps, but no handicap. I don't know what we would have done if you and Robin hadn't taken care of everything."

"Oh, Mary, you know all of us are happy we were able to help," Susannah said enthusiastically. "And you and Sean and Brian and Coleen will settle here—it is so nice to have new friends! But I do not want to get too far from my concern. Cameron, please say you will look at the books today."

"I'll be there."

Mary smiled from one to the other, then said, "Well, now that is settled, shall I tell you my good news?"

They both turned their attention to her.

"Robin will be here this weekend to take me to visit Fiona. His message says she is getting along very well, but he does not want her traveling yet. But I am fine—or nearly so. I feel as though I haven't seen her for years, rather than just a few weeks."

"Oh, Mary, I am so happy for you—and glad that Fiona will be all right," Susannah said, and leaned across the table, taking Mary's hands in hers.

Mary sniffed a little, her eyes bright with tears. "Robin is so thoughtful. I thank the Lord for the day He sent him to me. Robin sends those messengers back and forth almost daily. I don't know what I'd do if . . ." She paused and dabbed at her eyes, then looked apologetically at Cameron and Susannah. "Forgive me. I was never so weepy before."

"You have good cause," Cameron said. "Don't worry, you'll soon be yourself again. You have been so concerned with the health of everyone else, you haven't given yourself proper time to heal or rest."

"Well, nonetheless, without you and your brother, none of us would be here at all. And now, I'll leave you and Susannah alone for a moment." She got up slowly, but she smiled, her eyes twinkling. "And you'd better talk fast, for your privacy is not likely to last long."

It lasted barely a minute. Brian came in through the back door, and settled into the seat Mary had just vacated. Susannah gave Cameron a look.

Brian's eyes were red-rimmed, and his nose redder still. He coughed long and harshly, groping for the cup of hot tea Susannah poured. He let out a great sigh of relief as the hot, sweet liquid soothed him.

"What were you doing outside, Brian Campbell?" Susannah

scolded. "If Jane saw you, she'd skin you. You are still too ill to be out."

"I couldn't stand lying in that bed another minute!" Brian wailed. "I've never had such trouble feeling well before. I thought if I did some of my normal tasks I'd feel better."

"You've never been so exposed before as you were in the mountains," Susannah shot back. "You're very ill—you have a very bad chest."

"But I hate it!" Brian moaned, and set himself to coughing again.

When it abated Cameron asked, "How's Coleen? Has her fever broken?"

"Not yet, but Doc Marsh is encouraged. He says she's a good deal stronger than he thought. She'll be all right. She has to be. I'm going to marry her this fall. We've already decided it will be an October wedding."

"Jane told us," Susannah said, smiling. "This is going to be a busy household for months to come."

"Not just this one," Brian said. "It's not that I don't love my stepmother, but I want a place of our own. How about some help, Cam—you've got a good eye for land and cattle."

"Whenever you're ready, Brian. It will be my pleasure. But right now I'd better see to my own business. I promised Peter I'd meet him at Smith and Brannan's store in fifteen minutes."

"Don't forget to come by the shop," Susannah called after him. When Cameron had left she smiled at Brian. "It is difficult to find a free minute with him these days."

"I'm afraid Sean and I are part of the problem. We're all looking for a good piece of land. A man can't do better than to have one of the Gentrys with him when he's looking for good ground."

Susannah couldn't help the proud smile that lighted her face and eyes. "He is wonderful, isn't he?" she breathed.

Brian looked away. He barely suppressed a chuckle. If he were reading the signs correctly, his and Coleen's wedding would not be the only one to take place. It gave him a good feeling. Even though he was still weak from his ordeal in the mountains, he saw before him a bright future. The Gentrys, the McKays, the Campbells, his stepmother, would all be neighbors. He had never thought of being lonely before in this vast land, but he was inordinately pleased that there would be so many people here whom he liked and thought of as his family.

Susannah went to her shop and laid out her accounts on the desk in her back room, ready for Cameron. She became impatient expecting him, and wished she had named a specific time. Even while she was waiting on customers, her eyes kept going to the door.

When at last Cameron came in, it was obvious that he had enjoyed his meeting with the men, and that some of his tardiness was due to the bar Sam had in his store. She felt a quick pang of jealousy as once again she realized that there would always be a part of his life she would never share. But, she thought as he kissed her, there were other parts of his life she would have entirely to herself.

"Let's get at this," he said with a smile.

Susannah left him alone until he called to her. "Susannah, I need some information on some of these credit accounts. How did you determine these people were to buy on credit? Some of the amounts due are rather large."

"I asked Jane about each person. She told me I would have no trouble with payment from these people. Did I do wrong?"

He smiled at her. "No, you did right." His eyes stayed steadily on her so long she became uncomfortable.

"Why are you staring at me like that, Cameron?"

He laughed self-consciously, and shook his head as if to clear it. "I'm sorry—I guess my mind wandered."

Susannah pulled up a chair and sat down. She put her hands over the page Cameron was staring at. He looked up at her and she said, "What are you brooding about? Are you angry with me?"

"No, of course not. I just can't seem to keep my mind on business." He laughed shortly. "I don't know what's wrong with me—in the past Robin has claimed that I am too attentive to business." He smiled at her, touching the tip of her nose with his finger. "I think you've bewitched me."

Susannah smiled broadly. "That makes me almost happy."

"Almost?"

"Yes, almost. But I know that if you aren't doing something that gives you a sense of accomplishment, you won't be happy for long, no matter how we love each other. But—I've been thinking . . ."

457

Cameron made a face. "Uh-oh! That could mean trouble."

Susannah giggled. "Don't make fun of me. Oh, Cameron, you and I could do such wonderful things together."

"I thought we had been doing pretty well already."

She took his hands in hers, smiling. "I'm talking of business now. I want to present you a business proposition."

"I'm listening," he said, but an edge of wariness had crept into his voice.

"Well, I've been here nearly three months, and have seen people coming and going and talking about the future. I've listened to Captain Sutter too. He has great plans, and he is always trying to convince people to settle here. His sawmill will be built and running soon, and once that is done he'll have everything ready to make it inviting for people to live here. They will need acreage, lots, food, clothing—all manner of goods. I thought, perhaps, you and I could buy acreage, and when more people move in later this spring and summer, we could—"

"I thought you wanted to live in San Francisco, to be accepted there."

"I do, Cameron, I do. But the timing is wrong now. There are things for us to do here first, and it will be better for us. Most of the people in San Francisco now are Mexican or Mormon. It would take too long for me to be accepted there. Here, I am already. What we could do in San Francisco we could do here in half the time."

"My plans are for San Francisco."

"Does that mean we cannot do both? I am not asking you to give anything up."

"Both!"

"Yes, why not? We could do it. I want to go to San Francisco too—later on. You've said yourself it is a city that will one day be great, but that day hasn't come. And think of how long you'll be in New Helvetia anyway. You'll be here for a while yet helping Jane, and then you'll be here for Coleen's and Brian's wedding. Why not use that time profitably?"

He looked excited. "You're quite a woman, Susannah Morrison. What gave you this idea?"

"Cameron, I think I may have a head for business. I've been thinking this over for some time. It helped me endure, when I missed you so terribly while you were in the mountains. I've mentioned the lots and their sale, but there are so many other

458

things. With the sawmill there will be construction, and people will need furniture and tools. Except for Sam's store, there isn't a proper saloon or a decent restaurant, and—''

"Whoa! Enough! Let me think about it. I can see you don't suffer from thinking too small!'' He laughed, appreciation in his eyes.

"Well, there is just one more thing. What would you think of a house here? Not elaborate—something like Jane's. Just a front room, bedrooms, and a kitchen.'' Susannah was now boldly sitting on his lap. She began kissing his face, planting light butterfly touches on his eyes, cheeks, and ears.

Cameron began to chuckle. "Oh, let's make it a mansion. If we're going to think like emperors, we ought to live like them.''

"You're making fun of me again . . . I don't believe you think I'm serious.''

He kissed her. "Oh, I believe you, my love. And you'll have your house. But—''

"But what?'' asked Susannah, eyes wide.

"I won't build a house for you alone.''

Susannah stared at him for a long time, then she smiled and ran her tongue lightly across his lips before she kissed him. "Are you asking me to marry you? Last time you told me!''

"When will the wedding take place?''

Susannah threw her arms around his neck. "Spring! Oh, Cameron, I want to be a bride of the spring when the new growth is beginning and the whole year lies before us.''

"Not this fall?''

"No. I want our wedding to stand out from all others. Coleen is going to be married this fall. I want ours to be very special. Everyone must be invited, and be horribly jealous of us.''

Cameron smiled. He pulled Susannah closer to him. His hand slid along the lush curve of her hip and waist. Slowly, enjoying the feel of her under his hand, he sought the curve of her breast. "Close your shop, Susannah.''

Chapter Thirty-Nine

Sam Brannan was seldom in his fine new home for long these days. He had too many business interests to juggle; his fingers were trying to stop the leaks in too many dikes at once. But he thrived on excessive activity. He was strengthened by his growing reputation as an empire builder. His ambition was constantly spurred by his achievements to date.

Sam was proudest of his town, San Francisco. Less than a year ago his Saints had landed in a scruffy little village of fewer than two hundred inhabitants. Now, new buildings were going up everywhere, and the population numbered 451, including whites, Indians, Negroes, and Sandwich Islanders. It had been a good idea to give the town the name of the bay. Most pioneers heading their way found the place with no difficulty.

It had been a good idea to get rid of Bartlett too, the pompous scoundrel. Sam had bided his time nicely on that. Several days before Bartlett had issued his proclamation giving San Francisco its new name, Sam had run across valuable information. Using his position as *alcalde*, Bartlett was commandeering stock and other useful supplies ''as a war measure.'' Sam investigated further. Bartlett was also seizing lands and granting deeds—at a price. Another tidbit of interest was a print job Bartlett had ordered: notes of hand redeemable by the government. Bartlett was evasive concerning the terms of these notes. Sam went to Captain Montgomery with his proof. Montgomery promptly replaced Bartlett with another man. Sam published a full account of Bartlett's maneuverings in his *California Star*.

All in all, Sam told himself, it was a good reminder to keep one's own hands spotless.

Only ten days ago Sam had gone upriver to New Hope. He hadn't been there for a while, or received any reports, so he decided to observe progress first hand. Brother Brigham and his Saints surely ought to be arriving in California any day now, and Sam wanted things to be looking prosperous for them. After all the hard labor of so many people for New Hope, it would be tragic if Brigham's people were to find their heaven-designated New Zion not in working order.

As it developed, all was not well in New Zion. Sam was met at the landing by several of the Saints, who had seen his sails. They were humiliated, angry, uncertain of their next move. Will Stout, whom Sam had picked as such an excellent leader, had taken matters at New Hope into his own hands. For himself Stout had claimed the house and the first tilled acreage. Within the past few days Stout had sold the spring crops and kept the proceeds. The Saints were in turmoil, undetermined as to whether to notify Sam and admit their failure, or to throw Stout out of the house that was to have sheltered them all until President Young came and try to salvage something from their months of labor.

Sam called an immediate meeting of all the men at New Hope, including Stout, who, now that his spiritual leader was on hand, seemed less certain of himself. Sam's edicts, while not totally Solomonic, were practical. The men were to build a new community home on another site. Each man was to select one hundred and sixty acres for himself and his family. There was plenty of fine land right here, he told them, and they certainly deserved the first choice, since they were the ones who had developed the site for the New Zion. Having made their selection, they were to go back to work, giving to the Church the same amount of time they gave to their own land.

As for Stout, he was made to turn over the proceeds of the sale of crops to Sam. Sam noted the amount in his account book, and placed it in the funds being saved for President Young's party. Further, Stout and his belongings were removed from the house in question. When Sam returned to San Francisco, Stout would be going with him. Stout's actions at New Hope would be referred to the elders for suitable discipline.

461

Last, Sam, in the name of the Church, appropriated the house and the tilled acreage. "It is best," he said, "that this bone of contention be removed from further consideration at this time. We shall preserve these properties for the use of President Young's party."

With some reservations, Sam also appointed a new leader for the little community. In the present situation some natural leader should have come forth and taken charge, but instead, the Saints had milled about like sheep until Sam—by chance, if chance existed—had come to them. In most of his affairs Sam never let doubt creep in, but this colony at New Hope seemed to have slimmer and slimmer chances of success.

Where in *Hell* was Brother Brigham? He should be here by now, taking charge of the colony and getting it off Sam's neck.

Sam's fury at the entire situation had hardly cooled by the time he was back in San Francisco. And the birth of a daughter, who squalled all the time in a piercing tone, did little to soothe him. He'd had enough of waiting around for Brigham Young. By God, he'd go find the man himself.

On April 4, 1847, Sam rode out of San Francisco with a dual purpose in mind. First, he wanted to see for himself some of the survivors of the Donner Party, which he had gone to great effort to help. Second, he wanted to find Brigham Young, tell him of New Hope, present him with the copies of the *California Star* he had carefully packed, and bring him up to date on the Saints in San Francisco.

On his way to New Helvetia Sam stopped at the Gentry ranch, where he talked for a long time with Robin about business matters. He was greatly impressed with Fiona, whose radiance made him think of Catholic statues he had seen, with haloes around the heads. He did not question that Fiona McKay was a human being—would an angel's laugh be so spontaneous and carefree?—but she had an unforgettably ethereal quality about her.

Late in April Sam arrived at New Helvetia, bearing messages for Cameron, Susannah, Jane Pardee, and the McKay family. Observing Susannah with Cameron still had the power to pain him, although he knew he had lost her.

Before he left, Sam managed to see Susannah alone. Hesitantly, he put his hands on her arms, wanting to hold her close for one last time. They looked at each other and smiled tentatively. It was not the same as it had been aboard the *Brooklyn*.

He put his hand on her shining curls and kissed her at the corner of her full, sweet mouth. He asked, "My dear, are you happy?"

Susannah smiled, she blushed, she shone for the moment not unlike Fiona. "Oh, yes!" she cried. "Oh, yes, Sam!"

"Then I'm happy for you," he said. "But I'm selfish enough to be glad we had a little while together." As her face grew wary, he went on, "Susannah, you know I'll never forget you . . . I won't want to . . . in some part of me I'll always love you."

For a long moment she did not answer, searching his sparkling brown eyes. She answered softly, "The same to you, Sam. Everything you said."

He murmured, "But now it's Cameron?"

"It will always be Cameron."

He drew a deep breath. "Kiss me goodbye, my love. Wish me luck."

She took his hands, turned them palm up, and kissed each palm, closing his fingers over the kiss. "There now, nothing but good fortune can come your way. Goodbye, Sam." Their lips met tenderly, then he stepped back from her and vanished into the night.

On April 26, with a caravan of eleven horses and mules loaded with provisions and equipment, Sam and Charley Smith left Sutter's Fort. Sam's letters had at last reached Brigham Young. By good chance a messenger was at Sutter's on his way to San Francisco, and he informed Sam that Young would be waiting for him at Green River in Wyoming around July first.

Sam's caravan crossed the Truckee Pass, which had taken others so long and had cost the lives of so many, in twenty-six hours. He wrote later:

> We traveled on foot and drove our animals before us, the snow from 20 to 100 feet deep. When we arrived, though, not one of us could stand on our feet. The people of California told us we could not cross under two months, there being more snow on the mountains than had ever been known before; but God knows best, and was kind enough to prepare the way before us.

At Truckee Lake, Sam was appalled at the conditions under which the Donner Party had lived and managed to survive. To his astonishment Louis Keseberg was still there, dwelling in a filthy cabin where gnawed human bones littered the floor. Keseberg's weight and health appeared normal. He had a broken leg, he said, and was awaiting the arrival of the final rescue party. Tamsen Donner, who had refused to leave her ailing husband, George, had died. A tasty morsel, said Keseberg. The German was quite jovial, making further crude references to his own cannibalism, smacking his lips, and inviting the others to laugh with him at his description of the flavor of babies' flesh.

For once in his life Sam found it hard to extend forgiveness to a fellow human being. Louis Keseberg made his skin crawl. Sam and Charley left the man some provisions and a horse, and camped elsewhere that night.

By early June they rode into Fort Hall, near the junction of the Oregon Trail and the California Trail. The decrepit stockade there made John Sutter's well-ordered fort look all the grander.

On the clear sunny afternoon of June 30, Sam and Charley Smith came upon Brigham Young's encampment. For Young, who enjoyed company, it was extremely modest: his own Conestoga wagon, with two or three of his wives in ready attendance upon his wants; and the wagons of several bodyguards, who hung around fingering knives and rifles as Sam approached. The Green River, which flowed nearby, was swift and wide, fifteen feet deep in places, and three hundred feet across. Along its banks the long sweet grasses grew plentifully.

While Charley tended to the horses and mules, a guard conducted Sam to President Young's wagon. The conspicuous lack of welcome was supposed to make him nervous, Sam surmised; but it had the opposite effect of elevating his temper as for battle. He had never feared or even excessively revered Brother Brigham, taking Young at his word when he said that the power of the Church rested not with Brigham Young but with his priesthood. Sam himself had that same priesthood.

As Sam waited for Young to emerge from his wagon, he was feeling anger and dismay. He knew in his bones that Young no longer intended to come to California. What he intended instead, Sam might discover.

Brigham Young seemed larger than he was, which was large enough. He clasped Sam's hand in his own, and clapped him on the shoulder. He said heartily, "Well, boy, I see you made our rendezvous a little ahead of time." His heartiness did not extend to his face. The eyes were cool just short of hostile.

Sam bristled at being called "boy." And he did not understand why he was being treated as one completely out of favor. He let his hand in Young's go limp until Young released him. Then he said, "Brother Brigham, you're looking well."

Especially at this first greeting, Young did not appreciate being called "brother" by a man below him in the hierarchy of priesthood. He said gruffly, "Come, let's sit on the grass over here. I'm sure you have a great deal to report. I've been getting your letters from time to time. Trouble with the Saints, Brother Sam? We'll have to get that straightened out, won't we."

"Your advice would be most welcome," Sam said courteously. Prodded by Young, he told of the triumphs in San Francisco. He did not mention any of the difficulties he had been having with his flock. When Young brought him back around to that subject again, Sam, gathering his mettle against refusal, broached the topic of the New Zion. Young's baleful expression was not encouraging, but once started Sam felt determined to continue, painting as optimistic a view of it as he could.

"And so," he concluded, "we are eagerly preparing for your arrival in New Hope, Brother Brigham."

Young said abruptly, "That will be impossible, Brother Sam. I've already found the perfect spot for the New Zion, at Great Salt Lake."

"Great Salt Lake," Sam echoed, his head almost swimming. "But isn't that a wasteland—a desert?"

" 'The desert shall rejoice, and blossom as the rose,' " said Young reprovingly, " 'then the eyes of the blind shall be opened.' You should think on that, Brother Sam."

Sam tamped down his impatience, saying, "Tell me about this place."

Brigham Young smiled reminiscently. "That reminds me of what I said when we came upon it. I said, 'This is the place.' I felt I was divinely guided by God to my decision. You see, we are still outcasts in our religion. And this Great Salt Lake is ideal for us. The land is so poor that unless parties of movers stumble on us, they'll merely pass us by. In a few years we shall be firmly entrenched, our community thriving, and no one will ever push us out again."

465

Sam, a natural skeptic where other men's plans were concerned, said reasonably, "If the land is so poor, how do you expect the Saints to make a living on it? They must eat, and conduct business, until your millennium." Then, fully aware that his words had abraded Young, he added, "But I expect your plans for that are already in operation."

"As a matter of fact they are," Young replied stiffly. "We're bringing water down from the mountains by means of canals—" He stopped, his gaze on a small party of horsemen rapidly approaching. Looking around, he satisfied himself that his band of Danites, known as the Destroying Angels, were on the alert. He went on, "We're doing quite a number of things which would, I believe, astound you with their inventiveness. Oh, yes, the Lord has been generous with suggestions about ways we can improve the land to which He has led us."

Sam thought regretfully of the green and amply watered area of New Hope, rich with wildlife, to which he had thought the Lord had led him and his men. He wondered if Eden was different for every man. He would say nothing further of New Hope, and see if Brother Brigham mentioned it again.

Young stood up. "Excuse me, Brother Sam, there is a matter I must attend to." Quickly he walked away and disappeared into his wagon. Sam understood that Young had absented himself from sight until the riders came into camp. Once his Destroying Angels had assured him it was safe, he greeted the party.

The newcomers included a Sergeant Williams, of Captain Brown's company of Mormon soldiers recently discharged from service, who were attempting to reunite with their families in Young's party of emigrants. Young said, "Here, Brother Sam, is your perfect opportunity to observe for yourself what I have been speaking of. Your party will meet Captain Brown's company and guide them to the Great Salt Lake Valley. I'll return there, and we can discuss our business again after you have been enlightened."

It was mid-July before Sam and Charley Smith and their party intercepted Brown's company; in another two weeks they rode into Salt Lake Valley.

Sam's heart sank when he at last saw Brigham Young's New Zion. The town had been skillfully laid out; acres of parched earth had been irrigated with creek water, plowed, and seeded. Under construction were a fort and numerous dwellings. A "bowery" had been erected for public meetings. A site had been marked and construction started on the Lord's House.

So this was the answer to his expectations for New Hope, Sam thought. Perhaps this Eden on barren land was the reason for the failures at that perfect site on the Stanislaus River. Perhaps the Lord wished to show His power by sprouting seed in ground where, according to the mountain men who ought to know, it froze every month in the year. Sam could not accept that. This was Brigham's choice, not God's.

Over the next several days Sam and Young had several conferences. Young pressed Sam hard over every large or small difficulty Sam had had with his Saints. He was also insistent that the tithes Sam had been collecting for the Church be turned over to Young for use in Salt Lake City. All Sam's eloquent arguments that the Church in San Francisco was in equal need, and that the members there had made the contributions and were therefore entitled to the benefit of them, were useless. Young, as Sam's superior, was determined to have the money.

The men of Captain Brown's company had been mustered out in Salt Lake City and were entitled to their pay. However, their paymaster was in San Francisco with the records. Young decreed that Brown was to return to California with Sam, and bring back the tithe money. Brown was also to be entrusted with several letters from Young to the California Saints.

Sam's patience snapped when he heard this. He strode into Young's office without knocking and leaned toward the startled man, hands on Young's desk and his face aggressively close to that of his spiritual leader. "What is the meaning of this latest insult? I demand to know by what right you give Captain Brown letters which come under my purview. You may be head of the Church here in this Godforsaken wasteland, but in California I am head of the Church. You are infringing on my rights, and I require an explanation!"

"You require an explanation," Young repeated coldly. "You bumbling puppy, you will get an explanation. I've had my eyes on you for months. Asa Radburn has been watching your unworthy attempts to set up a kingdom for yourself at the Lord's expense. I've had your whitewashed versions of Church matters, but I have received true reports from Asa and other members of the Church under your so-called leadership. You have failed the Church in every way possible, Brannan. You have disgraced the

Saints who look up to you—you have stolen from the Lord's hoard for your private enrichment—''

"*Bull shit!*" said Sam forthrightly. "Asa is a liar. You know it, and I know it. Everything I have touched in Church matters, I've done with knowledge that God is my witness. I have not performed one deed of which I am ashamed before Him. But as for that, *Brother* Brigham, what of your agreement to bring your flock to California to join with mine? I had your word on that. Now I see what the word of a great man is worth. Nothing! You never meant to come to California. Only yesterday I learned that two years ago you picked this bitter little dot on the globe for your grand scheme—for one of Brigham's miracles. Well, you know where you can shove your miracles. This one will be small enough that it ought to fit.''

"Brother Brannan, you are blasphemous!"

Sam's eyes shot fires of deviltry and fury. "Have I used the name of God in vain? Or was it Brother Brigham's? Perhaps you are confusing the two."

Young rose from his seat, his face purple. "By God, I'll have you *used up* for an apostate!"

"Ah," Sam replied softly. "Blood atonement—your secret of success. If one of your Saints dares to disagree, then have him knifed or shot, for the good of his soul. I have heard that when Brigham gives his Danites the word, all the dogs howl."

Young's face was still mottled with fury. Breathing hard, he looked Sam up and down for several seconds. Then, with incredible self-control, he said, "One day, Brannan, you may discover that your spiteful tongue has brought down your own destruction. If you are a clever man, you will keep out of my sight from now on."

"My pleasure indeed—"

"But in the meantime, I expect you to conduct Captain Brown to San Francisco. I also expect you to turn over to him all the moneys which you have collected in the name of the Church of Jesus Christ of Latter-Day Saints."

Sam's expression was as blank as he could make it. He said, "I leave tomorrow at sunup."

"See that you do." As the door closed behind Sam, Young muttered, "Brannan, soon, very soon, the dogs will be howling for *you*. I'll arrange it myself."

*   *   *

468

It was the ninth of August when Sam, Charley Smith, Brown, and a few other men left Salt Lake City, heading west for California. Sam's feeling of being ill used, of being deliberately deceived and lied about and shoved out of the Church, had not abated in the days since he and Young had parted. He was never one to brood fruitlessly over his setbacks, but this situation gnawed at him. He was like a dog worrying a bone. His conscience was clear, but of what account was a good conscience when a liar's word was taken over his and Young would replace him with one of his lackeys? Every action he would take for the Church from now on would be subjected to the most critical scrutiny.

But that had been true all along. Young had seen him as useful, never as a friend. Now that Young was out in the open about his enmity, Sam supposed he should be more careful about his own person. Well, when he got back to San Francisco he'd hire some bodyguards of his own. He'd call them—the Exterminators. That was a good joke. Sam chuckled to himself.

Over the next weeks Sam came to some strong decisions. First of all came the Church. The Saints were his people. It was Sam they had followed from New York around Cape Horn to golden California. It was he who held their tithe money in his keeping. And it was up to him to protect the interests of the Church in California. If Brigham Young wanted the Lord's portion, then let Brother Brigham provide a receipt from the Lord. Signed.

As for his own future in the Church, that had always been in the hands of God anyway.

But Sam Brannan's life was made up of many interests. New Hope was one. He'd see how matters stood there upon his return. The easiest solution, of course, was to sell it. While he was at it, he'd sell out the assets of the Church-sponsored company they had formed aboard the *Brooklyn*, Samuel Brannan and Company, and divide the profits according to the amounts members had coming to them. Selling out, he thought, would be a great relief to everyone.

Sam would go on with San Francisco, of course—it was his city. He'd continue buying land there, and would put up some commercial buildings, a school, a bank, even a jail. And he wanted to keep both thumbs tight on the store he and Charley Smith had started. That had good chances of growing big. Charley was a sound manager and an honest man, and with him at the store and Sam out selling goods in lots to other merchants, they'd make a million.

Which reminded him, he and Charley would want to talk with John about putting in a general store at Natoma, where Sutter's gristmill was flourishing. And when Jim Marshall finished building Sutter's sawmill at Coloma, Sam would have a general store there too. The trickle of people to Oregon and California was becoming a steady stream now, and Sam would be ready for the river.

For some reason, the conversation he'd had with John Sutter about gold came back to him. All the mountain men he talked to mentioned that it was easy to find nuggets of gold in the California earth, so it stood to reason there must be a big deposit somewhere. Thinking of that, Sam pulled out a cigar, nipped off the end with his teeth, and lit it. He wasn't a man who'd go digging for gold himself, but say somebody else found it, a lot of it . . . Then who would be ready, owning land to sell, owning a newspaper always looking for news to print, owning general stores with goods to sell, living in the handsomest house in town, on first-name terms with the mayor, all the military officers, the governor? And who'd be waiting in San Francisco with his head full of ideas for advancement, for progress, for growth?

Sam Brannan, his brown eyes sparkling and his lips curved in a little smile, puffed contentedly on his cigar.

Dreams came and went, some down in defeat. But Sam had learned over the years that it was the distant dream which had the greatest glitter.

Chapter Forty

Coleen McKay's wedding might have been a quiet day but that was not taking into account her soon-to-be mother-in-law, Jane Pardee. Jane decreed it was to be a time of celebration of a new family beginning, and the return from the lost for all of them.

Jane's house had been overcrowded and busy for months, and now it needed to accommodate even more people and more activity. "Exceptin' my own, this house has never seen a wedding. We're goin' t'do it up right," Jane bubbled, and set about a thorough spring housecleaning in the heat of August.

Mary, Coleen, Jane, and Susannah washed every stitch of linen in the house. The men were set to dismantling the beds, polishing the frames, and airing and beating the mattresses and blankets. The house was scrubbed from rafters to root cellar. Sean wasn't at all sure he was pleased to be fully recovered. "It was easier gettin' through the mountains than it is keeping up with these women when they're in a wedding mood," he groaned, slumping down on the couch in the front yard. His rest was short-lived, for fast on his heels came Coleen with a bent wire beater.

"Mama said you were to beat every speck of dust from the couch, Papa."

Sean looked up, and put on his most miserable, long-suffering face. "Your mother has no mercy for an invalid."

Coleen laughed. "She said that when you said that, I was to

471

tell you exercise and hard work are good remedies for what ails you.''

Cameron did his best to stay away from the house, and be very busy with his investments, but he did not escape. Susannah seemed to have gone over entirely to the enemy, and she captured him at every turn. Because he was the strongest and healthiest of the three men, he was also given what he considered the worst jobs—like cleaning and polishing the stoves. At the end of every day he was certain the house and yard were clean enough, and that not even Jane could think up a new job. He was always wrong. He began to long for the wedding day nearly as much as Coleen and Brian did.

At last the day was nearing, and they all knew it when Jane announced that they would erect the large tent at the side of her house. When Rowena and Carl Gentry arrived, and Robin and Fiona, all the unmarried men would sleep in that tent, thus freeing the house for women and couples.

"I thought she'd never tell us to raise the tent," Brian said. "For a while there it looked like the wedding was going to be postponed till Ma was satisfied with the house.''

"She's a strr-rong woman," Sean breathed.

"And one of the best," Brian said. "She's been more mother to me than my own. I don't remember my own mother much at all, except for what Jane has told me about her. When Jane married my dad, she took me in hand and did everything that a mother does, but always insisted that I call her Jane and know her for my stepmother. She said God gives each of us one mother, and since I didn't have her in the flesh, I'd have her in the spirit. That was quite a gallantry considering Jane has always wanted children and never been blessed with them.''

Each of the men then reminisced about their mother or grandmother. Talking made the work go much faster. Since Jane had called them all to duty, the three of them had done more talking and remembering than at any other time in their lives. They also became good friends.

"How soon will it be that Robin brings Fiona?" Sean asked.

"They should be here day after tomorrow, with Mother and Father coming at the end of the week," Cameron answered between sledgehammer blows to the tent stake.

Sean chuckled to himself and said softly, "Fiona will liven things up when she gets here.''

*   *   *

Fiona would have disappointed her father at that moment, for as she stood in the bedroom in the Gentry house, her feelings were divided. She didn't want to leave Agua Clara. From the first moment she had opened her eyes in the warm soft bed, whose coverings smelled of home-made soap and sunshine, she had felt at home. She would never forget that day. She had hurt in all her joints, and her feet and hands still ached so badly that tears came to her eyes, but she had been *warm*. The warmth had meant everything to her; the sensation had become synonymous with safety.

She had wakened that first morning unsure of what she would find. Disoriented, she wasn't certain that she wasn't still in the mountains and the warmth was an illusion, the brilliant sunshine streaming into her eyes not the glare off the snow. Then, as she had turned her head slightly, she had seen *him*, the man with the gold and green eyes who had helped save Coleen, and though he didn't know it, had many times saved her. His eyes seemed to burn with life. Many times he'd given her the will to go on just a little farther when she had wanted to stop and curl up in the snow. Fiona had blinked, clearing her eyes, and wondering if he would still be there when she opened them again.

Robin Gentry wouldn't ever forget that day either. After he had brought Fiona to Agua Clara, she had remained in that bed asleep, almost motionless and deathly pale for days, so long he feared she would never again awaken.

"She is in God's hands, Robin," his mother had said. "Come away, you can do no good here, and you need sleep yourself."

But he hadn't left her bedside. He had sat beside her, stroking her hand, watching her every breath, always afraid that it would be the last. He cursed himself for having taken her on yet another journey after she had come from the mountains. It had been too much for her. He prayed to God that she be spared; and when she didn't awaken, he demanded that she be spared; then he railed at himself and God and all the powers of earth and heaven that they should have done this to her.

The morning she stirred and opened her eyes briefly, it happened so quickly he wasn't certain he had seen it at all. He had been sleepless for three nights, his beard was black and ragged on his face, and there were deep circles of fatigue under his reddened eyes. He leaned over her as if that would bring back the

473

illusion that she had looked at him for just a moment. Then slowly, she opened her eyes again, and their gaze met. Robin looked into the fathomless depths of her clear green eyes. They were like green fires that seared right through to the soul of him. His chest and throat were so tight he couldn't draw breath, then the expulsion of air came out in a hiccoughing laugh.

Fiona tried to smile, and just managed it. The effort made her sleepy, and her eyes closed again. She fought against sleep now, and tried to come back to him, to come back to the scents of sunshine and soap and all those things she loved.

Robin had his head down on the bed, his cheek pressed to her hand, when his mother came back into the room. Rowena was as worried about him as she was about the girl. She put her hand on his shoulder and gently rubbed the taut muscles. "Come away, Robin. You are not helping her, and you are making yourself ill."

He lifted his head, his tired face alight. "She woke up! Just a moment ago, she opened her eyes and smiled, Mother. She smiled at me—I think she knew who I am."

Rowena looked doubtfully at Fiona. She was as still and pale as she had been for days. Perhaps Robin had imagined the girl's awakening. But she said, "If she is beginning to come round, it will not be long before she will want food. Take a rest now, Robin, and you will be ready to help her with her meal."

He was agreeable to that suggestion, but not quite as his mother had envisioned. "Mother, tell Felicia to set up a cot for me in here, please. I will sleep, but I want to be near at hand."

"Robin, you cannot sleep here in the room with this young girl!"

Robin just looked at her, hurt and disappointment in his eyes.

Rowena couldn't stand it. What did it matter? The girl was most likely going to die, and they had been together night and day coming out of the mountains. If Mary McKay had wanted her daughter away from Robin, she would not have allowed Fiona to come to Agua Clara.

Robin got his wish. He was beside Fiona when she awakened the next time, and was far stronger. In fact, it was he who awoke to find her eyes fastened on him. She smiled as he pushed himself up on one elbow. "Good morning," she said in her lilting voice.

He lay back down on the cot and laughed, a soft, merry sound of relief and thanksgiving.

Rowena heard his laughter, and ran up the stairs to the bedroom. There she saw a glowingly lovely girl whose smile lighted up her whole face. Rowena was startled. There was no similarity between this girl and the pale waif who had been lying motionless in her bed. Almost shyly Rowena introduced herself. Fiona's mass of auburn hair seemed to have sprung to life with the rest of her. Riotous flaming curls twisted and sprang around her head and face. With a smile, Rowena recovered from the shock of the transformation and got to practical matters. She ordered a meal of broth and light biscuits, then found a hand mirror, comb, and brush for her young guest. A washbowl was brought, and a clean lacy nightgown that had belonged to one of the Gentry daughters. Robin was hustled out of the room with a foolish grin on his face, and Rowena and Fiona began a friendship that went deep and would last the rest of their lives.

From that day on, Fiona's recovery was swift and steady. Soon she was able to get out of bed, dress, and be shown the grounds of Agua Clara. Robin escorted her, with Felicia in attendance, over all the roads, to see all the cattle in every pasture where they were kept, to the fields of wheat, and to the new vineyard that was not yet completely planted and all the vines so young that little was expected of them. Fiona was enchanted by all of it. Her spirit was indefatigable. Only her body dictated that Robin could keep her out no longer. Even then, she refused to go to her room, preferring to rest on the cool tile in the courtyard, watching the birds and enjoying the flowers.

Carl Gentry was no less enchanted by Fiona than his wife and son were. He shook his head when the message came requesting that Fiona be brought back to New Helvetia for her sister's wedding. "I suppose that means she'll stay with her family," he said on a sigh.

Rowena smiled. "You don't want her to leave either."

He laughed. "It's been a long time since I've been jealous of another man, but I tell you, I'm going to have a hard time facing Sean McKay. I've come to feel as though his daughter is mine. I don't want to give her up. It's just like when our own girls left to live in some other man's home. I knew it was inevitable, and good—but I sure as hell didn't like it."

"I think Robin shares your sentiments."

"Umm. I wonder what McKay will think about that. She's very young—I don't suppose he's going to appreciate a man Robin's age coming around Fiona."

"Robin told me the mother already knows of his feelings for Fiona. Perhaps she can help." Rowena put down the sewing she had been working on, her eyes staring into space for a moment. Then she said, "Don't you think it odd with so few suitable women in the territory that each of our sons should bring home a young woman in need and fall in love with her?"

Carl grinned. "They're twins, aren't they?"

Fiona was in her bedroom, putting into a carpetbag the clothing that was her own as well as other things Rowena had given her. There were also gifts from Robin. She had expressed a fondness for Indian art, and Robin had bought her several beautiful pieces of Indian-made turquoise and silver. She picked up each piece, holding it in her hand, letting the light play on the colors and design before she placed it lovingly in the box he had given her to keep her treasures. She had never been given jewelry by a man before—she had never been given anything. She had been too young, and except for an occasional dreamy session of wondering what it would be like to be kissed, she hadn't thought of it before.

She had lost her early youth in the mountains, she realized. That part of her was gone now. There wouldn't be any more of the totally carefree days that could be passed by counting tents on the flats of a little city by a river. Her mind now held other things—herself, and the way she looked, in part. She wanted her hair done just right, and her clothing had far more importance than ever before. But even that was frivolous, and took up little of her thoughts. Fiona McKay now thought most of things like home, and security, and money, and the fragility of life.

Perhaps, at least partly, that explained her attachment to Agua Clara. Though she wanted to participate in Coleen's and Brian's wedding, she realized she did not want to lose the home she had here. So often she had wished that somehow Carl and Rowena and her mother and father could all be here—then she would have the whole world, and at the very core of it would be Robin Gentry. She couldn't keep tears from her eyes when she thought of never living that dream.

She most likely wouldn't have Robin either. Her father would say she was too young to be thinking of marriage, and Robin

476

would never wait for her. Never having had any experience, she wasn't even sure if what she saw in his eyes was really love—at least, the kind that made for a marriage. All she knew was that she ached for the sight of him when he was not at home, and she glowed with warmth when he was near. He didn't even need to touch her to make her body and heart sing, he had only to be there.

Her packing was going very slowly. With each piece of clothing she packed there came another memory. Every stitch she now owned had come from Robin and his family. There was nothing about her now that she didn't think of in terms of the Gentrys. It was almost as if she had really died in the mountains, and when she awakened again, she was a Gentry. Now, she was to go back to her own family, and she was finding it hard.

She looked up to see Robin standing in her doorway. "How long have you been there?" she asked.

"Long enough to know you are thinking about something that both disturbs you and pleases you."

She blushed, and her eyes looked greener than ever. "You've been there too long, then. You are not to be seeing my private thoughts without my permission."

He strode across the room and put his arms around her. Fiona's head rested against his chest, just above his heart. "Don't ever keep secrets from me, Fiona. You will never need to—unless you make the need yourself."

"Everyone must have secrets sometimes," she said, but with little force or assurance. When he held her as he did now, she did not want to keep anything from him.

Sometimes, when he held her like this, and talked to her, she got him confused with God or one of His angels. She was so completely at peace and safe with him. As long as they were together, there was nothing Fiona could not face or overcome. She listened to the reassuring beat of his heart, and felt his warmth and strength flow into her. It was almost as if he were a part of her. She wondered if he felt the same way, or if this was a feeling that was hers alone. She looked up at him, probing deeply into the light brown of his eyes. Today they looked like gold, a dark, dark gold. "Do you ever feel that some of what I am completes what you are?"

He didn't laugh, or pretend that he didn't know what she was talking about, but looked down at her and said, "The only time I am complete is when I am with you. It will always be that way for both of us, don't you believe that, Fiona?''

"I knew it for myself, but I wanted to hear you tell me it was so for you."

He laughed then, and said, "Now tell me what you were thinking about when I came to the door." He sat down on the love seat in her room and pulled her down beside him. "Tell me—and not a secret left when you're done."

It was easy to tell him all the things she had been thinking about, sitting with him as she was, and for that moment there was no need for secrets. When she finished, she looked up at him and smiled. "I am a foolish woman, aren't I? I have everything confused. My past and my present and my future are all a jumble, and I'm not very good at figuring it all out."

"Then allow me," he said grandly, adjusting their positions so that he could see her face better. "I think . . . no, I decree that you and I should marry. That will settle your future, so we need worry no more about that. Now, as to your past, your future husband says that you should return to your family, help your mother and sister settle into their new homes, and prepare for ours, for we shall need a place too. We could stay at Agua Clara, but—"

Fiona looked down at her hand in his. "But Papa is going to say I am too young, and it will never happen," she said, and an errant tear slipped from the corner of her eye.

Robin stroked her hair and pulled her head to his shoulder. "You can't think like that, my love. Your mother already knows how I feel about you, and—"

"She does? How could she know?"

Robin smiled. "I told her . . . when I brought you here."

Fiona looked wide-eyed at him. "So long ago . . . I didn't know . . ."

"I've loved you from the beginning, Fiona." He laughed a little. "Cameron always used to tease me and say I'd never find the kind of woman I wanted. He said she was a dream. Well, he was right about that, you are a dream, but I found you, and you're flesh and blood. When we go back to Jane's house, I'll talk to your father. Perhaps he will surprise us."

"You don't know Papa. I'm sixteen and lots of girls get married that young—some younger, but Papa thinks his daughters are different."

"Let's not borrow trouble, Fiona. Wait until I have talked to Sean."

"And what if he says I am too young?" Fiona asked, knowing her father would say just that.

Robin kissed her lightly on the tip of her nose. "Then I'll wait for you—for as long as I must. I will not live my life without you, Fiona McKay."

Suddenly she felt happy and full of energy. "Before we leave tomorrow, Robin, I want to ride over every acre of Agua Clara. May we? Will you have time to go with me? I don't want to go alone—I mean without you."

He glanced at the tangle of gowns and clothing around her room. "Pack up this jumble, and I'll go to the stables now. We'll go yet this afternoon."

By the time she and Robin were to leave for New Helvetia, Fiona was settled and content to return to her parents' home. There was a great to-do in front of the Gentry ranch house on the morning they set off. Rowena kept adding things to the already overflowing wagon. "Coleen is going to be starting a household with nearly nothing," she said, and handed up carefully packed crockery. Carl was behind her with a much larger urn. "For pickles," he said, and nodded at Rowena, smiling. "A necessity in every new house, you know."

By the time they were on the road they looked like a small wagon train. Robin and Fiona started out astride horses, but their carriage was behind them, driven by José, a man far more accustomed to driving cattle than a dainty carriage. Behind that came the heavily loaded wagon, bearing furniture and other household needs. Behind that came a smaller wagon loaded with food for the wedding feast, trunks of luggage for Rowena and Fiona, and personal gifts for Coleen, Jane, and Mary.

They had barely cleared the gates of Agua Clara when Fiona tossed a challenge over her shoulder to Robin, dug her heels into her horse, and took off at a gallop down the hard-packed road from the ranch.

With a high-pitched shout, Robin galloped after her.

Rowena and Carl Gentry stood at the huge gate on the road and watched the procession of wagons moving sedately in order. Carl reached out and took his wife's hand as his son and Fiona broke away from the body of the train and rode wildly after each other. Carl and Rowena watched until the two mounted figures were mere dots on the horizon, and they could no longer tell which was Fiona and which was Robin. "Those two make me feel young again," Carl said. "I hope they do marry someday."

Rowena smiled, and squeezed his hand.

Chapter Forty-One

Robin and Fiona rode into a beehive of activity at Jane's house. Had Sean and Mary not been outside, their arrival might have gone unnoticed because of all the work of setting up for the wedding. Mary immediately dropped the huge tablecloth she had been putting on the table under the tent and called to Sean as she ran to Robin and Fiona, her arms outstretched.

Robin helped Fiona from the carriage and into her mother's arms. Mary hugged her, kissed her, hugged her again, then stood back, examining her. With smiling eyes she looked approvingly at Robin. "You've taken good care of my little girl."

Fiona bristled instantly, leaned forward, and whispered in Mary's ear, "Mama, please! I'm not a little girl!"

Mary pulled her close once more.

"Hey! Isn't there room for an old papa in this gathering?" Sean asked, and enclosed both of them in his arms.

One by one others tumbled out of the house. Jane came out, her battle flags flying, for her workers were not working, but then she saw Robin and rushed over too. Coleen and Brian followed. Soon everybody was standing in the road talking, kissing, and asking after each other's health. Little more was accomplished at Jane's that day.

The families went inside, and Robin had the trunks of gifts and food and supplies brought inside. The rest of the afternoon was spent in trying on clothes, putting away edible delicacies, and talking about the wedding.

Robin tried unsuccessfully to find a time when he might take Sean aside and talk to him privately. By evening, when they were still in a group and beginning to play parlor games, he gave up. There was going to be no serious talk with Sean this night. With a toss of his head, he agreed to make a fool of himself playing Blindman's Buff, which wasn't too different from the Royal California Welcome.

But the next morning everything was back to normal. Jane Pardee had enjoyed herself as much as anyone, but now there were things to be done, and she was all business. Jane was a tireless woman and she saw no reason why others could not keep her pace. Her house had never had its door shut the past several days, and it would remain that way, for now there were guests arriving. Friends in town stopped by to wish Brian and his bride well. Jane kept a table covered with food and a bowl filled with a lethal mixture she called punch. At any time of the day or night well-wishers could be found around that bowl, or sitting on her front porch talking of weddings and weather and wanderlust. Mountain men with their weather-hardened faces and animal-skin clothing exchanged jokes and lore with shopkeepers and clerks wearing white shirts, suspenders, and visors.

In times past both Robin and Cameron Gentry would have been in the company of this strange and varied collection of men, but not so this time. Each of them had something more pressing on his mind.

Robin, having despaired of ever getting Sean alone in Jane's house, was spending most of his time with Sean, and sometimes Fiona, riding across Sutter's vast expanse of land searching for a suitable place for the McKays to settle. They moved in the direction of Sutter's mill, which was now under construction. The land up there was hillier, and parts of it were mountainous, but there was abundant water, and it was beautiful. Sean shook his head. "I thought I'd never want to see anything like a mountain again. Even a bump in the road was going to be something I avoided, but now I'm feeling more myself, and I find I like the hills and the trees and the sound of water near my door—not too near, mind you, but within hearin' distance."

They rode on a bit, with Sean taking in everything, and breathing deeply of the cool fresh air. He was no longer sweating as he had been at Jane's house. "I think I'm hearin' the music of my own hearth, Robin," he said, then looked at Fiona. "You know of what I speak, don't you, daughter."

Fiona smiled. "I think we both do, Papa."

"This will make a fine home for your family, Sean," Robin agreed. "There's plenty of grazing land, and surely enough farmland that you can raise what you will for yourself and the cattle. You'd be near self-sufficient here once you get it tamed a bit."

"I like it," Fiona said simply, and dismounted, preferring to walk now. They had stopped in a small glade. The odors of rich earth and grass and growing things was strong, and the sound of water rushing played with the sounds of a gentle breeze in the trees.

Before Sean realized it, he found himself alone. Robin and Fiona had walked nearly a hundred yards from him and were fast disappearing over a hill. Up until now he had thought little of Fiona accompanying him and Robin. She was but sixteen years old, and still Sean's little girl in his eyes. And he had been grateful for Robin's help and interest in his land.

Sean McKay, without any shame, admitted that he thought as much with his heart as with his head. He had always known that when he found it, the land itself would "speak" to him. He would hear and recognize its own music as being a part of himself. He had seen much acreage that would have satisfied all his needs, but none had been right, and time and again Sean had said no, that was not for his family. But this piece of land was. He'd try to purchase three hundred acres from John Sutter and begin his own—no, not farm, it would be his own ranch.

As always seemed the case, however, when one worry ended another began. Fiona was not behaving like a young tomboy with Robin. Nor was Robin Gentry treating Fiona like a youngster, Sean realized, and wondered why he hadn't thought of it before. Mary undoubtedly had, and had left him purposely in his ignorance. She always did when it suited her. But he frowned. He wasn't ready to lose both of his daughters quite yet. He wanted to keep his younger child to himself for just a time longer.

Robin was beginning to suspect what Sean was thinking. Robin was not a timid man, and he usually got what he wanted. When he had as much difficulty finding a time to talk privately with a man as he was now having with Sean, it was not coincidence. He was being put off. "Fiona, when we near New

Helvetia, I want you to ride ahead so that I can talk to your father," he said brusquely.

Not too long ago she would have thought his tone of voice was directed at her, but she had grown up a lot, and now she just smiled knowingly and agreed.

Robin remained tense and pensive. This was not the way he had envisioned his talk with Sean, and it was not the way he wanted it to go. When he and Fiona slowed their walk to allow Sean to catch up with them, Robin said nothing, but he took a longer, assessing look at Fiona's father. He saw a determined man, one with depths of emotions, one who would judge sternly any man who asked for his daughter's hand in marriage. For a moment Robin envied Brian his ordeal in the mountains. Whatever criteria Sean McKay used to judge the mettle of a man, Brian had met them.

As they rode back to New Helvetia, Robin and Sean talked about the supplies Sean would have to purchase to clear his land and begin planting, and those he could borrow from the Gentrys or from Robin himself. When they were two miles from home, Fiona said to her father, "I'm going on ahead. I've heard enough about bulls and cows and steers and—and all those things." She gave a gay laugh and spurred her horse to a canter before Sean could reply.

Robin suppressed a smile. "I asked her to make certain you and I had a few minutes alone, Mr. McKay."

Sean gave him a hard look. "It's Mr. McKay, is it? I suppose I know what you want to talk to me about."

"I think you've known for some time, and done a damned good job of avoiding me."

"If you're smart enough to figure that out, you ought to be smart enough to know I don't want to hear what you have to say," Sean said gruffly. "My girl is but sixteen years old. She belongs with her mama and her papa, and that's all I have to say on the matter."

"But that isn't all I have to say—or Fiona. I'm asking your permission to court your daughter, and to marry her."

Sean was silent for so long that Robin thought he wasn't going to answer, then suddenly he said, "What do you want to do that for?"

Robin was so stunned he stammered, "I—I love her. I—just love her."

Sean smiled and nodded his head. "You're not a bad fellow, Gentry." He rode on a bit, then added, "But you can't have my daughter. She's too young. Doesn't know her own mind yet. You're looking pretty good to her right now, 'cause you're the hero who rescued her. How much do you love her?"

Robin remembered the talk he had had with Mary. He had the same dizzy feeling with Sean. They were quite a family to contend with—asking questions that probed down deep inside a man where no one usually trod. "How much?" he asked weakly. "I don't know how to answer that. She—she is my heart."

"Are you willing to wait for her? Give her time—maybe lose her?" Sean asked, his eyes fixed fast on Robin's.

"I can wait, if I have to, but as to the other—"

"You talk to me about marrying my little girl on her eighteenth birthday. If you're still around, and she still wants you—then you'll have my blessing."

"But that's two years!"

Sean shook his head. "No, about twenty months. She was born in April. Is she worth twenty months to you?"

Robin swallowed hard. He thought of telling Sean that he could have his way with Fiona and it was likely she'd run off and marry him, but he said, "She's worth a lifetime of waiting to me, but that doesn't mean I have to like it."

"I wouldn't think much of you if you did. Now, can we get back to Sean and Robin and call this discussion closed?"

Robin laughed. "I don't have much choice, do I?"

Sean's eyes twinkled, and he let Robin know he had followed all his thoughts. "Not an honorable one."

Cameron was having as much difficulty getting Susannah to himself as Robin had had with Sean. With all the women looking to Susannah for advice on their gowns for the wedding, and asking her for help in fashioning them, he seldom saw her alone. That evening he announced that he was taking Susannah with him for the entire day tomorrow.

Susannah asked, "Where are we going?"

"No questions, no answers, Susannah. This is my surprise."

Susannah looked around at the others at the table. Even Robin shrugged, indicating he didn't know what his brother had in mind. Susannah smiled and said, "I guess I'll just have to go with you to find out. Can't I even have a little hint?"

"Not a one."

Fiona's eyes were nearly as bright with curiosity as Susannah's. She said, "You're mean, Cameron! Surprises are supposed to be given right away. It is terrible having to wait for something good to happen."

Sean laughed. "Fiona used to get mad at us on her birthday too, because we celebrated in the evening and she had to wait all day."

"But she's right, Cameron!" Susannah cried. "How shall I ever wait until tomorrow? Can we at least leave early in the morning?"

"At dawn, if you wish," he said, never suspecting she might hold him to his word.

The dawn was golden with promise and the breeze still chilly when they left New Helvetia. Cameron helped Susannah into the carriage and tucked a blanket over her knees. After a word to Juan, Cameron sat beside her, his arm warm against hers. Susannah loved feeling the solid, comfortable man next to her. Except that she was dying of curiosity, she hardly cared where they were going. Being near Cameron was enough. She managed to talk generalities with him for nearly half an hour, then she could stand it no longer. "Where are we going? Can't you tell me anything?"

He leaned over, taking her hand, and kissed her cheek. "Why must you always know everything?"

"No, not everything—just this. Please, Cameron. I can't think of anything else."

His warm brown eyes glowed as he looked at her. "We are going to San Francisco."

She blinked at him. "San Francisco? Whatever for? Nothing could be wrong with Papa or Mama, because you couldn't tease, or be happy about that. Does Papa want to visit with us?" He shook his head and she was quiet for a moment, then she squealed, "Landry! Has Landry come?"

Cameron put his hands on either side of her face. "No, sweetheart. I'm sorry, I never expected you to think that. Landry hasn't had time to come from New York. Even if he had wings and flew with the birds he wouldn't be here yet."

Susannah looked crestfallen. "Oh . . . I should have known."

Cameron took her hands. He felt terrible that he had stirred her hopes about Landry. He hadn't given her brother a thought, but he should have known that Susannah would. He asked her about her brother, and soon had her talking about him. The miles passed, and they were on the outskirts of the small town of San Francisco, which now boasted several new places of business and new houses.

He let Susannah finish the story about her and Landry playing hide and seek around the Croton Reservoir, then he asked, "How would you feel about seeing our new house?"

"Our *house*!?" she gasped. "Here? Cameron! You never said a word about a house here!"

He kissed her lightly, then chuckled, shaking his head. "If I'd told you, it wouldn't have been a surprise, goose."

"Well, where is it? I want to see it now!"

He laughed harder. "You can't wait a second for anything! It is on Montgomery Street. Another two or three minutes—can you manage that?"

"Only if you hold my hand," she said, smiling up at him. Then her attention went to the little village she had known when it was Yerba Buena. She was all eyes, looking around in excitement, peering at this house, that building, at people she knew. She saw Mary Addison Harris on the street, but looked straight through her for what she and Henry had tried to do to Sam. They went past Flora's tent, where two of her children were playing in a mud hole. In the mud hole was a hand-painted sign: San Francisco. Flora was a believer in Sam's idea. Susannah stuck her head out of the carriage, and waved. "Oh, stop, please!" she cried. Cameron helped her out of the carriage. She went to the tent and started to lift the flap and walk in as always.

One of the children yelled, "Mama's not home!"

Susannah turned her disappointed eyes to Cameron. He said, "Next time," and led her back to the carriage. Juan clucked to the horses and they moved along at a regal pace.

They stopped on Montgomery Street, where the foundations for a house had been laid. The workmen were now laying out the inside walls. Cameron helped Susannah out and they walked across boards placed over the mud so that they could stand inside. "This is your house, Susannah," he said. "Think it'll be big enough?"

She clasped her hands together like a child, grinning hugely in her delight. "It's enormous!" she proclaimed. "Oh, Cameron, tell me where everything is!"

He walked off spaces for her. "This is the parlor, where you'll receive important guests."

"Gentile guests," she said, giggling.

"Not exclusively," he said, giving her a look. "Over here's a big bay window, so you can watch for me when I come home at night from the big city. This is the kitchen . . . the dining room . . . and here's the bedroom." He grinned, his eyes burning through her. "Out in back there'll be a washhouse and a woodshed, attached to the house so you won't have to get your feet wet."

The workmen had stopped and were watching them, so she could not fling her arms around him the way she would have liked. "It's wonderful," she said, ecstatic. "I'm going to love it."

He put his arm around her waist, and they stood looking out the unbuilt bay window toward the open fields. "Think of what we can do, Susannah, together. We'll share everything. I think we are well suited to that. We'll own houses and hotels and little shops and a race track—and a whole lot more before we quit. We'll be leaders of San Francisco society, you and I. Think of that."

"All that," she marveled. "We'll be rich, Cameron."

"You bet we will!"

"I don't mean rich in money. I mean rich in each other."

He smiled down at her from his lovely height, and the smile and the look in his eyes were like the tenderest kiss she had ever known. Susannah had thought once she knew about being in love, but now as she stood in her partially built house, with Cameron's arm tight around her, she knew she was only on the threshold of it.

During the next week Carl and Rowena arrived, plus an assortment of guests who were housed at Jane's, in the tents outside, as well as in the homes of friends at New Helvetia, and even a few at Sutter's Fort. It was decided that Susannah's New Helvetia house should be raised, and used temporarily by the newlyweds, until their own was ready.

Susannah was excited about the idea, and amazed that a house could be raised in such short order. Cameron was amused, for Susannah's feet had barely touched the ground since they had come back from San Francisco. And he was enthusiastic about dividing their time between New Helvetia and San Francisco.

As Susannah watched the men stacking lumber near the wall they would be working on, he stood close beside her, and couldn't resist reaching out to touch the rose petal softness of her cheek. "I've never seen you like this before," he said in wonder.

"I am drunk with happiness," she said, leaning toward his hand.

"Are you certain you want to give your house to others even before you have had a moment in it yourself?"

"I would give it to Brian and Coleen, because I know how happy they will be. Besides, it will begin the life of the house in the best possible way—except, of course, if it were you and I who would be living there."

The house-raising was a riotously good time of hard work and play. There were as many straw bosses as there were workers, and when those who worked took a rest, they immediately became hecklers and advisers to those who continued to labor. There was always someone about to pick at a guitar, or play a mouth harp, or just to sing.

Coleen was excited and nervous. "Mama, this is like a circus," she said uncertainly. "I can't get married with all this—all this—I mean, a marriage is a sacred rite—a sacrament."

Mary pooh-poohed her fretting. "Does that mean you cannot laugh and have fun? Be thankful all this work is being done in a spirit of joy, Coleen. It is a wedding gift to you from the saints themselves."

"But, Mama, at home—"

"This is our home now. You'll never be happy here or anywhere else, if you try to mold it into the image of a place you've left behind you."

Coleen knew when not to argue with her mother, and she didn't actually want to. She had just wanted the assurance that all this lively good fun was all right for so momentous an occasion as her wedding. Now that she had been told in no uncertain terms that it was, she smiled broadly and rushed outside to join the others. The West was a strange place, almost like another world. Something was always happening, and when it wasn't, one simply waited, expecting it to. She supposed that after the wedding everything would settle down and become ordinary, as it had been in Illinois. Life could not always be an adventure. But until that day came, she was now free to enjoy the excitement.

The day of Coleen's wedding dawned clear and sunny. Jane's

house was festooned with as many flowers as they had been able to find, and where flowers were not available, they had substituted evergreen boughs—"For everlasting life and happiness," Mary said.

In the loft the women were all laughter and chatter as they dressed the bride in a gown of white Chinese silk trimmed with hand-tatted Irish lace. Coleen had wanted flower petals to be spread and tossed as she walked toward Brian, so Susannah, although a bit old for the task, had volunteered her services. She too was crowded into the room that seemed a jumble of darting elbows, flying petticoats, and squeals of pain and laughter. Mary and Jane felt as young as the girls as they dressed in their brand-new finery.

"By Jove, I've never had a dress like this on in my whole life," Jane boomed from under folds of satin as Mary lifted the dress over her head. "Why, these new underthings is prettier than the dress I got married in."

"Susannah, you are to be complimented again and again," said Fiona. "I don't know how you managed to design these gowns and then have your seamstresses get all of them ready in time." She glanced into Jane's pier mirror, admiring the rich summer-green of her gown.

Susannah glanced back, acknowledging the compliment, then started as she took in Fiona's appearance. A quick, sharp pang of jealousy shot through her as she saw a reflection of a stunningly beautiful woman. For that brief moment she was sorry she hadn't kept the green silk for herself, then just as quickly realized that it wasn't the dress that made the beauty, it merely enhanced it, and Fiona McKay needed little of that. Fiona's deep auburn hair now gleamed with health and red highlights. Her skin was soft and smooth, colored and brightened by the sun, and her eyes shone a deeper, more vibrant green than the gown she wore.

Susannah looked away. She put on her own gown of soft rose, adorned with yards of ecru lace at the neckline and the hem. Like magic her jealousy was swept away as she looked at her own reflection and realized what Cameron would see when he looked at her.

Shortly before noon three young and beautiful women walked into the garden, each with eyes only for the man of her heart. At the end of the garden stood a small dark-haired Spanish priest, and to one side stood Brian Campbell. The Gentry twins served as best man since Brian refused to choose between them.

Susannah's eyes were bright with happiness, and her gaze rested upon Cameron as she merrily tossed flower petals from her basket. Fiona came after her, her face soft with the many thoughts of her sister and herself that ran through her mind. But she, too, was very happy, very much in love. She had no idea what kept her feet fastened to the ground, for she felt she might fly away at any moment.

Sean, jittery and uncomfortable in his fancy clothes, stood hopping from one foot to the other at his daughter's side. He wanted to march right up there to the priest, but Coleen held him back, each step slow and graceful, her eyes modestly lowered.

Cameron and Robin came to stand beside Susannah and Fiona as soon as Brian and Coleen had said the words that pledged them to each other for life. In the moment that Brian took Coleen into his arms and kissed her for the first time as his wife, not a sound could be heard anywhere. For several seconds afterward as well, no one moved or said anything. It was as though this wedding had been for everyone, and in some way it had deeply touched all those who had participated.

Finally from the back of the garden, near the house, a fiddle began to play, softly at first, then with some verve, breaking the spell. People began to rush to the bride and groom, offering congratulations, and several gave gifts of money to the bride. The celebration had begun! The lone fiddler was joined by others, and then the sound of the mouth harps could be heard, and several couples began dancing.

It was very late when someone noticed that Coleen and Brian were no longer in the party.

"By damn!" an old mountain man yelled. "They think they got away! Let's go!"

En masse the group raided Jane's kitchen, taking from her cupboards every pot and pan they could find, then, shouting and singing and playing music, they walked and ran to the newly built house. All the lights were out, but that only encouraged the merrymakers. "They're in there, all right!"

"Let's give 'em a good start!"

The noise rose deafeningly, and went on for what seemed a long time, until a candle shone in the window Susannah knew to be a bedroom. Brian opened the window and stuck his head out. "Don't you people ever sleep?" he yelled, laughing.

"Where's the bride? We want to see the bride!"

Blushing, and hanging onto Brian, Coleen came to stand beside him. The revelers all cheered mightily, and threw rice at the couple and at each other. Brian and Coleen hastily dressed and came downstairs, and Brian began pouring drinks for their friends. Then once more the music began and in the front yard they all began to dance again.

Cameron and Robin and Fiona and Susannah slowly disengaged themselves, and walked down the relatively quiet street back to Jane's house. The four of them sat on the front porch and talked about the day. As they all quieted down and began to feel sleepy, Cameron put his arm around Susannah, pulling her against his broad chest. He looked at his brother. "I wanted to tell you first of anyone, Rob . . . Susannah and I will be getting married sometime this next spring. Maybe sooner, if she doesn't stop tempting me so," he added, grinning.

Robin and Fiona looked at each other, secret knowledge passing between them, but neither saying anything. They congratulated Susannah and Cameron, then Robin got up and brought out four glasses and a bottle of brandy. "A toast, brother. First to you, and my lovely future sister-in-law." They drank to Cameron and Susannah. Then he smiled and said, "Another toast. To us all—that our lives will always be as happy as they are at this moment, and that we will always be together."

The four of them lifted their glasses again, touched them to one another's, and drank deeply of the wish and the brandy.

Epilogue

On January 24, 1848, James Marshall, employee of John Sutter, went behind the mill he was constructing to check a tailrace built the previous day. As he walked along the ditch, he saw an object lying beneath the water. He picked it up, turned it over in his hand, then looked for more like it. As his eyes became accustomed to his search, he found more and more bits similar to the first. He felt the first small trembling of excitement. Taking off his hat, he placed the objects in it, bending over hurriedly each time he spied another.

James Marshall took his find back to camp and showed it to the other men. "It sure looks like gold," was the consensus, but no one was sure. One man, who had served in the army, had a five-dollar gold piece, which he took from his pocket to compare with the nuggets in Marshall's hat. The coin was lighter in color, but then none of them had ever seen gold taken straight from the ground.

"I know only one person who has," said one of the men. "Jenny Wimmer. She comes from Georgia. I heard her tell of a gold find they had once in Lumpkin County. She might know what this is."

Jenny took Marshall's nuggets, looked at them, smiled and shrugged. "I know the ways those ol' women back home used to tell," she said. She soaked the gold bits in vinegar. While the nuggets sat at the bottom of her vinegar vat, she set a vat of strong lye soap to boiling. She dropped some of the nuggets into

493

that, and let it boil all day and simmer the night. The following morning she retrieved the unharmed nuggets, smiled and said, "That's gold, all right. Yes sir, it's gold, boys!"

James Marshall and the other men who were building the mill hunted for more of the gold nuggets. Marshall finally became impatient, and on January 28, 1848, he rode through a pouring rain the thirty-six miles to Sutter's Fort to tell John Sutter about the gold. He wanted to be the first to break the news to Sutter, and to have credit for the find. Sutter made his own tests, and reached the same conclusion Jenny Wimmer had. It was gold.

John Sutter had great need of gold, for he was in his usual state of indebtedness, but he also needed a thriving community of busy working people to make his dreams of empire come true. He did not want men leaving their plows and their smithies to go hunting gold. He asked that the find be kept secret. He also needed to find out how the laws applied to mineral rights before he allowed anyone access to his land. To this end, he gladly gave freedom to the workmen and Marshall to take what they could find, and he set in motion a fact-gathering search to discover just what he could do with this gold and what his rights were.

The secret was barely a secret, but Californians had heard of other gold finds at other times, and for the most part they were more heartache and bother than they were heralds of wealth. The news of the discovery of gold at Sutter's mill was greeted mostly by smiles, nods of mild interest, and little else. From time to time a man would head for the forest stream high on a mountain and search around the tailrace for nuggets, and always came back with stories of having been successful. But there was no gold rush in California when gold was first discovered.

For over a year, those who had come to this land in search of their Zion and their own empires lived with the belief and expectation that those distant dreams would come true. Men like Sam Brannan, and John Sutter, and the Gentry brothers, women like Susannah Morrison, Jane Pardee, and Fiona McKay, lived their days one at a time, building their futures in a nearly empty land. None of them suspected the forces that would be brought to bear on them, or how drastically their lives would change once the Gold Rush of 1849 began.